AND WHEN I WAKE

The Fellowship Dystopia Book Three

LYNETTE M. BURROWS

ROCKET DOG
PUBLISHING

ISBN: 979-8-9861433-1-6 (pbk.)

ISBN: 979-8-9861433-0-9 (hardcover)

ISBN: 979-8-9861433-3-0 (Kindle e-book)

ISBN: 979-8-9861433-2-3 (epub)

Editors: Julie Glover and Sidekick Jenn

Cover by MiBlart

For information about this title or other books and or electronic media, contact the publisher:

Rocket Dog Publishing

rocketdogpublishing@gmail.com

www.rocketdogpublishing.com

Shawnee Mission, Kansas, U.S.A.

Thank You for Buying

AND WHEN I WAKE

Written by Lynette M. Burrows and published by Rocket Dog Publishing.

Become a Reading Rebel. It isn't just a mailing list—it's a readers' rebellion. Get a free e-book of Fellowship, informative and inspirational weekly blog posts, plus exclusive monthly news from the author about her writing life, events, and other news.

Chapter One

It should have been easy to find her murderous sister.

Miranda Clarke glowered at the diner's grumbling newfangled mechanical dishwasher. She had plenty of motivation to find her younger sister, but finding Irene Earnshaw, formerly the wife of the Prophet and the Lady of the Fellowship in the USA, wasn't as easy as Miranda had hoped.

Steam belched out between the rubber strips that hung over the end of the machine, and draining water gurgled. Miranda angled her face away from the extra heat of the steam. The steam condensed, gathered on the tendrils of hair that had escaped her hairnet, and made those hairs cling to her forehead. She swiped her forehead with the back of her hand. Got a whiff of the kitchen's ever-present stink of hot grease and cooked meats that seeped into her clothes and skin.

She smirked at the idea of Irene doing dishes in a diner. Unlike Miranda, her younger sister had chatted for hours about luxury clothes and cars and fancy things with her rich and powerful friends. Friends who might help her even when disgraced.

The word *friends* landed like a mountain of rock on Miranda's chest, stealing her breath.

A drainer of clean dishes pushed out from under the dishwasher's rubber strips and rolled onto the stainless-steel counter.

She pushed aside memories of falling rocks, steadied her breath-

1

ing, and focused on the latest load of dishes. Stacked the clean ones and carried them to the cooks. Placed one stack at the front-line cook's station and the other at the back-line cook's station. Their spatulas danced over the sizzling cooktop, flipping eggs and hash browns and burgers and plating meals.

Keith, the Blue Coffee Pot diner's front-line cook, was round from his wire-framed eyeglasses to his bushy mustache and his beefy hands. He nodded at her, picked up a clean plate and filled it. He turned, placed the plate of steaming food under the heat lamp, and pushed the buzzer to alert the staff in the dining room. Then he pulled the next order slip from the clothesline-like system that connected to the dining room. "Cuppa Joe and one houseboat." Even his end-of-the-shift-tired voice had a kindness to it.

On the other side of the cooktop, Chester, the back-line cook, was tall and as skinny as Keith was round. He had a long, straight nose, a youthful face, and an always electrified head of warm brown hair.

"There's been so many houseboats today, you'd think Baltimore was flooded," Chester muttered so the front of the house wouldn't hear. He set his spatula down and went to the ice cream freezer.

Keith adjusted the jaunty angle of his soda-fountain-style cap, then crossed over to the double-decker coffee pots. Despite the diner's name, the coffeepots back here, like in any other diner, were stainless steel and glass. "Hang in there, Chester," Keith said with a little more energy. "It's almost six-thirty, the—"

"The best hour of the day," Chester chimed in. The buzzer buzzed under his index finger. He placed a dollop of whipped cream on top of the banana split and placed the confection on the counter for the waiter. "One houseboat up."

"Hey, Miranda," Keith called. "Don't you think it's the best hour of the day?"

"This is our weekend for extended hours." Miranda cringed at her flat tone. But she wouldn't—couldn't join in their banter, be their friend. It would put them in too much danger.

"Yes, it is. But tonight we get to leave at regular time." Keith could find something good to say about everything, probably even Irene.

"What would you do if you didn't have to work?" Chester asked cheerfully.

Have more time to stop Irene and the Fellowship from hurting people.

Even if it's too late for Beryl...for Nick. The mountain of painful memories shifted back so fast, Miranda gasped. She retreated to the noisy dishwasher.

"Pretty girl like her?" Keith put a plate mounded with gravy-coated chipped beef and mashed potatoes under the heat lamp and tapped the buzzer. "Bet she'd have a date."

Nick and I never had an actual date. It hurt to breathe. She masked her pain with her old daughter-of-the-counselor smile.

"She has a date?" Chester's spatula stopped clattering against the cooktop. "Who's the lucky guy?"

Keith gave a playful chuckle and shot Miranda a mischievous look. "I'll bet it's Sam."

Miranda rolled her eyes. Pushed the next tray of dirty dishes onto the track and pushed the button. The machine's swish and grumble filled the space. She liked the noise. It protected her from chitchat. From fake words. Fake smile. And fake submission. From making friends. Friends who would die.

Nick is under that damn mountain. Beryl, too. Because of me. Ten months, and I still haven't found Irene. So how do I spend my time? She scowled at the steam leaking from the dishwasher's rubber strips. *Washing dishes—*

BANG.

Miranda's heart rocketed. She swallowed her gasp and kept from ducking, but her muscles twitched. *Don't look.* Her fingers gripped the cold stainless-steel counter in front of her, knuckles straining against her skin. *Don't look.* She couldn't help it.

The server backed through the swinging door with a tray stacked high with dirty dishes. "Make way," he shouted.

Sam. Miranda gritted her teeth to avoid shouting at him and getting her pay docked. Again.

She forced her muscles to relax. When she had started here, she'd flinched and ducked with every bang of the door. Sam had laughed himself silly over it.

Dressed in white slacks and a white shirt with the blue granite-ware coffee pot logo on his left shoulder, Sam took his time. Every step, every action, every word intentional, a chance to remind the non-Fellowship kitchen staff they weren't good enough to enter the dining room.

Behind him, the symphony of clatter and chatter from the

customers at the lunch counter swelled. The door swung on its hinges, back and forth, turning the dining room noises up and down like a conductor drawing the last notes to a whisper before the door closed.

"The place is hopping today," he said. "Rush shoulda been over hours ago." Sam slammed his tray full of dirty dishes down on the counter beside Miranda. "Scrub-a-dub-a-ding-dong, girlie." He didn't even look at her.

After I find Irene, he's next. She dredged up her daughter-of-the-counselor's smile again and loaded dirty dishes into the dishwasher's rack.

At six-thirty, the water drained from the sink with a final sucking sound. She dried her water-pruned hands on the damp towel. Tossed it and her soiled apron into the hamper and picked up the sack of leftovers Keith had divvied up between the three of them. Grabbed her time card off the rack and slid it into the slot in the time clock. *Ka-chunk.* Card punched, she put the card back in its slot and beat it out of there.

The mid-September setting sun stretched the shadows of the tall office buildings. With the temperature still in the 80s, even the shadows gave no relief from the day's humidity. Chin up, she reveled in the once unimagined odors of diesel fog and the rumble of delivery trucks. The demise of her former self, the Fellowship Counselor's daughter—an ignorant little princess—was one death she wasn't about to shed any tears over.

She turned the corner.

But at least seven Fellowship members in colorful, fashionable clothes waited under the bus stop awning. More than a dozen silent and somber non-Fellowship workers, clad in dull beige or brown, waited for the same bus, standing on the uncovered side of the yellow line painted on the sidewalk.

She huffed out a long sigh. So much for a seat to let her aching feet rest. If she dared go up Pennsylvania, she'd get home in fifty minutes. But Pennsylvania was too busy, too shop-lined, too Fellowship. She turned toward Howard Street.

Office buildings gave way to apartment buildings and then to neat row houses with manicured lawns. Children spilled out of the yards and onto the sidewalks in colorful clothing. They played carelessly, unafraid, unmarked.

She kept to the non-Fellowship side, the outside of the sidewalk. An officer from the Baltimore Police Department came around a corner. Her pulse thumped harder, and her neck and shoulders tensed. The BPD couldn't arrest her for walking down the street, but these past few months there were new rules every day. Thousands of excuses to arrest innocent non-Fellowship members. She bowed her head and, out of the corners of her eyes, watched him stroll past.

Once she was out of sight, she rubbed the back of her aching neck and glanced around. He hadn't followed. She balled her hands into fists and walked with a quicker, more forceful step. She didn't understand how Uncle Ethan could allow this abuse to continue. *He could order his Soldiers for the American Bill of Rights to hunt Irene, to make her and the Fellowship pay for his wife's death.*

Miranda ignored the pain in the back of her throat. Pretended she didn't know that Ethan and all of SABR knew Beryl's and Nick's deaths were her fault.

Slowly, the constant rumble of passing traffic faded. The row houses that lined the street grew tired-looking, then they wore peeling paint or graffiti on plywood shrouds and moved closer to the street until there were no lawns—nothing but littered, uneven sidewalks. The few people who ventured out of their homes sat on their stoops with nowhere to go. Even the air smelled different here. It smelled of factories and train yards and despair.

Miranda headed down a dusty alleyway. She didn't use the front door for fear of bringing Fellowship wrath on the host family that rented a room to her.

The Baxters' kitchen, with its faded yellow walls and worn white metal cabinets, was awash with searing heat and the mouth-watering aroma of fresh latkes.

Miranda let the screen door slam shut behind her to alert the women to her presence.

Face glistening, Evelyn turned a warmhearted smile on her. "Good evening, Miss Norwood. You had a good day at work, yes?"

Evelyn's mother-in-law, Mimi, stood at the scarred mint green gas range and flashed a smile and a soft "Shalom" at Miranda. She peered at the bottom of the spatula she held over the large, sizzling cast-iron skillet. Gave a satisfied nod.

"Yes, thank you," Miranda answered, a white lie that glossed over the hundred irritations of working in a diner owned by a bigoted Fellowship man.

"That's nice." Evelyn added water to the milk in the children's drinking glasses and filled them. Her golden hair wreathed the back of her head in the latest tight-roll style.

Miranda offered Evelyn the bag of leftovers.

"You always remember us. Thank you." She put it in the refrigerator, then placed the two glasses of watered-down milk on a tray laden with five watered-down cups of cold coffee. She turned and carried the tray of drinks down the narrow hall.

Miranda followed.

"Thea. Gene. Dinner," Evelyn shouted. "Bernie and ZeeZee, come and get it."

Two children thundered down the steps.

Their father, Bernie, stepped out of the living room into the hall.

The children rushed forward, made a U-turn down the hall in front of him, dashed in front of Evelyn, and into the dining room.

"Oh," Evelyn drew back, raising the tray she held up out of danger. Liquid sloshed in the cups and glasses, but not a drop spilled.

"Careful, children." Bernie gave them a stern look that his clean-shaven, boyish face couldn't hold. "If your mother spills my coffee, there's none until tomorrow morning."

Thea stopped. Faced him. "Sorry, Father." Then faced Evelyn. "Sorry, Mother."

Scrambling into his seat on the other side of the table, Gene looked up as if surprised. "I *was* careful."

Just home from work, Bernie laughed. "About as careful as an out-of-control garbage truck." He tousled the headful of sandy-brown curls his son had obviously inherited from him.

"Hey," Gene said. "I'm not garbage."

"No one said you were garbage," his sister said with all the superiority and disdain of a ten-year-old. She had golden hair too, but her curls were loose like her mother's.

Leaning on his cane, ZeeZee, Bernie's father, limped into the room and took his seat at the head of the table.

Sans apron, Mimi came into the room holding a plate piled high with latkes.

The aroma made Miranda's mouth water.

Mimi placed the plate in front of ZeeZee, then took her seat at the other end of the table.

The Baxters had a segregated table with the women on one side and the men on the other. Miranda would have thought it strange if Nick hadn't once told her about the custom at his Jewish grandfather's table.

ZeeZee picked up the plate of latkes and held it above his eye line.

The Baxters immediately fell silent. Even the children.

"Blessed are You, LORD our God," ZeeZee whispered.

When Miranda had first moved in, they hadn't trusted her. Then one day, she had arrived late and walked in on ZeeZee saying the blessing. She'd waited respectfully until he finished, then joined them at the table without comment. ZeeZee had led prayers in the windowless privacy of their dining room ever since.

ZeeZee served himself, then passed the bowl to his son. After the men were served, the women served themselves, eldest to youngest.

"I had a good day." Bernie always started the Baxter tradition of each of them sharing something about their day.

Fatigue blanked Miranda's mind, made her eyelids heavy and dulled the savory and slightly sweet goodness of the latkes fried to a perfect crunch.

Thea's voice cut through the fog. "Then I said I would not get married because I was going to be a scientist. Teacher said that single ladies weren't nice people." Thea flipped her hair over her shoulder. "She said I should want to get married and have children. I didn't tell her I knew a nice single lady named Miss Norwood, Father. But why does Teacher think single ladies aren't nice just because they're single? Miss Norwood is nice."

Startled, Miranda gaped at the girl.

"Why are you single?"

Why? Because I wouldn't marry the man my parents chose. And put off Nick, and Irene's Azrael killed him, and it's my fault his body's under a ton of rock.... She couldn't tell a ten-year-old that. She couldn't tell anyone. She stuffed her last bite of latke into her mouth.

"I am so sorry, Miss Norwood," Evelyn said. "Thea knows better than to ask personal questions like that."

Miranda faked chewing and smiling until she could think of

what to say. "Children are naturally curious," she muttered. "Excuse me." She stood. "I'm exhausted."

She left the dining room and headed down the narrow staircase to the basement. A handwritten sign taped to the stairwell ceiling warned, "Low ceiling," but the network of pipes and ducts didn't even brush Miranda's hair.

A bare light bulb at each end of the brick basement gave it a dark and unwelcoming atmosphere that didn't help Miranda's mood. She hurried past the large metal furnace occupying the center of the room and the old furniture and stacks of assorted boxes lining the other long wall.

Her room stood at the end of a row of raw wood shelves heavily laden with boxes. It was a utilitarian room. The cream-colored stucco plastered over the old brickwork gave the illusion of light to the windowless space.

She pushed the door closed behind her and crossed to the small table beside the full-sized bed, reached under the green glass shade, and turned on the brass table lamp. Stripped and dropped her crumpled uniform next to the ancient brown dresser that stood against the outside wall. Then crawled under the multicolored quilt that covered the bed.

But flashbacks of the cave's collapse made her heart thump harder, drove sleep away. Her heavy eyelids wouldn't close.

The cold, damp air chilled her shoulders. *I need to sleep.* She pulled the quilt up to her ears. Thea's question hung unanswered. The unbearably normal meals at the Baxter table taunted her. *Why couldn't my family have been normal?*

If her family had been normal, she never would have run away...

Never would've been sent to Redemption.

Never would've remembered —

She tugged her pillow into a more comfortable place and closed her eyes. Memories wouldn't quit. The cottage, Nick, the Azrael, falling rocks, dust; she gasped as if she were drowning. *My plan. My order. I killed and buried Beryl. Buried Nick*—and that had pulverized everything inside her into a million never fixable pieces.

Stop it. She lifted her head. Punched her pillow. *Stop wallowing. Dammit. Just let it fade.* She rolled over. *Let old memories fade away.*

Sleep tugged at her eyelids, weighed her body down. She was at

Nick's violin virtuoso performance again. Then she was back in the cave, desperately dodging falling rock…

A swirling, churning darkness flared inside, washing every bit of sleep from her. She sat up.

Ethan had insisted that Irene and at least some of the Azrael had survived. She didn't believe him. Until Irene's photo accompanied a Philadelphia newspaper story.

Miranda begged him to help her expose Irene and Felix as frauds, to destroy them and the Fellowship. He had a different plan.

She convinced Leslie and Wanda to help her end Irene and the Fellowship. For ten months, they had chased every rumor, every bit of false information. Found nothing. The two most important people in all the Fellowship made rare public appearances since the explosions last November. It made no sense.

Meanwhile, the Fellowship continued to impose more and more rules. More and more non-Fellowship had to break the rules in order to survive. And every broken rule increased the odds of being sent to Redemption or Taken.

A huge yawn overcame Miranda. She swiped at the tears that coursed down her cheeks. Every muscle in her body ached. *Dammit. Can't find Irene if I'm stupid-tired.*

She lay back down. Threw an arm over her face. Tossed from one side to the other. *Why am I single? Because I blew up a mountain.*

Clammy, she folded the quilt back, leaving only the sheet over her shoulders. Rolled over again. *Damn this humidity. Damn children and their curiosity.*

Every lump in the mattress pressed into aching joints. The sheet clung to Miranda's skin. *Children.*

Given it tied her to their parents' notorious crimes, Irene would abandon her maiden name. And the Council stripped away her married name. But what about the children? Did she change their surnames? Even though Felix remained the Prophet. Remained their father.

Their father.

They'll want to visit him, won't they?

Miranda sat up.

All we need to do is watch the Prophet's house. And when the children visit…

She threw on fresh clothes and hurried to tell Leslie and Wanda.

Chapter Two

I rene stepped off the trackless trolley with as much dignity as she
could, then stood at the entrance to Brown's Motel until the
trolley moved on, leaving her in a stinking cloud of diesel so thick it
left a nasty taste in her mouth. More than the oppressive humidity
heated her face. *Thank the Lord, Mother isn't here to see me, Irene Clarke
Earnshaw, the Lady of the Fellowship, use public transportation and a fake
name.* She strode down the asphalt drive that reflected the sun's heat
darkly, like her mood.

Five rows of white buildings radiated out like wheel spokes from
the drive around the central building, which housed the office. A
bell jangled overhead. She went straight to the vacant check-in desk.
Forced herself to wait like any commoner. Her former husband and
the Fellowship Council had orchestrated this humiliation. *They left
me a pauper with their pathetic stipend. Defenseless against the traitors.
Against Miranda.*

The motel manager opened the door of his family's apartment
and peered into the office. Her former husband's voice, giving the
Prophet's 8:00 p.m. blessing on the radio, drifted through the open
door.

Felix's voice tightened her jaw, her chest. *It was bad enough he let
them annul our marriage, but to take Sandra away too cut too deep to
forgive—ever.* Ten months ago, Irene had barely escaped dying in the
explosions Miranda and her rebels had set. Believed Felix had died

in the simultaneous rebel explosion that destroyed the Fellowship Center in DC. Feared she'd lost her only hope of finding her only biological daughter. Feared Sandra had died in the explosion alongside him.

The manager entered the office, his ribbed undershirt peeking out from his unbuttoned Oxford shirt. *He isn't even wearing a jacket.* A disapproving sigh nearly escaped her. She never imagined being a regular citizen would be so…casual.

"Good evening, Mrs. Elliot," he said and closed the door behind him. Buttoning his shirt, he scurried to the desk. A sheen of sweat quickly covered his round face in the uncooled office. "Is your cottage satisfactory today?"

"It is acceptable." *Barely.* She suppressed a cough triggered by the cloud of minty-lemon Aqua Velva aftershave surrounding him.

"Is there something I can do for you today?"

A muscle in her cheek twitched. Every day for the past four months. Every day, he asked the same two questions. *Why does he still ask? Does he think this is a game?* She steeled herself against disappointment. "Do I have any messages today?"

He disappeared behind the partial wall.

Irene had grown fond of Felix, even though her parents had arranged her marriage. Had been relieved when she'd heard the Fellowship Center was *unoccupied* when the bombs destroyed it. Overjoyed she had another chance to persuade him that Sandra needed her mother.

Then the Fellowship Council had announced Felix had taken a prayer retreat. A retreat that has lasted for months. Months when no one could see him. *Least of all me.*

The manager returned to his side of the desk and gave a sad shake of his head. "Nothing today. Perhaps tomorrow?"

"Thank you." Chin up, she left. Walked to her "cottage," determined no one would see her disappointment.

The cottage facade almost disguised that they were, in fact, not separate cottages but one long building filled with one- and two-bedroom suites.

Irene closed the door behind her and entered the modest split-room rental that was her temporary living quarters. Wrinkled her nose at the acrid stink of hot vinyl that hit her. A pull-out sofa stood against one wall and a pair of chairs at a small table sat against the opposite wall. An opening in the back of the main room revealed the double bed in the next room. She rounded the dinette table and chairs and rotated the dial on the little window air-conditioning unit that sat in the lower half of the window facing the main road.

The longer Felix's retreat lasted, the more her thoughts spiraled. *He's taken Sandra out of the country. He died in that explosion…and Sandra with him. No, the Council wouldn't lie about the Prophet, so Felix lives, and if he does, Sandra does.*

Irene strode past the worn Naugahyde chair that faced the rabbit-eared television set.

Juggling her purse, she peeled off her suit jacket on the way into the bedroom. Tossed her purse on the dresser and her jacket on the bed, then kicked off her shoes.

I hate motels. Her shoulders slumped under the weight of a sadness she could never show to the outside world. Across the room, a photograph in an ornate silver frame sat on the dresser. She picked it up, tears welling in her eyes. Taken on Prophet's Day 1964, she hugged her girls. Annabelle was eleven. Sandra was seven and short and adorable. *And now you're eight. I didn't even get to wish you a happy birthday.* Irene caressed Sandra's face with her index finger. The glass was room temperature, and hard and smooth—nothing like touching a living, breathing child of her flesh.

She hugged the picture frame and raised her face to the heavens. "I'm trying to count my blessings, Lord, but I could use some help. It's been nine whole months since Felix took Sandra from me, and I still have no idea where she is. Help me. She needs me. Amen."

She sighed. The Lord didn't talk to her like He did to Felix. But she had Annabelle.

For now, Annabelle was hours away in that creepy swamp. And had to hide, build the new laboratory, and pretend to work at the pleasure of the Fellowship Council. An irritating inconvenience that also meant access to certain agents in the Second Sphere. Agents who still regarded her as the wife of the Prophet and the Lady of the Fellowship.

She returned the picture to its place and went to what passed for the front room. Sat on the armchair, grabbed the pink Bakelite Princess telephone off the side table, and balanced it on her lap. The dial tone buzzed in her ear, followed by the swoosh and click-click-

click-click of the rotary dial each time she dialed a number. She let it ring three times, hung up, and immediately dialed again.

"Zekiah Swamp Bird Sanctuary," a female voice answered on the fifth ring. "How may I help you?"

"This is Irene Elliot. I need to speak to the manager."

"Yes, ma'am. I will have her call you."

The other end of the line went dead.

"Oh, for—" She slammed the receiver down. *It's 1965, for goodness' sake. Someone ought to have invented a way to hide telephone lines by now.*

Irene heated a bowl of spicy bean soup for dinner. Ate, washed and dried dishes, and stared at the telephone. Then went to the bedroom closet to choose tomorrow's outfit. The phone's shrill bell made her drop her aqua blue and olive-green suit coats. She left them in heaps and dashed to the phone. "Hello?"

"Mother," Annabelle said. "You know calling me is ill-advised if we want to keep the sanctuary a secret."

"Hello, darling. I haven't heard from you in a while and was hoping you had some information for me."

"I promised to call you the minute I hear anything about Sandra. What else can I do?"

"I don't understand how one little girl can be so difficult to find. At least tell me you have information about the rebels. Where Miranda is hiding? Or Beryl? Maybe Ethan?"

Was that static or did Annabelle just sigh at me?

"Be patient. After their mission failed, they went underground. And the Second Sphere continues its door-to-door search of all non-Fellowship homes in Baltimore."

Something about Annabelle's tone said there was more. "What?" Irene wrapped the handset's curly cord on and off her index finger.

"We don't know enough yet to alarm you unnecessarily."

Irene's pulse doubled. She shot to her feet, nearly dropping the telephone. "I'm alarmed now. What haven't you told me?"

"Someone is watching Papa's house and Sandra's old school."

"It's Miranda, isn't it? Why didn't you tell me? She's too close. I need you here with me."

"Mother, please calm down. We don't know it's Miranda. And you are in no danger. I have a team of three of my angels watching over you."

Her angels. The Azrael. A chill swept over Irene. She dropped back into the armchair. "You have Azrael watching me?" She swallowed and tried to sound happier. "I'd be much more comfortable if you were here."

"I am needed here. Soon I'll be able to leave it in the hands of my sisters and focus on finding Sandra. Regardless, I will deal with Miranda the instant we think she is headed to Baltimore.

"We need to talk in person, Annabelle. I need to—we need a, um, a solid plan to, um—on how, on how to deal with my big sister."

"I have to go. Something here needs my attention."

The dial tone buzzed. Irene held the handset out in front of her and gaped at it. *This is how you treat your mother? The person who gave you the last of my inheritance to build that place?* She replaced the handset, and another chill swept through her.

Lord, I didn't mean any disrespect. I am only human. Sometimes I forget my adopted daughter isn't my daughter, isn't eleven, but your ageless angel. She mopped her handkerchief across her damp forehead, then her sweaty palms. *Still not a whisper of cooler air? Nothing at this motel ever works.* She crossed the room to the air conditioner. The little machine whirred and blew as if it were trying its best but blew tepid air. She turned the knob to maximum and focused on how the setting sun highlighted the pitiful strip of yellow and orange marigolds planted alongside the main road. *Maybe the Lord doesn't talk to me like He talks to Felix, but His light will show me the way.*

Chapter Three

The odd mixture of the whistle-tweet of birds in the trees and the whoosh of traffic on the road made Leslie jumpy. Sure, she was always tired, always on guard, but this was different. She paused at the fork in the asphalt path leading deeper into the park. Scanned the area for Second Sphere agents. *Of course, they wouldn't be stupid enough to walk in the park that has collected so many dead bodies the locals call it an "open-air cemetery."*

The phrase brought back the old breath-robbing pain. She pushed the memories aside and pretended to enjoy a random stroll. She took a deep breath rich with the unique perfume of greenery after the rain mixed with exhaust from the cars traveling the nearby roads and followed the left fork.

Within a few feet, the trees turned dusk into late evening and grew darker with every step. Certain she'd heard a Fellowship goon or worse behind her, she did an about-face. Her palms sweated inside her white cotton gloves. Another couple of yards and she whirled to peer at the way she'd come. *You'll never get there if you don't calm down. Play the part. You're a local.* She gave a snort. *A local who's stupid or a murderer.*

Leakin Park, the second largest woodland park in the country, stirred memories of the terrifying weeks she and her siblings had hidden in the wooded mountains near her home. Her pulse quickened, and she knotted her fists to stop her tremors.

The city sounds and smells blended and then disappeared behind aromas of wet earth and the sounds of birds singing, squirrels scolding, and her shoes squishing against the mud. She reached the unpaved ramp to the creek bank. She followed the instructions she'd memorized, stepped off the paved path and up a gentle slope thick with trees. The message from her brother had promised that the gruesome reputation of the park made it the safest place for rebels. She wasn't so sure.

Branches creaked. She checked behind her to see if she had a tail. No one was in sight. She reminded herself that being jumpy wasn't a bad thing. Not when the Second Sphere had increased its presence on the streets. She forced herself to continue. The path wound through trees and grew narrower, more uneven. *If anyone other than Ian had asked me to come here….* Her hands were clammy.

She hated the Fellowship. They'd sent Azrael to Take her parents and older brother. Forced her and her brothers to hide in the Blue Ridge Mountains with what they could carry. She hated them for making her send her younger brothers away for safety, for warping the country and for turning her from a healer to a rebel. Her shoulders sagged. She hated that she felt so much hatred.

The path forked again. This time she went right.

Where are you, Ian? She couldn't turn on her flashlight for fear of drawing unwanted attention. But she was worried. She had the night shift at the clinic this week. It would take half an hour to get to the clinic if she caught the trolley. If she missed it and had to walk, she'd be late, lose her job. But…

The hair on the back of her neck stood at attention. She caught her breath and slowed, uncertain of what had spooked her. It was quiet. Too quiet. The crickets had stopped chirping. Only the murmur of leaves filled the air. Then, faint footsteps approached. *Ian?* Adrenaline sent her pulse into a frenzy. Told her to run away. But the footsteps were regular. Unhurried. "Hello?"

The footsteps grew closer and closer.

Her muscles quivered, tensed to run. "Ian?"

A man's shadowy form passed on her left. "No talking. Follow me."

It was *him.* She blew out a long breath, wished her knees weren't quivering as much, but followed.

They walked a serpentine path through the undergrowth between trees for a few minutes.

Ian stopped, swept the hood back from his head, and gestured toward a small campsite hidden in the shadows.

She had vague impressions of a stone fire ring, a sleeping bag under a tented tarp, and a motorbike.

"Welcome to my place." His tone sounded hard and grim. Like Ian but not like him. "We can talk here, but keep your voice low."

"All the comforts of home." She tried to strike a lighthearted tone but failed.

Ian wrapped her in an awkward hug. "I missed you."

She'd imagined the Ian she knew before her parents were Taken, then hugged him back. "Ditto." Her voice trembled. He wasn't that Ian. Not anymore. And though she wished he were, he wasn't here because he missed her. Missed the family. She pulled away and looked up at his face, but shadows hid his eyes. "Why are you here? Is there something wrong?" "Have you seen the boys?" Her questions spilled out, uncontrolled. At least she'd sounded tense instead of angry. "Did you—"

"Whoa. Slow down. Let me see…I'm here 'cause you are. I didn't see the boys. As for your last question, I'm guessing you want to know if I found the one who killed Ma, Pop, and Junior. No, I didn't."

Leslie's chin quivered. Surprise and a little suspicion tumbled with disappointment, as out of control as her words had been.

"Come over here," Ian said in his I-am-in-charge tone. "I've got a comfy log sofa. We should catch up. Talk about—stuff."

"I can't stay. I have to leave for work in about an hour." Friday was the second busiest night of the week.

"Okay. We can keep it short tonight. Sit. Please."

She toe-tapped along the ground, trying to find the log. Found it. Lowered one hand to it, kept it there, and turned and sat.

The rough bark bit through her uniform pants, stirred memories of huddling in the cold, terrified… She forced the memories away, turned to Ian. He was a study in shades of gray. She wished they'd met somewhere else, somewhere with light. "Ian?"

"Yeah." He was next to her but somehow sounded far away.

"Did you want to talk about something?"

"You didn't come back."

"You thought I would?" *Why doesn't anyone listen to me?* "I told you why I had to leave. Not just because of the doll. What we were doing wasn't working." If he thought he could get away with treating her the way he had the last time they'd seen each other, he would be sorry. Very sorry.

"I thought we'd done pretty well." His voice stayed soft, but the old familiar heat lurked behind his words.

Sourness coated her throat. She didn't say *if we'd done so well, how come we didn't find the killer?* She didn't want to argue.

Ian rested his elbows on his knees, folded his hands together, and sat still as a fog-shrouded mountain. Didn't look at her. Didn't speak.

She didn't fill the silence. She was tired of trying to help angry people, tired of the fruitless searching, tired of all the deaths.

"Did *you* find anything? Anything about—you know." He squirmed a little when she remained silent. "I heard about the explosions," he said after a while. "You weren't at one of those places, were you?"

She closed her eyes and heard it all again—the explosions, the screams—and smelled the smoke and dust and fear. Her stomach twisted.

"Oh. You were."

"I was at one site. Made it out before the explosions started." She'd thought joining SABR would be a good thing. "The doll was a solid lead." Figured she could do more with the rebels than what she and Ian could do alone. "But no. Nothing about—our family." But life with the rebels turned into more and more lies and running and hiding and deaths of people she cared about. She rubbed her burning eyes, then turned to Ian. "Did you? Find anything, I mean?"

"No. Not a thing."

Leslie tried to find something other than *I told you so* to say. Settled on "I'm sorry."

Ian shot to his feet. Loomed over her. "Why are you sorry? You said we'd never find him—the person responsible for killing Ma and Pop and Harry Jr." He still didn't raise his voice, but the heat of his anger sparked hers.

The ever-present fury in Leslie's blood shot her to her feet. She stepped forward, stood toe-to-toe with her brother, her knotted fists straining at her sides. "You know I want to make someone pay for that too. But finding and killing one person won't help. It won't bring Ma and Pop and Harry Jr. back. It won't stop the killings. Make it safe for us to be with the little ones. We have to stop it. Stop the Fellowship. End this. Forever." She heard how murderous she sounded and caught her breath. *I've been with Miranda for too long.* "I mean, restore our rights, our democracy."

Ian stomped away, disappeared into the deeper shadows. His footsteps grew lighter and then, suddenly, he was close again, as if he stomped around in a circle. "I'm not angry with you. I'm angry that I—that we—lost our parents, our family, our lives." His voice cracked.

"Then help me—help us. We can force the Fellowship out. Get democracy back." *And finally, go home, be a family again.*

"That's why I'm here."

"Oh."

She sat down hard. The log wobbled under her.

Ian sat beside her. "I told Monkshood I wanted to join the fight. He said he needed me here."

Her mouth dropped open. "With me? I mean, with Miranda's team?"

"Yeah. I can help Miranda if she'll have me."

Leslie couldn't speak. When Ian said he wanted to fight, he meant he wanted someone to take his anger out on. Part of her was glad he was here, alive, safe. But she was furious that he was forcing her to police him again. She wasn't sure she could handle his and Miranda's anger. But he was blood. Family. Even if only part of her family.

"It's okay if you don't want me on your team," Ian said, even softer than before. "I understand."

He sounded so…lost…her chest hurt. "Of course it's okay with me," she blurted.

He let out a huff. "I was afraid…"

She gave him a side-eye. "Of what? That I wouldn't want you here?"

"Yeah." His voice had a sheepish tone. His shoulder and thigh lightly brushed hers. "I said some pretty mean things before you left."

He had. The memory of their argument still burned. She shook it off. "Brothers and sisters get angry at one another. Say hurtful things, but—oh, Ian." She threw her arms around him in an awkward side hug. "I can't stay angry or hurt. You're my big brother. You saved us." His shoulders relaxed in her embrace.

He gently pried her arms off. "So now what? When do I meet Miranda?"

"I don't know." She had to think about that. *Would Miranda accept him? Or the always-suspicious-of-strangers, Wanda? Well, they accepted me. If they believe he's here to help Miranda find her sister, they'll accept him.*

"There are an awful lot of agents on the streets. And I'm working night shifts. We weren't planning to meet until next week." She tried to see her watch. Couldn't. "I want to hear all about what you did after I left, but I've got to go to work. I can't afford to lose my job. I'll lose my room." *A proper bed and water out of the tap instead of a creek...*

Ian laughed, the first time he'd sounded natural all night. "It's okay. Give me a time and place. I'll meet you whenever and wherever."

"Come to the clinic. Be there about 6:30 tomorrow morning. We'll make a plan after my shift." She gave him directions and then headed back toward West Baltimore, flashes of joy alternating with dread at the prospects ahead.

Chapter Four

At the end of the Baltimore Zoo's polar bear exhibit, Miranda paused near a mother with two toddlers and a crying infant. No Second Sphere agents so far, but that didn't mean they weren't lurking nearby. She scanned the area again.

One of the massive dirty-white bears approached Miranda. Him inside the three-quarter round cage of iron bars embedded in a low stone wall, her on the walkway on the opposite side of a moat surrounding the cage. Him panting. Her sweating. His a primal, predatory stare. Hers a distracted one. *Bet you wish you could get to some prey. Wish I could get to mine too.* The other three bears had taken refuge against the building's cool stone walls. She glanced at her wristwatch. It was time. She slowly followed the walkway around the exhibit. The restless bear shadowed her all the way to where the cage met the tall stone wall of the bear house, stopped when she did.

She glanced around again. Still no one suspicious.

The bear rose on his rear feet, rested his front paws on a crossbar, stared at her, and panted.

"You've got a cage of iron. Me?" She shrugged. "Somehow I traded the cage my parents kept me in for one built by my uncle."

The bear raised his head and growled.

She winced. "I hear you loud and clear, buddy." Gave him her best daughter-of-the-counselor smile, then went inside the bear house.

A damp animal muskiness hung in the air. Four vacant cages lined each side of the viewing area. All the bears were outside, seeking whatever cool corner they could.

She hurried past the empty cages to a short hallway. At the end of the hallway, light filled a doorway. The room beyond held two more vacant cages and a large open space, vacant except for two familiar women who sat in a couple of metal folding chairs against the wall.

Miranda nodded at petite and ginger-haired Leslie, the young woman whose evidence had led them to the caves that should have ended Irene and the Azrael. The mangled ruins of which now held Beryl and Nick.

Wanda raised her head at Miranda's entrance. Her long rows of braids bounced and swayed, and her wide, full lips blossomed into a smile.

Miranda managed a small smile for her former crewmate, who had stuck with her despite the destruction of their ship. But both Ian and Uncle Ethan were absent. Miranda's gut tightened. *If Uncle Ethan wasted my time…* "Where's Monkshood?"

"He's probably been waiting for all of us to arrive." Wanda's Midwestern accent still sounded funny. "He said he'd be here, so he will."

"Where's Ian?"

"He wasn't invited." Leslie rubbed one hand over the other.

After a glance at her wristwatch, Miranda said, "We're on time." She spoke softly and peered suspiciously back the way she'd come.

Behind her, a door opened. She whirled, ready to fight.

Leslie and Wanda scrambled to their feet.

Uncle Ethan Mitchell, a.k.a. Monkshood, came through the door, his bearing as tall and straight as ever. He gave her a warm smile.

She didn't return it. He looked even skinnier than he had the last time she'd seen him.

He seemed to grow uncomfortable under her stare. Brushed a stray lock of once raven black, now almost pure white, hair off his gaunt face. His aura, his eyes, still commanded attention.

"Why are we here?" *Great Miranda. Start off by antagonizing him.*

"Sorry, it *is* good to see you." Her mutter was only marginally better.

"It's good to see you three as well." He upped the wattage of his smile and turned to the others. He motioned for them to sit. "Excuse us for a moment. Miranda and I have a family matter to discuss. We'll be back in a moment or two." He extended his hand to her.

Miranda hesitated.

He dropped his hand. "Please." He turned and walked toward the back of the room.

She bit her lip, hoped he meant to apologize and offer to help. She followed him into a shelf-lined storage area tucked into a corner.

"You left while I was still at the memorial tree."

She stiffened. "There was no reason for me to stay."

His eyes darkened, and his lips tightened. After a moment, he relaxed a little. "I would have—we needed to—talk. About Beryl. She and I talked. Before we went into the cave. It was something we did before—before she went to Redemption."

Miranda cocked her head. "And I need to know this because?"

"We made a plan."

"Come on, Uncle Ethan. Spit it out."

"Before every mission, we'd plan our no-return scenario—"

She gave him a blank look.

He took a deep breath. "Share our—last wishes—in case."

His words wedged in her throat. *They knew one of them would die because of me?* She bit the inside of her cheek.

He turned, took a thick alligator-hide briefcase down from the shelf behind him. Faced her, but his eyes were on the case. "Beryl wanted you to have this."

Beryl's pistol case? The thing in Miranda's throat mushroomed into a boulder. She took the case. Placed it on an empty section of the shelf beside her. Unlatched the locks and opened it. Red silk lined the case, surrounding two stainless steel 1911s with white pearl grips. The sight of Beryl's pistols stole her breath.

Attached to the lid of the case, an engraved plaque read, "The fiery trial through which we pass will light us down in honor or dishonor to the latest generation." Abraham Lincoln, Annual Message to Congress, December 1, 1862. Below that was a personalized inscription, "A grateful nation thanks you for your service." Signed, Abraham Lincoln.

She touched the smooth white pearl. She never expected Beryl to —Her insides seized. *Beryl was a prisoner. The Azrael would have taken her guns. How could he—?* Rage instantly scorched her veins. "You got to her and didn't bring her out?"

He looked as if she'd slapped him. An instant later, kindness oozed from him. "She left them behind to avoid ricochets. Thought her knives would be enough."

Her eyes burned. She blinked and blinked. Snapped the case closed. "Anything else?"

"I—I guess not."

She whirled and returned to where the others waited.

Wanda and Leslie shot her curious looks but said nothing.

The silence grew heavy.

Miranda's patience wore thin. *Is he going to make me drag him out of there?*

He stepped back into the room. Tilted his head in a follow-me motion and led them into an office.

A gray metal desk, an uncomfortable-looking metal roll-around chair, a wall of filing cabinets and three even more uncomfortable-looking metal folding chairs filled the room.

Ethan stood behind the desk. "Take a seat."

Miranda stopped herself from rolling her eyes. Pulled the chair forward. Its feet screeched across the concrete. She grimaced, then sat on the cold metal with the briefcase on her lap. A shiver ran through her.

Wanda sat on one of the two chairs against the wall.

Leslie settled on the chair beside Wanda.

Ethan sat in the roll-around.

"Before I tell you why I'm here, I'd like to hear how your search is going."

Miranda ignored her pounding pulse. "About as well as you'd expect."

"I didn't have any expectations; that's why I asked."

"We're three mosquitoes searching a forest of concrete and metal for a bit of flesh to bite."

"In other words, you've had no luck finding Irene? Any run-ins with the Fellowship?"

"None to speak of."

"Speak anyway."

"There's nothing to say."

He eyed Leslie for a long moment, then Wanda.

"Like Miranda said, it was nothing," Wanda answered. "An indirect nothing."

Miranda shot a heated glare at her teammate.

Ethan cocked his head.

Wanda watched herself stroke the fingers of one hand with the other.

"Care to explain how you had an indirect run-in with the SS?" Uncle Ethan's tone was mild, but his look demanded an answer.

Leslie's chair creaked. She shot an apologetic look at Miranda, then said, "Agents showed up at one of the host family's homes this past Friday."

"It was one of their routine searches," Miranda said before either of the other two could say anything else. "We observed from a hiding place. No one got arrested or hurt. We shouldn't even have mentioned it." She shot a look at Leslie and Wanda, then turned to her uncle. "Why are we here?"

Ethan shifted his weight in the chair and leaned forward. "I don't think you're telling me everything. Whose home did they search?"

"The Baxters' house," Miranda said grudgingly.

"*Your* host family's home? What happened? What aren't you telling me?"

Miranda returned his piercing look with a quiet and unruffled one of her own.

"Was it just a routine search, Wanda? Leslie?"

Miranda pressed her lips tight, willing the other two to keep quiet.

"We think so, but..." Wanda hesitated. "One agent behaved badly toward the little girl. It upset—us."

Miranda shot a shut-up glare at Wanda.

"Behaved badly?" Ethan's gaze went to Miranda, then Leslie, and finally Wanda. "How?"

Wanda sighed audibly. "It was nothing. I shouldn't have said anything."

"But you did. What did the agent do that upset you?"

Miranda clutched the briefcase to her chest and shot to her feet. Her chair screeched and fell backward. The metal rang against the concrete. "So *now* you care?"

Ethan's face creased with confusion. "Of course I care. I've always cared."

"Right." She crossed her arms over her chest. "You cared so much you let me think you were dead for years."

"I was a hunted man," Ethan murmured. Then, louder, "It didn't mean I didn't care. That I don't care."

"Like you cared for Beryl, leaving her in that place for ten years?"

Ethan's jaw tightened. "You can doubt all you want. It changes nothing. I cared then and I care now."

Miranda swept the room with a glare, then allowed her anger to blaze at Ethan. "And I quote, 'I can't indulge in reactions based on my emotions. I must remain steadfast, for the people, for SABR, for our country.'" She placed her hands on the edge of the desk and leaned toward him. "So what is the emotionless, steadfast leader of SABR doing here, asking about an insignificant incident?"

Ethan smoothed his face, scooted his chair back, and stood. "I *am* the leader of SABR. *I* decide what I need to know. And you are evading my question with a tantrum. What happened?"

Look who's evading the question. She straightened and gave Wanda and Leslie a what-did-I-tell-you look. Neither of them raised their heads. She locked eyes with Ethan.

"Answer my question, soldier," he said in a commanding voice. "What did the agent do that upset you?"

"He touched her and leered at her inappropriately, okay? And that upset us—upset *me*. Okay?" She stomped to the door, thinking about leaving. *But something else is up. Something big or one of Ethan's flunkies would be here instead of him.* She faced him, hands on her hips. "Now will you tell us what we're doing here, or do you prefer we get caught?"

"I'm sorry," Ethan said softly and crossed over to Miranda. He gently placed his hands on her shoulders. "I understand—"

Miranda shrugged out of his grasp. "You can't possibly understand..."

"You're right. I don't know what you feel." He stepped back.

"May I ask what you did after you saw that?" His tone returned to that of a commander.

She shot an accusing look at Leslie and Wanda, then glared at Ethan. "I didn't do anything. I wanted to hit him, but I didn't. Thanks to Wanda and Leslie, I didn't even warn her parents."

"Good. The Second Sphere, the Fellowship—they're making up lies about how we are criminals. They wouldn't hesitate to—" He sighed. "If the Baxters knew, they'd put themselves into more danger trying to protect their daughter. They'd put you and Wanda and Leslie in danger too."

"It isn't fair. They trust me, and I trust them. If something happens to Thea…"

"I know the weight of that kind of secret, Miranda."

Something flitted across Ethan's face.

Pain, maybe?

"I don't know how to tell you to bear it. All I know is, it's not about who *you* trust. Even when it's people close to you. It's about whom *they* trust. Sometimes you have to protect the ones you love, and that means keeping dark secrets that eat at you."

Miranda's blood thundered in her ears. *He thinks he can get all fatherly?* She never thought she'd be grateful her mother had taught her how to play the game. Yet, here she was again. She slipped on a submissive mask and used her most submissive tone. "I realized I might have misread the situation." *As if that could be misread.* "I said nothing to either Evelyn or Bernie." *To protect Evelyn and Bernie, not you or Wanda or Leslie.*

"Thank you. I know that was a difficult decision. Please sit back down. I'll tell you why I'm here."

"I'm good," Miranda said, folded her arms across her midsection, and leaned against the wall.

Ethan returned to the desk, pulled a photo from a large manila envelope. "One of my guys in a cell in DC gave me this photograph. When the cell leader saw it, he rushed it to me. I had the photo analyzed by a knowledgeable photograph processor in our ranks. He said it was genuine. Not retouched or changed in any way." He held the photograph out toward Wanda and Leslie. "Do any of you recognize this man?"

It appeared to be someone in a hospital bed, but Miranda

couldn't make out much more from the door. She sighed and went to the desk.

Ethan handed her a black-and-white photograph of someone lying in a hospital bed. She wasn't sure why she thought it was a man, but she did. White bandages swathed his head, hiding all of his features except his eyes, the tip of his nose, and his ears. His *jug-handle* ears.

Heat rose from the center of her chest. *No wonder we haven't been able to find him or Irene. I should have known he wasn't on sabbatical. They lied. They always lie.*

He should have died. Irene *should have died in that explosion. It would have been poetic justice— Wait. What is Ethan saying?*

"—at least four months ago. Our source says his injuries appeared severe, but the source isn't a medical person so cannot give more details. Our source went to where this picture was taken before he sent me the photograph and didn't find any evidence of the Prophet being there."

Miranda tried to find clues in the photograph. But all it revealed was a bland room that could have been in any hospital or building, for that matter.

"After a month of attempting to find the Prophet," Ethan continued, "we've found not one person who has seen him since before Thanksgiving last year. That and this photo suggest he was inside the Center when it blew and received severe injuries. It also suggests the Council is keeping his injuries a secret, and that is why I called this meeting. This is an opportunity we cannot afford to overlook."

Miranda leveled a copy of her mother's scorn at Ethan. "You think we haven't been looking for Felix?"

"You were looking for a healthy man. We need to consider that he's in a nursing home or a rehabilitation center or—"

"A private care situation," Miranda finished for him. *They could afford it. Does Irene know? Is that why she's so hard to find? Would she care for him herself even with their marriage annulled? For Sandra's sake, she might.*

"I was going to say—or a cemetery. If his injuries were that severe—he could have died."

"Why would the Fellowship hide that?" Wanda asked.

"Wouldn't they make a bunch of noise about the rebels killing the Prophet?"

Ethan gave her a grim smile. "Probably. But we can't rule anything out. I've got folks checking death certificates and cemeteries. I need you three to look for places they'd hide an injured man, an injured Prophet."

"Baltimore has a million people in it." Miranda shook her head. "There must be dozens, maybe hundreds, of hospitals and nursing homes and private care situations. How do you think the three of us can check them all out?"

Ethan's look of impatience smoothed to a more neutral expression. "As I said, I have teams searching out other options."

Teams. Plural. "How many other teams?" *How many do we have in Baltimore? One or two could help us search, cover more ground.* "Shouldn't we coordinate our efforts with the others?"

"That's why I'm here. I am coordinating." Ethan's tone said that was not up for discussion. "If any cell needs to contact you, they will use a dead drop. Should they have something time sensitive, they'll drop something as they pass you on the street and say, 'I'm sorry, I have a back problem. Could you pick that up for me?' Your response is 'Certainly. Happy to help.' Their confirmation response is 'Your kindness will be rewarded soon.' Then they'll give a place and time to meet."

He rose from his seat. "Since the Council is keeping this a secret, I don't think the Prophet will be in any of the public nursing homes or rehabilitation centers. Maybe not even the private ones. But I have teams on that and at the hospitals. The three of you will search for health care supplies being sent to private homes or hotels. If you'll accept this assignment." His gaze rested on Miranda.

"We accept," Miranda said. *I know what to look for now. No matter where they're hiding, I will find Felix. And Irene. And I'll make certain they never, ever hurt anyone again.*

Chapter Five

Annabelle darted silently from one squalid row house to the next, intoxicated by the thrill of the hunt and the promise of another step toward her ascension. Twilight's rosy glow illuminated the western sky. It was light enough to keep the streetlights off, but dark enough that most people had taken refuge inside their houses.

For the ten months since she had become the Chosen One, the leader of the Azrael, she had sent her angels on many missions to Take someone from the list of sinners the Council gave them each week. She had been so busy with the building of their new home and laboratory, she couldn't recall when she'd last Taken a soul herself. Today her inner angel had grown insistent, so she had allowed herself to choose one from the Council's list.

Tall and skinny, with unruly brown hair, he reeked of fry oil and pickles and carried an oil-stained paper bag with big blue letters that spelled out "The Blue Coffee Pot." He plodded through the sultry evening breeze that tossed bits of trash and paper down the street in one of Baltimore's mandated non-Fellowship neighborhoods.

She didn't know what his sin was. She didn't care. She would follow him to his home. Sate her inner angel's hunger and be lifted.

His shoes clacked against the sidewalk in time to the melancholy secular tune he hummed. He turned into an alleyway.

Annabelle's heartbeat slowed. The power of the slow, steady beat helped her inner angel come out. She followed him into the dark.

Thirty feet down the alley, a light pierced the darkness. Under the light, sagging carriage-style doors revealed an empty garage. The young man passed under the light. Turned into the deeper shadows cast by the garage and into the yard beyond it.

A door opened and closed. A moment later, dim light glowed in the door's window.

She paused on the porch steps, listening to the chirping of crickets and the intermittent murmur of the breeze. No humming. Unexpectedly, a woman said, "Well, your father says so, and your father knows best." The trills of a harp followed by the swell of theme music from a popular radio show reassured Annabelle the woman would not interfere.

She opened the door just enough to slip inside. Eased the door shut. Entered a dark, narrow kitchen. Dim light spilled into it from the next room. She inched forward.

"Yes, it's *Father Knows Best* transcribed in Hollywood starring Robert—"

The sound of water running intermingled with the radio and became a low, unintelligible murmur.

Emboldened, Annabelle moved into the next room.

A single bulb cast an uneven glow over a cramped room with peeling wallpaper. A small dinette table and two chairs huddled against the same interior wall as the kitchen. The crumpled bag from the Blue Coffee Pot slumped atop the table, unopened. The static-filled murmurs of the radio came from the center wall. A small dresser and bowed daybed lurked in the diagonally opposite corner. Two doors stood between the end of the bed and the dining table. From the sound of the water running, the young man was behind the closest door—the bathroom.

She slid her fingers across the bubbling wallpaper to find the light switch. Turned off the light, then darted to the bit of wall next to the bathroom door. A muted sound of the young man humming the *Father Knows Best* theme song reached her. The radio show narrator launched a description of where this episode took place, a convenient cover for the snap of her garrote. The hunger within grew unbearable.

The weight of her Azrael jumpsuit and body armor grounded her. She'd have known whether her suppressed Mauser VP60 automatic pistol was even one round light. Pressing a button on her wrist pad would light her goggles with the eerie green glow of night vision. Instead, she kept her visor up, relying on her own powers. Her every muscle, every nerve—vibrated with anticipation.

A toilet flushed. Water ran again. Then, the door opened, and the young man stepped out, wearing only a towel around his waist. He glanced up at the ceiling light, puzzled.

She stepped behind him. Whipped the garrote over his head and dragged him three steps into the gloom.

He made a soft choking sound. Clawed at his throat with one hand and groped for her with the other.

Elbows braced against his back, she forced him to bend forward, nearly toppling him.

He dropped to his knees. Clawed at his throat with both hands.

Knee to his back, she tugged.

His struggles weakened.

Tighter.

Blood spurted.

His body spasmed and flailed.

His struggles grew weaker and weaker, then ceased.

Annabelle's nostrils flared, taking in the coppery odor of death. A lighter-than-air sensation filled her chest and made her skin tingle. Her angel within lifted, and they hovered above the lifeless body. Above her own body. A blessed bliss flooded her. Ascension at last.

The bliss faded. Gravity pulled at her. She returned to the earth. Her heart ached from the weight of her mortal being.

She soothed her inner angel. *Fear not. We will ascend. I saw it in my dreams.*

We have the lie to atone for. We must choose targets of higher value.

It is not a lie. Just as the Lord does not share all His plans with His followers, I must not share all of mine with the angels. My duty to find Sandra is mine alone.

She kneeled beside the body. Curled her gloved hand into a fist, dipped the edge of her fist into his blood, then pressed it to his forehead. "Thy will be done."

Annabelle stood and cleaned her soiled gloves with a blood-specific solvent from her equipment belt.

Her inner angel was right. They needed a higher value target. But that had to be put aside. First, she had to find Sandra.

She tapped her throat mic twice to signal the cleaners. Slipped out the door and faded into the night.

Chapter Six

A surge of energy lengthened Miranda's stride. The next street sign identified the cross street as Laurens. *Almost there.* Soon she could rest after washing every dish in the Blue Coffee Pot at least five times.

A faint jingle drew her attention to Virgil's Grocery, a wedge-shaped building on the corner of the neighborhood where her hosts lived. A petite, strawberry-blonde young woman stood in Virgil's corner-facing door. *That looks like—*Miranda's steps faltered. *It is Leslie. She looks worried—something's wrong.* Miranda's throat tightened. She did a quick scan of the area. Saw nothing alarming. Hurried forward.

"Hon," Leslie used the local greeting and fell in beside Miranda. "You don't want to go home yet," she whispered.

"I don't?" *Please say you've found Irene.*

"Unexpected *visitors* are there."

Miranda's jaw twitched. Leslie's tone meant Second Sphere agents, Fellowship enforcers. "How do you know?" *Did the Fellowship find me? How? The Baxters don't know my real name or that I'm a rebel.*

"Wanda and I wanted to talk to you." Leslie gave her a tight-lipped grin. "We arrived just in time to see the agents entering the house."

"This is the second inspection this month." *Are they getting suspi-*

cious? "When did they arrive?" *I can't—won't—lose anyone else.* "Any arrests?" She fought the urge to run the next four blocks. Forced a friendly smile and a slow stroll for the porch-sitting and window-watching neighborhood busybodies.

"They've been inside a half an hour."

"That means they've found nothing yet." Not that she kept anything incriminating in her room. *Still, if the SS even suspects I'm staying there, they will immediately arrest or execute the Baxters, including their two children. And they'll never know why.* "We have to distract them."

"What? How is that a good idea? We have no sign this is anything more than a random check."

"I can't just stand around and wait for them to get arrested or—worse." She peered up Baker Street. Saw nothing out of the ordinary. Didn't really expect the SS to have parked this far away. It was a long rectangular block, and the Baxters' row house was near the far corner. Unwilling to wait any longer, she hurried forward to Cumberland.

"Wait." Leslie followed. "We've been watching from one of the empty houses across the street. Wanda's still watching. Waiting for us."

Miranda hesitated beside the corner building. She'd be in plain sight for a full block before she reached the Baxters. "What's the plan?"

"Keep you from accidentally walking into trouble. Observe."

"What about the Baxters?" *Don't have time to go to the bus station lockers for Beryl's guns.* She chanced a quick glance around the corner of the red brick building. No Second Sphere posted along the street.

"We were waiting to see what happened. Waiting for you."

"Take me to Wanda."

"That's why I'm here," Leslie muttered. "This way." She did an about-face and strode back to the alley behind the corner building. Ducked into the alley.

They darted across gravel driveways, hugged the occasional sun-bleached wood privacy fences, and skirted the edges of backyards. They entered a postage-stamp-sized backyard of nothing but dirt and tall weeds, up the steps to the boarded-up back door on the first level.

Leslie glanced in both directions, then rotated the plywood up out of the way, creating an inverted V-shaped opening.

Evening sunlight, dulled by dirty, slat-covered windows, provided the room's only light. Once white kitchen cabinets with doors askew lined one dingy pale blue wall. There was a raw hole in the peeling Formica counter where a sink must have been. The range stood by itself against the opposite wall. It had no oven door.

Like all the row houses around here, the hall was long and narrow. A stairway to the second level filled one wall. Peeling flowery wallpaper adorned the other wall. Its entryway ended with raw plywood instead of a front door.

The double-wide arched doorway into the living room opened on her right. Wanda was barely visible, crouched at the broken front window, peering through a hole in the plywood. She still had her dark, kinky hair tied up in the Fellowship-approved beige house-keeper's kerchief.

"How many are in there?" Miranda asked, then without waiting for an answer, "Anyone come out yet?"

Wanda flashed her a tight smile. "No. Two cars arrived at six-thirty. The two drivers haven't left their vehicles. But four went in. Someone pulled the front drapes closed soon after they entered. Can't see anything."

"That's not good," Miranda muttered. "Have you checked out back?"

Leslie turned away from the crack between two pieces of plywood. "I did recon earlier. No Second Sphere guard. All curtains closed."

"We can't leave the back unguarded. They could have—"

"Done what?" Wanda pulled away from the knothole and gave Miranda a come-on-now look. "Left their cars and drivers out front and walked somewhere?" Wanda's tone was her crankiest.

Miranda bit back the thousand and one reasons that ran through her brain. Arguing with the one person she trusted would serve no useful purpose. She stepped around Wanda to the other side of the window. Peered through another crack between the boards. Could only see half of the house. She tried not to let it bother her. Shifted her weight from one foot to the other. Tried to be patient and quiet. But waiting was not in her these days. "You need a break, Wanda." It came out more of a command than she'd intended.

Wanda gave her a side-eye. "Sure. I'll take a nature break." She stood. The upside-down bucket she'd been sitting on rocked with a hollow plastic sound.

Miranda settled on the bucket. She was too short to see through the hole while seated. She half stood, half crouched.

The knothole gave her a fisheye view of the Baxters' front door.

The house stood at the end of a long string of row houses, third from the corner. Distinct from the other red brick homes because of the alternating bricks of cream and dark gray. A little wider home than most in the area, the Baxters' house had two narrow front windows instead of one wide one. The front door and window trim were painted white. The red awning over the front door and window stood out. Maybe the color was why the Second Sphere harassed the Baxters.

Leslie and Wanda were right. There was no way to see inside. Two black sedans waited on the street, facing North Calhoun. One driver appeared to be napping. The other had a newspaper spread open across the steering wheel.

The agents have been inside too long. What are they doing? Not for the first time, Miranda wished the home weren't a row house. *One entrance front and back. And—the old coal chute to the basement. If I could fit through the chute, no one would know I'm there.* She stood.

"Someone's coming out," Leslie whispered.

Miranda stooped to peer across the street. The door stood open, and a shadowy figure of a man paused on the stoop under the light. She couldn't tell if the Baxters were near. "Move," she muttered.

The agent descended the steps, followed closely by a second. They wore traditional dark trench coats over dark suits and went straight to the first car. A third one followed but went to the second car. The fourth agent stopped on the stoop. Almost as tall as the door, he had a light brown crew cut. His unbuttoned trench coat revealed the usual dark suit and Fellowship-red tie. He held the hand of the Baxters' flaxen-haired ten-year-old daughter, Thea.

Thea looked up at him with more gravitas than any little girl should wear.

Miranda's heart stuttered.

He stooped to be at eye level with Thea. One hand caressed her cheek, then drifted to her shoulder and down her shoulder to her chest. Thea's parents stood helplessly behind them.

A primal rage ripped through Miranda. Set her veins on fire. She clenched her fists. *In public? How dare he? He dares because he's Second Sphere. But he's going to learn better on my watch.* She whirled and took two determined steps toward the doorway.

Wanda appeared out of nowhere, blocking her path. "You go there like this, and you won't help her. Your anger will burn you and everyone around you."

"I can't let him get away with this." Miranda raised her hand to push Wanda out of the way.

Wanda grabbed Miranda's wrist. "What do you think you're going to do? Alone, unarmed, and against six agents?"

Miranda glared at her. "Get out of my way."

"It's okay. *She's* okay." Leslie called from the window. "He let go of her and went to his car." Her tone was irritatingly soothing.

"Trust me, she is *not* okay," Miranda said through her teeth.

"The cars just pulled away. She's safe," Leslie said. "And Mr. B just came out and picked Thea up. I can see Mom and little Gene, too. They're safe." Leslie joined them.

"No. They are not safe. Thea's not safe. I have to warn her parents and kill that son-of-a—"

Leslie moved to stand with Wanda, putting a hand on Miranda's arm. "Killing the agents who just searched their house will be a death sentence for everyone in that house."

"We can't protect them 24/7 from whatever retribution the Fellowship dreams up," Wanda added. "Not and work *and* search for your sister."

Miranda stood very, very still. Fought the urge to knock Leslie and Wanda aside and run across the street. Struggled to keep from blurting out, *You don't understand. The Fellowship...men like that...they won't stop. They have to be stopped.* Struggled to calm herself. Struggled to find the daughter-of-the-counselor mask she'd used so easily before.

She unclenched her fists, slowed her breathing, and deliberately relaxed her shoulders. Smiled at the irony of using her daughter-of-the-counselor mask on Wanda and Leslie.

"You're right; now is not the time," she said in her calmest voice. *I won't let you hurt the Baxters, or Thea, Mr. Agent. I will find you.*

Chapter Seven

Irene stood in front of the tepid air of the window air conditioner. Fighting the hollowness of another day as a childless pauper, she stared at the yellow and orange marigolds that lined the motel's asphalt drive under the sultry sky. Seeing and not seeing the flowers, her thoughts pinwheeled, searching for some of the Lord's guidance, some inspiration, where to find Sandra.

Movement caught her eye. A sleek white limousine came down the main road and turned into the lane her room faced.

Who on earth would take a limousine to this Lord-forsaken motel? She turned away, reached atop her head for her pale blue pillbox hat, and walked toward the bedroom.

Knock. Knock. Firm. Authoritative.

Every muscle in her body tightened. Her stomach dropped and then thrust upward, stopped only by the tightness of her throat. *That is not the manager's knock. And Azrael don't knock. But no one else knows I'm here.* She sucked in a breath and pushed her hatpin back into place.

Knock. Knock.

Whoever it is isn't going away. She tiptoed to the door and put her ear to the wood. "Who's there?"

"Lucas Matthews, I need to speak to you."

Her breath froze in her chest. *What's he doing here? How did he find me?* Her hands shook. "Counselor Matthews? Um—" *He's here to arrest me. No, he'd just send his goons.* She straightened, forced herself to breathe normally. *He can't hurt me anymore. I've got nothing left.*

"Irene?"

She pasted a smile on her face and opened the door enough to stick her face in the crack. "Counselor Matthews. What a surprise."

"Hello, Irene. May I come in?"

What choice do I have? "Of course." The taste of acid burned the back of her tongue and throat, and with every ounce of self-respect she could muster, she swung the door wide.

He swept his fedora off his head and lumbered into the room, as round or rounder than when she'd last seen him. From his well-tailored white linen suit to his shiny black and white buck shoes, and the faint spicy scent of his cologne, every inch of him exuded, *I am the most important person here.*

She closed the door after him, composed herself, then turned. "Please," she said with a bright smile. "Be seated." Swept her hand toward the Naugahyde chair.

He pulled out one of the straight-backed chairs at the table and waited with gentlemanly patience for her to sit before he settled into the opposite chair.

Her smile hid her loathing. She was certain he was behind the annulment. *Just say what you came to say and get it over.*

"Why are you hiding here?" he asked.

Irene bristled. *Because you and the other counselors annulled my marriage and made it clear I am not wanted here. Because I have to find my daughter, to protect her—from Felix and you and the rest of the Council.* "I didn't want the Council to think I was trying to ingratiate myself back into the Circle." Her tone had just the right amount of submissiveness.

Lucas tilted his head. "Why would we think that?"

Oh no. You don't get to play the injured and innocent. "Let me count the ways." She kept her tone civil but taut and ticked the list off on her fingers. "Annulment after nine years of marriage, banned from any leadership role in the Fellowship, and last but most important, taking my daughter from me."

A flush appeared on his face. "The annulment was an unfortunate bit of business."

Unfortunate? She couldn't—wouldn't—play this game. Not anymore. She bit the inside of her lip hard enough to hurt, but not enough to make it bleed. Steadied herself so her tone wouldn't betray her. "Why are you here? Is this about my daughter?"

"There have been many—events that have transpired in the past ten months, some tragic like the loss of your daughter Annabelle in one of the terrorist attacks, some enlightening. We've learned we all made mistakes."

She pulled in a deep breath, released it slowly. Lucas had just given her more information than he realized. *He doesn't know Annabelle is alive. And he didn't react to Sandra being taken away from me.*

He cleared his throat. "I'm here to extend apologies on behalf of the council. Your annulment was *our* mistake, one we are ready to rectify."

Rectify? Her frenzied pulse battered the echo chamber of her ribs. She kept her expression mild to disguise the onslaught of dizziness that threatened to topple her. She kept her seat. Kept her composure. Kept her hands folded in her lap. *The Council doesn't admit mistakes unless its self-preservation is threatened. Lucas, the Council, or both want something from me.* Lucas looked like he expected her to say something. She didn't trust her voice. Instead, she tilted her head. Her dizziness returned in full force. She braced her feet with a click of her heels against the floor.

"I can't say more here. But there is something you should see in person. Would you take a ride with me?"

The last time I went with a representative from the Council was the worst day of my life. Even if he wants to take me to Felix, dare I discuss Sandra in front of him? A surge of weightlessness filled her hollow spaces. Finally, she found her voice again. "A ride where? To see— Sandra?"

His thick lips twisted into an almost apologetic smile. "This is supremely confidential. And your...place is"—he glanced around the room—"not secure. All will be explained when we get where we're going."

Her mind spun out a dozen scenarios, both good and bad. "And you want me to go with you now?"

"Yes."

Though slower, the dreadful thumping of her heart continued. Part of her guessed his coming here, begging her to go with him, was a very good thing. Part of her screamed, *Don't be a fool! You can't trust him. But if there's the tiniest chance he's taking me to Sandra, I have to go.*

She disappeared into the bedroom, retrieved her purse from the dresser, returned and faced Lucas. "I'm ready."

———

THE SMELL AND FEEL OF SINKING INTO THE LEATHER SEATS overwhelmed Irene with a rush of memories. Not all of them good. *If I were a lesser woman, I would cry.*

The limo's soft hum remained uninterrupted. The privacy glass was up. He could begin if he wanted. But no matter how hard she willed him to speak, he didn't.

For fifteen minutes, they headed toward the city. She clutched her purse tightly in both hands and tried to convince herself this wasn't a mistake.

She tried to read Lucas's expression.

He stared forward, his pudgy fingers laced together. The car rode so silently, so smoothly, his heavy breathing filled the space.

The limo turned up North Broadway. Toward Johns Hopkins Hospital.

Her mouth went dry.

They circled the hospital until they reached a drive marked deliveries. Drove past the loading docks to an unlabeled, unassuming door in the back of the building. The car stopped, but neither the driver nor Lucas moved to get out.

"There is no easy way to say this." Lucas continued to stare forward. "So I'm just going to say it. Felix was badly injured in the explosion."

What? But... She shook her head and sputtered, "The news... they said he...."

"They said what we told them to say."

Her insides quivered. *Of course, they did.*

Lucas reached forward and opened a hidden compartment that held a bottle of whiskey. "Drink?"

"You said 'badly injured.'" *Don't want to know. Must know. For Sandra.* She pulled herself together. Spoke in a calm, clear voice. "Is Sandra with him? *Was* Sandra with him?"

"No."

Relief washed over her, followed by fear. "Is Felix dying?" *Am I too late to get answers?*

Lucas snapped his head around and stared at her. "You still care for him?"

"What I feel for him is none of your concern. Answer my question."

"The doctors say he is stable." He avoided her eyes.

"Stable? For now? For a day? A week?" The car's idling engine hummed until she wanted to scream. "A month? A year? For forever?" Her tone wasn't as demanding as she had wanted.

"I am a humble servant of the Lord and do not know His intentions. The Prophet is still with us, and I have faith that the Lord will heal him in due time."

In due time? Almost a year since, and he's not healed himself? Lord. If Felix's death is Your will, please keep him here until he tells me where Sandra is.

The car door opened. Startled, her stomach lurched. She hadn't noticed the chauffeur getting out.

He offered his hand for her to disembark.

———

She followed Lucas silently through a series of the hospital's long and dark and vacant hallways. The smell of medicine and sickness tested Irene's control of her stomach.

They took an elevator that clanked and moaned until it opened onto an unlit hallway. Lights flickered on the moment they stepped into the hall.

They passed a dozen empty hospital rooms. Then, Lucas paused outside the only room with a closed door. "One more thing you need to know." He locked eyes with her. "He's here under the name John Doe and under the strictest security, for obvious reasons. I'm counting on you not to reveal his true identity. Can you do that?"

"I can and will." A tremor of weakness ran through her body. *The most famous person in the entire United States, maybe the world, and they've given him a fake name? This is not good. Not good at all.*

"Good." Lucas held the door open. "I'll give you a few minutes. His nurse can answer any questions you may have."

Irene squared her shoulders, prayed she'd learn where Sandra was today, and entered. Wrinkled her nose at the unpleasant odors of soap and medicine.

A nurse rose from a desk laden with papers, a stethoscope, and slatted with light and shadows cast by a wall of vertical blinds. "Come on in; we've been expecting you." She nodded toward the occupied bed across from her.

Irene turned and swallowed a gasp.

Thin and pale, Felix lay in one of those narrow hospital beds with metal rails caging him in. The left side of his face drooped; his eyes were closed.

The smile she'd maintained so far slipped for a half-second. "Dear," she whispered, unable to call him John.

He didn't respond.

Louder. "Hello?"

"Excuse me, ma'am," the nurse said. "He can't hear out of his left ear. Stand on his right, and he'll hear you fine."

Irene walked around the bed to his right side. "Hello."

Felix's eyes opened, his lips writhed as if he didn't know how to form words. "Hello." His voice sounded—flat.

She strained to keep her smile in place. "I'm glad to see you are getting better. How do you feel today?"

"Bbbb—" His brow furrowed and his mouth moved soundlessly, then he blurted, "Butter." He gave a slight shake of his head, sighed, and closed his eyes.

Irene gaped at him. *Butter?* She stood waiting for more, for Felix to laugh and say it was a joke. But his eyes stayed closed.

She marched over to the nurse's desk. "Is his mind gone?"

The nurse gave her a sad smile. "He suffered significant brain trauma when the building collapsed on him. His speech and the left side of his body were adversely affected."

"Adversely?" *Why can't doctors and nurses use regular words?* "Say what you mean in plain English."

"He is paralyzed and has dysphasia."

Irene pinned the younger woman with a glare. "That's *not* plain English."

"I'm sorry, you're right. He's unable to feel anything or move the left side of his body. He has trouble recalling—remembering the right words to use—and trouble getting the words he remembers out. He also has trouble understanding what we say to him."

"How long?"

"He was critical and in a coma for almost eight months. With therapy, he regained some speech."

Are you an imbecile? "That is not what I asked. How long until he's completely recovered?"

The nurse's expression told Irene everything she needed to know. A wave of dizziness hit again, weakening her knees. She put a hand on the nurse's desk to steady herself. "So," she whispered, uncertain why she was whispering, "he could be like this for the rest of his life?"

"I couldn't say. You need to talk with his doctor." The nurse busied herself with her paperwork.

That can't be right. He's the Prophet. A miracle worker. A healer. Sadness, fear, and anger swirled inside. *Oh! Dear Lord.* She gripped the edge of the desk tighter. *What if he can't tell me where Sandra is? Does he even remember?* The Tilt-a-Whirl in her head spun out of control. She focused on a black smudge on the institutional beige wall behind the desk. The whirling stopped. *Why did Lucas bring me here?* Behind her, the click of the door latch sounded. She turned slowly. Glared at Lucas.

"I'm sure you have questions," Lucas said before she could speak. "Let's go to the lounge so we don't disturb the patient."

The patient. Not the Prophet. She strolled down the hall with a nonchalance that didn't help her subbasement stomach.

What Lucas called a lounge was an alcove at the end of the hall with two vinyl-covered chairs and a matching sofa in a pale imitation of a living room. Absent the windows and harsh overhead lighting of Felix's room, it was dark and unwelcoming.

Lucas stopped in front of one of the two chairs. "Sit down, Irene." His tone was kind—for Lucas. "It's been a shock to see him like that, I know." He crossed to a small buffet table at the short end of the room. "Would you like a cup of coffee?"

Coffee? Who could drink coffee now? Here? She shook her head and sank onto the palm-leaf printed vinyl of the sofa. It gave a most unflattering creak.

"I am sorry I couldn't prepare you better, but I couldn't be certain we spoke in absolute privacy until now."

She glanced around. His people must have emptied the entire floor.

He took a cup from the upside-down stack of disposable cups and folded the handles out. Taking his time, he poured himself a cup of coffee. Added two sugar packets and two creamers to the dreadful paper cup, then settled onto the chair. It expelled air with a vulgar sound.

His alternate blowing and slurping of the steaming coffee tortured her. There was only one thing she wanted from him. "Why did you bring me here?"

"Everything we—the Council—have done has been to protect our Prophet."

To protect yourselves, you mean.

Lucas set his cup on the side table. "But we've taken things as far as we can." His tone, so carefully controlled, held a new note.

You still haven't told me why the Council forgives me. "What do you mean, 'as far as you can?'"

"We've kept Felix's condition from the public."

Felix? She kept her face neutral. *That's twice Lucas has avoided calling him the Prophet.* Her stomach churned with enough acid to burn through the six floors below them.

"We've prayed for his health for hours, provided him with the best around-the-clock care, but—" He spread his hands as if beseeching the Lord then quickly braced them on his legs.

But she saw his tremor. *He's afraid. Afraid the public will lose faith in the Prophet. In Felix. No, more than that. In the Fellowship.*

His expression showed expectation at first, then uncertainty, and settled on resignation. "Well, you've seen him. He's in no condition to appear in public. That's why we had to find you—we need you. Rather, *Felix* needs you."

An ugly suspicion grew in her. Her pulse doubled. She stiffened. "How?"

"He cannot stay here any longer. He needs long-term care."

"Please say what you mean."

"You said you still care for him. Don't you want to take care of him?"

She stared coolly at Lucas, tilted her head. *I wasn't good enough to be married to him when he was the Prophet, but now that he's the patient, I'm your best option for a nursemaid?* She fought to keep her tone civil. "The Council didn't consider what I wanted ten months ago when you annulled my marriage."

Lucas looked down, shifted his weight. He met her eyes again. "We are but humans, trying to serve the will of our Lord. We made a mistake. The Lord will forgive us. We hope you will too."

Her heart thrashed inside her chest. Words stormed against her throat. *A mistake? Annulling our marriage was a mistake? And you want not only my forgiveness, you want me to...? Of all the nerve!* The stirrings of an idea quieted her anger. *Think, Irene. If the annulment is reversed, am I the Prophet's Lady or Felix's little wife?* "Long-term care, you say? But won't the people expect the Prophet to—" Her jaw dropped. "You've hired someone to pretend to be Felix. Someone who sounds like him. Have you also hired someone to act as the Lady of the Fellowship?"

A glint appeared in Lucas's eyes. "When we said we'd erase the annulment, we didn't mean you would only take care of Felix. You'd help keep up appearances."

I'd be the Prophet's Lady again? But... "A Prophet's Lady needs certain things...."

Lucas cleared his throat. "The Council expects she does."

"I must ask for the Lord's guidance on this matter." *Mrs. Wynter will have to give me my driver and guards back.* Irene stood. "Take me back to the motel."

Lucas smoothed his face. "Of course. Perhaps you would like me to pray with you?"

Wouldn't you love that? She smiled. "I must pray in isolation so I may clearly hear the Lord's wishes." *And figure out the best way to make the Council pay for my humiliation.* She led the way out of the little sitting area, followed eagerly by Lucas.

Chapter Eight

With one hand on her apron tie, Miranda was ready for quitting time. She dabbed the back of her other hand at the sweat that dripped from her forehead.

The door to the dining room banged open.

"Make way." Sam waltzed through the door with a tray heavy with dirty dishes balanced on his upturned hand over his right shoulder. He brushed past Miranda and dropped the tray on her freshly cleaned "dirty" counter. "Scrub-a-dub-a-ding-dong, girlie."

She gave him a mock smile. "Those will have to wait for the night-shift girl."

"Uh-uh." He wagged his index finger inches from her face. "Night girl overslept. You gotta cover until she gets here."

"I'm off in ninety seconds." She pulled her apron string, untying it from her waist.

"Ding-dong, girlie." Sam grabbed her apron strings from where they fell. Wrapped his arms around her waist.

He stank of bubble gum and Brylcreem. She cringed and turned her head away. "Get your hands off me." She kept her voice low, menacing.

He laughed. "Aw, come on, doll, I know what your type likes."

She gritted her teeth so hard they hurt. "I don't like."

He tightened his grip.

"Get off." Louder.

His breath was hot on her ear. "Your mouth says no, but I've seen how you look at me."

The temptation to beat him off her with those dirty dishes nearly won, but she didn't dare. Someone turned Chester in. And that someone could have been Sam.

"Is he bothering you, Miss Norwood?" Keith brushed his belly against Sam's arm.

Sam released Miranda and dusted his hands together. "Just having a little fun after a long shift." Sam tipped his hat to Miranda. "See you tomorrow." He held the dining-room door open and turned back to her. "Oh, and the boss-man said he'll let you know when you can leave." He winked, then disappeared. The door swung back and forth until it closed.

Miranda released her fists, tried to slow her breathing down, to relax her jaw.

"You all right, Miss Norwood?" Keith asked, his face wrinkled with concern.

"I'm fine." *Too sharp.* "Thank you." *Better.* She smiled belatedly.

"Want me to wait for you outside, make sure you get home all right? Can't be too careful after what happened to Chester."

This smile came more naturally. "That's kind of you, Keith, but I don't want to get you in trouble."

A dubious look clouded his face. "You sure?"

"You saved me from Sam. That's enough for one night. Don't worry. Dishwashers don't get Taken. You go home, be with your wife and kids." She had a hard time believing Chester had been Taken. Couldn't help but wonder if Keith was so unnerved because he knew why.

Keith peered through the door's porthole window into the dining room. "Yup. He's gone an' won't bother you no more tonight." He tugged his apron off. "You go straight home, y'hear?"

She threw an "I will" over her shoulder and tackled the stack of dishes.

Almost two hours later, she trudged under a darkening sky with air thicker than any syrup served at the Blue Coffee Pot. Every muggy step added to her outrage at Sam's touch. She couldn't scrape off the memory of it. It didn't help that she had missed the last non-Fellowship trolley.

Most Fellowship members avoided non-Fellowship as if they had some disease. But a righteous few appointed themselves behavior police and harassed the unwary "rule-breakers." Miranda almost hoped one of them would...

In the no-man's-land between Fellowship and non-Fellowship, a teenage boy on the Fellowship side of the sidewalk bumped into her. A second and third boy followed suit. With each bump, Miranda ground her teeth tighter.

The boys hooted and hurled insults at her and each other, running toward the non-Fellowship border.

Miranda slowed. *Someone ought to teach those boys some manners.* But they were Fellowship. Safer not to draw attention to herself.

Midway down the block, still in no-man's-land, two young girls in brown non-Fellowship rompers cast anxious glances at the boys behind them and hurried toward safety, but the boys caught up.

Miranda tensed, and her fingers curled. *Why are those girls out at this hour?* She drew closer to the scene.

"Get out of our way, stinky."

"I'm sorry," the smaller one said. Her soft, youthful voice held a note of terror.

The boys jostled and taunted and herded the girls into the space between the stoops of neighboring row houses.

Miranda stared at the gray sidewalk, focused on the pain of her fingernails digging into her palms, and told herself the sooner she got to the Baxters', the sooner she could wash Sam's touch off her body. She tried to ignore the bullies...but couldn't.

The biggest boy pushed the smaller girl.

She fell backward, landing hard. Cried out in pain.

"Leave her alone," one girl stepped between the boys and her smaller friend.

"Dogs like you can't tell us what to do." He wrapped a finger around the thin strap of her jumper.

Tears welled in her eyes, but she stepped forward, forcing the boys back.

"I think we need to teach this foolish little apostate a lesson, boys." Two other voices shouted their agreement, and they surrounded the girl.

Ignored, the smaller girl scrambled to her feet, then slipped around the stoop until she was clear of the boys, then ran and disappeared into the non-Fellowship zone.

Steps from the scene, Miranda set her jaw and moved to the outside edge of the sidewalk. *Stay out of trouble. Focus on Irene.* But the girl reminded her of Thea.

"Aw, the little unbeliever's crying." The boy who spoke wiped his thumb across her cheek. "Ugh! Harlot cooties!" He wiped his thumb down her dress. The strap on that side ripped loose.

"No!" She tried to cover herself.

One of the other boys jerked the loose strap from her and held it tight. Her breath came in ragged sobs.

"What d'ya think'll happen if I pull this one?" He asked his buddies.

A surge of blood pounded in Miranda's ears, sending strength to her muscles. In three strides, she pushed past the other two and curled her fingers around the hand of the boy holding the strap. "Let go of that."

"Whoa, what have we here? Another harlot!" The tallest leered at her. "Two for the price of one."

"I said, let go." She glowered at the one whose hand she held, dug her fingernails into his palm, and pressed her thumb against his middle knuckle like Beryl had taught her. "Drop it."

The boy tried to pull away. "Ow, that hurts." He dropped the strap and leaned toward Miranda.

Miranda glanced at the girl. "Go, get somewhere safe. I'll take care of these hoodlums."

The girl hesitated a half second, then whirled and ran without a backward glance.

The boy twisted and pulled against Miranda. "Make her let go of me."

"Get your filthy hands off him." The tallest boy shoved Miranda.

She stepped back without losing her balance. "You boys need lessons on how to treat a lady."

"You bitch!" The tallest boy drove a fist into her side. His fist connected with her ribs. Drove the air out of her lungs.

Her vision darkened. She dropped the boy's hand, spun, and drove a punch into the tallest boy's face. Bones crunched.

The boy howled in pain. Both hands flew to his face. Blood spurted.

One down. Two to go. She whirled toward the other two boys. The shortest one was halfway up the block.

The one with the injured hand went to his friend. "Let me see it." He gasped, whirled on Miranda. "You broke his nose. Our father's a Second Sphere agent. He's gonna kill you for that!"

Energy coursed through her. "Not if I kill you first." She stood her ground, fists ready. Gave them an evil grin. Took a menacing step toward them.

The boys shot a glance at each other, then with their eyes riveted on her, they backed away, five, ten feet, spun and ran back the way they'd come.

"Remember this the next time you pick on someone less fortunate," she called after them. "Stupid boys," she muttered. "You're lucky I didn't accidentally kill you." A shudder rippled through her. *Stop it. Being a wimp got Beryl and Nick killed. Be like Beryl.* She squared her shoulders. *Kill them all, and let God figure it out.*

Chapter Nine

Leslie opened the door to Virgil's grocery. The bell overhead jangled. The store's cool air brushed her sweaty skin. A chill skittered down her arms. Faint aromas of fruits and onions and baked goods were a welcome change from the sour smog outside.

Virgil looked up from his cash register, nodded a friendly greeting, and continued ringing up his customer's purchases.

She rubbed her arms and strolled to the refrigerated soda case. *What's so important that Miranda's risking a meeting while Virgil's is open? I certainly don't have any new information.*

Virgil's customer feigned outrage over his choice of high school football team. The woman waiting behind her laughed at their antics.

Leslie pretended she couldn't decide on a flavor and wished the customers would hurry.

"Later," the customer said cheerfully, picked up her two bags of groceries, and left.

The ring of the bell over the door jingled and mingled with the ringing of Virgil's register for the next customer.

He responded politely to the thanks of his customer, mentioned she was his last of the day and that he expected to see her next week.

He locked the front door behind her, flipped the open sign to closed, and pulled down the blinds on the door and the front windows. He turned his smile on Leslie. "The others are already back there."

She set a quarter on the counter for her grape Fanta.

The storeroom doubled as a lunchroom for Virgil and his wife, the owner-operators of the grocery. Filled with sweet scents of oranges and lemons and apples mixed with a faint hint of disinfectant, the room spanned the width of the building.

Seated at the lunch table in the far back corner of the room, near a stainless-steel sink, Miranda and Wanda sat in the wooden captain's chairs opposite one another. Ian straddled the black-and-white vinyl-and-chrome chair nearest the stainless-steel sink, his arms crossed and propped on the top edge of the chair's back.

"Before you ask," Leslie said. "My coworker said she'd told me about the only seller of black-market health supplies she knows about."

Miranda grunted and scrubbed her face with her hands.

Leslie sat across from Ian in the remaining vinyl-and-chrome chair. "At least we know where not to look." She tried to sound upbeat but doubted she had.

"Where else do we look?" Wanda's tone held an edge.

"I can't do this anymore." Miranda pushed her chair back. Paced away from the table. "Monkshood was wrong. We *were* making progress. I say we go back to our old mission."

There she goes. Leslie took a long pull on her Fanta. The burst of cold, sweet grape flavor couldn't rid her of the wretched feeling of impending doom.

Ian straightened. "I don't know what your old mission was, but you're right. We'll never find the Prophet by searching through thousands of medical supplies purchases. What if he went home needing nothing more than a few bandage changes?"

"This is all we can do for now." Leslie set her soda down. "Monkshood said his guy at the hospital had nothing else. And he sent other people looking in other places."

Miranda interrupted her pacing. "What if..." She returned to stand behind her chair. She leaned forward, planted her hands on the table. "What if they couldn't find any information because they didn't know what to look for?"

"What do you mean?" Wanda asked.

"If the Council wanted to keep the Prophet's identity and condition a secret, they would have scrubbed the hospital of any sign he'd been there. What if they missed something?"

A surprised "huh" forced its way out of Leslie's mouth before she could stop it.

Ian's face lit with a slow smile. "They could have missed something, couldn't they, Les?"

Can't get their hopes up, but I won't lie to them. Not anymore. She rubbed her lower lip, then spoke in a soft, reasonable tone. "Every patient has a patient care record and central supply records, records of blood work and other tests or procedures, records of transfer, and probably old hospital records. Monkshood is a smart man. He would have had people look for those. We should stick to his plan."

"You know he would have told us if he had?" Miranda asked. "And he needs that information, doesn't he?"

"Of course he does." Leslie stood in front of Miranda, trying to read her eyes. "But he's our leader and coordinating this mission. It's his decision."

Miranda stiffened. "I'm just doing what he wants all cell leaders to do. Make independent decisions in the best interest of our cause."

"We both know Monkshood expects us to go to him for this mission," Leslie said, a little hotter than she'd intended.

"Say we send him a message right now," Miranda answered in an infuriatingly reasonable tone. "Who knows when he'll get it? In the meantime, we what—wait? Every second we wait makes finding the Prophet harder."

"Sis." Ian put a hand on Leslie's. "You know more about hospitals and medicine than any of us. And you're the one with the busiest schedule. We can't miss this opportunity."

She had to try one more time. "Those records won't be under his name, not even his fake name. They file records by medical number. And some patients have records scattered across a dozen departments."

Wanda slouched in her chair. "So how do we find the right medical number?"

"It'll be next to impossible. Johns Hopkins has been operating for more than seventy-five years. I can't even guess how many patient records they keep. Not to mention how many patients they have in the hospital right now."

"There's no master list?" Miranda asked.

"There should be. But *his name won't be on the list.*" She doesn't *want* to understand.

"So the master list is just a list of numbers? Surely they have something else on the list: ages, conditions, something."

"Yes, but we don't know what his condition was." *Why do I bother?*

"Aren't you just the Negative Nancy?" Wanda set her bottle of RC Cola down with a thump. "You'd think finding a patient who'd survived being buried under a bombed building would be easy."

"If his age is on the list, that's something," Ian said.

Leslie rubbed the back of her neck. It didn't help. "We don't know what his birthdate is or how old he is. Heck, we don't even know if he has any other medical conditions or distinguishing marks that might identify him."

Miranda gave a twisted grin. "Do big ears count as distinguishing marks?" She made a noise that might have been a swallowed laugh. "His birthday? I don't think I remember. Is it important?"

Leslie pressed her tongue against the back of her teeth. *They won't give up on this.* She sighed. "It's the one thing they won't fake."

"Okay." Miranda drew her brows together. "If I remember correctly, he's ten years older than Irene. Irene's two years younger than me. So he'd have been born in nineteen" —she looked up at the ceiling, mouthing numbers to herself— "twenty-seven. Oh. Now I remember." A look of triumph flashed across her face. "His birthday is September twenty-seventh of nineteen twenty-seven. I remember because of the two twenty-sevens."

Resigned. "That and the date of the explosion will narrow the list of possibilities. Do you remember anything else about him or his medical history? Any chronic conditions?"

Miranda gave a shake of her head. "Isn't that enough?"

"The last time I looked up the Johns Hopkins Hospital, there were seventeen buildings. Could be more by now. They could have a thousand patients, maybe more."

"That is a lot," Wanda said. "You'll need time to search for the list and for his records."

"And that means she'll need a lookout," Miranda said. "You'll need your housekeeper outfit."

Wanda leaned back in her chair, arms folded over her chest. "Who else?" She scowled at the wall.

"What time will we do this?" Ian asked.

"Now."

"I should do some research," Leslie said in a last-ditch effort. "Find out where Medical Records and Central Supply are. Not to mention, we need to learn what hospital security is like."

"Might as well do that research there," Wanda pointed out. "We're all off tonight. Don't know if or when that will happen again."

"Les, what time do you think is best?"

"Typically, there's only one person in Medical Records after eleven," Leslie said, surrendering to the inevitable.

Miranda nodded. "All right. We know what to do. Meet back here at eleven."

At the corner where they each went in different directions, Ian looked at her and grinned. "Looks like I'm driving you to Johns Hopkins Hospital tonight."

The pit of Leslie's stomach hollowed out. For the first time in her life, she wished she had never become a nurse's aide.

———

In the twenty-five minutes it took to cross town, Miranda questioned Leslie about hospital routines and made a plan. A plan for Leslie to steal from the hospital of her top-choice of nursing schools—back when she had a prayer of going to nursing school.

The Johns Hopkins Hospital complex had large and stately red-brick buildings with blue sandstone trim. Most of the buildings were silent shadows ablaze with light from dozens and dozens of windows, but light flooded the glassed-in patient entrance, the newest addition to the hospital.

Ian drove around the campus. One by one, the others fell silent. Leslie figured they were finally understanding how big the hospital was. How impossible the task was.

Wanda broke the silence. "They didn't have to move the Prophet to another hospital. They could just switch to another building."

"Not just any of them. Each building has a specialty—psychiatric, women's health, children, and so on," Leslie said.

"But they wanted to keep his identity secret, so he could have been—could be—in any of them."

The humid night air grew thick in Leslie's throat. "If you're right, we'll never find him."

"Stick to the plan," Miranda said. "You're searching records, not buildings."

"But the records could be—"

"Don't think like that, sis," Ian said. "We have to start somewhere."

Leslie quirked her mouth into something resembling a smile. "Right."

"Don't worry," Wanda muttered. "This little ol' maid will warn you of any danger."

"And your getaway driver and outside protection will be ready when you are." Ian's reflection in the rearview mirror winked.

The domed Queen Anne administration building surrounded by a black wrought-iron fence with red brick columns stood out from the rest. Gates closed off its circle drive and the sidewalk entrances on either side of the drive.

The walk from where Ian had dropped her off to the administration building's drive was one of the longest of Leslie's life. She walked parallel to the brick and wrought-iron fence. *Almost there.* Her out-of-control pulse and her heartache fought a crack-a-rib contest. *If I'm caught, I'll never be able to— Focus. That dream died along with Ma, Pop, and Junior.*

She opened the gate and closed it behind her. Followed the sidewalk to a side door. The door opened with a squeak. She squared her shoulders and entered the building.

Every other overhead fluorescent light was on down the long, straight hallway. Framed portraits marched down the interior wall as far as she could see.

She kept moving and silently rehearsed, *What? Of course, I have a name badge. It's right—oh. No, it must have fallen off. I've got to go find it.*

Who am I fooling? That wouldn't work at home. Then again, her hometown hospital only had five nurses and twenty-five beds.

The hallway ended in a brightly lit octagonal rotunda with polished marble floors. A white marble statue of Jesus stood in the center. Behind the statue, a wide, gleaming mahogany staircase led upstairs. Mahogany railings surrounded the three balconies above. Overhead, the dome's translucent glass panes glowed with moonlight. She hugged the shadows beneath the first balcony. Searched for the building directory.

Glassed in, the directory hung on the south wall. *Patient Records —oh no. It's in another building.* She studied the schematic map of the campus.

She turned and strode out, practically running over Wanda.

Wanda's mouth shaped an *O*.

"Wrong building," Leslie said under her breath and kept her purposeful stride. If she had any chance of success, she had to act like she belonged here.

In the correct building, a sign suspended from the ceiling pointed at the door to Medical Records. Expecting the door to be locked, Leslie reached for the handle—

It popped open.

"Oh!" Leslie yelped, an octave higher than her normal voice.

"Sorry." Dressed in an off-the-rack woman's suit, the tall skinny woman gave her a distressed look. "I'm on my way to deliver a STAT request. I'm the only one in the department tonight. Do you need something quick?"

Leslie forced a soft chuckle. "When is a records request ever quick?"

"I can't get it for you right now." The woman glanced at her wristwatch.

The exterior door down the hall opened, and a muttering black woman bumped a housekeeping cart through the doorway.

"That's all right," Leslie said in her most soothing voice, drawing the medical records woman's attention away from Wanda. "Is it okay if I wait inside? I wouldn't mind a few minutes off my feet."

The woman smiled warmly. "Of course. I know how hard you nurses work." She unlocked the door and held it open for Leslie. "There's fresh coffee and paper cups on the shelf by the visitors' chairs. Help yourself. Won't take me long. I'm only going next door."

"Thanks. I'll be fine." Leslie smiled and hoped the woman's trusting soul wouldn't mean she'd be in trouble tomorrow.

The door sighed shut.

Leslie stood in a small, well-lit, and totally silent waiting area. The aroma of fresh, strong coffee made her nervous stomach twitch.

A row of interconnected chairs with wooden backrests and seats stood along the wall on either side of her. Across the way, a reception desk divided the room. Behind the desk stood row upon row upon row of floor-to-ceiling shelving stuffed with thousands of manila folders.

Never assume. "Hello? Anyone here? I need some records."

No answer.

She swiped her sweaty palms down her skirt and advanced on the reception desk. Each end of the desk opened, barrier-free, to the records storage area.

"If you don't mind, I'll find the records I need myself." She rounded the desk. No alarm sounded. No one yelled at her.

The desk was clean. No master list. Not a single piece of paper. None. By the typewriter sat a neat stack of paper requests. Not what she was looking for.

Leslie crossed quickly to the first shelving unit. Metal file sorters hung on the end of each shelving unit. Under those stood carts stacked with files. *This is impossible. How can I find one record in all this?*

The shrill ring of a nearby telephone made her dive into the shadows between the nearest shelving units. The phone rang three more times, then silence. No footsteps rushed to answer. Only a soft mechanical sound and the brush of cool air against her skin. She blew out the breath she'd been holding and resumed her search.

On the cart at the end of the third row, she found a clipboard. It held ten typed pages with rows of medical numbers, ages, genders, seriousness of condition, service, and admission dates. *The master list.* A sigh escaped her.

She scanned for a forty-year-old male admitted in serious condition on or after November 11, 1964. Eight pages in, she found one. *Admitted November 30, 1964. Discharged today?* She memorized the number.

Like a library, a range of record numbers identified which records were in the rows of shelving. She focused on those numbers.

"What are you doing back here?" The tall, skinny medical records woman was back, and her tone was more than a little suspicious.

"I'm sorry," Leslie said, moving toward the waiting room as she spoke. "My supervisor paged me to come back. I thought I could find real quick—my supervisor's gonna kill me. I've gotta go."

The woman followed her. "You know the rules. You have to wait for one of us to get the records. What's your name?"

"I'll have my supervisor call you," Leslie said and bolted out the door.

Chapter Ten

Miranda leaned against the shelving unit full of canned goods in Virgil's storeroom and suppressed the urge to tap her foot at Ethan. *We should be out searching for Irene.* Instead, he'd chewed her out in front of her team for triggering increased security at the hospital when Leslie was the one who almost got caught. On top of that, he was wasting their day with a home movie.

Ethan and Ian bent over a movie projector on the table, fiddling with something on it.

"There." Ethan straightened and patted the projector. "I think Ian and I got this figured out."

The projector whirred and clicked, slowly at first, then faster and faster until it sounded like a playing card strumming the spokes of a bicycle wheel.

Black and white images from a drugstore security camera flickered across the concrete block wall. It was a long, silent, boring montage of people entering and leaving the small shop.

"Stop," Ethan instructed Ian. "Back it up a little."

The people walked backwards.

"Stop. That's him. The one we think is the Prophet."

Miranda studied the man who stood frozen just inside the doorway. Bandages swathed his head, covering everything except his eyes. She tried to estimate his height by comparing him to the door frame. "It could be Felix," she said grudgingly. "But why would the

Prophet go to the drugstore himself? Wouldn't he have someone fetch whatever he needed?"

"Maybe he's alone so observers would think it couldn't possibly be the Prophet," Wanda suggested.

"When was this?" Leslie asked.

"A month and a half ago," Ian said from behind the projector.

Miranda quirked her mouth and glared at Ian. "How do you know that?"

"It appears at the bottom of the frames when the day changes." Ian backed the film up and played it again at the lowest speed, stopping it when the man appeared outside the door.

Tiny yellow letters at the bottom of the image gave the date—August 11, 1965. The odor of a hot machine filled the storeroom. Ian turned off the machine's light. A fan whirred.

"That was nearly two months ago. Do we have anything any more recent?" Miranda asked.

"No," Ethan said. "That's why we have to investigate."

We? This is my team. We search for Irene. Still, Felix could lead to Irene. Ethan hadn't said where this drugstore was. "Where?"

"I'll give the name and location to the team I send to investigate," Ethan said.

He's going to take over my team. She gave a tight-lipped smile. "Of course. Need to know. But remember, I'm probably the only person who can positively identify Felix."

Ian snorted. "I think we've all heard his voice enough to recognize it."

"True. But through bandages? And what if he can't speak?" She glanced at her team. They were all focused on Ethan. Fine. *I don't need a team.* "I know Felix *personally.*"

"You don't have to convince me," Ethan said, and spoke louder. "Come in, Pokeweed."

A dark-haired young man about Miranda's age entered, stood at ease.

"Silverthorn, you and Pokeweed will go as a couple, new to the neighborhood and establishing your new pharmacy."

Miranda opened her mouth to object. *I don't need a partner. But...I need this intel. Okay. I'll play for now.* "If the bandaged man comes to the pharmacy while we're there, do we follow him?"

"No. Once we've confirmed he's still in the area, we'll set up surveillance. Thorn will cover the night shift since Bluebonnet and Zinnia have jobs to keep their identities intact." He nodded to the two women. "You two will split the day shift. Work out a schedule." He turned back to Miranda. "You and Pokeweed need to be a couple for the next stage of the operation."

"The next stage of the operation?"

"Once we know where he's staying, you'll work on something we'll call 'Operation Good Neighbor.'"

Miranda nodded. *Your plans. Being a good neighbor isn't even a tiny part of my plans.*

"So all we do is follow him and find out where he's staying?" Ian said. "Why? If no one knows who he is, we could kidnap him. No matter who he is, he's got information you could use."

Ethan smiled. "I'm glad you're all so eager to help, but yes and no. You'll take pictures, find out where he's staying and how many Fellowship or Second Sphere guard him. But the next stage is about turning the public against him and against the Fellowship." He faced Miranda. "I know you have reasons to want a more, shall we say, immediate decision about his fate, but this is about more than us, about more than what we've lost."

"When do we start?" Pokeweed asked.

Miranda stood. "I'm ready."

Chapter Eleven

Radiating as much genteel respect as possible, Irene sat in the upholstered Bentwood chair with her right hand over her left, properly stuffed in white cotton wrist-length gloves and resting on her lap. The tick-tick-tick of a nearby clock grated, shortening what patience she had left. She picked up the fine china teacup decorated with blue cornflowers without a sound and pretended to take a slow sip of the hot tea.

Opposite her, Mrs. Wynter sat on her dazzling sapphire sofa. Her elegant white-on-white room hadn't changed. Neither had Mrs. Wynter's penchant for heat. Despite September's high temperature and humidity, a fire blazed in the fireplace, giving the room a nasty, wet sock smell.

"I have to say, this is quite unexpected." Mrs. Wynter's gravelly voice was even breathier than on Irene's last visit. She wore a classic, tailored suit in a soft beige, and though she sat straight-backed, she was paler, more wrinkled, more tired-looking than Irene remembered.

Maybe Lucas was right; maybe Mrs. Wynter has changed. Maybe it'll be easy to finagle her into offering to host a charity event for the Prophet and me. At the very least, I must get my security team back.

The old woman picked up her own teacup. "When you disappeared last November, I thought I'd never see you again." The brown liquid in her cup sloshed to the edge but not quite over the lip.

Her age is showing. I can use that. Irene gave a polite smile above the rim of her cup. "Nothing nefarious was going on. But after the Council" —*annulled. What a nasty word*— "did what they did, I needed some time to myself."

Mrs. Wynter's sly smile showed her yellowed and crooked teeth. "Well, dear, from what I hear, you made some rather *interesting* friends while taking time for yourself."

With slow, measured movements, Irene set her teacup onto its saucer, then casually settled back in the chair. "Just what have you heard?"

Mrs. Wynter giggled in her wheezy way. "Let's just say it didn't end well. Thank goodness there was an autogyro handy."

Irene sucked in air without a noise, and her chest quivered. *She once said a wise woman always has more information than she needs. But sometimes all a woman can do is play the game.* She locked eyes with Mrs. Wynter and, with a steady voice, said, "You know why I'm here." Not a question. A statement.

"No, I don't, dear." She lowered her cup. It clinked against the saucer repeatedly until she eventually let go of it. "But first, why did Lucas Matthews take you to the hospital? Are you or the Prophet ill?"

It took every ounce of control Irene had not to gasp. How much Mrs. Wynter knew was unsettling. *But she doesn't know—can't know —everything.* After a slow inhale and exhale, she trusted her voice enough to ask, "What makes you think anyone is sick?"

An approving smile flickered across Mrs. Wynter's lined face. "You're learning." She waved a hand in the air. "I know Lucas Matthews has taken pains to hide the fact that he visits someone in a different hospital about once each month. He started this habit after the destruction of the Fellowship building. Security is tight enough that even my people can't find out who the patient is. Obviously, he's moving this person from one hospital to another in order to keep his—or her—identity a secret. You're here, so it's not you. Nor your siblings. I don't believe you'd be here if it were one of your daughters. That leaves one possibility. Are you going to deny it?"

She needs confirmation. Dare I? I need her to host a party, but I also need her advice. Maybe this is the dues I pay for that.

"Come now, dear. Your mother and I kept no secrets from one another."

"I doubt that." Irene snapped her mouth closed. *Why did I let her get to me?*

"Never mind, dear. You've all but confirmed it. And I'm certain Lucas threatened you in his usual way. I tire of these games. You came here for a reason. Out with it." Her pale blue eyes bore through Irene.

Irene interlaced her fingers and held them tight against one another. *Let her think she has power over me.* "All right. You're right. Lucas has threatened me. I was supposed to convince you to host a fundraiser for one of the Prophet's causes." She gave her tone a note of holding something back.

Mrs. Wynter pursed her lips. "There's more, isn't there?"

"I need your advice."

"Advice about what, dear?" A sly smile made her eyes sparkle.

Irene leaned forward and lowered her voice. "Confidentially, Felix *was* in the Fellowship building when those terrorists blew it up."

Mrs. Wynter cocked her head. "His injuries were severe enough that he's been in the hospital all this time?"

"Well, yes. Of course, he's healing faster than the doctors thought possible, but he still tires quickly and, according to the doctors needs a month to grow stronger. But the Fellowship Council is afraid" —*Mrs. Wynter, dear, I will keep some secrets.*— "the SABR terrorists will take advantage of his condition. The Council—Lucas —asked me to go with Felix to a secret location and help Felix until he's stronger."

"Did they now?" Mrs. Wynter's cup clinked against her saucer again. "And you want to know if I'd advise you to do that?"

"They offered me something in return."

"Do tell."

Irene focused on Mrs. Wynter's neutral facial expression. "They're going to reverse our annulment."

Mrs. Wynter's expression didn't change, but she tilted her head a tiny bit. "Now that's interesting. Anything else?"

Irene smiled. "That's what I wanted to talk to you about. The Council stole my reputation and dignity. I think they should pay to restore that too. Don't you?" She picked up her cup again.

Mrs. Wynter steepled her fingers in her lap. "True, the annulment harmed your reputation, but that is all the more reason you'll want to be a good Fellowship member and act in accordance with the Council's wishes. I certainly wouldn't want to antagonize the Council."

What is she up to? "I most definitely do not wish to provoke the Council, but if you were me, you would not let the Council ignore the damage they've done."

The cackle Mrs. Wynter released set off a coughing fit. After a couple of sips of tea, she recovered and gave Irene a gleeful smile. "Dearie, I think they owe you a great deal."

Irene lowered her eyes, sipped tea, and peered through her lashes at Mrs. Wynter.

"It's insulting, don't you think? After their appalling behavior, they expect the Fellowship's First Lady to become a caregiver." She shook a finger at Irene. "Shame on them. The Council must make amends. They must promise to provide the Prophet with round-the-clock help, say private duty nurses, and in-home doctor's visits."

"Of course," Irene said. *I would have thought of that.*

"You'll need comfortable furnishings for your new residence. And you'll need a budget—one that will provide everything the Prophet needs, plus a new wardrobe." Her glance measured Irene's outfit with some distaste.

Irene tensed and pressed her lips tight. But the old woman was right.

"And if they want you to appear publicly, not only must they provide for the elevated lifestyle suited for such a worthy couple. They should allow the Prophet's Lady the authority to guide the women of the Fellowship in matters of the home, childcare, and the like."

Warmth bloomed inside Irene. "That is a wonderful idea. There is so much I could do to help the women and children of America." *With that kind of authority and Felix unable to countermand, there's no limit to the changes I can make.*

"I will, of course, host a fundraiser." Mrs. Wynter waved her hand, interrupting Irene's attempt to say more about her authority. "You and the Prophet will be the guests of honor. The Council, having provided the financials, will attend to support the reunited couple. I might even persuade President Kennedy to appear. It'll be the event of the year." She sat back, smiling in satisfaction.

That'll keep Lucas happy… "Thank you." Irene beamed a warm smile of gratitude to Mrs. Wynter. "I knew I could count on your being helpful." She picked up her teacup, then set it down and put on a concerned face as if she'd just had a thought. "Should the Council provide us with some security?"

Mrs. Wynter snorted. "You don't have to be delicate with me. Yes, the Council should provide security. But of course, you'll need a team loyal to you as well. I'll see if I can round up your old security team."

Irene dipped her head in thanks. *Now I'm ready for whatever Lucas has planned.*

Chapter Twelve

Miranda and Pokeweed hammered out their fake relationship on the twenty-minute streetcar ride in whispers. Newlyweds. Oliver and Mandy. She'd chosen an old nickname so she would remember to respond to it and wondered if he had done something similar. He kind of looked like an Oliver.

The small, mom-and-pop drugstore sat between a hat shop and a grocery store in the Tuxedo Park shopping center on a busy street in a popular Fellowship-centric neighborhood.

She and Oliver held hands and stood at the corner closest to the drugstore. Adrenaline made her stomach flutter. *If this is Felix, Irene has got to be nearby.*

The street was busy but not rush-hour busy. She stepped off the curb. Oliver pulled her back onto the sidewalk.

She shook loose of his grip. "Darling," she said through her forced smile, "don't you want to go with me to the pharmacy?"

"Sure. But I don't want to risk my bride of three months against these Bal'more drivers." He raised his eyes to glance over her head, then looked at her again. Twice.

She got the message. He wanted to observe first. "Can't stand here all day. We don't know how long it's open." *Ethan should have named him Slowpoke instead of Pokeweed. Good thing he agreed to be the one distracting the pharmacist.*

"The traffic will clear in a minute."

A steady trickle of customers went in and left the pharmacy. No one seemed to stay long.

The traffic cleared, and Oliver offered her his arm. "Ready, Mrs. Webley?"

At last. She placed her gloved hand inside his elbow. "Ready, Mr. Webley."

Inside the shop, Pat Boone crooned softly in the background, and a woman greeted them from behind a short soda fountain counter.

Miranda sniffed the scent of peppermint and smiled. "Do you think we can afford some peppermint ice cream?" It had been a favorite treat during her childhood.

Oliver played his part with an indulgent smile. "It would be nice, wouldn't it, Mrs. Webley?"

She gave him an adoring gaze. "We can share a bowl. Why don't you go place our order, and I'll see if the pharmacist has any of my stomach powder."

He hid his surprise in the blink of an eye. "How about this: you go get your stomach powder, I'll do the rest of our shopping, then we meet at the soda fountain?" He took her hand, and his eyes sent her a *be careful* message.

"Perfect." She couldn't bring herself to bat her eyelashes at him. Instead, she sashayed down a narrow aisle.

At the back of the store, above the shelves crammed full of cures for everything, a lighted sign identified the prescription department. She went straight there. Had to wait for the pharmacist to finish accepting payment from a stooped old man.

"Hello, how may I help you?" the pharmacist said in a pleasant voice.

"I need some *stomach* powder, please." She leaned over the counter and whispered, "I'm a newlywed, and wouldn't you know it, my time of the month came early."

The pharmacist ducked his head but not quite fast enough to hide his smile. "Yes, ma'am, I've got something that will help your stomachache." He crossed over to the row of shelves behind him and pulled down a three-ring binder. "I'll need your name and address." He dutifully wrote the fake name and address she gave him.

"This is a lovely shop you have," Miranda said in a chatty tone.

"We're new to the area and so happy to find a pharmacy so close. But my darling husband is a worrier and wouldn't let me come here alone, as we don't know how safe this neighborhood is. Is it full of non-Fellowship scum as my husband fears?"

"Not at all," the pharmacist answered. He put a small metal bowl on his scale, then poured some powder into it. "I don't believe there are any of those people within two miles of us."

"But he said he saw a man with a bandaged face come in here last week."

The pharmacist looked up at her. "Not to worry. That gentleman is an upstanding Fellowship member who had some surgery on his face." He added a little more powder, then poured the contents of the metal bowl into an envelope.

"Poor man, you'd think his wife would fetch his bandages and such for him." Miranda watched the pharmacist closely.

"Bet." He nodded, wrote a label, sealed the envelope, and fixed the label to the front of the envelope. Then he picked up an index card, carefully copied the information from the envelope onto the card, bent and put the card in a drawer beneath the counter.

"Maybe his wife's sick too?" Miranda hoped the cave-in had caused Irene some well-deserved pain.

"Don't know. Haven't met her." Irritation crept into the pharmacist's voice.

Out of the corner of her eye, she saw Oliver come down the aisle across the back of the store, toward the pharmacy desk. He turned and vanished from her sight. She figured he circled around behind her, playing the part of a stranger who needs the pharmacist's help.

"Well, it's good to know he's not a stranger with bad intentions."

"Rest your pretty little heart; we only serve locals here." He rang up her purchase. "That'll be seventy-five cents."

"That's good to know," Miranda gushed and handed him a dollar bill. "So sorry to have bothered you." She gave a little laugh. "My husband says I'm all aflutter since we've moved."

The pharmacist gave her her change. "You'll grow to love Roeland Park as we all do."

"Thank you." She took her change and the envelope. Tucked them into her pocketbook. "I'll see you soon." She drifted toward a display of health pamphlets.

Oliver gave no sign of recognizing her and stepped up to the counter she'd just vacated.

"How may I help you, sir?"

"I was wondering if you could help me find the right ankle wrap for my little girl." Oliver's Baltimore accent had grown thicker for this role.

"My wife's at the soda counter; she can—"

"I'm sorry, but she's busy serving ice cream to a family. And I really need to get this now so I can take it home to my girl and then get to work on time."

"Of course, be right with you," the pharmacist said. He came out the door and locked it, then crossed over to Oliver. "The ankle wraps are over here. Why don't you tell me a little about why your little girl needs an ankle wrap?"

"The doc said it was just a sprain and wrapped it, but she spilled her milk all over it." Their voices receded into an indistinct mumble.

Miranda hurried to the counter. A quick glance around, no one in sight. She sat on the edge of the counter, swung her legs over to the other side, and hopped down. Crouched behind the counter and scanned an impossible number of file drawers. *It would be easier to wait for and follow bandaged-man.*

Four wooden card catalog units, each about three feet wide, stretched underneath the counter. Forty drawers each. *And I have a minute, maybe two.* A hand-written label on each drawer had a range of letters in the alphabet.

She yanked open the drawer labeled E. *Earnshaw. Earnshaw. Earnshaw. Nothing.* She peered over the countertop. No sign of Oliver or the pharmacist. She remembered the pharmacist had written something behind the shelf when filling her order. Dashed back into the shelving, where a faint medicinal odor lingered.

Beside the tall metal shelf stood more shelving, including one with a built-in desktop. On it, a three-ring binder. Entries were by date. Index tabs by month. She flipped back to August, paged to August eleventh. Six double-sided pages of date, time, customer name and address, plus medication information. *Holy crap.* She'd thought to remember the date, but the time? *Morning, I think.*

"Excuse me, sir." Oliver's voice was inordinately loud. "One more thing..." His voice faded again.

Out of time. She tore the first page for August eleventh out of the notebook, folded it and stuck it in her bra. Ran to the counter, slid over the top, and slipped into the next aisle.

"Thank you for your time. You've been very helpful." Oliver's voice drew close.

"Hurry home now. Wrap it like I showed you, and soon she'll be good as new."

"I will, thank you."

Miranda strolled up and down the aisles, picked up a random object here and there, considered it, then put it back. She glanced up at the big clock above the pharmacy window. *Finally, time to meet Oliver and get out of here.*

She rounded the end of the aisle smiling, her Mrs. Webley persona intact, and froze. Oliver wasn't alone. Two men in suits stood on either side of him. *Second Sphere agents.*

Dry-mouthed, Miranda gulped air. She pretended to search the items on the shelf but kept Oliver in her peripheral vision and tried to eavesdrop.

The brassy sounds of "I Got Rhythm" from the overhead speakers garbled their conversation. Miranda chewed her lower lip and picked up an object here and there from the nearest shelf. *What gave you away, Oliver?* She stared at the small green bottle in her hand and put it back on the shelf. As casually as she could, she moved to the other side of the shelving and partly down that aisle, pretending to shop while searching for another exit. *Should have done that first thing.*

Ignoring the urge to run, she drifted through the store. Made her way to the door and left.

––––––

An hour later, she delivered the bad news to Ethan, who had waited in Virgil's storeroom.

"Well, that's just great." Ethan's tone said it was anything but great. "Why did you split up?" He glowered at her.

He still thinks I'm his little niece, someone to entertain instead of someone who actually knows how to run an operation. She gritted her teeth and took a deep breath before she spoke. "Two different casual conversations can yield quicker results."

"Instead, you've got nothing more than what we already knew, and you burned the location for us."

"I wasn't the one who got caught," she blurted out, fists clenched at her sides. *Besides, I got more.* She relaxed her fist, preparing to retrieve the paper still hidden in her bra.

"I didn't get caught either," Oliver said, appearing from the shelf holding canned vegetables.

She smiled and put her hand back down at her side. "That's a relief!"

"Is it?" Ethan asked.

She gave him an indignant look. "Of course it is."

"Why did you leave?" Oliver asked. "Our Fellowship identities were intact."

"How was I supposed to know that? Was I supposed to walk into what looked like an arrest?"

Oliver gave her a puzzled look.

Ethan fixed her with a dark stare. A muscle in his jaw jumped. "I send people in pairs in the city for a reason, Miranda. Remember that if I send you on another assignment."

If? Seriously? Her fists ached from clenching them so tight. "I thought Ian was supposed to be watching our backs? Where was he? Why didn't he warn us?"

"Unlike you, Ian is doing what I told him to," Ethan said. "Watching the pharmacy."

Miranda glared at Ethan. "Oliver and I did what we needed to do, but we shouldn't have. You put him in danger because you didn't do proper surveillance first."

Ethan scowled at her, looked away, then turned back again without anger. "How do you think I knew the Prophet had been at the pharmacy?"

She propped her fists on her hips. "So then why didn't you know that Second Sphere agents were watching the pharmacy?"

"Miranda, you don't know everything I know." He ran a hand through his hair and sighed. "This war is taking too long, taking too much from us; it's made us all short-tempered and suspicious. Take a breath. Go home. Get some sleep. We'll discuss the next phase tomorrow."

Operation Good Neighbor? Bah. He doesn't care about making Irene pay for what she did. The way he's been acting, he'd probably burn the list if I gave it to him.

When the Prophet, his wife, and *his Azrael are dead—then we can talk about a next phase.* But she couldn't say the words out loud. *It's pointless. He'll never concede I'm right.* She forced out a conciliatory "Yes, sir" and walked out, determined she'd show him who was right.

Chapter Thirteen

Leslie carried a narrow, rectangular wooden box down the hall of the former offices converted to the Clinic. Muted conversations surrounded her. Here and there, doors opened or closed. She loved working here. Even loved how the place smelled of alcohol and cleaners. It felt so good to be helping people—almost homelike. She turned into a patient exam room. "Good morning. In for a blood pressure check today?"

Her patient, a matronly woman with greasy hair, sat in a metal chair beside the exam table. The woman gave Leslie a nervous smile. "Yes, and I've been picturing the ocean on a peaceful day just like you said."

"Good," Leslie said. "That, with the changes you've made in your diet and the medicine, ought to help lower your reading." She opened the box and made certain the blood pressure monitor attached to the lid stood straight, then wrapped the cuff around her patient's arm. She pumped the squeeze bulb to inflate it.

Her patient winced a little as the cuff tightened.

"The ocean is so calm today. I love walking in the wet sand and letting the warm waves lap at my feet." Leslie had never been to an ocean, but her patient needed help to lessen her anxiety.

The thump and swish of the woman's pulse came through the stethoscope, then faded away. Leslie smiled and took off her stethoscope. "Your blood pressure is still a little high, but not as bad as last time. Keep taking the medicine and doing what you're doing, and it'll be even lower next time." She placed the cuff into the wooden box and closed the lid. "Is there anything else we can help you with today?"

"No, Miss Leslie. Thank you."

Carrying the box with her, Leslie escorted her patient down the hall to the reception area. "See you next week."

Behind the reception desk, Leslie picked up the next patient folder, opened the door to the crowded reception area, and called, "Mr. Smith."

The three men in the waiting area stood up.

Leslie sighed. So many people needed to use pseudonyms in public spaces these days when the only criminal thing they'd done and wanted to hide was names that gave away their culture or race for fear the Fellowship would use their names against them. "Sorry. I need D.R. Smith."

Two of the men sat down. One came toward her.

"Hello, Mr. Smith. We'll get your weight first." She stopped at the scale and waited for the man to unload his pants pockets.

Buzz. Buzz. Buzz.

The soft sound made Leslie's pulse surge. "Mr. Smith," she whispered. "That buzzer means Second Sphere agents are here, in the clinic. If you need to leave, there's an exit out the back way down that hall." She pointed to her right.

Mr. Smith scooped up his belongings from the counter and hurried away.

Patient folder in hand, Leslie ducked into the vacant patient room she'd planned for Mr. Smith and opened a drawer beneath the patient table. Pulled a surgical mask out of the drawer and put it on. She took Mr. Smith's folder, walked calmly, and put it back, then headed for the clean room.

A door slammed.

Despite the growing lump in her throat, she didn't turn around but pressed on.

Made it to the clean room. Closed the door behind her. Swallowed. She wasn't safe, but here, amongst the autoclave and sterile solutions, she had a reason for wearing a mask.

She put on a sterile gown and a pair of gloves and set about cleaning the thermometers and various small instruments they'd used.

Thirty minutes later, she emptied the autoclave contents onto a sterile towel.

The door opened. Two Second Sphere agents barged into the tiny room.

She threw a sterile towel over her clean instruments and exclaimed, "Can't you read? This is a sterile room. Where are your masks?" Her mouth was so dry she lisped.

The two agents didn't hesitate. "We're here by order of the Fellowship Council."

"Don't take another step," she commanded. "You will contaminate these instruments. You don't want the doctor or his patient, Mrs. Johnson, mad at you because I had to clean these instruments all over again."

"Step aside. We have a job to do. You, your doctor, and your Mrs. Johnson will have to wait." They both squeezed into the small room with Leslie.

The two men opened every cabinet and rummaged through the supplies.

The over-warm space became suffocating. Leslie's pulse rumbled double-time. Every second the agents spent in here increased the possibility they'd discover her real identity. "Please, if you tell me what you're looking for, I can help."

"We're looking for any signs of rebel activity."

Leslie tried to smile under the mask. Smiles affected tone, and she needed all the help she could get right now. "We're a free clinic. The rebels leave us alone."

The clean-shaven agent gave her a kind look. "There is at least one notorious rebel criminal hiding in the area."

"We are a clinic. We don't fight. We heal the sick."

"Rebels don't ask permission," the younger of the two agents said.

"They use disguises and fake identities and violence to get what they want," the older agent said. "This is what the sketch artist came up with based on a witness description."

Leslie stared at the sketch. She had thought her throat could get any drier, but staring at the sketch of Miranda, it had gone from desert dry to haven't seen rain for five hundred years. Never had she been so grateful for a surgical mask.

"Do you recognize her?" The older man peered at Leslie intently.

She returned his stare steadily. "I've never seen her before." Somehow, she kept her voice natural. "You say she's hiding in the area? Here? In Baltimore? I haven't heard of any fighting here. How do you know she or any rebels are around?"

"She broke the nose of the twelve-year-old son of the agent who heads our squad."

A gasp escaped Leslie. *She broke a boy's nose?* Leslie gripped the edge of the table to keep her hands from shaking. "That poor boy," she squeaked out.

"The boy injured her as well. Which is why we are here."

Wait. Miranda's injured? "When did this happen?"

"This past Monday, before school."

She didn't seem injured on Wednesday or yesterday.

The agents both drilled her with eyes that demanded some kind of response.

Leslie searched for something to say, some way to get the agents to say more, but there wasn't enough air in the tiny room. She swallowed, which didn't help her dry throat. "I've been in here all morning. No one's hiding here. Who could fit in any of these cabinets?"

The younger man laughed and got a sharp elbow from the other agent, who opened the door and left. "Thank you for your cooperation," the younger man said and followed the other agent. He left the door open, and they marched down the hall, banging doors open as they went. At the end of the hall, they opened the last door. A woman shrieked.

Still shaking, Leslie caught her breath. *Why hadn't that patient left when the buzzer sounded?* When the agents exited alone, she heaved a sigh of relief. A flush of anger stopped her shaking. *The Fellowship's lack of respect for our rights has gotten worse.*

Leslie pulled the door closed behind her and hurried down the hall, wondering if she should warn Monkshood or Miranda first.

Chapter Fourteen

Instead of walking home after her shift, Miranda rode the trackless trolley north through a faint haze that made Baltimore's streets look wet without the benefit of rain. *Who does Ethan think he is? I don't need an assignment from him. I know where to go and what to do. If he'd have listened to me, he'd know too.*

She stepped down off the trolley. Slipped on the slick pavement. Jerked her arms wide like a tightrope walker. Balance regained, she continued with determined steps toward the address of the bandaged man's apartment.

Only a block down the street, the back of her neck prickled with the feeling that eyes were on her. With a sideways glance, she spied an old woman in a rocker on her front porch, who stopped rocking and stared.

Up and down this section of Roland Avenue, two-story traditional-style houses with large, immaculate front lawns lined both sides of the quiet residential street. A Fellowship neighborhood. Her drab non-Fellowship clothes didn't belong here.

Damn it, Ethan. You distracted me, so I didn't think. Reluctantly, she put her head down like a submissive non-Fellowship worker. The limited visibility that afforded her, the chuffing of window air conditioners, and the whine of traffic passing kept her alert for any sound or sign of danger.

The quiet residential homes gave way to small shops, then to rentals and apartments. Tall, block-long red-brick apartments for students and faculty from any of the three nearby universities. Also quiet.

Miranda's pulse quickened. According to the address, she was close. She walked a little faster. Cursed Ethan again that she was unable to run because of what she wore.

A small sound startled her. She spun around jerkily. Searched for the source of the sound.

A Second Sphere agent headed away from her and straight into a three-sided enclosure full of dumpsters.

Every muscle in Miranda's body tensed. *What the hell is he up to?* He faced the other direction, but she had to be careful not to draw his attention. She turned slowly back north, toward the address.

Her gut tightened uneasily. Something was wrong. Really wrong. Her steps faltered.

She cast a glance behind her to be certain he hadn't turned. Glimpsed a young non-Fellowship woman with her arms full of thick textbooks backing away from him. Miranda sucked in a breath. *Nope. None of my business.* She took a step forward.

"Please don't," a soft, barely intelligible voice pleaded. "I'm late for class."

Miranda heaved a sigh through gritted teeth. *He wouldn't dare. Not in daylight. Would he?* She glanced over her shoulder again.

He'd backed the young woman deep into the garbage enclosure. Its tall fence shielded the trash containers—and anything that happened in there—from the street. He leaned close, his nose inches from the woman's face. She turned away. He pulled her hair and drew her close for a kiss. His other hand reached under her skirt.

The sight rekindled the fire in Miranda's heart. Her fists curled. She took slow, measured steps around the corner. Then darted to the side of the apartment building. Didn't move. Didn't breathe. *What am I doing? I'm not armed.* Agents are. Always. Statue-still, she listened intently. The noises of daily life surrounded her: vehicles rumbled down the street, machines growled, and trees whispered. Traffic in the distance.

She couldn't stop herself. She had to see what was happening. Rounded the corner.

From this angle, heavy shadows shrouded the man and made the girl invisible. Muffled sobs came from the area.

Loathing scorched Miranda's veins. She had to do something. Stop this. She didn't know what she would do without a weapon, but she had to try.

Neither the man nor the girl noticed her, too absorbed in their struggles.

Eyes targeted on the man, the threat, she slowed, took a deep breath, and entered the garbage enclosure.

He faced the corner, his legs spread wide. One hand tight against the girl's mouth.

Her dark eyes were terror-wide and riveted on him.

Zip.

"Uh-uh, uh-uh, hm-mm-mm."

Miranda's heart lurched. She slid one foot in front of the other. Her toe bumped something solid. The hair on her neck rose.

She bent slowly without taking her eyes off her target. Groped for the object. Books. A pile of them. *The girl's textbooks.*

The man's breathing grew louder, faster, harsher.

Miranda picked up the thickest book. Tested its weight. *Heavy.* Raised it like a baseball bat.

Dove forward, struck the man on the side of the head. Hard.

He released the girl, staggered sideways. Stunned.

The girl's mouth worked soundlessly.

The man clawed at the dumpster.

Miranda pulled the girl out of the corner with her free hand. "Run."

Gasping, shaking, the girl pointed.

The agent stumbled toward Miranda, groping for his sidearm. His face twisted with pain and confusion, then he snarled, "I've seen your face…"

Miranda lunged. Drove the book into his throat.

His head jerked back. His eyes fluttered, and he fell to the ground.

Miranda straddled his body, peered down at him.

His mouth opened and closed spasmodically, gasping for air.

Rapist recognized me. She smashed the book into his face with all her might.

His body jerked. One arm feebly tried to protect his head. His other hand fumbled at the snap holding his gun in his holster.

Blood pounded in her ears. She raised the book over her head and brought it down again.

Bones crunched. He took rapid, gurgling breaths. Shuddered. Sighed. Stilled.

Straddling his body, she stared at him, book raised and ready. She drew great, ragged breaths. Prodded his ribs with her foot.

He didn't move.

Book ready, she bent and watched his chest. His motionless chest. She stepped over the body to the enclosure's entrance. The girl was out of sight, thank goodness.

She tossed the book into one of the stinking bins. Strode out of the enclosure determined to finish her mission. At the corner, crossed the street.

A scream came from behind her.

Miranda caught her breath. *Act normal.* She paused, glanced behind her. Saw no one. She shrugged and resumed walking.

A young man hurried toward her.

She swallowed hard. Cast her eyes down. *My hands. Clothes. His blood.* A tremor shook her. She knotted her fists. Tucked them into the folds of her skirt, drew them close to hide the worst stains.

The young man hurried past as if he hadn't even seen her.

She breathed out in relief but didn't relax. *Have to find a place to clean up. Please let there be a gas station or a Dairy Queen soon.*

But she was closer to West University Avenue than she remembered. She drew even with the corner sign she had been looking for.

The rectangular red-brick building sat on a triangular piece of land. Three stories tall, four if you count the dormers that dotted the sloped roof. A sleepy building, without a soul in sight.

Miranda took a deep breath, walked up the wide steps, across the columned porch, and went inside.

———

CLIMBING THE NARROW STAIRCASE TO THE THIRD FLOOR, MIRANDA could scarcely breathe, certain someone would appear and see her. See the blood.

But the only thing that filled the hallway was a nauseating blend of fish, hot oil, and something burning.

She reached the end of the hallway and a door marked 311. She grabbed the knob.

It didn't yield.

She checked both directions and pulled out her library card. Slipped it between the door and frame. Manipulated her card until the latch clicked.

She stepped inside the dark, empty room. Closed the door. And released the breath she'd held. An intoxicating rush filled her. *I saved that girl. With nothing but a book, I saved her.*

The rush floundered, turned. Her neck grew warm. A wave of lightheadedness swept over her. *I killed a man.* She bent, hands on her knees. Took a slow, deep breath. *He wasn't a man. He was despicable.* Another breath. *A would-be rapist.* A steadier breath. *A monster.*

She straightened. Got a look at the apartment. Empty. Not a single piece of furniture, scrap of paper, or sign anyone had ever lived here. Pristine vacuum marks on the rug were the only evidence anyone had been inside.

Miranda raised her hand toward her face. The sickly-sweet odor of blood made her gag. She scanned the room. On her left, the bathroom stood ajar.

She rushed inside. Stood uncertainly over the lid-up. Squashed the memory of being violently ill after she had killed. *I'm not that Miranda anymore.*

Her stomach pitched up and down. She took deep breaths until she beat the nausea. Faced the sink.

Reflected in the polished mirror above the sink was a stony-faced woman she barely recognized. A woman with blood splashes on her face and neck. Miranda's hands trembled. The trembling spread. *I'm stronger now. I stopped his brutality.* The trembling lessened. *Strong enough to save that young woman and stop evil. Strong enough to stop Irene. Strong enough to stop the Fellowship. On my own.* The nausea receded. She turned on the faucet.

Pipes gurgled. The gurgling grew closer, morphed into a sloshing sound. Water splashed into the sink. She plunged her hands into the water. The unheated water chilled her. She scrubbed her hands together. The water turned pink. She kept scrubbing until long after the water ran clear.

She washed her face and arms and neck. Peered at her blood-spattered skirt and legs. Noticed bloody footprints on the floor. Gasped. *I've left a trail for anyone to follow.* She balanced on one foot and examined the bottom of her shoe. *Damn.* She took her shoes off. No way she could erase the footprints outside leading back to the dead man, but she damn sure wouldn't lead anyone from here to anywhere else.

No towels hung on the walls. She searched in the small vanity. Nothing in the drawers. She groped around the space under the sink. Her fingers closed on something wrapped in paper. Grinned. *They missed something.* A soft something in paper. She pulled it out.

A gauze roll.

Evidence. He was here. Triumph flooded her. She hated to open it, but it was all she had. She tore off a section with her teeth. Scrubbed her clothes, her legs and her shoes. Got her legs and shoes clean. For once, she was grateful for the drab brown clothes. The former blood splatters, now wet splotches, blended with the older stains gained from the diner.

Someone's bound to follow those footprints. Been here too long. Avoiding her bloody footsteps, she made her way to the front door. Scanned the room one more time, and left.

Sirens filled the twilight. She walked north on Roland Avenue, away from the building, away from the garbage enclosure. But the scene in the enclosure played on repeat in her brain. She fought to bury the memory. *Beryl didn't second-guess herself.* She passed the first bus stop. *The rapist was Fellowship through and through. He'd probably committed countless atrocities in the Fellowship's name...*

She walked past the second bus stop. *I did what I had to do. What Beryl would do...*

No, Beryl would have done worse. He got better than he deserved.

At the third bus stop, she boarded the bus headed for home.

Chapter Fifteen

Still vexed by her mother's latest phone call, Annabelle waited, alert but comfortable in her gray cotton jumpsuit. Outside the French doors before her, twilight deepened the shadows which hid the nocturnal animals of Zekiah Swamp, who chirped and trilled, hooted and screeched. The sharp, sweet smell of the recently varnished wood in the new fighting arena covered the scent of her opponent.

There. Her bare feet picked up vibrations in the floor. Vibrations of the stealthy approach of a twelve-year-old. The sound of her cocky young opponent's breathing came next, broadcasting eagerness and overconfidence. Annabelle almost smiled. *I will deliver a message she won't forget.*

The rhythm of the girl's approach changed.

Annabelle pivoted with her right arm extended straight and rigid.

The girl's eyes widened, but her out-of-control momentum drove her forward. Her soft neck smacked into Annabelle's arm. The girl gasped and fell backward onto the thick green floor mat.

Annabelle bent and drove an elbow into the girl's solar plexus with enough force for the girl to feel it for a few days.

The girl wheezed spasmodically. Tears streamed from her eyes. Her kicks, ineffectual.

Annabelle stepped back, out of reach.

The girl bared her teeth, leaped to her feet, and drew her knife.

"Hold," Annabelle said.

The girl immediately sheathed her knife. Assumed an at-ease stance with no sign of her earlier aggression.

Annabelle inclined her head to the girl. "You would do well to remember Azrael anticipates her opponent's next move and avoids it."

The girl bowed her head. "Yes, Blessed One."

Annabelle strode over to the instructor, who stood near the French doors. "Her skill still lags."

"We fear the damage from the explosions has crippled her inner angel." The instructor's tone hinted she thought this youngest survivor of the SABR attack needed termination.

Annabelle quelled the rage that festered inside. "It is His will that we reawaken and re-train her inner angel." She drilled the instructor with a commanding look. "We cannot afford to fail." *There are too few of us remaining.*

The instructor's eyes focused on a point over Annabelle's shoulder. "Yes, Blessed One. His will be done now and forever."

Annabelle marched to the door, slid into her loafers, and left. Being called Blessed One was only marginally better than Resurrected One. But her not-sisters insisted on an honorific. *No longer not-sisters. My angels. My command.*

A gaggle of geese honked from the far edges of the fast-moving, shallow water off the boardwalk and drew Annabelle's attention. She stepped up to the safety fence, a single strand of rope that looped from one wooden stanchion to the next. Breathed in the breeze-freshened earthy aromas of the swamp. Annabelle loved the swamp more than any other place she'd lived. But this night, the Lord's most tranquil place did not ease the tension in Annabelle's shoulders or calm her thoughts. *Am I so weak that a call from Mother reduces me to my lesser, human half?*

She turned and strode down the elevated boardwalk, past the building with the canteen and kitchen.

All the materials needed to construct this sanctuary had to be brought in by small boats. Construction workers, men, drove stilts deep into the Earth and built the boardwalk and all the buildings. Men chosen from the wicked.

Men, you denied to us, her inner angel complained.

I must see to my angels' needs first.

We hunger.

*My dreams signify I will build this place for all our angels here…*and *find Sandra…*Her dreams did not tell her which to do first, nor when she would ascend. She wished she could talk to the Prophet directly. Learn the Lord's will from his lips.

She stepped through the doorway into the laboratory. Cool air quickly dried the perspiration on her face. Gooseflesh riddled her skin. She pulled the sliding door shut. The pulsing mechanical sounds of dozens of pumps replaced the songs of the swamp creatures.

"Resurrected One!" Anna leaped off her stool and stood. Embroidered on the right shoulder of her white lab coat was YST 2891.

Annabelle nodded politely. "Good morning, YST 2891. How are our children this morning?"

YST 2891 bowed her head. "Good morning, Blessed One. All are progressing. I anticipate they will be ready for decanting on schedule." She offered a clipboard to Annabelle.

On the clipboard were pages and pages of readings from the various gauges on the many pendulous, semitransparent artificial wombs that hung from the ceiling.

Annabelle declined the clipboard.

YST 2891's brows tightened the tiniest bit.

"You say they are progressing as they should. That is enough for me."

The tightness faded from YST 2891's face. She was among the youngest who had survived the collapse of the caves with only minor injuries. She gestured toward the nearest artificial womb. "The articles you found have been most enlightening." Her voice took on a more animated tone. "The scientists have new, advanced techniques. The United Federation of Germany must be very rich."

Almost as tall as Annabelle, the heavy artificial womb with its crown of gauges and tubing that snaked up to the ceiling held a girl-child curled in a fetal ball. Tinted pink by the redness of the womb, the girl floated motionlessly in nearly fifty-five gallons of a viscous, nutrient-filled fluid. Pale and skinny, the girl nearly filled the womb. Though Annabelle had known what to expect, the size of the girl inside shocked her. It had nearly doubled in size over the past week.

YST 2891's animated chatter continued. "They have a laboratory filled with magnificent equipment. They transplanted a nucleus into an egg and grew a frog. They called it a clone. I like that word."

Annabelle waved her hand, silenced the chatter, and moved up and down the rows until she'd visited all sixty wombs. Each one held another child-Azrael. Each child-Azrael fed through tubes connected to an intricate network of overhead pipes attached to large stainless-steel vats on each side of the room.

This is the Lord's work.

YST 2891 shadowed Annabelle around the room. Hovered at her shoulder and explained again that the first gauge's needle showed the pressure inside, the second one the ratios of oxygen and other nutrients, and the third one, a graph rather than a gauge, measured the heartbeat and other vital signs. That and the relentless pulsing in the room ratcheted the tension in Annabelle's shoulders up to headache-inducing.

At the end of the last row, her weekly inspection complete, Annabelle gave her usual response. "We look forward to the day our children will stand beside us. Then we shall sing of your mighty acts and excellent deeds, forever and always. His will be done."

YST 2891 bowed her head. "His will be done."

Annabelle asked her usual question. "Is there anything you need?"

"I wonder if—" YST 2891 began. Contrition clouded her face. She bowed her head and stared at her feet. "Forgive me. My angel-within hungers, and that weakens my faith in Doctor Galloway's notes. I shall fast and spend an hour in prayer this evening to realign my spirit."

"I understand. As Angels on Earth, each of us must be vigilant and work to overcome the weaknesses of our present forms," Annabelle said with a small smile. *I hunger too.*

YST 2891 raised her head to gape at Annabelle. "Even you?"

"Yes." *Even me.*

I must feed. I will feed soon.

Annabelle endured the wave of dizziness that washed over her. *My duty to my charges comes first.*

"I will instruct my lieutenants to spell you so you may partake from the donors," she said, unhurriedly. "Excuse me." She exited on the other side of the building. Hurried down the boardwalk, past the arm that led to the dormitories, past the storage building, to the single, one-room cabin-on-stilts that was her sleeping quarters, her refuge.

It held a functional navy-blue blanket and some white sheets on the bed that stood along the long wall on the west side. No pictures on the walls, not even a family photo on the single three-drawer dresser across from her. A kneeling bench sat beneath the curtainless, east-facing window. In here, the swamp's song, muted by the walls, added a level of peace and reverence.

She went straight to the window, kneeled on the bench, and prayed desperately for strength. Ten months since the explosion. Ten months of keeping the search for Sandra secret from her lieutenants and angels was a heavy burden.

Prayer after prayer went unanswered. Annabelle looked up into the heavens. "Without the Prophet to guide me, what am I to do, Lord?"

The Lord has abandoned us because of your weaknesses.

Weaknesses?

You've gone soft. Allowing the imperfect ones to live.

One. One who is Azrael. Surely if the Lord wished to Take her home, he would. How could trust in the Lord be a weakness?

Two. Her. The Prophet himself removed her from his office and life.

Mother? A sour taste rose in Annabelle's throat.

If she is holy, why does she refuse to let us speak to the Prophet?

She is holy. She saved me. For that alone, she remains a holy member of the Fellowship.

She is human, and her losses cause her too much pain.

She saved me. I must save Sandra, thus save her.

The Prophet saved us. Even the Council judged her unworthy. It is our duty to Take her.

No. He healed the dengue fever, but Mother healed my despair. It is my duty to grow the ranks of the Azrael and to honor and respect Mother. I will find Sandra and save her. You will see.

Annabelle burst out the doors and strode down the elevated boardwalk, grabbed a walking stick, and struck out across the swamp and into the trees.

Six minutes later she reached the shelter. The rough-hewn wooden building was the size of a large closet. Meant for meditation and prayer, she'd turned the place into something else.

She turned on her torch and entered. Closed the door behind her. The foulness of human waste and sweat and blood repulsed her. She peered at the man tied to the cane chair in the center. His shirt bloodied. His slacks soiled. Blue and green bruises marked his face. His shoulders slumped. A weak shadow of his former self.

Faster than he could blink, she slipped in closer, shot out her fist, and smashed his nose. She followed that with a one-two shot to his ribs and danced out of reach.

He moaned pitifully. His head drooped and rolled between his shoulders. Blood dripped from his nose and mouth.

She grabbed his hair, raised his head, and stared into his pain-glazed eyes. "Where is Sandra?"

He spat at her. "I've told you I don't know any Sandra."

She drove her right fist deep into his belly.

His mouth worked, trying for more air.

She bent. Put her mouth next to his ear. "You were in the Prophet's home. Had Sandra's clothes. Tell me where she is. And I will set you free."

He could not hold his head up. Stared at her out of the corner of his weary but defiant eyes. "Kill me, you mean."

She drew back a fist. Drove it into his chest, which gave unnaturally.

His breath gurgled, garbling the words he mumbled.

She jerked his head back up. "Say again."

"She's just a housekeeper." His voice held the wispy nature of near-death exhaustion.

"A housekeeper? Why would—?" Annabelle inhaled sharply. "She works for those who hide Sandra. Yes?"

His eyes fluttered.

She glared at him. "Open your eyes. I need an address or a city."

He gave a weak smile. "DC." He released a long sigh, and his eyes drifted closed.

Her angel within inhaled the essence of his death. It lifted her. But only for a moment. Annabelle reclaimed her body.

Relief shook her. She *had* understood the Lord's message in her dream. At least part of it. *But a housekeeper in DC?* That did not narrow her search. DC had hundreds, thousands of housekeepers.

The aroma of a sweet-smelling garden enveloped her. The tomb-stones of Miranda and all her fallen rebels replaced the rough-hewn walls around her. The air filled with the voices of joyful Azrael. Her earthly sister and parents and her Azrael children enjoyed a picnic at her enormous feet. She loomed over everyone and everything. While she watched over them, the Lord touched her shoulder.

The rough walls and the stench reappeared. She stumbled outside. Heart full, she tilted her head up, faced the heavens. "I understand. My search will be fruitful. I will find Sandra, destroy Miranda and the rebels, and Mother and Papa will rejoice with us."

Chapter Sixteen

M

iranda climbed the Baxters' narrow stairwell and stifled her yawn. She hadn't meant to sleep so late, but she'd had four sleepless nights and days since she'd killed that agent. No agents or angels had come for her at the diner or here. *Of course they haven't. Only that girl knows what I did, and who's she going to tell?*

"Gene." A desperately drawn-out word came from the top of the stairs. Frantic pounding. "You've been in there forever!"

Miranda stepped onto the second floor and covered her mouth to hide her grin.

Thea stood outside the home's bathroom, fists propped on her hips. "It's my turn. Hurry up. We'll be late for school." She flipped one and then the other of her shoulder-length braids. "Gene, pleee-ase." The bows in her braids matched her lacy beige pinafore dress.

By comparison, Miranda's own childhood in Virginia featured a palatial home with four bedrooms and two bathrooms, but she and her sister and brother didn't dare create such a scene. Her throat tightened. Her family only looked normal on the outside.

"Breakfast," Evelyn called from downstairs.

The bathroom door banged open, and Gene dashed out. Thea slammed the door behind her.

"Get it while it's hot." Evelyn's tone held a warning that the family knew was toothless.

Thea bolted out of the bathroom.

Miranda washed up and dutifully appeared at the dining room table. The Baxters were all seated and waiting for her.

After the morning blessing, they passed the bowl of white rice and the butter keeper.

Thea leveled an anxiously curious look at Miranda. "Is it boring? Washing dishes all day?" Her question broke the usual silence around the breakfast table and startled everyone.

"Thea, don't be rude." Evelyn's kind tone took the edge off her words.

Thea flushed and looked down at her half-empty bowl of rice, properly chastised.

Unable to bear the girl being rebuked for an innocent question, Miranda pretended to wipe her mouth with her napkin and considered her answer. "I guess it is a little boring, but..." *What? Wanda and Leslie were right. Anything I say will put them in danger.* "Well, when you're an adult, sometimes you do what you must for now," she finished and ignored Evelyn's sharp look. *What did she want? No answer? A lie? I won't lie to the girl by giving her platitudes about being grateful for work during this challenging time.*

Thea picked up her fork and muttered, "Sometimes you do that as a child too."

Miranda's breath caught in her throat. *That's how I felt as a child.* Everything else receded. Voices became muted and indistinct. Even her bowl seemed to be very, very far away.

The table lurched, and something thumped against the wall.

Startled, Miranda grabbed her wobbling bowl.

Voices cried out, "Oh!" "Whoa." "What the—" "Thea!"

"Not my dress. My new dress."

Gene snorted. "Klutz."

Thea stood back from the table, her chair trapped between her and the wall. She held her wet pinafore out from her body. Milky fluid pooled on the table and dribbled to the floor.

Thea stared down at her soiled dress and wailed, "I can't go to school like this."

Evelyn rose and went to her daughter. "Are you hurt?"

Thea shook her head.

"Quick, go upstairs and change."

"I can't be late again," Bernie said. Concern made a deep line between his eyes. "They'll fire me."

Evelyn turned to him. "You and Gene go on ahead. I'll walk Thea to school."

"You're supposed to deliver the ironing to your customer," Bernie said.

"Yes, but I don't want Thea walking to school by herself."

"I can walk to school by myself."

"The roads are too busy—"

"I have an appointment in that direction," Miranda interrupted. She could do that, then search for Irene. "I'll walk her to school." *That'll give me time to talk to her in private.*

"Are you sure?" Evelyn asked.

"Of course. It's on the way." Miranda smiled at Thea. "Go on. Change. I'll wait for you." *If that agent, or anyone, is hurting you...*

Thea ran upstairs.

Her parents, grandparents, and brother hurried off to their morning appointments.

———

THE WALK TO SCHOOL WITH THEA WAS NOT QUITE WHAT MIRANDA HAD expected. Even when Miranda asked friendly questions, Thea's answers were minimal.

Across the street, a girl about Thea's age wearing a non-Fellowship brown dress walked alone. A group of three Fellowship boys walked alongside her, taunting her with shouts of "sinner" and "someone forgot to take out the trash." The girl slowed to a snail's pace, which earned her more taunts. She ran. They kept pace and continued the taunts.

Miranda bit the inside of her cheeks raw. Swallowed the metallic taste and her burning rage. Anything she did would put Thea in danger.

The crowded schoolyard came into view. "Stop for a minute, please," Miranda said.

"I don't want to be late." Thea kept walking.

"There's something private I've wanted to talk to you about," Miranda said.

Thea stopped, turned, and looked up at her.

"You're growing up into a young lady."

Thea rolled her eyes.

"I'm sure your mom has talked to you about that. I wanted to tell you that if—that sometimes—What I'm trying to say is I can teach you to protect yourself."

Thea cocked her head. "Protect myself?"

Miranda tried for a smile. "From anyone who might try to hurt you—or scare you."

Thea's expression changed.

Miranda recognized the fear. "You know, you can tell me about any people—or things—that make you afraid. I will protect you."

Thea quirked her lips in a *yeah, right* expression, stared at the poor girl across the street, then at Miranda.

Couldn't tell a ten-year-old, I can. I killed one agent, I can kill again. "I can't protect the world. But I will protect you."

"Sure," Thea said in her most skeptical tone.

She's right. "I can't protect you all the time." *I have to work at the pot and some catering with Keith.* "But I'll teach you to protect yourself too."

Thea pressed her lips tight and stared, then said, "I don't want to be late." She hurried toward the school.

Miranda knotted her fists and hurried to catch up.

Chapter Seventeen

Irene sat back in the limousine Lucas had sent for her. *Well, if the Council was going for unimpressive, this fits the bill.* The limo parked in a deeply rutted parking area of gravel and weeds beside a long rectangular, one-story warehouse of red brick set on a white concrete base. Nestled among a bunch of other warehouses, it looked like any other warehouse.

Behind the brick front of the building was an elevated dock area, made of concrete blocks painted white. Six iron beams supported the roof over the dock. Widely spaced between the beams were three garage doors for loading and unloading. All of them closed.

Irene pruned her lips. She'd warned Lucas that if her accommodations weren't up to her standards, their deal was off. Looked like he wanted to test her resolve.

Inside was worse than she'd expected. She passed through a dingy hall of grimy doors that smelled of dust with a hint of a floral note all the way to the lobby at the front.

Dark fake wood paneling lined the walls. A worn three-seat bench sat near the door. Directly opposite the front door was a metal desk that held a sign stating, "Ring for service," with an arrow pointing to a red button.

"Hello? The driver said someone was waiting for me."

She pressed her lips tight. Waited, but no one appeared. Took a deep breath, and under her gloved index finger, a muted buzz sounded.

Distant footsteps approached.

She crossed her arms and glared at the hallway.

A wisp of sound came from her left. She swiveled and gaped.

Lucas stood in an open doorway in the middle of the paneled wall. A wall where no door had been visible. "Welcome," he boomed in a ministerial tone. "Follow me and see your new home."

She followed him through a room with high ceilings, white walls, rows of empty shelving, and echoes. Something didn't add up. *Aha, it's what I am* not *seeing.* Only one garage door was visible.

They went down an aisle of empty shelves to a second secret door and stepped into a park-like area. Memories of the cave and rocks falling hit her with a surge of lightheadedness. *This is not the cave. No rocks over my head. Only a metal roof.* She forced herself to breathe slowly and savor the scent of the flowers that surrounded her.

"Can you hear me? Are you all right?" Lucas's voice sounded far away.

She shook off the unpleasantness and beamed at him. "Of course, silly. I'm just…taking it all in."

"Come, your home awaits on the other side of these bushes."

The bushes were taller than him by at least two feet. On each side of the arched break in the bushes stood a pair of black stone angels with folded wings on Roman-style columns. She stepped under the arch. Gawked at the stone-clad house to her right. The house had a Spanish tile roof, a vaulted porch, curtained windows, and an extra-wide wood door with a rugged wood lintel. It looked exactly like the Mar del Plata home of her dreams. *Inside the warehouse.*

She didn't wait for permission but went straight through the front door.

"Oh," she exclaimed softly. Stared into the long room that functioned as living and dining room, and kitchen. A stunning vermillion sofa. She ran a hand over the sofa's soft fabric. Above the sofa, an oversized cubist painting dominated the room. The painting picked up the vermillion, and so did the base of the rounded-triangle coffee table and the cone chairs at the glass dining table. Soft dove-gray walls allowed the furniture to shine.

A rich, modern, and decadent home? She suppressed the excitement bubbling up inside.

"I take it you like it?" Lucas asked.

Determined not to give him the satisfaction, she murmured, "So far, so good."

Down the hall, there was a nicely appointed guest room, a serviceable bathroom, and the primary bedroom. Her bedroom. The dark rafters of the vaulted ceiling matched the dark wood of the furniture. The bedclothes were royal blue with a pink floral print. It was serene and perfect.

"This will do for now," she said aloud. She did an internal Sandra-style victory dance. The memory of her daughter sobered her. "Where's Sandra?"

Lucas scratched his nose. "Well, now you can't expect miracles. We've only just started looking." He motioned for her to follow him. "There are a couple more things you need to see."

She followed him back to the kitchen.

"There are emergency exits hidden throughout the warehouse." Lucas opened the door. Inside appeared to be a slightly wider-than-usual pantry. "Release the latch here." He reached inside the doorframe. *Click. Pop.* He pushed the shelves, canned goods and all, inward and revealed a steep, dark staircase that had a faint earthy, musty smell.

Irene peered down the uninviting exit. "Where does it go?"

"Down to a buried culvert."

She inhaled sharply. "You mean one of those built-over rivers that crisscross Baltimore?"

He gave her a sly grin. "It's a small tributary of the Jones Falls Stream."

Irene's heart jumped erratically. "How deep is it?"

"Don't worry. We made certain it's safe. Your shoes will get wet, but it's only six blocks before you reach a ladder to the surface."

Her chest hollowed. "Why do I need this?"

"It's a precaution. One you probably will never need." His smarmy smile did not reassure her. "Come, there's more to see."

He led her to the kitchen, out a sliding glass door, and onto a beautiful courtyard full of flowers surrounded by another set of tall bushes with another pair of stone angels gracing an archway between them.

Beyond that opening stood two buildings, one on each side of another small courtyard. One building had a facade similar to her new home. The other looked like a miniature Fellowship Center. The one the rebels destroyed.

He led her to the one similar to her own new house. "This is Felix's home," he said, and ushered her into a large room that was an extraordinary mix of hospital and home.

The nurse beside Felix's bed put a finger to her lips and mimed that Felix was asleep.

The two-toned walls, with an earthy green on the lower half and a soft sky-blue on the upper half, gave the room serenity. Soft notes of a songbird almost defeated the otherwise hospital aura of the room. The sight of Felix in a standard hospital bed sent a shudder through her. She placed a hand on her chest to imply the shudder was heartbreak.

On the wall behind Felix's head, there were spigots labeled oxygen, suction, and air. Soft drapes curtained off other medical equipment and a bathroom.

The nurse's desk area sat on one side of the room and had a wall of cabinets behind it. There was a sitting nook with a lush row of green plants beneath a window—to the outdoors? *No, not an actual window—an excellent fake.*

Irene nodded at the large sliding door that took up half the rear wall. "What's that for?"

"Shhh." The nurse cautioned.

Lucas took Irene out into the hallway. "That door opens to an alley-side dock for ease of access if he has a medical emergency."

"Right. I've seen my place and Felix's. What is the third building for?" The fake Fellowship building was too large to store garden supplies. *Home for the nurses and housekeepers, perhaps. Or security?*

"Why don't we go see?" Lucas said with a sly smile and led her inside.

Irene turned a look of disbelief on Lucas. Less than a third of the size, the space was otherwise identical to the old Fellowship Center. "Are we going to hold worship here?"

"Don't be silly." He gestured at the replica statue. "This is where you'll practice."

"I'll what?"

"Maybe practice is the wrong word; prepare. Yes, that's better. You'll use this space to help prepare for official appearances."

Her ears filled with the rushing, pounding of her blood. "You think that I've forgotten how to be the Prophet's wife in the past ten months?" She struggled to keep her tone civil.

"Oh, no. No, that's not what I meant. I meant you would help prepare Felix for appearances." He must have seen the look on her face. "Not the real Felix, his stand-in—until the real Felix can make appearances himself."

Outrage blurred her vision. "You said nothing about a stand-in. Who could act as a stand-in?" She half-turned away from Lucas, gasped. Whirled to face him again. "You don't mean a stand-in as in —a *husband*—do you?"

Lucas laughed a little too heartily. "That thought never crossed my mind." He led her to the auditorium.

Tiered levels of chairs, enhanced by paintings of chairs in perspective, gave the illusion of a full-sized auditorium.

"No," Lucas continued. "The people believe the Prophet has been on sabbatical these past ten months. And though we've had helpers create new prayers out of old ones, our people need to see the Prophet, so we've hired an actor to...stand-in for Felix. Until he's healed, of course."

An actor? Immediate images of handsome young men strutting about came to mind. Irene shook her head. "There's not enough makeup or an actor so talented that anyone will believe he is Felix."

Lucas led her into a windowed room at the back of the theater. Its only fixture—a control desk. "And that is why it took us so long to get the right person for the job." He touched a button on the control panel.

The house lights dimmed, and a spotlight lit the stage. In the spotlight stood a man in Felix's robes. A man with Felix's hairline. A man with Felix's ears.

No. Not Felix. She strode toward the stage. "Is this man supposed to be a long-lost twin brother or something?"

"We had an excellent plastic surgeon work on him. It took a little longer to heal than we'd hoped, but here he is. Healed. He's been practicing his walk and speech, but you will help refine his act." He nodded to the actor.

"Ah, here comes my dear wife, now," Fake Felix said. He came forward and offered to take Irene's hand to help her up onto the stage.

She ignored his hand. "Felix would never help me up. He knows I am perfectly capable."

"Of course." Fake Felix dropped his hand. "Forgive me."

"And you're speaking too slowly and too clearly." She turned to Lucas. *I will not let you and this charlatan destroy me. Not again.* "This" —she waved her hand at the actor—"will never work."

Lucas's smile stayed on his lips, but his eyes gleamed. "You are here to make it work. The two of you will make certain no one suspects he is not the real Prophet." His tone had a hint of or-else to it.

Irene met Lucas's look with one of her own. "This man's three inches too tall, his voice is all wrong, and…" *Maybe they want him to fail—us to fail.* The thought chilled her deeply.

"If he's too tall, wear taller heels. Teach him. You will appear before the public in two weeks. You will make this work, or the Council will take action. Trust me, neither of you wants that."

You dare to threaten me? She composed her face into a submissive daughter of the Fellowship expression. *If you could buy him…* "Then we will be ready," she said. *Annabelle and her angels will persuade him to help me. Then they'll make certain you and the Council can never threaten me or my family ever again.*

Chapter Eighteen

Leslie closed the last patient's chart, placed it in the basket by the door, and flipped the blue flag for the doctor to come. For once, she had all her charting finished so she could leave when her last patient left. Out of habit, she checked the hall for orange flags, the ones that meant a nurse was needed. *Wait. There's one. That's odd. I could have sworn the patient in that room had gone home.* She hurried down the hall to the last room and hesitated. *No chart? Doc must have forgotten to push the flag back again.* She opened the door.

Wanda looked up from the chair in the room.

Leslie's pulse slammed against her throat. She glanced up and down the hall, then slipped into the room and shut the door. "What's wrong? Is Ian okay? Are you?"

Waving her hands in a calm-down motion, Wanda shook her head. "No one's hurt. Just listen."

"We can't talk here." Leslie's insides quivered. She swallowed, forced herself to breathe slower. "What's so urgent you'll risk my job and all the people here?"

"Ian and I got to talking and—"

"Ian?" Leslie's chest tightened.

"Calm down," Wanda said with exasperation. "Ian's fine. We need your help."

"Medical help?"

"Oh, for—" Wanda looked up at the ceiling. Took a deep breath, then looked at Leslie again. "Just listen for a minute. Okay?"

Leslie nodded and pressed her lips tight against the million and two questions that roared inside her.

"Miranda's been leaving us out of whatever she's doing, so Ian and I did a little searching on our own. We think we've found someone. Someone important. I've reached out to Monkshood but got a message he's out of state."

"Okay." Leslie drew her brows together. "He'll be back, won't he?"

Wanda gave her a look that shut her up again. "We need him now. No one else can or will give us the go-ahead."

I thought Miranda and Ian were problems. Not you. "It's late. What do you want me to do?"

"We need your help to follow a woman. A cleaning woman. She goes to a house in DC every day. This house has Second Sphere agents guarding it. We've never seen the person hiding in there. We think it is the Prophet or Irene."

"There are thousands of reasons someone never comes outside. Not to mention the weather. Maybe they don't like the humidity or the fall chill in the air or—."

"What if we have found the Prophet? Monkshood would want us to confirm that, wouldn't he?"

"That's what he asked us to do." Leslie laced her voice with her I-don't-understand tone. "You just need to wait for Monkshood to come back."

"We don't know how long that'll be. What if we lose our best chance?"

"Could we talk about this later? I'll be off in—" She glanced at her watch.

Wanda gave her a side-eye. "Why are you resisting? Are you afraid of making Monkshood angry, or is it something else? Maybe you don't wanna upset Miranda. Or you don't want to work with Ian?" Wanda's mouth dropped open. "That's it, isn't it? It's Ian? Your own brother? What's going on between you two?"

Leslie took a big breath to blast Wanda for wasting her time and jeopardizing her job. Clenched her face and fists. *Can't make a scene here.* She forced herself to relax, blew out the breath she held. "Nothing is going on." She crossed back to the door, hand on the doorknob. "I'm tired of hiding and sneaking around and lying and all of—." She threw her hands up in the air. "I like my life here. It's...almost normal."

"Normal." Wanda rubbed her mouth and eyed Leslie. "This life" —she waved a hand showing the exam room and beyond—"is a lie. You aren't Leslie, normal girl. You don't belong in Baltimore. Girl, do you honestly think living this lie, with the Fellowship breathing down your neck all the time, is normal? Or something you can keep up forever?"

Leslie locked her jaw. She wanted to shout, *yes, yes I do.* But she couldn't. *Wanda is right. This isn't normal.* Her shoulders drooped. She studied the floor in front of her feet. "Say I agree to help you, and we find out that the Prophet is hiding there, then what?"

"If Monkshood isn't back, we do what he'd do if he could. Capture the son of a bitch."

Leslie sputtered, "We do what?" Her knots in her stomach had knots.

"I can't think of any faster way to destroy the Fellowship than to show the sheep that their Prophet is a fraud."

Leslie opened her mouth, but Wanda was right again. She met Wanda's gaze. "Give me five minutes. I can't leave until the last patient's done." And that wasn't a lie.

———

Two hours later, she was in DC. She sat in the backseat of the Chevy, behind Ian and next to Wanda. She stared at a quaint stone-and-brick, two-story house on a corner opposite two abandoned churches. It didn't look special. It had a stone entry and trim, high-peaked roofs, one windowed attic room, a cupola on the side that didn't rise to the second story, and a stone chimney. No security fence, not even a picket fence. A heavy line of trees between it and a third abandoned church building next door and a stand-alone garage opened onto the alley behind the house. A man in shirt-sleeves stood on the porch.

They turned the corner. Another man stood in the cupola of concrete and stone facing the side street, and a third man stood on the back porch.

She craned her neck looking at it until they'd moved too far down the block. *How can anyone expect to be secretive in a corner house?*

The picturesque neighborhood of historic homes had trees lining the green space between the street and the sidewalk.

"We saw two Second Sphere agents enter the house yesterday after the housekeeper left," Ian said. "We didn't see the car that dropped them off or see them or anyone else leave. The blinds are always closed, so we can't see inside. All I know is that some men are hanging out around the house. Why do you think the Prophet is inside?"

She suspected Ian wanted to find the Prophet so badly he couldn't be objective.

"They get groceries every day," Wanda added. "A lot of groceries. And a nurse visits every couple of days. She stays inside for about thirty minutes. Why else would there be a nurse?"

"Many people need a nurse," Leslie said. "Based on the age of the house, the occupants are probably of the age when many people need nurses."

Wanda grunted. "Why would a nice old couple have Second Sphere agents staying at the house?"

"There's got to be lots of reasons. Maybe it's a former counselor or some dignitary."

"What we need is proof," Wanda said reasonably. "That's why you're here."

Leslie gaped at her. "How am *I* going to get proof you couldn't?"

"You're gonna go to the door, act like you're selling something or maybe you're lost—that's it. You're lost and you need to use their phone."

"You expect people living in an obviously Fellowship neighborhood to open the door to a random non-Fellowship person?"

Ian glanced over his shoulder. "You can say you're on your way home from the pharmacy down the block."

"Right," Wanda said. "They don't need to know where you live, how far you need to walk. And if they won't let you in, then delay them closing the door as long as you can. See as much as you can and let us know."

"I'll loop around the block and drop you off on that side of the street," Ian said. "You walk a block to the house. See what you can, and we'll wait for you down the side street at the next corner."

Leslie couldn't meet the reflection of Ian's eager gaze in the rearview mirror.

"Second Sphere agents don't guard a house for no reason," he added.

"They might guard a counselor or a dignitary."

"My gut tells me it's the Prophet."

She knew Ian too well. He would never give up on this. She sighed. "If I don't get arrested and I see nothing important, we're done here. Right?"

He flashed her a grin. Turned down the side street.

She had a bad feeling about this mission of Ian's.

She got out when he stopped the car and walked the block back to the house. She took a deep breath, and then went up the walkway to knock on the front door.

Surprisingly, the guard said nothing to her. Did nothing except watch her.

It seemed she stood under his scrutiny for hours instead of minutes.

A muted metal-on-metal sliding sound came from inside. The door opened with a creak. "How can I help you?"

Leslie wasn't sure what she'd expected, but the woman who opened the door looked like any other housewife. She wore the same from-the-rack pink floral print dress many of Leslie's patients wore.

The woman peered into Leslie's face. "Are you all right?"

"Yes, I mean, not really. I'm sorry," Leslie stammered. "Sorry to bother you, may I use your phone? I need my brother to come pick me up."

"What happened? Car broke down?" The woman craned her neck and peered both up and down the street.

Leslie opened her mouth. Shut it. *If I work at the pharmacy down the street, why didn't I go back to the pharmacy to use the phone?* She tried to think quickly. *What can I say?* "I'd planned to walk home today, but after a very busy day at the pharmacy, and it's so hot and well—I'm afraid I'm going to faint. I need him to come pick me up." She hoped her smile looked a little pathetic.

The woman gave Leslie a look up and down, shrugged. "Make it quick."

Leslie stepped into a modest living room that could have been her own parents' home. Nothing out of place. Nothing hinted at anything nefarious.

The woman beckoned, "Follow me," to Leslie and led her into the kitchen.

A man stood at the counter chopping carrots, looked up and smiled.

The woman said, "She's going to use the phone." The man—*her husband?*—nodded and continued chopping.

The woman gestured at a light green Bakelite phone on the wall.

Leslie tore her eyes from the man whose haircut looked suspiciously like a Second Sphere agent haircut and picked up the handset. Shielded the dial and dialed the number for the recorded weather. Spoke into the receiver. "Hi Joe, I need a ride home, please." Waited as if she were listening for an answer. "Yes, I'm at the corner of 16th Street Northwest and Webster Street Northwest." Pause. "Sure, I'll meet you there. Thank you. You're my hero." Pause. "Bye." She turned slowly, studying the very normal kitchen. "Thank you so much." She smiled, including the man who still chopped carrots—*how many carrots do two people eat?*—in her smile.

"No problem," said the woman. "We girls need to stick together."

Leslie walked back through the living room. A hallway door squeaked. Out of the corner of her eye, she spied a young girl's curly blonde head peeking out.

"Ocean," a male voice called.

The little head disappeared, and a door closed.

Leslie pretended she hadn't seen or heard anything. Stopped at the front door and faced the woman again. "Thank you again. I really appreciate the use of your phone."

The woman smiled a smile that seemed a little off. She reached around Leslie, blocking Leslie and forcing her toward the door as the woman opened it.

An icy knot rose in Leslie's throat. She smiled and walked out backward. "You have no" —the door slammed shut—"idea..." She turned, nodded goodbye to the man on the porch. Her back crawled under his watchful stare down the steps and until she followed the sidewalk around the corner. The man in the cupola porch.

Leslie continued on her way as if she had noticed nothing

strange. *Wanda and Ian are right*. She couldn't say either the Prophet or Irene was there, but as Ian said, Second Sphere agents don't just watch any old house. Whatever or whoever was in that house, it was strange enough that Monkshood needed to know.

Chapter Nineteen

Miranda reached for the curtain to Virgil's storeroom and hesitated. *Would the others know she'd killed that agent?* She blew out an impatient-with-herself breath. *How could they? After a week and a half, there were still no news reports, no public search.*

"We should wait for Miranda." Wanda's voice came from the other side of the curtain.

"I'm not sure we should tell her," Leslie said.

Miranda burst through the curtains. "Tell me what?" She glared at Leslie, then Wanda and Ian. "What has Ethan got you doing behind my back?"

"It was my idea." Seated at the table, Ian pointed to his own chest. "Ethan has nothing to do with this—yet."

"We found something." Wanda sat opposite him. "Not sure it's anything important."

Leslie thinks it's important I don't know. "Why don't you let me decide if it's important?"

Ian leaned back, balancing his chair on its back legs. "Wanda came to me about a week ago. She had heard a rumor through housekeeper gossip."

"I kept hearing rumors about a housekeeper getting paid a lot of money to keep quiet about a house she was cleaning," Wanda said. "It made me curious. At first, it seemed like it was just a rumor. But an acquaintance I trust confirmed the rumor. Gave me the housekeeper's address. Ian and I followed her. She went to the same house every week. It seemed normal at first. Then yesterday, we saw them."

"Who?"

"The house is guarded by three Second Sphere agents," Wanda said.

Acid churned in Miranda's stomach. "You think they protect someone. Who? The Prophet?" She glowered at Wanda. "And you didn't come to me?"

Wanda raised her hand as if that could stop the burn of Miranda's stare. "Ethan sent you to the pharmacy. Ian had been relieved of watch. Besides, it was just a rumor. We drove past, and we saw the agents, and we didn't dare get close enough to find out more. You were working, so we asked Leslie to help."

"I only found out about it yesterday," Leslie said. "But when I was inside, I didn't see any proof that the Prophet or Irene were there. It could be a counselor's or a deacon's home or even someone the Second Sphere is interrogating."

"You were inside a house where the Prophet and my sister might hide, and you don't think that's important for me to know?" Acid rose from Miranda's stomach to the back of her mouth.

"I didn't want to get your hopes up."

Miranda aimed a slow burn at Leslie. "You think hopes are bad?"

Leslie sighed deeply. "I don't mean it like that. I'm just…"

"You're just what?"

Leslie stood, came around the table to Miranda, and touched her arm. "I'm concerned."

Miranda shook her off and searched Leslie's face, amazed she hadn't seen how duplicitous Leslie was before.

"You've been so full of anger and hate, and I heard about the boy you punched, so I—"

"Excuse me?" The pressure inside Miranda built until it was unbearable. "The boy I punched? Who told you I punched anyone?"

Leslie bit her lower lip. "The Second Sphere searched the clinic the other day, looking for someone fitting your description who punched a young schoolboy and broke his nose. They said the boy was a Second Sphere agent's son."

"Whoa," Ian said with what sounded like respect. "You broke a Second Sphere brat's nose?" He chortled. "I'd have paid to see that."

Leslie shot him a quick disapproving look. "I'm sure you had a reason, but you risked everything." She waved her hand in a sweeping gesture. Faced Miranda, with a look of pity on her face. "I know what you're going through. When they took my parents and big brother, I was angry, too…"

Miranda jammed her tongue into her cheek. Couldn't hold back. "Are you pointing a finger at me for needing to make Irene pay for Beryl's and Nick's deaths when you spent five years searching and planning revenge?" Miranda focused her glare on Ian and Wanda. "And you two agree with her?"

"I didn't have time to object before you charged in," Wanda said dryly.

"It's a damned good thing I *charged in.*" *I'm tempted to send Leslie back to Ethan.*

A shadow flickered across the redhead's face.

I knew it. "There's more to this, isn't there?"

The three of them stared anywhere except at Miranda.

"Do I have to pry it out of you? Damn it, someone tell me what she saw."

Leslie spoke in a quiet voice. "The woman who answered the door acted normal until a little girl poked her head out of a hallway door. Then everything changed."

Miranda's pulse pummeled her throat. She opened her mouth to demand more information, but if she did that, Leslie would clam up. Miranda clamped her lips shut and waited.

"A man called her Ocean," Ian said. "Who would name anyone Ocean? It's gotta be a code name."

"What did this little girl look like?"

"Like a little girl," Leslie answered.

"You know what I mean." The need to scream "just tell me" bubbled in Miranda's chest.

"I just got a glimpse."

"But you saw something. What color were her hair, her eyes?"

"Blonde. I don't know how old…over five…but grade school maybe. Wasn't close enough to see eye color or anything else."

"Skinny?" Miranda couldn't slow her heart but held her breath. If the answer was fat or chubby…

"I didn't see enough of her—she had chubby cheeks."

That's got to be Irene's daughter, Sandra. If Sandra's there, so is Irene. Maybe Felix too. "We've got to go there—now."

"We should watch the place for a while first," Leslie said.

"So let's go watch." She strode toward the door.

"Whoa. Whoa. Miranda, stop." Wanda reached her, gripped her arm. "You can't go off half-cocked like this." She glanced at Leslie. "Even if Leslie's wrong, and you didn't break that kid's nose, the Second Sphere *thinks* you did. They're looking for you."

"What's new about that?" *I killed an agent, that's what.* She glanced down at Wanda's hand on her arm. *Have I lost Wanda?* Smiled a fake smile. "I'm not as out of control as Leslie has suggested."

Wanda let go of her. "We saw three agents; there could be more."

"Look, I didn't plan on breaking his nose," Miranda said grudgingly, "and I can't take it back, even if I wished I could, which I don't. That can't stop us from finding Irene, who will lead us to Felix." She had an idea. "Ethan will not be happy if this causes us to miss finding Irene and the Prophet." She focused on Ian. "Take me there. If I get the tiniest glimpse, I'll be able to identify the girl."

"She's got us there," Ian said. "Ethan wouldn't be happy if we blew it." He lifted his chin. "If she confirms it's the Prophet and his family, we'll speed back here to make a plan."

"They are keeping the girl inside, out of sight of visitors," Wanda said. "But the housekeeper had to have seen the girl. What if we follow her after she leaves there tonight?"

Miranda smiled. "We could question her away from the house, and those inside would never know."

"Yes," Leslie said. "But *I'll* ask her a couple of questions, then we will leave her alone." She aimed a look at Miranda. "Agreed?"

"Agreed," Ian and Wanda chimed.

———

LESLIE HID IN THE TREES THAT BORDERED ONE SIDE OF THE PROPERTY. Miranda perched on the edge of the back passenger seat.

Wanda fidgeted beside her. Ian fidgeted in the driver's seat. Miranda gritted her teeth, determined to watch the house guarded by the Second Sphere agents. At least Ian had stopped drumming his fingers on the steering wheel.

A sliver of silvery moonlight sliced across the yard and the silent two-story, stone-and-brick house on the opposite corner. The house looked like a place Irene would choose to hide in.

They'd been at it for a couple of hours before the front door opened. A crack of yellow light spilled onto the porch, and a woman in a brown pinafore came out. She became a shadow that moved along the shadowed walk.

Leslie emerged from the tree line. Followed the housekeeper.

Ian guided the car out of the parking space, inched forward well below the speed limit, and followed his sister.

Miranda peered through the windshield at Leslie's shadowy figure, lagging far behind the housekeeper. Ian hung back so far the housekeeper was out of sight. The woman probably would take a trolley. Miranda would not risk losing her. She slipped out of the car.

"Miranda," Wanda whispered harshly. "What do you think you're doing?"

Miranda timed her exit from the moving car. Stumbled but didn't fall, and hurried to the sidewalk, and followed parallel with the housekeeper.

The housekeeper waited at the next trolley stop. Leslie took a place behind the woman.

Miranda held back. Pulled the scarf out of her pocket. Fashioned it over her head, shadowing her face.

The trolley arrived with a squeal of its brakes, surrounded by a nose-wrinkling cloud of diesel.

Miranda waited until Leslie had taken a seat and then hurriedly hobbled to the stop with a stooped posture. The door moved to close. "Hey," she hollered. The bus driver opened the door again.

The trolley reeked of sour sweat and fear. Head bent, Miranda took the first available seat.

The trolley bumped and swayed down the street. Both it and its seats creaked and groaned with every bounce and turn.

Forty minutes later, the housekeeper got off, closely followed by Leslie.

Miranda stood, limped slowly down the aisle, and off the bus. Trailed Leslie by half a block.

Leslie picked up her pace, forced Miranda to lose her fake limp.

A moment later, Leslie walked alongside the housekeeper. They stopped outside an apartment building south of the Anacostia River, just barely inside the District of Columbia. *Were they chitchatting?*

Miranda pressed her lips together. *I wouldn't trust anybody approaching me on a dark street. Leslie will be lucky to get the woman's name.* She marked the placement of the apartment building in her head and hid in the shadows between the nearest stoops.

Leslie called a cheery goodbye and walked away to meet with Ian at the next side street.

Miranda moved quietly to the housekeeper's building and slipped inside without drawing Leslie's attention.

Heavy footsteps moved up the stairs. Miranda followed.

The second floor was dark and silent.

Too quiet. Miranda continued up to the third floor.

Before she reached the top step, a door closed softly on the left.

Two doors stood at the left end of the hall, staggered across from each other.

Miranda edged to the door on her right, put her ear to the painted wooden door. Silence. She crossed the hall. At the muted sound of movement within, she knocked.

The door opened a crack. "Hello? Is there something—?"

Miranda pushed her way in.

"Wait, stop. Who are you?" The housekeeper, still in her pinafore, backed away. "Get out or I'll scream."

Miranda closed the space between her and the woman. Clamped her hand over the woman's mouth and forced her back against the wall. Miranda whispered in the woman's ear, "I mean you no harm. You have some information I need. Promise me you'll be quiet. I'll take my hand away."

The woman's pale hazel eyes were wide; her breath came fast and hot against Miranda's hand.

"Nod if you agree to be quiet."

The trembling woman swallowed and searched Miranda's face. She nodded.

Miranda slowly released her hand from the woman's mouth but kept her pinned against the wall. She was younger than Miranda had expected. She had thin brown hair, dark circles under her eyes and saggy skin as if she had lost a lot of weight.

"Who are you? What do you want?"

"Tell me about your employer at your last house."

"I don't know anything about anything. I'm just a house cleaner."

Miranda glanced around the room. It had a combined living room and kitchen, a door to a bath, and a door to a bedroom. Gold-colored brocade drapes framed a windowed door at the end of the living room, which opened onto a tiny balcony. Copper pots hung from a rack in the kitchen. The sofa and chairs matched, and plants and knickknacks covered every surface.

"One look around your home, and I can tell you're not *just* a housekeeper. Tell me who you work for, what you've seen and heard, and I'll leave you alone."

"What is going on? What is it about that house? Are you with that woman from the bus?"

Damn. I should have thought... "Just tell me about the people you work for."

"What do you want me to say? They're just people."

"'Just people' don't have Second Sphere guards."

"Please, I don't know anything. I've never seen the mister. or missus."

Miranda did a double take. Cocked her head and fixed on the woman's face. "You're in the house at least once a week. And you have *never* seen them?"

The housekeeper's lower lip quivered. "The nanny is there, the little girl is there, and the guards are, but that's all."

There was no deception in the woman's expression. "Tell me about the little girl."

"I don't know her. I rarely see her."

"What's the girl's name? What does she do all day? What's she like? Happy? Sad?"

"They call her Ocean. She seems lonely, but not unhappy."

"About how old is she?"

"She just turned nine."

"How do you know that?"

"There was a birthday cake on the kitchen counter a week ago."

"What name did it have on it?"

"No name. Just happy birthday."

Miranda chewed her lower lip. The age was right, but there had to be hundreds of nine-year-old girls in DC right now. Maybe information about the adults would be more helpful. "Who signs your check?"

The woman tried to sidestep out of Miranda's hold.

Miranda pressed her forearm against the base of the woman's neck. Just enough pressure to feel her pulse throbbing. "I'll ask one more time. Who signs your check?"

The woman's mouth moved, but no sound came out.

Miranda eased the pressure off but kept her arm in place. "Try again."

"There's no check. I get paid in cash."

"Never a check?"

"Never."

"Okay. Tell me about their clothes, their shoes—"

The woman shook her head.

"Why are you shaking your head?"

"The bedclothes are never disturbed, and the closets and dressers are empty."

Never slept in? No clothes? Miranda was confused. *Do they really have a house just for a nanny and Sandra?* She studied the woman. *Either she's telling the truth, or she's exceptionally good at withholding information.* "Are you going to tell anyone about me?"

"No. I promise." Her voice and her lower lip quivered.

"Whose side are you on?"

"No one's."

Miranda clicked her tongue. "You're wearing non-Fellowship colors but work for the Fellowship. Are you non-Fellowship, or are you a sympathizer?"

"That's who you are." The woman's eyes widened. "You're the woman they're looking for. The one with a price on her head. There's a reward." The woman clamped her lips tight.

Shit. She recognized me. Miranda watched alarm grow into panic in the woman's eyes. *Gotta think.*

Tears streamed down the woman's face. "Are you going to kill me now?"

I'm going to have to take her with me. "Pack a bag."

"Why?"

"You're not safe here. You're coming with me."

Miranda dragged the woman into the bedroom. An old battered

six-drawer stood opposite a full-size bed with a wrought-iron head-board. "Pack." Miranda shoved the woman toward the closet.

Visibly shaking, the woman reached for the closet doors and, without facing Miranda, asked, "How long am I gonna be gone?"

"A day, maybe two." At least Miranda hoped so.

The woman packed slowly.

"Too slow." Miranda pushed her aside. Threw some clothes into the bag. Seized the bag in one hand, gripped the woman's arm with the other. "We're leaving."

The woman grabbed a couple of items out of her dresser, held them in her fist, and stumbled after Miranda.

Miranda paused at the apartment's entry door. "Am I gonna have to gag you?"

"You don't have to take me with you. I won't tell anyone, I promise."

"I can't leave you—in danger. Let's go."

Chapter Twenty

Annabelle stood on a quiet little street in a non-Fellowship suburb of the District of Columbia on a moonless night. The windows of the apartment building she sought were dark.

She'd lost count of how many housekeepers she'd Taken trying to find Sandra. But the last one had given her the name of an agency responsible for placing housekeepers in homes of the elite. It had been simple to break-in and find a list of addresses. A long list.

Slipping inside the unlocked building, Annabelle quickly found the apartment with the correct number at the back of the building. She eased into a one-room apartment with an occupied Murphy bed in the center of the room.

She stole to the bed, looked down at an old woman. *Older than Mother.* Gray-haired. Wrinkled skin. Toothless mouth gaping and issuing a regular but coarse snore. Annabelle silently thanked the Lord that she would ascend long before she grew that old. She put a gloved hand over the woman's mouth.

The woman's eyes opened and closed. Flew wide. She kicked and tried to roll away.

Annabelle hopped onto the bed, knees astride the woman, drawing the blankets taut across her arms and legs. "Peace, woman. I have questions."

The woman tossed her head but couldn't free herself.

Annabelle pressed her hand more firmly against the soft mouth. "The Lord means you no harm. We need answers. Calm yourself so that you can hear and answer."

The woman quit struggling. Her eyes pleaded with Annabelle.

"You are a housekeeper, yes?" Annabelle kept her hand over the woman's mouth. "Nod."

The woman nodded.

"Is there a young girl in the house you clean?"

The woman's eyes grew wary. She shook her head without taking her eyes off Annabelle.

"No?" Annabelle glared at her. "Are you certain?"

The old woman nodded vigorously.

We hunger. We must feed.

Without removing her hand from the woman's mouth, Annabelle pinched the woman's nostrils closed.

The woman tossed her head from side to side, but Annabelle was stronger. The whites of the old woman's eyes grew larger. Trapped between Annabelle's knees, she thrashed. Kicked her feet against the bed.

Annabelle waited patiently. Waited for the thrashing to weaken. Waited for the fighting to stop. Waited for the blessing of acceptance.

The woman's eyes closed. She sighed the long last sigh of death and stilled. The tension in her face, her arms, her legs vanished.

Annabelle lifted her face to the heavens, but no lighter-than-air sensation flooded her.

The stench of an old woman's wastes filled the air. Something stirred inside Annabelle. Not her inner angel. She knew that one. This feeling…unsettled her.

This creature robbed us. She was one of the Lost Ones. She had no soul to lift us.

Annabelle climbed off the woman and off the bed. Lifted an eyelid. Peered at the large black pupil.

She robbed us. Wasted our gift of death.

Annabelle cocked her head and studied the lifeless body. She gently brushed the woman's hair out of her eyes. Straightened her bedcovers.

The clock on the wall said two o'clock. Annabelle figured she could visit the next address and still be back at the lab before her angels missed her. Only being able to do two every few nights was testing her patience, but until she found Sandra, this was the Lord's and Mother's mandate.

She listened at the door for signs of movement. Slipped out into the silent hallway and into the dark of night.

Chapter Twenty-One

It was past midnight by the time Miranda got the housekeeper to Leakin Park. She answered all of Pokeweed's questions, and he finally agreed that the housekeeper wasn't above suspicion and warranted further questioning.

Miranda carried a paperback fragrant with the aroma of hot meat into the tent, sat on the crossbar of the cot, and stared at the housekeeper.

"Thank you for saving me." The woman's voice had more rasp to it than it had earlier. She sat in the lone camp chair, and in the glare of the kerosene lantern, her skin had a sallow cast.

The cot had a blanket, and there was a waste bucket in the corner. But kerosene was the strongest odor, so she hadn't used the bucket yet.

"You're non-Fellowship by your clothing," Miranda said in a mild tone. "But you don't live like one. Why?"

"I'm just trying to survive."

"Looks to me like you're doing better than surviving."

The housekeeper's eyes sparked with defiance, and she returned Miranda's stare without answering.

"How many days a week do you work at that house?" Miranda didn't take her eyes off the woman.

"I go for four hours every morning and six hours on Saturdays."

The woman kept eye contact with Miranda. Her breathing remained regular and even.

"Wow." Miranda did the math. "Twenty-six hours a week. That's a lot. What do you do?"

"I fix lunch and prepare supper, tidy up—clean." She must have seen something on Miranda's face. "It's a big house."

"How many Second Sphere agents guard that place?"

The housekeeper broke eye contact. "I've only seen the one at the back door."

"Only one? What about the one on the cupola?"

She gave an insincere chuckle. "Sorry. I forgot. I don't see him much." Her breathing grew more rapid.

Miranda moved, stood close enough the woman had to look up to make eye contact. "There's a young girl in the house you called Ocean. What's her real name?"

"Ocean."

"You think I don't recognize a code name? What's the child's real name?"

"What do you mean? Do you think Ocean's a nickname?"

Miranda cocked her head. "You tell me."

The woman swallowed. "Um, could I get a drink of water?"

"Look around you. Does this look like the Belvedere?" She circled and stood directly behind the housekeeper's chair.

The woman cranked her neck to follow Miranda. "It's been hours since I had anything to eat or drink."

"How thoughtless of me." Miranda bent and whispered, "How many guards are upstairs? Are any of them armed?"

The woman blinked rapidly. "How many times do I have to say it? I don't know. I saw only one guard at the front door and one at the back."

Miranda sighed. "Make it easy on yourself." Moved. Stood in front of the woman. "Tell me what you know."

"I swear I'm telling you everything I know."

"Damn it!" Miranda slammed her fist onto the arm of the camp chair.

The woman yelped and drew her arms to her chest.

"Are there armed guards in the yard?"

"I don't know."

"Does the nanny ever leave?"

"I don't know."

"Does the child have visitors?"

"I *don't* know." The housekeeper clasped her hands and twisted them nervously.

Miranda returned to sit on the edge of the cot, pulled a paper-wrapped sandwich out of her brown paper bag. Unwrapped the sandwich. Took a large bite. "Mmm." Miranda took her time chewing. The small morsel of roast beef in her sandwich was dry and tasteless. She took another bite, groaned as if in ecstasy, and spoke around her mouthful. "Love me some roast beef."

A stomach growled. Loud. It wasn't Miranda's.

"Hungry?" Miranda held the sandwich out as if offering it to the housekeeper.

The woman reached for the sandwich.

Miranda took another bite. A wave of déjà vu mixed with nausea rolled through her. She re-wrapped the sandwich and put it back in the bag. Stood. Casually walked behind the woman again. *What would Beryl do? She wouldn't ask nicely.* Miranda whipped her scarf out of her pocket. Yanked the housekeeper's arms behind her.

The woman tried to pull away. "What are you doing?"

Miranda didn't answer. Wrapped the scarf around one of the woman's wrists. Trapped the other wrist. Tugged the scarf against the woman's struggles and tied the woman's wrists together and to the back of the camp chair. Bent to the woman's ear. "How many guards are there?"

"I don't—"

Slap. The back of Miranda's hand stung from where it had struck the woman's neck.

The woman gasped. Sucked in quick short breaths. Watched Miranda out of the corner of her eye.

On edge and twitchy, Miranda wanted to do more than hurt the lying housekeeper again. To calm down, she paced behind the woman.

Calmed, she circled to stand in front of the housekeeper. "How many guards are there?"

"I only see the guards at the front and back doors because I make coffee for them first thing."

Miranda's open hand smacked against the woman's cheek. "How many guards?"

Tears shimmered in the woman's eyes. Her voice quaked. "I've told you—"

Smack. Smack. "How many?"

A red handprint marked one side of the woman's face. The other side of her face held a red blotch that was darker where Miranda's knuckles made contact. Tears rolled down her face and dripped from her chin. She shook her head and lifted her chin. Watery eyes regarded Miranda. "I. Don't. Know."

Miranda ground her teeth. Her muscles quivered. Her hands curled. Her fist lashed out. Connected with the woman's breadbasket.

The woman bent as far as her bindings would allow. Her muscles spasmed. She gurgled and arched backward. Noisily sucked air. Then she gagged and spewed.

Miranda danced out of the way of the gush of sour-smelling stomach contents that splattered the cozy rug on the tent floor. She waited for the woman to clear her throat and breathe more normally. Part of her watched as if from outside herself. The part stunned by her actions. The part that cried silent tears. The part that wanted to be the old Miranda.

"If I tell you what you want to know, they'll kill my parents and my sister and her family," the woman cried tearily.

The old soft Miranda is useless to me now. Miranda drew back her arm to deliver another punch.

"Four. There are four guards."

Look at that. Beryl's way gets answers. "Where are they stationed?"

The woman sighed. "Patrols outside. One stays on the cupola, one at the back door. And the one inside changes positions."

"They have sidearms. Any other weapons?"

"Each of the agents has a long gun. Rifles, I think."

"When do they change shifts?"

She gave Miranda a wary look. "How am I supposed to know what happens when I'm there?"

Miranda let that one go. "Who visits the child?"

"I don't know. I'm not there. Please. I'm just the housekeeper."

"You saw no one visit the child ever? Who leaves their child alone like that?"

"No one other than the nanny and the Second Sphere agents can be with the girl. She's never there when I clean."

Pressing her lips together, Miranda took a step closer to the woman.

"There is a man who comes to the house on Saturdays sometimes. At least he walks like a man." The woman shook her head emphatically. "He wears a heavy, hooded robe. Comes into the house and goes straight upstairs. I'm never to be near the stairs when he arrives."

"What's upstairs?"

"A guest room with…a full-size bed, a large desk, papers, maps, books—oh, and a telephone."

Would Felix appear at the house without visiting his daughter? She had so many questions. "Tell me more about the papers, maps, and books."

"Maps of DC. A big one on the wall, with colored thumbtacks marking dozens of places."

"Just thumbtacks?"

She nodded.

"What did his voice sound like?"

The woman's chin quivered. "Do you know what it's like to know if you do anything wrong, say anything wrong, your family will die?"

The stench of vomit was overwhelming. Miranda untied the woman and stepped outside to clear her head. She wasn't alone. Startled, she drew a quick breath.

Wanda faced her. "What did she tell you?"

She released her breath slowly. "Why do you want to know?"

"Girl, you have a nasty habit of not listening to me." She kept her voice low, but her simmering rage was as strong as when they'd first met. "You don't wanna tell me, that's fine. On the very first day we met, you heard me. You saved me when nobody else saw me. So hear me now. I hear you. I see you. I owe you. Been waiting. Ready to fight *with* you."

Miranda swallowed the lump in her throat. "That's a pretty speech. But it wasn't long ago I heard a different tune."

"Not coming out of my mouth, you didn't."

"Right." She hadn't meant to sound so sarcastic, so hurt. *I can't do this. I need to think.* She strode into the forest.

Wanda kept pace with her.

Miranda ignored her. *Why can't I figure this out? Four Second Sphere agents to guard one child? Maybe a counselor child—but heavily guarded and alone? It only makes sense if the child is Sandra.*

"You just figured out what something she said means, didn't you?"

Miranda stalked away. But couldn't shake Wanda. She stopped abruptly. Faced her old crewmate. "Why did you send Leslie into that house?"

Wanda gave her an incredulous frown. "You were working. And Leslie—well, people seem to trust her automatically."

A wry smile escaped Miranda's control for an instant. "I meant, why did you send her into a place with Second Sphere on duty?"

Wanda's lips stretched in a grimace. "I thought they were hiding the Prophet until Leslie saw that little girl." She shook her head. "I don't get it. Who would want to keep a child hidden?"

"Maybe she's so well-known they couldn't keep her identity a secret any other way."

"But what kid is that well-known?"

"The Prophet's daughter."

"Oh-kay," Wanda drawled. "Should we tell Monkshood—or Pokeweed until Monkshood gets back?"

"No." Firmly. Definitely. Miranda rubbed her aching knuckles. "We need proof." She glanced up at the sky through partly bare tree branches. The moon had faded. It would be dawn soon.

"Maybe we ought to find out who that child is and why they are hiding her."

Miranda gave Wanda a long look. "What are you proposing?"

"We need to go on what the police call a stakeout."

"We who?"

"We may be on dry ground, but you are still my captain. Give me your orders."

"If we're going to do it right, we have to watch the place twenty-four hours a day. I can quit my job, but I promised Keith I'd help him cater a party on Saturday…" *She doesn't need to know it's a party for the Prophet…not yet anyway.*

Wanda quirked her mouth. "I can watch the house while you do that."

"What about—" Miranda stopped. She saw it on Wanda's face.

She'd lost her job again. Fellowship families didn't like intelligent housekeepers.

Miranda gave a sharp nod. "Let's do this." She wasn't sure she forgave Wanda for not defending her against Leslie's doubts, but... *the two of us just might pull this off.*

Chapter Twenty-Two

Leslie's pulse fluttered in her throat. Sweat beaded on her upper lip, and her head ached. She reached under her full skirt and pulled the legs of her jeans down to her mud-caked shoes. Her only pair of shoes. She sighed heavily and kept following these directions.

She knew why meetings at Leakin Park had to be after the park closed for the night. But geez, it got darker and quieter and scarier. Monkshood's messenger had also said this meeting was a secret. So she'd told more lies. Told Miranda and Wanda she had to work. The band of pain circling the top of her head squeezed tighter.

She walked the path without a flashlight. At step one hundred, she peered into the shadows. That was the tree that had a sharp bend in it. Monkshood should have been waiting for her here. She turned in slow circles, checking the path in front of and behind her over and over. A trickle of sweat slid down her back. Her skin crawled.

"It's good to see you, Leslie."

The voice in her ear startled her, but she recognized it. She swallowed the shout that had bubbled in her throat and whirled to face him. "Monkshood? Where did you come from? Sorry," she stammered. "I mean, here I am, as you requested."

"Relax, Leslie. I just wanted to ask you for some help in private." He stood in the shadow of a thick oak tree.

Relax? Monkshood was an extraordinarily intense person. *"You need my help? You've got to be kidding."* She scanned the area. *Where is his security team?*

"This isn't a joke."

She waited.

No one jumped out from behind a tree. Monkshood's expressions didn't change.

Her insides squirmed under his fierce gaze. "So what do you need me to do?"

"I know what I'm asking isn't easy. But I can't begin until you promise to keep everything I tell you confidential. You must tell no one. Not your brother, or Wanda, or Miranda. Especially Miranda." He leaned slightly forward. "I wouldn't ask if it weren't critically important."

A weight dragged at her. *More secrets mean more lies.* "Will I eventually be able to tell them?"

A brief smile flickered across Ethan's face. "If everything goes according to plan, yes."

She pressed her lips tight. *This is for something bigger than me or lies that don't have to stay lies.* She swallowed three times, but the lump in her throat didn't go away. She blew out a big breath. "Okay. I'll keep whatever you tell me a secret." *They'll understand when I explain it was critical to SABR's success.*

"Follow me." He led her a little further into the woods, to a tent guarded by one of his lieutenants.

The four-person tent sat in a clearing barely big enough for it.

The lieutenant held open the tent flap, and Monkshood gestured for her to enter first.

Inside sat four small card tables surrounded by chairs. Monkshood went to the table where a small, shielded lantern gave off a dim glow.

After they sat, Monkshood seemed reluctant to speak. "You need my help with this plan?" Leslie prompted.

"Not exactly."

The hair on her neck raised. "What do you need me to do?"

"We have a way to stop the conflict. But it's delicate. Everything, and I mean everything, must go according to plan."

"Stop the conflict? You mean stop the Fellowship? As in get rid of it?"

"As in kick them out of our government, out of the District, and make them so small they can't hurt anyone ever again."

Leslie caught her breath as if she had received a physical blow. What Ma and Pop had worked toward might actually happen? A tiny star of hope glimmered. "How certain are you that this plan will work?"

"I can't say much. I can tell you that this time we have help from the right people in the right places at the right time. But it's absolutely critical that they can do what they must without interference."

"So you're asking me to make sure we, Miranda's team, don't get in the way?"

"I need you to keep *Miranda* under control. Keep her from doing damage. If she uncovers part of the plan during her search for her sister, it will expose people and plans we cannot afford to have exposed."

She shook her head in disbelief. "What you're asking is impossible. You know how Miranda is. She charges into things without thinking."

He ran a hand through his hair. "I know that's how she is now. She's hurting and doesn't know where to put the pain. We have to help her find herself again."

"Why ask me to do this? Why not ask Wanda? She knows Miranda better than I do."

"I'm not sure Wanda's the one to help Miranda do nothing and be calm."

Leslie couldn't argue with that.

"So look, I've been trying to decide whether to meet with Miranda and give her an assignment. Do you think she'd do better if I showed her we're working toward the same end?"

Leslie wove her fingers together to keep from fidgeting under his stare and studied the dirt in front of her. *Working toward the same end?* "You mean the ending of Irene and the Azrael or the ending of the Fellowship?"

"They are the same. So, how do you think she'd react to an assignment from me?"

Would Miranda accept an assignment to do anything other than look for Irene? I did. But it took four years of fruitless searches before I understood Ian and I were fighting too small a fight. Ian didn't understand that —doesn't—even now. Her chest tightened.

She raised her gaze to Monkshood's and shrugged. *A brother-in-law isn't the same as a brother.*

Monkshood's expectant look grew more intense.

"I don't know. I guess it depends on the assignment." She ended her statement as if it were a question.

"Of course." Monkshood's somber gaze swept across the tapestry of trees around them.

Leslie sighed silently. She got that the leader of a rebel organization had to be secretive, but the secrets and the fighting kept going on and on and….

Monkshood's gaze returned to Leslie. His lips curved upward in a poor approximation of a smile.

Her smile wasn't much better. She'd only known Monkshood for a little more than a year. Didn't know exactly what she had expected, but this left her struggling to understand. "Want me to give her a message?"

"No, it's better she doesn't know you talked to me first." His head jerked to the right as if he'd heard a sound.

Leslie followed his gaze, but she had heard nothing and saw nothing.

"I'm needed elsewhere right now, but I'll send a message to Miranda and set up a meeting with all of you. In the meantime, keep Miranda calm and quiet. Use the same drop to inform me of her intentions and movements."

She scoffed in frustration. "In order to know what to tell you, I'd have to quit my job and never sleep. Can I recruit help to get this done?"

He pinched his lips together, shook his head. "I'm sorry. No, you need to keep your job, your cover, and figure out some way to keep Miranda calm."

Leslie sat back in the camp chair. "If SABR can stop the Fellowship, I'll do my best to keep Miranda from interfering." She had no clue how, but she'd try.

He smiled at her with sad eyes. "Good. Thank you. Now, I really have to go." He took several steps away, stopped, and turned back to her. "My lieutenant will make sure you get out of the park safely." He turned and hurried away.

Chapter Twenty-Three

The low, flat-roofed building was dark except for two security lights—one above the front door and one at the far end of the dock. All around Annabelle, machinery hummed, but no sounds came from within the target building. The place sounded as abandoned as it looked.

She circled the building Mother had said was where to meet Papa. Her options were the front and side doors or four garage doors, three of which stood next to one another. Mother had instructed her to use the side door.

The only light on the building was two floodlights. One covered the front of the building; the other covered the parking lot on the side of the building. She avoided both security lights, slid under the railing, and popped up on the dock. The doorknob turned easily. She slipped inside.

"Come on in, Annabelle." Mother's voice had that tinny quality industrial speakers always had. "Follow the hall to the entry area. I'll buzz you in."

Annabelle stepped through a secret door, past empty shelves, and finally into a restroom and waited for Mother's next instruction.

"Shield your eyes from the lights, darling, and I'll open the door."

Annabelle did.

There was a buzz, then a click, and the door opened.

Mother stood six feet away amid a riot of sweet-smelling red, pink, and yellow blooms, bathed in a soft dim light.

Annabelle scanned the area, but there were only flowers and Mother.

"Welcome, darling." Mother swept her hand over the surrounding gardens. "Beautiful, isn't it? You should see it when the lights cycle back to daytime brightness—it's breathtaking." Her tone held a bright note Annabelle hadn't detected since they'd left Buenos Aires.

"The Prophet is expecting me."

"Oh, Annabelle, as blunt as ever. Yes, you're here to see the Prophet, but we must talk first. Come, you must be thirsty after your trip."

Annabelle did not show Mother her displeasure. Mother always did things her own way, and if the way to see the Prophet was to please Mother for a few extra minutes, so be it.

They walked on a flagstone path, past two stone heavenly angels that kept watch over a break in the bushes that were about seven feet tall.

Beyond the bushes stood a stone-clad building with a Spanish tile roof. Mother led her inside to a brightly colored, modern-style living room.

"You're living here with Papa?"

"In a way. I have a lot to tell you."

"I am listening."

"Please sit down." Mother gestured at a bright red sofa.

Annabelle pressed her lips together, reminding herself to do whatever it took.

Mother sat on the sofa too, turned toward Annabelle. "I'm sorry to have to tell you this. It was as I suspected. Your father was in the Fellowship Center when those apostates blew it up."

Annabelle eyed her mother suspiciously. *I would have felt his death. The Lord would have—*

"He survived, but his injuries were..." Mother took Annabelle's hand. "Severe. Possibly permanent."

Annabelle peered deeper into her mother's eyes, searching for a reason she would say such a thing. Saw only truth and concern. Annabelle's chest tingled. *How can this be? He brought me back from the dead. He is the Chosen of the Lord, the Prophet.* "Go on."

"He cannot walk, nor take care of his simplest of needs, and can barely speak. His memory—his..." Mother swallowed, then gave a sad smile. "He's not the man he used to be."

Annabelle's breath caught in her throat. "Are you saying he cannot carry out his duties as Prophet?"

"He cannot." Mother pressed her lips together and squeezed Annabelle's hands in hers.

Annabelle's chest ached, and something blurred her vision. She pulled her hands gently from her mother's and stood. "I must see him." She didn't say, *for myself.*

Mother wordlessly led her out of the kitchen to another flower garden. They followed a path between an identical line of bushes and a pair of stone angels. Beyond them stood two more buildings. One looked similar to Mother's house; the other looked like the now-leveled Fellowship building. A clever paint job, but Annabelle saw the buildings for what they were. Fakes.

Inside the house like Mother's, the odors of citrus-scented cleaning chemicals and medicines partly masked a hint of bodily fluids in the air. They entered the room without knocking.

A medical bed with chrome railings stood on one side of the room. The frail man on the bed was Papa, but not Papa.

Something inside Annabelle twisted, and her chest ached like a child's.

A dumpy woman in a white uniform hovered near Papa's head. She straightened his blue blanket, then gave them a soft smile. "He's been waiting for you," she said, then retreated to a desk across the room.

Annabelle hurried to his bedside. "I am here, Papa."

Papa's eyes sparkled, and one corner of his mouth lifted. "Thister."

Annabelle didn't allow her body to react, but inside she recoiled, speechless. *He does not know me?*

"No, Felix," Mother said. "Annabelle is your daughter."

"I know," he said irritably. "Fluff my pillow."

Mother lifted his head and took his pillow, shook it, then replaced it under his head.

"No!" Papa cried. "Pillow fluff."

The nurse hurried toward them. "He means raise the head of his bed." She took a tear-shaped control from under his left hand and pushed the button. Mechanical gears clanked and whirred, and the head of his bed raised up.

"Praise," Papa said. Spittle collected on the drooping side of his mouth.

Annabelle saw it with her own eyes but couldn't believe it.

"He means thank you," the nurse explained.

He no longer has spiritual guidance for us or anyone.

The words of her inner angel, returned Annabelle to her human self.

Mother and the nurse discussed Papa's condition. But Annabelle paid no attention. She didn't understand. *Why did the Council keep this from us for so long? Why hasn't the Council searched for a new Prophet or chosen a First Apostle?*

The Lord is testing him, the Council...and us.

Annabelle faced her mother. "He is the Prophet. Can he not heal himself?"

Mother glanced at Papa, then returned Annabelle's look. "The Lord works in mysterious ways, which is one reason your father wanted to see you. We have a plan."

Annabelle cocked her head, glanced from her mother to her father and back again. "A plan?" *For the Azrael? Perhaps...* "You found Sandra?"

Mother pressed her lips together, blew out a breath, and faced Annabelle again. "Your father doesn't remember...yet." She took Annabelle's hand, patted it. "No. Our plan is to keep our followers, the Fellowship, believing. And we need your help. Don't we, Felix?"

Papa lifted his head off the pillow and gave a wobbly nod. "Help." He laid his head back down and worked his mouth. "Mother." His mouth opened and closed, opened again. "Lord's will." He closed his eyes and pressed his lips together. "B-b—" He opened his eyes again and gave Annabelle a pleading look. "Believe." He took several deep breaths.

"That's all right, Felix, dear," Mother said with a sideways glance at him. She moved toward the door. "I'll fill Annabelle in the rest of the way. You rest now. Get your strength back."

Mother took Annabelle out into the garden between the buildings and sat on a bench made of wood and iron. She closed her eyes and blew out a long breath. "I'm sorry you had to see him like that."

"Weak?"

She grimaced. "Sick. Unable to heal himself, yet." She gave a smile Annabelle recognized as her brave-face smile. "He will, but our Fellowship members are upset since they haven't seen him in public for so long. So your father, the Prophet, the Council, and I have decided we must appease the members for now."

"Appease?" Annabelle's inner angel stirred. Her stomach rolled uneasily.

"We're going to have a very good, holy actor fill in for the Prophet."

The uneasiness inside grew more agitated. "An actor?"

Sacrilege. Now you see how unworthy she is. She lied to us for months and now asks us to lie too.

"Only for a short time," Mother said. She smiled in a bemused way. "He's surprisingly good."

"The Prophet and the Council approve of this?"

Mother laughed lightly. "You can't think this is my idea. Counselor Lucas Matthews came to me."

Annabelle's glance took in the garden and the three buildings. *Mother couldn't do this on her own. The Fellowship Council is behind this.* Her inner angel gave a ferocious roar and beat against Annabelle's ribs. "Why do you show me this? What is it you wish me to do?"

Mother took a deep breath. "The um—stand-in Prophet and I have our first appearance one week from now. With the Lord's help, and yours—you and the Dark Angels—the people won't lose faith before the true Prophet can heal."

Annabelle's inner angel's skepticism flooded her. *Lie to protect a pretender because the Prophet failed a test?*

She has lost a daughter and her husband. She is lost.

She is a sinner. It is our duty to Take her where she stands.

She is Mother. My first duty is to honor her. Annabelle squared her shoulders. *I will find Sandra, reawaken her faith.* Aloud she said, "We are the instruments of our Lord, the Fellowship Council, and our Prophet."

Mother patted her hand again. "I knew you'd understand."

Chapter Twenty-Four

Miranda stood at the food prep counter of the Mayflower Hotel in Washington, DC, slicing fancy breads into tiny squares so Keith could create tea sandwiches for the party.

When Keith had mentioned he and Chester had a side job with a caterer in DC and that the fundraiser's guest of honor was the Prophet, she had eagerly agreed to help. Reassured him she had experience with this kind of party and could plate food like a pro.

"Look lively, people." The owner of the catering company burst into the kitchen from the Grand Ballroom. "The hostess and first guests have arrived." Waitstaff and busboys bustled in and out of the kitchen carrying trays of hors d'oeuvre or soiled dishes and champagne glasses. Every time the doors opened, the cacophony of a thousand Fellowship members in the ballroom rose. The noise subdued only during the short times the doors stayed closed.

She plated food Keith prepared as fast as she could, and as fast as she did, the waitstaff carried the trays she filled out to the ballroom.

"I served the Vice President of the United States," one of the waitstaff announced. Picked up a tray and left again.

A Second Sphere agent came into the kitchen for a drink and a snack.

Miranda's pulse surged. Her slicked-back hair, chef's hat, and catering uniform had fooled two agents on the way in. *Let it work magic again.*

The agent downed his snack in one bite, washed it down with a long drink of water, then hurried back out to the ballroom.

Miranda smothered a giggle at the irony of being mere feet away from agents sworn to catch rebels like her and remaining unrecognized.

"Glad you're enjoying this, Miranda." Keith's broad smile flashed white against his red and sweaty face. "I owe you. Chef said he'd fire me if I didn't find a replacement."

Miranda's gut twisted. *He'll hate me after the Prophet shows up, and he gets fired…or worse.* She hated to do this to Keith, but this was her best shot.

"You're good at this," he continued. "If you're interested, I could probably get you hired for more jobs."

"And work this hard on my days off? No. Thank. You."

He put a warm, beefy hand on her arm. "I'm serious. I owe you. You need anything, anything at all. Ask."

Her throat tightened. *I'm sorry.* She made a show of mopping her sweaty brow with her right sleeve. Mustered the best smile she could for him.

The crowd noise poured in, followed by a crash and clatter of metal trays and breaking china. A waitress and a busboy struggled to their feet, the floor littered with broken plates of food, their uniforms covered in food and drink.

"You oaf!" Boss shouted, purple-faced. "That's coming out of both of your paychecks. Girl, you can't go out there like that. Change into a clean uniform."

Shamefaced, the waitress murmured something inaudible.

"What? No spare uniform? You're fired. Get out before I have an agent throw you out." Boss looked around the kitchen. "You." He pointed to someone behind Miranda.

Miranda turned to see who he pointed at, but no one stood behind her.

"You, filling that tray."

Miranda's pulse doubled. "Me?"

"Yes, you. Take off your apron. You'll take out the next tray."

"But I'm kitchen staff, sir. Not waitstaff."

"You're waitstaff now. Hurry. There are hungry people out there."

I can't go out there. If Felix sees me… But, if I refuse, he'll throw me out too. I can't miss this chance at Felix. Miranda gave Keith a you-owe-me-big-time look, took off her apron, and picked up a tray.

"Smile," Boss said. "And take that thing off." He pulled off her chef's hat and gave her a shove through the swinging doors.

Her throat dry and her blood filled with get-me-out-of-here adrenaline, she took a deep breath and walked among the tuxedos and furs and pearls.

Crystal chandeliers hung from the ceiling two floors above them. Arched balconies and doorways adorned with shiny gold *fleur-de-lis* lined the long luxurious room.

Roaming around the room serving guests gave her odd flashes of déjà vu. It seemed a lifetime ago when she had been the daughter of the Counselor at parties like this. Working as a staff member was the same and yet very different.

A gentleman called, "Hey, girl."

Miranda turned to him with her fake smile. "Sir?"

"Bring that over here."

She wound around the guests standing between them. "Would you like a tea sandwich?" She lowered the tray in front of him.

"Attention, everyone," a disembodied voice called over the loudspeaker. "Please line up on either side of the red carpet."

The man Miranda waited on hemmed and hawed and took his sweet time picking two sandwiches. Most of the crowd had lined up on each side of the carpet down the center of the room by then.

Miranda tucked the now-empty tray under her arm and made her way toward the kitchen, trying not to disturb anyone.

"It is my pleasure to introduce the Prophet Felix and Lady Irene."

Miranda sucked in her breath and did a slow turn.

A sea of silk dresses and furs and tuxedos blocked her view. Gentle applause began, grew louder. She pushed through the crowd until her toes touched the edge of the red carpet. Peered toward the grand doorway.

"Ex-*cuse you*. Hey! What are you doing? The help shouldn't be here."

Miranda ignored the complaint and leaned forward to see.

Twenty feet away, arm in arm, Felix and Irene came toward her. Miranda wished she'd planned to see Irene. She could have had her vengeance now. A hand grabbed her shoulder. Her chest seized. *Second Sphere?* She couldn't breathe. Looked down at the hand, a white shirt with ruby cufflinks and a hairy wrist peeked out from under a navy-blue jacket's sleeve. *Not Second Sphere.* She breathed out a bit of relief, whispered "Sorry," then hurried into the kitchen.

She went to the counter where Keith had trays of artfully arranged finger sandwiches on dainty plates. Picked up the next serving tray. Her trembling made the dishes clatter against the tray. Hastily gripping the tray's edges, she sent furtive glances toward Keith and the boss. Fortunately, the kitchen noises kept them oblivious.

"What are you waiting for? Get back out there." The boss waved his hand in a shooing motion. "Go on."

She braced herself and walked out into the party again.

For the rest of the evening, she kept watch for Irene and Felix and positioned herself at the opposite end of the room. It wasn't as hard as she'd expected. The party guests usually paid no attention to her, often rudely grabbing a plate without so much as a please or thank you.

Another serving tray emptied, she tucked the tray under her arm and glanced up to see where Irene was. The crowd parted, leaving an opening directly to Irene, who stared at Miranda with a puzzled expression.

Chapter Twenty-Five

A rap on the door of the Mayflower Hotel's Grand Ballroom warned them. Irene watched Fake Felix turn on his persona, from his ramrod posture to his beatific smile. He held out his arm for her. She placed her hand lightly on top of his.

The doors opened to a bright, hushed room, as if everyone held their breath. Sparkling crystal chandeliers hung from gilt ceiling medallions on the arched ceiling. People in elegant evening gowns and tails crowded the second-floor balconies and behind each side of a red carpet that ran down the middle of the ballroom to the stage.

Fake Felix gave a regal nod. A smattering of applause rippled through the crowd, growing in intensity until it was thunderous. The weight of preparing for rejection slid off her. They were welcoming her back. Her vision cleared, and her smile grew broader and more relaxed.

They walked down the aisle slowly, shaking hands and greeting dignitaries. From the vice president to the cCounselors and their wives, everyone who was anyone was here.

As their walk progressed, Fake Felix relaxed into a charm almost as endearing as the real Felix. Though when he shook Mickey Mantle's hand, she detected a slight slip in his fake persona.

They reached the stage and turned to face the crowd. The crowd surged over the red carpet and toward the stage. Lucas stood front and center. Applause filled the room again. Fake Felix signaled the bandleader. A trumpet flare and drum roll quieted the room.

"My lovely wife, Irene, and I wish to thank you for coming out to raise money for the Johns Hopkins Orphanage tonight. Your presence and your generosity honor us. With your indulgence, I'll make a few remarks before the band continues to entertain us.

"As you can see, Irene is here by my side as she has been since our first day of marriage. Yes, we heard the rumors of annulment. We have said nothing until now because we didn't wish to make it a bigger issue. Unfortunately, many people believed the lies. We're here tonight in part to show you that marriage is a sacred sacrament that we each take seriously. I don't know who started the rumors, and frankly, it doesn't matter. We forgive them."

Applause interrupted him.

He held up a hand for silence.

"One more announcement. I am saddened to report that the recent increase in vicious crimes by the unbelievers moved the Lord to send his angel Gabriel to me."

Gasps and whispers stirred and then quieted.

"Gabriel instructed me to deliver this message...." Fake Felix delivered the Council's message with the right amount of gravitas and humility.

The band struck up some soft jazz tunes. Soon the crowd relaxed, and friendly chatter and generous donations resumed. Felix and Irene acted like a couple, chatting with people at the event for hours.

Irene longed to get out of her heels and rub her aching feet but couldn't. It would reveal Fake Felix was too tall.

"Well, Irene." Mrs. Wynter's gravelly voice grated on Irene's ears. "I've mingled and listened to the chatter. It seems the people are accepting your annulment was fake."

"It was," Irene said with no irony in her voice. "Our people are smart enough to see that."

Mrs. Wynter cocked her head. "They are smart. I wonder if they have noticed the same things I have."

Irene had to take a sip of her sparkling orange lemonade to speak. "And what have you noticed?"

"Felix isn't quite himself yet, is he?"

"Surely you can understand that being attacked by evil leaves one a bit—unsettled." Irene held the glass cup to her lips but didn't dare test her throat. The aroma of oranges filled her nose.

"Of course, my dear, of course." Mrs. Wynter looked out over the murmuring crowd. "I'm curious about how those who don't know the extent of his injuries view this." She waved a hand. "Don't mind me. I'm just an old woman who worries too much. It's been a fine evening. The Prophet has done a fine job for the orphans." She raised her glass of sparkling water in a salute. "Enjoy the rest of your evening."

She moved to a couple Irene didn't recognize and chatted with them.

Irene kept an eye on Mrs. Wynter.

The governor's wife approached her. Shook her hand and spoke of how much she admired Irene. The compliments almost erased the unease Mrs. Wynter had stirred.

Irene rejoined Fake Felix, and another hour passed in pleasant, if superficial, chitchat. She emptied the champagne flute of sparkling orange lemonade that she'd been nursing all night and looked for and glimpsed a waitress across the room.

A vaguely familiar waitress. A waitress who resembled... *She's much too skinny and has short, dark hair, but she looks a bit like— Miranda.* A wave of heat spiked Irene's heart rate. She made her way to the Second Sphere agent standing nearby. "Find her."

"Find who, ma'am?"

"Only the second most wanted rebel in the country. She's one of the waitstaff!"

The agent, whose eyes had never stopped scanning the crowd, gave her a direct look. "Go to your husband, m'Lady. We will take care of it." He whispered nonsensical code words into his lapel and moved toward the kitchen.

She strolled away from him. By the time she wound through all the people between her and Fake Felix, two Second Sphere agents had positioned themselves near him. The agents stuck nearby for an hour but didn't rush them off to safety. Irene forced herself to relax.

"Prophet, Irene, you've done a splendid job raising money for the orphans tonight." Lucas pumped Fake Felix's hand up and down. "I'd say this evening is a success."

She smiled a little stiffly. "Of course it is. The people love their Prophet for his generosity and his holiness."

"Yes, they love him."

Her smile wavered. *Did Lucas place a little extra emphasis on the word him?*

"I hope you had a pleasant afternoon paddling the river with your adopted daughter."

All she could hear was the frantic beating of her heart. It was as if the crowd of people who had pressed to see her all night had vanished, and she and Lucas were in a dark, claustrophobic tunnel. All she could see was Lucas's bloated face. She tried to keep her voice quiet, steady, sure. "You've had me followed?"

"I want to be certain you have everything you need. That you… and the Prophet…are safe."

"Of course." *Did his men follow us downriver?* She tore her gaze from Lucas, scanned the room. They were in a bubble of isolation. *How?* Another scan of the room revealed his men, discreetly directing people away from them. She smiled a public smile and turned her attention back to Lucas. *Intimidation. Again? This is intolerable. What you should be doing is finding Sandra.* Her frantic pulse became thundering fury. She narrowed her eyes and fed her gaze all her rage. "You already know what I need," she said in a barely controlled whisper. "I need *both* my daughters. Have there been any developments?"

Lucas shed some of his intensity but none of his arrogance. "We will inform you when there is. Enjoy the rest of your evening." He turned and made a wake through the dwindling crowd.

Irene watched until he and his men became part of the anonymity of the crowd. She didn't know how much longer she could tolerate him. Annabelle might not know how long it would take to train the newly born, but some things couldn't wait much longer.

Chapter Twenty-Six

S *hit!* Miranda kept a straight face and calmly walked back to the kitchen, expecting a shout or the touch of an arresting Second Sphere agent at any minute.

Shaking, she put the tray down. Sucked in air, but there wasn't enough in the kitchen. She whirled toward the exit.

The boss stepped in front of her. "Where do you think you're going?"

"The little girls' room, sir."

"Be sure to wash your hands and get back here pronto."

She hurried out and onto the dock without even speaking to Keith. But outside was no different. She couldn't breathe. *Irene is inside.* Miranda wobbled. *Dizzy. So dizzy.* She bent, hands on her knees, and took deep breaths.

I was close enough to kill her. Why did I leave Beryl's guns in the locker? Could've told Ethan. Had a whole SABR cell here, ready to take out the entire Fellowship Council and Irene right now. Should have told him. Her vision darkened, narrowed.

Irene and Felix here. In public. Somehow they're back together. How does Ethan not know about this? Ethan. I have to find him. Surely he'll help when he knows what I've seen.

He's got more bombs somewhere; I know it. If I hurry, he might be able —I can take care of everything tonight. Purpose replaced dizziness.

Getting out of here won't be easy. She could see four Second Sphere guards from here. *Could be more. But the guys at the gate had already cleared the van. And Keith left the keys in it.*

She climbed into the van and grabbed the keys out of the glove box. Drove to the dock's entrance, where the gate guard stopped her.

"Where are you going, ma'am?" he asked, peering inside. "The party isn't over yet."

"I've got to get more pâté from our kitchen before we run out. You can't have a party without pâté."

"How long do you think you'll be gone?"

"Thirty minutes tops." The lie rolled off her tongue.

"Right. Hurry back. I wouldn't want to be you if Mrs. Wynter's guests get hungry."

She pulled away from the gate and slowly turned onto the street. She watched the Mayflower shrink in the rearview mirror. A black car pulled up to the gate. The guard gestured in her direction.

Miranda regretted her decision to take the van. The Johnson's Catering logo of a burgundy ribbon with bold black letters outlined in gold on its sides made her easy to spot, and the van was much slower than the agents' cars.

She zigzagged through the side streets of DC, knowing her pursuers in their black Mercury would easily run down the van on a straightaway.

The Mercury behind her cornered more speedily and narrowed the distance between them to only half a block behind.

Can't leave the van on the street. Parking garages are closed. Her heartbeat rivaled her vehicle's speed. Her shoulders tensed, expecting a bullet. The bullets didn't come.

The stoplight turned red. She turned off 6th Street NW onto S Street NW, jammed on the brakes. Slammed the van around in a U-turn to avoid the blockade of black cars ahead. An ear-splitting screech of metal on metal rent the air, and the parked car moved onto the curb.

Accelerator to the floor, she scraped the other side of the van on the black Mercury following her. Mashed the brakes at Georgia Avenue NW and turned. Turned again and entered the visitor parking lot of Howard University Hospital. Parked in the darkest shadows as far as she could from the street and left the van.

Crouched low, she darted between parked vehicles. The sound of a rumbling V8 made her flatten on the cool pavement.

She held her breath. The rumble faded and she could breathe again.

She slid into the driver's seat of a dark green Plymouth Valiant. Fumbled with the ignition wires, got it started. Pulled out of the parking lot.

A mile later, a black Mercury traveling south passed her. It didn't turn and follow her.

She took the northern route back to Baltimore. Parked the Plymouth in the Walters Art Museum's parking lot at about four in the morning.

An hour and a half later, deep in Leakin Park, the hunting screech of a barred owl split the air. She answered the sentry with the correct trill. Got the all clear and went straight to Ethan's tent.

His tent was empty.

She entered the closest tent. Shook the shoulder of the man sleeping on the ground. "Wake up."

"Wh—? What time is it?" He raised up on an elbow. "Whatcha want?"

"Wake up. I need to talk to Monkshood. Where is he?"

"Go away till morning."

"It's urgent. I have to talk to him now."

"He's not gone."

"Where?"

"How would I know?"

The man rolled over, his back to her.

She grabbed his shoulder and pulled him back toward her. "Where does he keep the ordnance?"

The man perked up, more awake. "Why? Are we in danger? Do we need to wake the camp? Bug out?"

Ready to explode, Miranda kept her voice down. "No. I have some information that needs to be acted on now. Where are the guns, ammo, and explosives?"

"Dunno exactly." The man yawned and stretched. "Wanna tell me what this is all about?"

I don't know you. She shook her head.

"Then leave. I'm going back to sleep." With a yank and a twist, he escaped Miranda's hold and pulled his sleeping bag over his head.

She stomped out of the tent. "Damn it. Someone has to know."

"What do you want to know?"

She whirled to face the person who'd snuck up on her so quietly. *Pokeweed.* Relief flooded her. Pokeweed will know. "Where's Monkshood? I need to speak to him now."

Pokeweed took her by the elbow. "Let's go over here so we won't disturb the sleepers."

Miranda allowed herself to be guided to the circle around a stone-lined fire ring full of old dead coals.

Pokeweed gestured for her to sit on a log ringing the fire circle. He sat first. "Now what's so urgent you risked getting shot for waking up strangers in the middle of the night?"

She glanced around. Saw no one. "It's about the Prophet," she said, almost whispering. "I've seen him. If we act now, we can wipe out him and—and many of the counselors and Fellowship supporters."

"He is in a very important meeting. We cannot disturb him."

Of course he is, damn him. She locked eyes with Pokeweed. "Then it's up to you and me. We need guns and explosives."

"Explosives?"

Exasperated, she said, "To blow up the Mayflower Hotel's ballroom."

"The Mayflower in DC?" Pokeweed rubbed his jaw. "First, it will take time to get to our weapons stash, then it'll take more than an hour to get to the Mayflower. It'll be long past checkout time. Will anyone still be there?"

Startled, she looked at the sky. "Dawn." She hadn't realized how long she'd been driving.

"Second, I really hate that I'm the one who has to say this."

A sudden chill washed over her. "Say what?"

"Monkshood left instructions."

Miranda huffed. "I know. He can't be disturbed. You said that. That doesn't mean—"

"Monkshood appreciates your passion, but he's left orders that you—that we—"

Every muscle in her body tensed. "Say it."

Pokeweed gave her a sympathetic look. "Look, I don't know

what's going on between you. No one here can help you. You must have Monkshood's approval first."

"That's what I was trying to do. But he's not here. And this won't wait."

Pokeweed gave a shake of his head. "It will have to. Monkshood will be back in a day or two."

She tore her gaze from Pokeweed and glared into the black firepit. *Who does Ethan think he is?* Miranda walked away from the firepit, from Pokeweed, and from the rest. *Doesn't matter. Irene's in the city. And she's with Felix. Someday soon, they'll visit Sandra at the house. And I'll be there. Then they'll pay for what they've done. And the price will be biblical.*

Chapter Twenty-Seven

"I will be brief," Lucas said without sitting down on the sofa like a respectful gentleman. "From the description, we believe your sister broke his nose." He towered over her, red-faced, brows scrunched, lips drawn down in an ill-boding frown.

Despite the molten fury coursing through her, Irene kept her hands in her lap, her face smooth. She met Lucas's eyes, then coolly and pointedly looked at the chair to her left. Said nothing. Waited.

He huffed, then sat on the edge of the chair, leaning toward her. "Your sister Miranda."

"I know who my sister is."

"You have no opinion about this?"

"Oh." Irene leveled a shocked and innocent look at him. "You want my opinion about my sister breaking the nose of a Second Sphere agent's boy?"

Lucas pressed his lips together. "About your sister *and* about whether you think New Felix is ready for an appearance for the general population."

Now we're getting down to it. "Well, of course, I denounce my sister and her atrocious behavior." *And in a couple of hours, I'll inform Annabelle.* "As to *Fake* Felix,"—she couldn't think of him as anything else—"he managed the party, didn't he?"

Lucas screwed up his mouth and did a slow blink. "At the reception, yes. The Council feels we need—New Felix needs—to give the people need some guidance."

The knot in Irene's throat was unbearable. *Mrs. Wynter was right. The Council hired Fake Felix to be their puppet, and they think I'm going to go along with it.* "What sort of guidance?"

"We've set up a press conference where he will *encourage* our membership not just to resist temptation but to *help* us bring the non-Fellowship to a place of learning."

Her stomach churned and her jaw ached, but she kept her voice pleasant, cooperative. "I suppose you have a script for us?"

Lucas's face and body relaxed a little. "Of course, but you need to rephrase it." He handed her a slip of paper with a typed paragraph. "Put it in Felix's words. Make his followers *want* to help him."

She read the typewritten statement.

There is no authority except from the Lord. And the Lord commands you to heed His words. Obey all his commandments. You who obey the Lord shall show the apostates no mercy. You shall take them into custody and deliver them to the Second Sphere, who will commit them to Lord's Redemption or to the fires of Hell.

Irene bit the inside of her cheek to keep from crying out. *Apostates belong to the devil, and we should return them to him. Especially Miranda.* The coppery taste of her own blood fueled her anger.

She ran her tongue across the back of her teeth until she calmed enough she could think. *Mrs. Wynter, Lucas, and the Council believe they can use me. Too bad I need their support to get congressional approval for my Youth Spiritual Aptitude and Assignment Act. So for now, I'll allow them to think they use me. In time, Annabelle and I will make them see differently.* She raised her gaze to Lucas. "Under the circumstances, I think the Lord would move Felix to remind the Fellowship that the apostates have had years of opportunities for Redemption. He'd say we should protect the Fellowship; there will be a curfew on all apostates from henceforth, and we will send violators to Hell."

"That would amount to martial law," Lucas said, "which is a federal power. The Council would have to propose it to the President."

Irene's cheeks stiffened. "I suggested a curfew, which is not martial law. Public authorities issue curfews. The Prophet is such an authority."

Lucas lowered his head and steepled his fingers. "There may come a time when a curfew is appropriate, but the Council decided this is what the new Prophet will announce." He shifted his bulk in the chair and raised his head. His face composed. His eyes hard. "We will have a law-abiding society across all stations of life."

The implied threat only fueled Irene's determination. "You said you wanted this in Felix's words," she said in a tone of utmost reasonableness. "I am attempting to advise you as you asked me to do."

"We ask that you choose words or phrases Felix would use to deliver *this* message." His tone grew harder, almost threatening. "The Council will decide when and if we declare martial law."

"Of course." Irene dipped her head deferentially. "Tell me when and where, and we will do as you asked." *You're in charge...for now.*

———

TWO HOURS LATER, IRENE GRIPPED THE EDGES OF THE FLAT-BOTTOM boat that wobbled with each stroke of the oars. She wished there were a more dignified way to visit Annabelle. One of Annabelle's lieutenants, posing as Annabelle, had picked Irene up at the Wicomico Riverboat launch for a mother-daughter boating date.

The swift current carried them into the wetlands. Irene longed for her family's yacht, but it drafted too deep for the swamp's braided streams.

Annabelle waited at the dock and helped Irene disembark. "Mother, it's good to see you."

Stunned, Irene couldn't speak.

Annabelle's expression grew concerned.

"I'm pleased to see you as well," Irene said, "and look at this place." She swore Annabelle had grown into a woman overnight. *How? I just saw her a few weeks ago. I must be misremembering.*

She scanned the new buildings. If it had been anywhere but in a swamp, it would have looked like a luxury tropical vacation spot.

"I was going to show you around, but we have to hurry." Annabelle led the way down the elevated boardwalk.

"I didn't miss it? They're about to be decanted?"

"They are."

Irene stepped into a room that definitely didn't belong in a swamp. A mechanical pump sent a bone-throbbing rhythm through Irene's ears and body. Little girls curled in fetal positions inside translucent red bags hung in rows. The number of pipes coming out of each bag made Irene think of a spider. An upside-down spider.

Beside each bag stood an Azrael with a roll-around stretcher. Blankets and washcloths and portable oxygen tanks lay on a shelf under each stretcher.

An Azrael in a lab coat approached Annabelle. "Blessed One, it is time. Shall we start?"

"Yes."

The one in the lab coat went to the first canister and fiddled with the dials on the canister. Under the pulsing beat of machines, there was the sound of liquid draining.

The scientist and an assisting Azrael moved quickly, sliced open the first red bag. They reached in together and lifted a girl's wet body the size of a small ten-year-old. The assisting Azrael slid her arms under the lifeless child's arms, and the scientist suctioned the newly born's mouth and nose. The child remained limp and lifeless.

Irene held her breath. Willed the child to breathe. But the child didn't.

The Azrael wrapped the child in a blanket and placed her on her side on a stretcher. The scientist suctioned the lifeless child's mouth and nose, then rubbed her chest and back with a dry towel.

The newly born threw her arm up in a startle reflex. Gasped. Coughed. Cried out. Her eyes flew open, and her arms and legs flailed. She made high, terrified animal cries.

The attending Azrael patted the child's back. "Be calm, Anna ZAE 0001," she said in a soft but commanding tone. "You must take time to adjust to the outside." She hummed a soft tune.

The child quieted.

Irene turned to Annabelle with a wide, proud smile. "The Lord has blessed you. Well done. Soon you will lead a legion of Azrael and rid the Earth of Miranda and all those who seek to destroy us."

Annabelle gave her a strange look. "First, we find Sandra, right, Mother?"

That tone. That look. Irene kept her smile in place despite the painful writhing of her stomach. "Of course. I wasn't forgetting her.

Praising the Lord, you, and the rest of His angels does not diminish that. And my worries about Sandra do not take away from the miracle of you, this place, and your new sisters."

Annabelle's eyes swept slowly across the room with a maternal smile on her face. "This is just the beginning, Mother."

"Yes. It is." *Not only the beginning—a sign. I will defeat Lucas, Mrs. Wynter, and Miranda and her rebels, and I will restore everything they stole from me in abundance.* An extraordinary sense of calm filled Irene.

Chapter Twenty-Eight

Fresh out of the first bath she'd had in a week, Miranda sat cross-legged on the bed in her basement room of the Baxters' home. She didn't like putting the Baxters in danger, but the unoccupied house in DC had no running water or beds. And even without a job, the past eight days covering the house in DC, First Fellowship Church, and Sandra's school were exhausting. She and Wanda couldn't keep this up much longer. She had to find help.

A timid knock at her door startled her. "Who is it?"

"Mimi. I have some soup for you."

"Thanks, but I'm not hungry."

"May I come in?"

"It's your house." Miranda ran her fingers through her damp hair.

The door opened, and Mimi stepped into the room. Frizzy gray hair framed her face, though her bun was tidy. Her face crinkled in a wide smile. She carried a wooden tray with a sweating glass of lemonade and a large steaming bowl. The aroma of matzo ball soup accompanied her. She set the tray on the small bedside table. Straightened, folded her hands over her stomach, and gave Miranda an appraising look. "You don't look sick. What is troubling you so that you have no appetite?"

"Please. Just go on back upstairs. I'll eat tomorrow."

"You didn't eat the day before yesterday. Yesterday. And now, not today. It's not good for a young woman to go so long without food. Not good for your stomach to hold troubles inside. Tell Mimi all about it while you eat."

Miranda looked away from Mimi's warm eyes. "It's personal."

"OK. So it's personal." Mimi put a papery hand on Miranda's chin and gently raised it. Looked into Miranda's eyes. "Something bad happened, heh? Your friends treated you badly and now you wish to die, hmm?"

I don't wish to die. I wish others to die. "I'm not gonna die after missing a few meals." Miranda curled her lips in a wry, half-hearted smile.

"You know, you came here. We didn't know you. But you've shown us you are a good person."

Her stomach twisted. "I'm glad you think so." *My friends think I'm poison, and my uncle thinks I'm worse than useless.*

"Ah, so that is what not eating is about. Someone has said you're not a good person? Bah. They were being a schmuck when they said that. You are goya, but you are a good person."

"You just said you don't know me. How can you know I'm a good person?"

"A good person doesn't offer a little girl protection from *mishegas*, the crazy people in this town. A good person doesn't bring us extra food from her job when she can. A good person doesn't skip a meal so that the children have plenty to eat. I'm here to tell you, you can eat. We will always have enough matzah for you."

Miranda swallowed. It didn't ease the ache in her throat. "What if I have done or plan to do something bad—something you don't know about?"

The old woman looked at her hands, twisted her wedding ring in silence. "We are living in difficult times, dangerous times. We can hope for a miracle, but to rely on that hope is foolishness. Sometimes the bad is so big we must do a little bad to fix the big bad. Your family knows you are a good person."

Miranda didn't know what made her feel worse. Knowing she'd done more than a little bad or that she'd done that to family. And she was going to do worse. But she couldn't tell sweet old Mimi that.

Mimi peered at her with an intense look. "I see. Family said you are no good, heh?" She patted Miranda's knee. "Family sees all of us." She shrugged. "You are human. You have good. You have bad. But family is good and bad too. It's like the rabbi said, we all have two voices in us."

"Two voices?"

"*Yetzer ha-tov* and *yetzer ha-ra*. Yetzer ha-tov is the voice that moves you to give, to be kind, and to do the right thing. Yetzer ha-ra is the voice that is only interested in having lots of fun and money and does not care about the right thing. Many people think they must crush Yetzer ha-ra out of existence, but they are wrong. The voices live in you. Which you choose and how you balance them— that is the difference between wisdom and foolishness."

Miranda couldn't look at Mimi. *Irene has left me no choice. I must crush her and the Fellowship.* Aloud, she said, "You are very kind, but you should go back upstairs before ZeeZee gets worried. I don't want him to come down those stairs."

"But you haven't eaten yet. Here,"—the old woman picked up a spoonful of soup—"I feed you."

"Thank you, Mimi." Miranda put a hand over the old woman's hand, took the spoon from her. "I can feed myself."

"Good. Matzah is good for what ails you."

"You don't know—"

"I know I don't know what I don't know, but I know matzah makes everything better. I don't go upstairs until you've finished this bowl. And if I don't go upstairs, ZeeZee will come fuss over me, certain that I've fallen. Then B will come down worried about…"

Miranda forced a laugh. "All right. I give up." She sipped the hot soup. Its mix of salty chicken broth with a touch of dill and parsley and doughy matzah balls soothed her dry throat and the ache inside.

"Evelyn and I—we talk." Mimi smoothed her dress. "We see you are home more now and want you to know that if you lost your job—"

"I can—"

Mimi motioned shush with her hand. "Eat. I talk."

Miranda pressed her lips together and looked down at her soup.

"We don't say you lost your job. Maybe you did. Maybe you didn't. But we say that we want you to stay here without worries. You bring us food or supplies, or you pay us a dollar. Whatever. You stay here. You are safe here. Family is blood, but family is more than blood."

Stunned, Miranda stopped listening. *Family is… I still have one family member I can count on.*

The old woman rambled on.

David will help me. Ethan will forbid it…if he finds out I've asked… I need someone SABR doesn't know…

Mimi placed her hand on Miranda's knee. "You are Baxter now. This we have decided. You need money or food or anything, you ask. We will help."

Miranda gazed with open-mouthed wonder at the old woman. "I can't ask you to help with—what I need to do."

"You ask. If we can help, we help. If we cannot, we will say so."

Miranda lightly rubbed her fingertips across her lower lip. *Could Bernie or Evelyn get a message to David?* "There is a message I need delivered …" Miranda shook her head. "It's too dangerous."

"No one pays attention to a little old gray-haired lady." Mimi gave her a sly smile. "You tell me who or where to deliver this message. I deliver it."

"This would be a message to someone who's hiding from the Fellowship." *And he could have moved by now.* She shook her head again, more emphatically. "No. I need someone other than me to address it. To do these things would put you in too much danger."

Mimi pulled back, with an expression of disbelief on her face. "I take it to the post box or I take it to a house." She shrugged a shoulder. "These are hard times. I just deliver a letter for a quarter. I know nothing."

Miranda tilted her head and stared at and through Mimi. *She could deliver it to a dead drop, and Ethan would never see it. But it would have to be far enough away that neither Wanda nor Leslie would see it either.* There was one place… "You know the twenty-four-hour laundromat on Pennsylvania Avenue?"

"Near the Laurens Street bus stop?"

"That's the one."

Mimi's brows creased. "You want me to take a message to the coin laundry?"

Miranda met Mimi's puzzled stare. "You can't tell anyone. But yes. I'll give you an envelope, and you're going to go into the laundromat and drop the letter behind a washing machine that's empty, put a coin in the machine so it doesn't lay flat, and push in the thing until it gets stuck. Then you'll tell the attendant that machine is the kind of broken that stays broken. Say that."

"The machine is the kind of broken that stays broken. Like that?"

"Exactly like that." Miranda couldn't help it. "Do you think you could get the letter delivered by six p.m. tomorrow?"

"Of course."

Miranda took Mimi's papery hand, locked onto her warm brown eyes. "Give me ten minutes. I'll give you the letter and tell you what to write on the envelope. You take it to the laundromat. Don't take any risks. Just say what I said for you to say, and no one will be the wiser."

Mimi went upstairs to wait for Miranda to bring her the tray of dirty dishes with the letter under the bowl.

Miranda got a piece of paper and an envelope from the dresser. Finished her note to David, then, hungry for the first time in days, she finished her soup.

Chapter Twenty-Nine

Leslie followed Pokeweed to Monkshood's tent. Dread shivered down her spine. *He's going to blame me for Miranda's behavior or for not stopping her. But Miranda has her own agenda, her own plans, and she keeps them to herself, so how was I to stop her?*

Monkshood's tent was indistinguishable from everyone else's except at this hour it was the only tent with a faint glow of light from within. Inside it smelled of coffee and kerosene.

"Good, you're here." A haggard Monkshood rose from a camp stool, approached Leslie, and shook her hand. "Thank you for coming. Please take a seat."

Two of his lieutenants, already here, sat on camp stools.

She sat. *Is he going to reprimand me in front of everyone?*

Pokeweed sat next to her.

Monkshood raised a tin mug. Gestured with it. "Anyone want some coffee? It's hot."

At this hour? As if my stomach isn't queasy enough right now.

No one took him up on his offer. Leslie wondered if the men were as anxious as she was.

Monkshood ran a hand over the dark stubble covering his chin. "Sorry for my appearance. I think it's important for the four of you to hear this information as soon as possible."

"You all know I've been out of town recently. What you don't know is why and what that means for us, for SABR. In order for our movement to be successful, we've had to have funds and quiet military and political backing. Unfortunately, one of our most important backers—our guy inside the military—died last year." He looked down as if studying his shoes. Cleared his throat and raised his head again.

"I've just returned from meeting one of our friends in DC. They have convinced me it's time to bring down the Fellowship forever. What I tell you next is information you cannot share with anyone. Not a wife, a family member, not even a trusted member of SABR. This information goes nowhere except here with us. If you think this secrecy is too much of a burden, leave now. No hard feelings." His intense eyes locked on each of theirs until he received a nod.

Open-mouthed, Leslie couldn't believe she was here, hearing this. "Did you really mean for me to be here?"

"If keeping this secret from your brother or your friends will be an issue—"

"No, it's not that. I—why me?"

"You, like everyone here, have more than proven your loyalty to your team, to SABR; you have shown you can perform hard tasks under difficult situations."

She tilted her head, stunned. *Is this why he asked me to spy on Miranda?*

"Our friends in Washington have been moving behind the scenes for some time. They have been garnering support for SABR and for a return to democracy. And not just in DC. All over the nation. But we cannot respond to the Fellowship with violence during this waiting period. In the next couple of weeks, there will be a revolution, one that will help SABR overcome the Fellowship. But first, we must do certain things to support this. Make no mistake, there will be chaos and bloodshed. It's our duty to help keep the bloodshed to a minimum, to make this as peaceful of a transition as possible. No more bombs. No more terror. We need to show the people we can return our government to the people through mostly peaceful means."

"I don't understand," the older lieutenant said. "What are you asking us to do?"

"You've each displayed an ability to influence your squads and a strong desire for a less violent alternative for ousting the Fellowship leadership. In the coming days, I will rely on your steadiness, your calm, to keep our people calm. You will lead peaceful demonstrations at strategic times and places."

"But the Fellowship won't just watch us demonstrate. What if they attack?" one of his lieutenants asked. "Can we defend ourselves?"

"Of course we can defend ourselves. But we must not be the aggressors. At least right now. I'm not saying our aggression before was wrong. But we've entered a new phase of the revolution. And there is no other way to describe it. It is a revolution. And we have help. But for our revolution's success, we must get more support."

Leslie's stomach twisted in so many knots she wasn't certain she'd ever feel normal again. "Um, may I ask a question?"

"Certainly."

"There are some who won't understand this change."

"Who might actively work against a period of peace, you mean?" His wan smile said he understood who she meant.

"Right." She wasn't sure whether she meant Miranda or Ian.

"We have to do our best to curtail or at least minimize those activities. At least for now. There will be a time when everything will become clear, but...look, I know I'm asking a lot. I can't give you any more information. If this were to get out in even the smallest of ways...." Again, that intense gaze swept across them, drilled into each of them. "Do I have your word?"

"Yes, sir," each of the men chorused.

"Of course, sir." Part of Leslie wanted to jump up and down. Peace, the way Ma and Pop had envisioned? Yes. Part of her didn't know how she would convince or control or even counter the reactions she knew Ian and Miranda would have.

A man poked his head through the tent flap. "Sir?"

"Coming." Monkshood stood.

Leslie and everyone else stood too.

"I've been here too long." He glanced at the four around him. "You may not see much of me until this gets rolling. Pokeweed will distribute envelopes with your assignments. If you need direction or advice, look to him." He gave each of them a long, softer look. A goodbye look. "Be careful." He strode out of the tent.

"Don't read these here or where someone might see you," Poke-weed said. He handed Leslie an envelope. "Memorize and burn this as soon as you can."

She accepted the envelope, folded it, and slipped it in her pocket. She exited the tent with her future simultaneously stuck in her throat and burning in her pocket.

Chapter Thirty

Miranda avoided touching the cold cinder block walls and squinted against the glare of a brilliant orange sunset that haloed the house across the street.

Ah, there he is. She snapped a photograph with the Polaroid camera she'd borrowed from the Baxters. *Second-shift guy. Right on time.* He and the guard inside the cupola exchanged a few words, then the second-shift guy took over.

She placed the developing picture on the sill of the casement window and then wrote the time and change of guard in their spiral notebook. The long list of dates, times, changes of shift, and no other information made her stomach knot up.

So far, the housekeeper had told the truth. Four guards. One on the cupola, one on the back steps, one inside, and a fourth one who appeared and disappeared at random intervals. But nothing else even remotely interesting had happened.

The aroma of hamburgers and French fries preceded the click of the door latch behind her. Her stomach grumbled.

Wanda entered with the carryout bag in hand. "Sidewalk's quiet, but I came through the alleyway to be safe."

"I don't get it," Miranda whispered.

"What's that?" Wanda asked only slightly louder than the crinkle of the paper bag she set down on the discarded crate they'd placed upside down so they could use it as a table.

"What are they guarding? It's been a week and absolutely no one has gone in or come out of that place."

"Give it time. Someone has to get groceries at least once in a while."

Miranda reined in a forceful *maybe you're willing to wait but—*. Dragged in a deep breath to avoid alienating her only helper. She hoped David had gotten her message and was on his way. The paper bag crinkled again, and her stomach gnawed at her. "I'll take over so you can eat while it's still warm," Wanda said in her ear. They switched places.

Miranda circled the upside-down crate, picked up the burger, and took a big bite. Chewed once or twice and swallowed. It hit her stomach, which sharpened its twisting. She straddled the metal folding chair they'd found and sat on the cold metal, grateful for the chance to sit despite the chill that raced up her arms and back. Her feet burned from the hours of standing on a concrete floor and staring out the casement window.

She took a bite of a limp French fry that tasted like cold grease. Forced herself to swallow it. Didn't touch the rest of them but finished the lukewarm burger.

She yawned. "Think I'll take a nap so I can take watch tonight." She climbed into the sleeping bag in the back corner and dropped instantly into the insensible sleep of exhaustion.

"Wake up." Wanda's voice reached her through the fog of a dream. "Miranda, wake up."

"Whacha want?" she mumbled.

Snap. "Something's happening." *Snap. Snap.*

That's the camera. "What?" Miranda scrambled out of the sleeping bag and lurched to Wanda's side. "What's happening?"

Wanda huffed. "It's too late." She glanced at Miranda. "The girl was in the window. I thought she was going to open it. She's gone now."

Miranda peered at the first-floor windows. "Which window?"

"Middle of the first floor."

In the darkness of a cloudy night, leaves slightly lighter than the house tumbled in turbulence under the window. "What happened to the streetlight?"

"Burnt out, I guess. It didn't come on tonight."

"How long was I asleep?"

"An hour or so."

"I don't see any—wait." The curtains moved, and a pale face appeared. Miranda gasped. *It is her! Sandra. I've found you, Irene.* Snap. Snap.

"What's going on?" Wanda asked. "You saw her, didn't you?"

"Yeah, she's—wait. I think you're right."

Sandra raised her arms and strained.

"She's trying to open the window." *She's young for the slip-out-of-the-house while-the-parents-sleep thing.* Miranda bit her lower lip. *What about the guard on the cupola?*

She glanced at the cupola. *Wait. No guard? Is he helping Sandra, or does Sandra know something I don't?*

Sandra moved closer to the window, lowered her body, and strained some more.

This is my chance. Miranda willed her niece to lift with all her might.

"I'll grab her when she gets out," Miranda whispered.

Wanda made a sound in her throat. Came back to the window.

A flash of light came from the cupola.

"Wait."

The guard returned and closed the door behind him.

In the window, Sandra whirled and disappeared behind the curtains.

Light glowed around the curtains. Then another window showed a strip of light around its curtains. One after the other, lights glowed at every window and door. "I think she got caught. But something weird's happening. Switch."

Wanda took her place at the window. "Why are they turning on all the lights at this hour?" She breathed the question softly. "Something's happening out front."

Miranda returned to the window.

A beam of light reached across the front yard. Flashed on and off twice. An answering flash of light came from the bushes on the far side of the front yard.

"Shit. An extra agent just showed up in the front yard."

Wanda gasped quietly. "Another agent arrived. Backyard. Twelve o'clock."

Miranda sought the backyard agent.

The porch light from the house across the alley illuminated the agent for half a second before he disappeared again.

Miranda's pulse surged. "Something big is about to happen. You watch the front. I'll watch the back."

"Got it."

Long minutes ticked past. Wanda's steady breathing played counterpoint to the crickets outside the window.

"Vehicle approaching," Wanda said.

Miranda held her breath.

"Passing by."

Pursing her lips, Miranda blew out a long breath. *Come on. Show us something.*

The wait continued.

Miranda's eyes burned. She had to get sleep soon but not until whatever—

"Three sets of headlights approaching," Wanda whispered. "At the stoplight now."

Three? Maybe this is it. Stay calm.

"Green light. All still coming this way...wait. They just turned off their headlights. Running lights only. First one's turning in—oh —second one too, a Lincoln Continental." Wanda's hushed tone held a controlled excitement. "Third one's following."

The first vehicle—a dark sedan with dark windows—moved past slowly.

"Lincoln's turned into the alley, no, the driveway," Miranda said, her voice a little shaky. "Third vehicle moving on."

The Lincoln came to a full stop, but no one got out. A minute or two later, the driver's door opened.

The driver got out.

Miranda strained to see his face, but he wore a trench coat with the collars turned up and a fedora pulled down over his face.

The driver walked around to the other side of the car, opened the back passenger door, and the passenger got out. The passenger wore a dark hooded robe.

"I can't tell who they are," Miranda said. "I've gotta get closer."

"You can't go out there now," Wanda whispered emphatically. "They'll see you."

"Keep watch," Miranda ordered. "I'll be back in a minute." She slipped out the door and upstairs. Eased the back door open.

Stepped into the screened porch. Listened. The night was warm and quiet. Even the crickets had hushed.

Grateful for the cloud cover that deepened the shadows, Miranda moved as stealthily and as quickly as she could. Arms outstretched, she crossed the heavily shaded backyard toward the side street.

Across the street, a light flashed on. She ducked behind a tree trunk and froze. Soft footsteps and muffled voices came from the target house and moved from her left to right. *They're going inside. I'm going to miss my chance.* She squatted low and dared to peek around the tree.

The pair from the Lincoln stood in the cone of light at the top of the porch. The hat and the robe's hood did a thorough job of hiding their faces even in the light. Miranda cursed herself for not bringing the camera with her.

The door opened, and the driver let the passenger enter first. Then they were inside, and the light went off. *Maybe Irene or Felix left something identifiable in their car.*

Miranda took a step away from the tree, realized she'd been so intent on the two from the Lincoln she hadn't located the additional guards, and pulled back. Sank to the ground, banged the back of her head against the trunk three times. *It has to be Irene and Felix. Who else would visit Sandra now?*

A quick peek around the tree confirmed a guard stood at the back door as usual and at least one extra stood by the car. He appeared settled in for a long wait. Miranda sighed. *What if they stay overnight? Or for days? Worse, what if they leave while I go inside? What if this is my one and only chance?*

The distant whine of an engine interrupted the quiet. Miranda wondered at the sudden influx of traffic in the area. A pair of head-lights swept across the lawn. Gasp. *The escort vehicles...* She pulled back behind the tree. Prayed she'd been fast enough to avoid being seen.

A dark sedan rolled slowly down the side street.

The timpani of her pulse pounded in her throat. *Should've known they'd reappear.*

She counted. At one hundred-sixty, the second vehicle crept in the opposite direction past the house. At least she thought it was the second vehicle. *It had to be, right?*

Why the patrols? What do they expect?

She figured she had about thirty seconds left to cross the yard if she was going to go back inside before the first car came back around.

After a second peek confirmed the guards were stationary, Miranda snuck back inside and hurried to Wanda.

"Don't take your eyes off them," she blurted. "I came for the camera."

"So it *is* them?" Wanda asked without taking her eyes off the house.

"They're meeting someone."

"They are? Who? How do you know?"

"The extra guards… the patrolling cars…" Miranda grabbed the camera. "I'm going to get pictures for Ethan."

"All these,"—Wanda waved her hand showing the photographs on the windowsill—"are way too dark. It'll be worse outside."

"I've gotta try." Miranda slipped out the door and back to her position behind the tree.

After twenty minutes of crouching, Miranda's leg muscles twisted in painful knots. Her heart and lungs strained as if she'd been running for miles. She drew deep draughts of the thick air but couldn't regulate her breathing or her pulse. Too much was riding on this.

She scanned the house from front to back and back to front over and over. Then, the extra guard detached from the shadows around the garage.

She snapped a picture.

The distinctive putter of a Mercedes-Benz engine grew louder. The dark sedan rolled around the corner, then into the alley and into the drive. It stopped next to the Lincoln.

Miranda expected the porch light to come on this time and closed her eyes for a second, then opened them again.

The driver stepped out, circled the car, and opened the back passenger door. The passenger climbed out and stood with a military bearing. He wore a uniform, but in the dark Miranda couldn't identify which service it represented.

Miranda pressed the shutter button, clicked again too soon. Kept clicking the button and placing developing photographs on the surrounding grass.

The driver saluted. The guard at the top of the stairs also saluted. The passenger returned their salutes and strode across the yard.

The passenger stepped into the porch light. Harsh shadows on his face gave him a stark, vaguely familiar profile, but Miranda still couldn't identify him. She hadn't been paying attention when Ethan had discussed the military at one of their briefings.

The military man entered the house, and the porch light went out.

Miranda heaved a sigh. Then, she set about carefully waving her photographs until they each had dried. Waited as long as she could bear it, then scooped them up and hurried back inside.

"Well, that's an interesting development," Wanda said.

"Do you know who that is?"

"I can't be sure, but it looks like Admiral Moorer."

"Is he important?"

"Haven't you been paying attention to the morning briefings?" Wanda's voice held a tone of disbelief. "He's next in line for Chief of Naval Operations."

"What would"—she almost said Irene—"the Prophet want with the soon-to-be Chief of Naval Operations? We aren't about to go to war with anyone, are we?"

Wanda gaped at her. "I don't think so. But whatever it is, it's bigger than us. We need to get this information to Ethan." She peered back at the house.

Miranda shook her head. "We need to find out what the plan is first. You distract the guards, and I'll—" She stopped herself before she said kill Irene. "Listen to what they're saying."

Without taking her eyes off the house, Wanda harrumphed. "How am I going to distract three guards in the front and at least two in the back?"

Miranda paced the room. "Maybe you could feign an injury and task them to help you."

Wanda eyed Miranda, her skepticism clear. "All three of the guards in the backyard would help lil ole black me without shooting me on the spot?" She made a face and focused on the house again.

"Okay, not my best idea," Miranda said impatiently. "We don't want all the attention we'd get by opening fire on them, so what do you suggest?"

"You need to go back to camp," Wanda said. "Tell Monkshood. He'll make a plan and bring a team back here."

Miranda faced Wanda, fists clenched at her sides. "This is the first time we've seen them in days. What if it's the only time they come? Or they don't come back for months? We don't have time to get the team." *Not to mention Pokeweed had said she couldn't do any missions.*

Wanda gave her that look. The look that said, you're wrong, and I'm gonna die trying to help you.

Miranda turned away, paced to the end of the room and back again. "What if you walk into the yard and distract them that way?"

"How does my getting arrested or killed help capture Irene and Felix or help the cause?"

"Sorry, I didn't mean…"

"Yes, you did. But even if I would do that, it wouldn't help you. They will be on high alert if anyone tries to infiltrate their space."

Miranda sighed. "I can't give up now."

"Who said give up?" Wanda turned to her again. "I will stay here and keep watch while you go to camp. Monkshood will use everything he has to kidnap the Prophet. Then he can finally end the Fellowship."

"That'll take too much time."

"Well, I guess you can go running into that house and try. I don't see how you won't get shot."

She was right, of course, though Miranda would not admit it out loud. "Maybe I should stay and watch, and you go to the camp." *Pokeweed wouldn't say no to Wanda.*

Wanda sighed. Kept her eyes on the target. "I don't have the relationship with Monkshood that you do." Under her breath, she added, "No one listens to me."

Miranda glared at the house. It remained lit up, but she couldn't see a thing. *What is happening in there?* She started to tell Wanda she would go to the camp, but movement and a faint squeak warned her. She focused on the back door, which stood open. The hooded-robe person, who had to be Irene, came out. The Admiral came out, closely followed by Felix, still shielding his face with the coat and hat. Miranda's heart sank.

They paused in the yard, exchanged words, then the Admiral

got in his car, and Felix and Irene got in theirs. Moments later, the cars pulled out and drove away.

"Well, at least we have time now," Wanda said.

Deep inside, disappointment and resentment swirled into a massive fiery ball in the pit of Miranda's stomach. She cast a what-the-hell glare at Wanda. "You're just like the others. Well, fine. Go back to camp on your own. I'll do what I have to do."

"Whoa." Wanda's hands went up, and she took a step back. "Who is talking out of your mouth right now?"

Beryl. Miranda kept her glare aimed at Wanda. *No, it's not. Beryl never spoke that way. Never spoke that much. She just acted.*

"All I meant was that we have more time to plan. We'll be ready the next time." Wanda let her hands drop to her sides. "We can assume they won't come back until tomorrow night at the earliest. So we can catch a few hours of sleep. You can make yourself presentable and make your case to the team."

Miranda's anger evaporated, leaving only the massive dead-weight of extreme exhaustion. Her muscles quivered with the effort to stay upright. Maybe Wanda was right. After a few hours of sleep, she could make a better plan. "You should take the first sleep shift."

"I just got up, remember? I couldn't sleep even if I wanted to. You go ahead."

Miranda's knee muscles gave in a little, causing her to sway. "You'll keep watch the rest of the night while I sleep and tomorrow while I go to camp?"

"Of course."

"Maybe…" Miranda gave Wanda a head tilt. "The plan is to take over the house now, when there are fewer guards. Then we wait. When Felix and Irene return—then bam! We've got them."

"That might work. But first, sleep."

Sleep. Miranda made her way to the sleeping bag, each step more difficult because somehow her body carried double, then triple, her weight. She sank onto the sleeping bag so quickly she sent a jolt of pain through her bones. "Wake me in three hours, then I'll clean up and change and take watch so you can take a nap before I leave for camp." Somehow she kept her tone steady, though her eyelids were so heavy she could barely see.

Wanda opened her mouth. Shut it. "Yes, captain. Three hours."

Chapter Thirty-One

Annabelle stood in a corner of the training room and frowned at the new Azrael. *YBZ 2891 said the scientists coined a new word for the newly born. Clones? No, they are new sisters.* Each of them had an older Anna helping them to their feet. The fourteen-day-old new sisters' limbs wobbled and would not hold their weight. They'd been at this all day and into the night. Still, the new sisters underperformed. "Now," Annabelle commanded.

All the Annas released their hold on the new sisters. Every single new sister flopped to the ground like Sandra's rag dolls and cried. Their piteous cries shattered the peace of this place and made Annabelle's head pound.

YBZ 2891 turned to her. "My apologies, Blessed One. This batch lived until decanting, but obviously they are defective. I will terminate them."

"Did I order that?" Annabelle asked in a sharp, imperial tone that surprised herself. Her insides fluttered in a most confusing way.

YBZ 2891 gaped at her, then stammered. "No, Blessed One. I overstepped. I deserve punishment, if that is your desire."

Annabelle strode away without a word. She'd watched the live birth of cows. Their offspring stood almost immediately. Surely the Lord's Angels should stand by now. She stopped at the nearest of the newly born and motioned for the older Anna there to move.

Annabelle bent, slid her arms under the new one's arms and yanked the girl upright.

The new one cried out in pain.

Surprised by a sudden tightness in her throat and a burning in her eyes, Annabelle stopped.

The new one sobbed, and tears ran down her face.

"You will stand." At least her voice sounded commanding. "It is the Lord's will."

The new one straightened her legs, but the girl's weight hung heavily on Annabelle's arms. "Stand!" The weight lifted, and Annabelle dropped her arms.

The new one collapsed to the floor. Her cries tore at something inside Annabelle. Something that made Annabelle's stomach squirm. Something that churned and spoke of a need. A need to fix this. She scanned the room.

Wearing her lab coat, hands clasped behind her back, YBZ 2891 crossed the length of the room, paused at one pair and then the next.

Annabelle strode over to her. "Why can they not stand? Did you follow the doctor's plan?"

YBZ 2891 studied the floor. "We did, Blessed One. We bicycled their legs until they kicked and pushed against us. Still, they fall like the dead. I fear—"

Annabelle quirked an eyebrow. "You think they hunger?"

A flash of surprise crossed YBZ 2891's face. "No, Blessed One. Not that. Though even if they did..." She waved her hand at the loose-limbed performances around them. "No. The good doctor's book has pages missing. I fear those pages tell the secret of making them strong."

Annabelle studied the new sisters. In the too-big workout clothes of their older sisters, the new ones looked even smaller than they were. *Perhaps they need clothing their size.*

Her inner angel scoffed. *Clothing does not make an Azrael strong. These must be defectives like the last two attempts.*

That need churned again. *They are or will be my charges. It is my duty to fix this.* Aloud she said, "The dengue fever robbed me of my memories. But surely you remember *your* days like this. We can do what you remember."

YBZ 2891 cocked her head to one side then the other. Her eyes became unfocused for a moment, then she focused on Annabelle. "I remember the games we played. And the tests I passed. I do not remember being weak."

Annabelle sighed. They looked and acted like Sandra's rag doll. She had a vague memory of mocking Sandra when her sister appeared holding the doll by its arms with its feet stuffed into her socks. She'd claimed she was teaching the doll to walk.

Annabelle raised her eyes to the heavens. *But these are not rag dolls. I cannot stuff their feet into my socks.*

The memory morphed, and in her mind's eye she stood in the park of her dreams, towering over her family. At her feet were dozens of Azrael. No, not *at* her feet. *On* her feet. She blinked, and the vision vanished. All around her lay the sobbing newly hatched. The churning need grew stronger. "Thy will be done."

She positioned herself behind another new one. Bent, slid her arms under the new one's arms in a tight embrace and lifted the girl. "Put her feet atop mine."

The Anna who had been teaching the girl blinked without understanding.

YBZ 2891 stared.

Annabelle nodded at YBZ 2891. "Put her feet atop mine." She kept her tone soft and even.

With the new one's feet atop her own, Annabelle walked forward. "This is how we walk," she whispered in the new one's ear. "Our legs are strong. Our backs are straight. One foot goes, then the other."

The girl sniffled and hung limp in Annabelle's arms. It was an awkward, ungainly shuffle hampered by the girl's dangling and inexperienced limbs. Slowly, the sniffling stopped. The girl's legs moved independently of Annabelle's, making them wobble for balance. The girl laughed a high, delighted laugh that sent a flush of warmth through Annabelle.

She walked the girl back and forth across the room and finally weight settled on Annabelle's feet and the girl's legs moved in coordination with Annabelle's.

After uncounted passes, Annabelle stopped in front of YBZ 2891. She lifted the girl and set her feet on the floor in front of her. "You can do this," she whispered to the new one. "Stand."

Slowly, Annabelle supported less and less of the girl's weight.

The girl stood free for several seconds, then wobbled. She waved her arms like a tightrope walker and steadied.

Annabelle circled to face the girl. "Walk."

The girl took a stiff-legged step. Tottered for a moment. Waved her arms around. Her eyes lit up, and she took another stiff-legged step, then another.

"Good." Annabelle couldn't help but smile. She backed away. "Keep coming."

Her inner angel scolded, *You grow soft.*

Annabelle stopped smiling.

The girl shuffled forward five more steps, then her knees bent into a precarious squat that teetered until she landed on her bottom. She laughed.

The desire to smile grew strong again, but Annabelle resisted. She looked up at YBZ 2891. "That is how you shall teach them to walk."

The expression on YBZ 2891 didn't change, but a stillness came over her. That stillness spread throughout the room.

Annabelle lifted her chin and her voice. "The Lord sent me a vision. It is His will."

The stillness remained.

Annabelle let her angel within blaze from her.

One by one, each instructor bowed her head and repeated, "His will be done."

Chapter Thirty-Two

Miranda's clothes were damp with perspiration. She'd waited in the stuffy tent since a couple of hours after daybreak. Patience thin, she tapped the toes of her right foot.

Still, Pokeweed waited. He said there was one more to arrive.

Unexpectedly, Leslie appeared. Took a seat at one of the card tables alongside one of the other lieutenants.

Miranda wanted to ask, *why are you here? Are you a lieutenant now?* She stuffed those questions down. *Must focus on my mission.*

The final two lieutenants arrived and took their seats. Exchanged greetings and the insults of shared history around the tables.

Pokeweed, in crisp clean clothes, walked to the front of the tent radiating a ready-for-anything energy.

How the hell does he look like that in this humidity? Miranda tugged her shirt straighter.

"Something has come up," Pokeweed said. "An opportunity we need to discuss and decide whether it fits our mission. Miranda will brief us on it."

She moved to the center front.

The men and women around the table looked to Pokeweed. *Wanda may have been wrong about who they'd listen to.*

Miranda took a big breath. "All right. Here's what I know." She told them about how Wanda and Ian had found the house, the housekeeper, and how they'd watched the house. "These pictures are the best shots we got of the child, Sandra." She passed the stack of Polaroids to Pokeweed, who having already seen them, passed them on to the first table. "And these are of the Prophet and his Lady." Miranda passed those pictures to Pokeweed and told them about the neighborhood, the backyard, and the neighboring church. "But that's not all."

"You all know who this guy is," she said when the pictures had returned to the front. Handed Pokeweed the photo of Admiral Moorer. That one went around the table more slowly.

"Obviously, that meeting is something we need to know more about. The photographs show us something is being planned that the Prophet doesn't want anyone else to know about. From what I learned from our prisoner—our guest, the former housekeeper there —I'm guessing the Prophet keeps documentation of his meetings in the upstairs room."

"You're assuming a lot," one lieutenant said, his head tilted and expression skeptical.

Miranda tried again. "Those photos of Felix, I mean, the Prophet, and Irene…"

The bald lieutenant crossed his arms. "The photographs are too dark. Anyone could be in them, and there's nothing that tells us when or where this is." He leaned back in his chair and extended one leg. "Nope, I'm not convinced."

She couldn't argue that any of the photos of Irene and Felix were clear. Without a flash and farther than ten or fifteen feet, the Polaroid simply didn't record what she saw. "Trust me. I know them both." She sounded more desperate than she'd intended.

"She wouldn't lie about this," Leslie said. "And if the Prophet is meeting with the Admiral in secret, that is something Monkshood needs to know about."

Miranda sucked in a breath. *Leslie speaking in favor of this? What is she up to?*

"Maybe we should check it out," the bearded lieutenant said.

Miranda tried not to look too hopeful.

"You said according to the housekeeper," the bald lieutenant said. "those Second Sphere agents have sniper rifles and shotguns. They can do a lot of damage before we even get near the place."

"But," the youngest lieutenant said. "If there are documents inside, it could mean a guaranteed success for us."

"Or it could mean the end of SABR if we're caught." The bald lieutenant crossed his arms.

The people at the table erupted in arguments for and against raiding the house.

Pokeweed whistled.

The shouts quieted and stopped.

"We will discuss this rationally. But first, Miranda, we need you to wait at the firepit for our decision."

You're sending me outside? Heat burst inside, fueling a fist-clenching rage that shook Miranda. She opened her mouth, but a second look at Pokeweed's face changed her mind. "Yes, sir," she said in a controlled tone and stumped out of the tent.

———

FOUR HOURS LATER, MIRANDA PACED AROUND THE FIREPIT. HER HANDS twitched open and closed. She would tell Pokeweed to forget it; she had to get back to Wanda. Apparently, she and Wanda were braver than the rest of SABR.

She marched back to the tent.

The tent flap flew open, narrowly missing her face.

"Oh. Miranda," Pokeweed said, clearly unsettled by her being so close. "I was just coming for you. We've made our decision."

She followed him and came to a halt inside.

The lieutenants crowded around a table, discussing something in hushed voices.

"You had questions for Miranda," Pokeweed said.

The voices fell silent, and all eyes rested on her.

Leslie stepped away from the table. A collection of oddly placed plates and cups, and stones sat on the table. "The plates are the churches you told us about," she said. "The cups are the buildings along the alley. The stones represent Second Sphere agents. Show us what we missed or got wrong."

Miranda took in the items on the table, then studied Leslie suspiciously. "Does this" —she nodded at the table—"mean you're going to help me get inside?"

Pokeweed cleared his throat. "It means we're going in as a team. Help us plan and execute the plan so we get the most information for the least risk."

She pressed her tongue against the back of her teeth. "I can't stay. Wanda has been on watch for hours and hours."

"I could send Ian to relieve her," Leslie said.

Pokeweed dipped his head in agreement.

Leslie stepped outside.

"Tell us what you think." Pokeweed swept a hand toward the table.

Miranda licked her lips and stepped forward to study the layout. She moved the two cups to be opposite one another and drew a finger between the plates that represented the church and the house. "This is a thick row of bushes and trees."

One lieutenant produced a clean handkerchief and laid it where she'd said the tree line was.

"You said you kept track of when the guards arrived and left," one of them said. "If we hit them right before the next change, they'd be tired and sloppy."

"The next change will be after sunrise tomorrow," she said dryly. "As much as I hate the delay"—she didn't say because they had taken so long to decide—"we should wait until after everyone has gone to bed tomorrow night. Rush the guards and the house. Focus on searching the upstairs office and rescuing Sandra and getting out."

Pokeweed gave her a deadpan look. "You want SABR to kidnap a child?"

She returned his look. "If we can't get the Prophet, how better to influence him than to have his child in our safekeeping?"

"Safekeeping." Pokeweed rubbed his chin. "Interesting word choice."

"We both want to stop the Fellowship, right?"

"Of course."

Miranda made eye contact with him. "Then we do what it takes to get the job done."

Chapter Thirty-Three

This housekeeper's apartment sat in one of a row of apartment houses south of the Anacostia River, just barely inside the District of Columbia.

Annabelle slipped inside the fully lit room of the fourth-floor apartment. Stood in the tiny vestibule with her back to the door and listened. Stifling heat brought beads of sweat to her forehead. Nothing stirred. Not even a curtain. There were only muffled street sounds and an occasional raised voice from outside the room. The still silence told her no one was home. Annabelle's insides quivered, caught in an unfamiliar, uncomfortable unease. Even her inner angel remained silent.

The apartment was a large all-in-one-room. And vacant from the kitchen, through the dining room, and into the living area. Each area boasted more things than the one before. At the far end of the room, gold drapes framed a door to a balcony dripping with plants.

Annabelle checked the lavatory. Also vacant. A quick search confirmed that the woman wasn't hiding in a cupboard, in the closet, or under the bed.

The Lord shows you another false lead. We must stop this and pursue ascension.

Our target is but human. They often work late. Or make trips to the grocer. It is late, so she will return soon. Annabelle carried a hardback chair from the dining table to the far corner of the room. Angled it so she could see all entry points. She sat and waited. And waited.

After an hour, Annabelle searched the apartment for clues. She looked in every drawer, every book, and even inside the copper pots hanging from the rack. As a last resort, she went through the papers on the desk. Electric bill, telephone bill, bank statement, and a list of dates, times, and locations. *Her jobs. The stupid woman has it right there. In plain sight.*

Annabelle frowned. One address seemed familiar, but she couldn't remember why: 4326 16th Street NW. It was the numbers. Four, three, two, six. Annabelle caught her breath. She and Sandra made a game of the numbers four, three, two times three was six. *Oh, Papa took Sandra and me there once. He called it his Gethsemane and made us swear we'd never tell a soul about it, not even Mother.*

Her chest filled with righteous vindication. *It is a sign from the Lord. Sandra is at Gethsemane.*

She hurried out of the apartment, ignoring the open cupboards, cushions thrown on the floor, and papers strewn about. Didn't matter who found it that way. Didn't matter that she hadn't burned the shield into the door. Didn't matter if the agnostics or the Fellowship declared it was the work of the Azrael. The Lord's command was hers to follow. She would find Sandra this day. This hour.

Chapter Thirty-Four

When Pokeweed gave the signal, Miranda didn't wait. She barreled through the door of the Prophet's secret house, up the stairs, and through the door to the room the housekeeper said had the maps.

The agent inside whirled to face her. Finger on the trigger, he raised his rifle with a silencer attached, aimed—

She drove her shoulder into the shooter's waist and plowed into the window frame behind him.

The trigger clicked.

Bang.

Her ears rang.

He lost his rifle, grappled with her.

They slid together down the wall, rolled across the floor.

His hands wrapped around her throat. His thumbs pressed down, choking off her air.

Her mouth gulped, but no air could pass the pressure of his thumbs. She scrabbled and scratched and scraped at his hands. Her lungs contracted. Her vision darkened. Her arms weakened.

His grip slackened, went away.

The first gasp brought a straw's worth of air. A little more air rasped through her raw, swollen throat. Her lungs expanded over and over. Air rushed in, and the desperate hunger of her lungs subsided. A muffled and distorted voice called to her from a deep well. She opened her eyes. Blobs of color swam before her. She gulped more air and blinked.

Pokeweed's face loomed over hers. His lips moved.

She barely understood the words.

"Still with me?"

"Still here," she croaked. "Alive." She pressed her elbows to the ground, levered herself to a shaky sitting position. Discovered that she sat on a large wool area rug with a frame of ivy leaves and floral medallions in the corners on each side of her.

A body lay to her left. His blank face stared up at the ceiling without seeing. From the blood pooled behind his midsection and awkward position, she figured he had a knife in his back.

She turned to Pokeweed. Her head swam. She swallowed, drew slow deep breaths. "You did that?" She side-eyed the body.

"Had to."

"Thank you." Miranda's voice sounded harsh in her ears. She gathered herself to stand.

"Take it slow." Pokeweed's voice still had that empty echo-chamber timbre. He grabbed her free hand and helped her to her feet.

She swayed and quickly opted to lean against the closet door behind her rather than fall.

"Sit back down."

She shook her head. Once. The tilt-a-whirl in her head was slower, but she decided not to shake her head again anytime soon.

She waited until the dizziness faded. Then scanned the room, surprised it took up half the upper floor. A dark wood lowboy dresser stood a couple of feet to her right, and against the intersecting wall was a matching highboy chest of drawers.

To the right of the door was a full-size bed with a tall wrought-iron headboard of curlicues and flourishes and a white chenille bedspread. Someone had folded a deep green throw and placed it neatly at the foot.

Chair-height dark-wood wainscoting surrounded the lower half of the room. Above the wainscoting, the walls and ceilings were a pale yellow-green.

At the far end of the room, bookshelves lined the wall and turned the corner until they reached the round window above a large wooden desk. On the other side of the window hung a large map of the East Coast dotted with gold, silver, and black pushpins.

"Is the house secure?" Her bruised throat made her voice low and harsh.

"Yes, got the signal a minute ago."

"Good." She steadied herself with a hand on the wall. Dropped her hand to her side, relieved her legs held her. "Let's find out what's in this room that's worth dying for."

Pokeweed hesitated as if he wanted to say something else. Instead, he reached for his walkie-talkie. Clicked the button twice, paused, and held the button down for three seconds. Listened to the static. Then, one click, a pause, and a hold for four seconds answered him.

Shit. Secure but no Sandra? Miranda pressed her lips tight against the niggling doubts that nagged her. *Wanda and Ian would've said something if she'd seen them take Sandra away.* "I'll search the desk."

"Right." He didn't have to say, if we don't find something, I won't ever trust you again.

He turned and opened the top drawer of the dresser that stood next to the door.

She crossed the short distance to the wooden swivel chair at the desk and sank into the chair to hide her weakening knees. The desktop held a metal desk lamp and a black Bakelite telephone on the right. A green desk blotter sat in the center with a heavy glass ashtray so clean it sparkled in the desk light. Only a thick, hard-bound Bible sat on the left corner of the immaculate desktop. She turned her attention to the three deep drawers on each side of the pencil drawer between them.

The top right drawer held a stack of leather-bound ledgers. Memories of reading her mother's ledger flashed through her, accompanied by the shock and hurt of discovering her mother had known about and hid the creation of the Azrael.

Miranda paged through the first ledger. It listed household expenses and registered payments to the housekeeper and the electric, telephone, and water companies. Under that ledger, a manila envelope held receipts and check stubs that seemed to back up the ledger's notations. Under the envelope were four more ledgers, two blank and two that were also detailed household accounts.

The second drawer held a bunch of random papers: maps, and

pamphlets, and prayer books, and handwritten letters and sermons. *Finally. Evidence to prove Felix was here.* Miranda pulled the drawer all the way out and dumped its contents onto the desktop. She sorted the papers into handwritten, handfuls of printed promotional materials, and dozens of street maps. Puzzled, she leaned back in the chair and stared from one pile to the next. Some of the handwriting could be Felix's, but some of it was a precise block print that looked nothing at all like Felix wrote it. There were maps of the District, of Baltimore, and Maryland and Virginia, and a map of Pennsylvania. And the promotional materials were for all the tourist sites in DC. *Why? And why street maps? His chauffeur did all the driving.*

She opened the top-left drawer. Crammed inside were more leather-bound journals. The second drawer held even more journals. Loose, handwritten notes filled the bottom drawer. The most recent ones held handwriting that looked nothing like her brother-in-law's penmanship.

"Find anything?" Pokeweed asked.

"The Prophet's handwritten sermons." An omission, not a lie.

"The whole desk is full of sermons?" Pokeweed had a dry, disbelieving tone in his voice.

"Of course not. If you want the whole catalogue list, ledgers of household expenses, maps, tourist brochures, and miscellaneous notes."

"Where's this girl you saw?"

"She's probably frightened and hiding. We'll find her." Miranda hoped she sounded a lot more certain than she felt.

"I meant, is there any evidence of her in those ledgers?"

Miranda's cheeks grew warm. "I'm looking." She opened the first ledger from the top left drawer. Paged through it. Slowly at first. Faster when the pattern of bill paying got repetitive.

Their walkie-talkies erupted with signals for Pokeweed to come to the cellar.

Miranda closed the ledger. "Bet that means they found her."

Pokeweed left.

She stared after him, eager to join him, but he hadn't asked her to come. She'd give him a minute and then arrive and comfort Sandra. Show him only she could calm and talk to her niece.

Without Pokeweed's presence, the room grew unnaturally quiet.

Occasionally she heard a muffled sound from downstairs, but mostly she heard the internal static of silence.

Ahchoo!

Startled, Miranda jumped to her feet. The chair rolled into the wall behind her. *That sounded as if…* She prodded the agent's body with her shoe. He was still dead.

She peered under the bed. No one. She straightened. Took soft steps toward the dead agent. "Sandra? Is that you?" Miranda strained to hear another sound, but there was only silence.

"It's okay, honey. It's Aunt Miranda. I came to save you. I know you didn't know it was me. And some of my friends. You found a really clever hiding spot, didn't you? Come on out now. You're safe."

"Are you really Aunt Miranda?"

It is *Sandra. I've got you now, Irene.* Miranda laughed. *I've got you.* "Of course it's me, you silly goose. I've missed you so much. Come out and give me a hug."

"But you sent us away."

Air burst from Miranda's lips as if someone had punched her in the gut. It took a couple of breaths to steady her voice. "I didn't want to, but your mommy and daddy wanted to stay with Grandma and Grandpa, and *they had* to go away."

Pop. A panel between the highboy and the bookcase wall swung open on silent hinges. Sandra sat cross-legged inside a cubbyhole just big enough for her. "Why?"

Miranda resisted the urge to drag her niece out. *It'll be better if she comes willingly.* "They did some bad things to some people who would have hurt them if they stayed." *If she's happy, eager to come with me, I can convince Pokeweed to change plans. We take her back to camp. Force Irene to come to us for once.*

Sandra's face crinkled in concentration. "But Grandma and Grandpa—" She crawled out, perched on her knees in front of the cubbyhole.

"Sweetheart, you're too little to understand."

Sandra crossed her arms over her chest. "That's what everybody always says."

Miranda sat on the floor, in front of Sandra. "I know. Sometimes adults say that because they want to protect kids from adult things. This time it's because it's very hard to understand. Even for adults."

"Even for you?"

Miranda didn't have to fake her sad smile. "Even for me."

Sandra sighed and looked toward the window. Her face paled, and her eyes widened. "Is he dead?" She pointed at the agent's body.

No hiding that. "Yes. My friend Pokeweed had to stop him from hurting me."

"Did the bad man do that?" Her cool fingers touched Miranda's throat.

"Why do you ask?"

"It's real red, and it looks like it hurts."

Miranda smiled at the tender concern on her face. "It doesn't hurt now."

"Good." Sandra's expression changed. "Are you going to take me to Mommy and Daddy?"

"They'll come again soon, like they did last night."

"Huh?" Her face scrunched up. "I haven't seen Mommy and Daddy in a really, really, really long time."

Miranda tensed. "What do you mean? Who came to see you then?"

Sandra's shoulders drooped. "Nobody. Uncle Lucas came last night, but he doesn't like me to see him. Sometimes I hide so I can see him, but he can't see me."

"But I saw your mommy and daddy come here last night. That's why we knew you were here."

"I told you. Uncle Lucas was here last night to work on his papers. I had to—wait." Suspicion crept into Sandra's eyes. "You were watching?"

"I'm confused," Miranda said. "How long have you been here?"

"Since before Christmas. No, before Thanksgiving."

Shock waves cascaded through Miranda. "Wait. Are you telling me you haven't seen your mommy or daddy since before Thanksgiving?"

Sandra made a sad, pouty face.

Since the explosions at the cave? Miranda could scarcely breathe. *Maybe Irene didn't escape unhurt. But I saw her...* "Did anyone tell you why your parents couldn't visit?"

Sandra sighed. "Bad people put Daddy in the hospital. So they hid me and Mommy to protect us."

"They hid you and Mommy—in different places." Miranda's breath came in short bursts. Her chest tingled. She swallowed and tried to breathe more calmly. "This is important, honey. Do you know where your mommy and daddy are now?"

"They won't tell me 'cause I'm a kid. They think I don't know how to keep a secret." She drew her crossed arms tighter, looked down at the floor. "You didn't come to take me back to Mommy and Daddy." Her words were slow but grew in heat. She lifted her head and glared at Miranda. "You're gonna send me away again, aren't you?"

Miranda sat still. Summoned up her most apologetic tone. "Oh, sweetheart. I'm so sorry. I made a big—no, humongous—mistake when I did that. I'd never ever do that again." That part was true. She put on her sincere face. "I can't make it happen today, but I will help you get back to your mommy and daddy as soon as I can. Cross my heart." She made the motion, never taking her eyes off Sandra.

Sandra's face softened, but her arms remained crossed tight against her little body.

"Let me take you away from here to some place that's safe until I can find your mommy and daddy." Miranda held her arms open.

Sandra's gaze went inward. Her eyes shifted left and right.

Miranda's chest tightened. *She's going to make me grab her. That is what Beryl would do. But I don't want to frighten her. Think. There's got to be something else I can say or do.*

A warm little body collided with hers. Little arms snaked around her neck in a tight hug. *I can finally make Irene come to me.* Elated, Miranda kissed the top of Sandra's head. Drew in a deep breath of bubble-gum-scented shampoo. Deep inside, an ache stirred and uttered nasty descriptions of who she'd become. She lifted her chin with a toss of her head and sealed that off. *I am who I must be.*

Chapter Thirty-Five

Annabelle slowed her motorcycle to a crawl, grateful for the modifications that made the engine no louder than a car. She parked two blocks away and closed the distance, darting from shadow to shadow. The sight of the house at 4326 16th Street NW with its high peaked roofs and stone-wrapped brick made her breath catch. It had once meant time with Papa when he wasn't the Prophet. He was just Papa.

Her inner angel growled impatiently.

Though the house was dark, a single sedan sat in the driveway behind it. Someone was home.

She switched on the night vision in her helmet's visor and turned into the alley behind the house. Nothing moved in the soupy pre-dawn stillness.

Against the backdrop scent of lavender and the musical chirps of crickets, the only other sound came from the traffic in the distance. She made her way through the bushes to the side of the house. Still no human sounds reached her. She made a quick dash across the open side yard and a creep along the back of the house to the porch. She climbed the steps two at a time.

The doorknob turned easily. Soundlessly. She slipped inside.

It was dark and quiet. Too quiet. She stole from the kitchen to the dining room.

Her heartbeat quickened at the sight of someone sitting in a chair, slumped over the table. An adult's body. Not Sandra. But it didn't bode well. *If someone has hurt Sandra…*

The body didn't move.

She moved closer and bent to peer at the chest, a female chest, for signs of life. The chest moved.

Standing behind the woman's chair, Annabelle placed a gloved hand over the woman's mouth.

"I am Azrael," Annabelle whispered in the woman's ear.

The woman jolted upright, uttered a muffled scream, and writhed to free herself.

"Calm yourself. I am not here for you."

The woman stopped making noise but whipped her head back and forth struggling to see who was behind her.

"Be still," Annabelle said, trying to be patient with this stupid, frightened human.

The woman's shoulders trembled violently and her breath sobbed, but she stopped thrashing her head about and nodded.

"I will remove your gag. Tell me where the child called Sandra is, and I will not harm you." Annabelle removed her combat knife from its holster and slid it behind the woman's head.

The gag fell to the table, and the woman's sobbing breaths slowed to quiet, air-hungry snuffling.

"Where is the girl child?"

"Rebels," she croaked. "Surprised us. Killed our guards."

Something squeezed Annabelle's throat tight. "And the girl?" Her voice squeaked. She cleared her throat. "Where's Sandra?"

The woman gave her a startled, open-mouthed look. "How does everyone know?"

"Tell me."

"They told me to tell only the Prophet and his Lady."

Annabelle made a strangled noise. She wasn't entirely certain if she had made the noise because her throat was too tight or if her inner angel had made it.

"Please don't hurt me." The woman swallowed audibly. "You're one of the Prophet's angels. I'm sure the Prophet would want you to know. The rebels said to tell the Lady that Sandra was with her favorite aunt."

The roar of her inner angel sent holy fire through Annabelle.

"Did they give the aunt's name?" she asked, though she knew the answer.

"Miranda."

"Where did Miranda take her?"

"I swear they didn't say. The only other thing they said was to tell the Lady that Miranda would be in touch."

Annabelle whirled and stalked across the room. Paced back to the woman. "Who brought Sandra here?"

The woman blanched. "I'm just the nanny. I don't know anything."

Humans lie. It's in their nature.

Annabelle didn't glare or grimace or threaten. She simply waited.

The woman squirmed in the chair. "My hands are numb. Please untie me."

Annabelle didn't move.

The woman licked dry lips. "Honestly, I don't know who brought the girl here. All I know is that the counselor hired me to take care of her."

Another wave of certainty hit Annabelle. "What's the counselor's name?"

"Counselor Matthews is the only one I saw."

Fury filled Annabelle. *Lucas.*

"He told me the Fellowship Council"—the woman's demeanor changed from defeated to proud—"chose me for this honorable duty. So you should untie me now."

Annabelle turned, strode through the kitchen and out the door.

Behind her, the woman cried, "Wait. Don't leave me like this. Untie me. Pleeease."

Annabelle ran to her bike, kicked the motor into life, and roared down the street.

Her inner angel cackled. *The lives of a rebel and a counselor. We will ascend!*

Chapter Thirty-Six

Irene sat frozen in the first of four rows of "donated" pews in the Azrael chapel. The small chapel lacked stained-glass windows, an organ, and other niceties, but high on the rough-hewn wall beyond the altar hung an oak, hand-carved Fellowship Shield. A twelve-foot-long white cross bisected the blood-red shield. Three graduated angular planks on either side of the upper portion of the shield represented the wings of Ascension. On any other day, Irene would have said it was the most magnificent Fellowship Shield she had ever seen.

Fury blazed from the pit of her stomach to her fingertips. *Lucas? I knew he was devious, but—he knew? All this time, he knew where Sandra was?*

Silent now, Annabelle stood in front of the altar rail, beneath and to the right of the shield.

Unable to sit still any longer, Irene shot from the pew, past Annabelle. Paced down the main aisle to the door and back again.

Annabelle didn't budge, but her eyes followed Irene's movements.

"Are you sure Miranda has Sandra?"

"Yes, Mother."

"Why am I just finding this out?" She wanted to throw something, hit something, kick something. A small piece of her remembered the sanctity of the chapel. She sucked in a deep breath.

Expelled it explosively. Tried another deep calming breath, but calm wasn't possible.

Sandra could have been with me all this time? Oh, he'll pay for this. She ground her teeth, whirled to face Annabelle. "Considering what you've just told me, I have changed my mind about something." She stopped directly in front of her adopted daughter. "The Prophet, your father, had a message from Gabriel yesterday that I didn't pass on to you. God forgive me. I—I thought there had been a mistake."

"And what was Gabriel's message, Mother?" Annabelle's tone was cool.

"That Lucas was to be Taken," Irene blurted and hoped her tone held enough shock and confusion and compassion to be believable.

Annabelle tilted her head. "The angel Gabriel told Papa that Counselor Matthews had veered into a sinful life and must be Taken? And you didn't believe it?"

Irene's throat instantly tightened. She cast her eyes downward. *Annabelle questions me more and more.*

With prayer hands positioned below her chin, Irene put every ounce of piousness she had into her tone. "Your father and I prayed about it. We've been under such terrible attacks by evil forces that we feared somehow they had given Felix this vision. That they were trying to undermine the Fellowship Council. So we asked the Lord to give us a sign that this was His command." She stepped forward to stand closer to Annabelle. "And you have just answered our prayers." She smiled warmly. "You have provided us with the answer. Lucas *has* fallen. He *must* be Taken." She held her tongue, hoping Annabelle felt the sincerity she projected.

"Perhaps Lucas isn't the only one who has strayed under the constant attack of evil."

Irene fought to keep her smile unchanged. *Mustn't allow Annabelle to question my faith. A miracle sooner rather than later might be the thing to restore her belief in me.* "Darling, we are so blessed to have you. You who are above the pettiness and trials and tribulations of being human. We trusted the Lord would send an answer. And praise the Lord! He did…through you."

Annabelle's expression didn't change. She didn't blink.

Irene squirmed inside. "But you may be right. The stress has been great. You should increase your surveillance of the Council.

Others may have fallen under the same evil influence that turned Lucas."

"That is a wise decision, Mother."

Relief washed over Irene. To hide her moment of weakness, she firmly gripped Annabelle's hand in both of hers. "I am guided by the Lord and my beautiful daughter who serves Him."

Annabelle's gaze fixed on Irene's hands holding hers.

Uncomfortable, Irene patted Annabelle's hand and released it. "Enough unpleasantness. I wanted to say how much I love this chapel you've created for your angels." She did a slow turn as if admiring the gloomy chapel. "It is perfect."

"It suits our needs."

"Your humbleness inspires me." She dabbed her sweaty brow and neck with her already damp pink handkerchief. "I need some air."

Outside on the boardwalk, the air was no cooler, but frogs and birds and other creatures she couldn't name sang. Pretending to listen gave her time to regain her composure. Finally, she turned her proud-mother face on Annabelle. "Darling, while I'm here, may I see how the newest batch of Azrael have progressed?"

Annabelle's face lit up, and her posture somehow relaxed and puffed up at the same time. "Of course, Mother. Follow me."

Irene followed Annabelle down the boardwalk at a quick pace.

At a newly constructed building on the east side, Annabelle opened the door and they stepped inside a small, unfurnished foyer-like space with three walls of smooth boards and a fourth wall covered in heavy, royal blue drapery.

Annabelle spread the drapes open, revealing a large, thick window in the wall.

On the other side of the window were a dozen identical ten-year-old girls. They sat at school desks, all their attention focused on an Azrael in the front.

A warm feeling lifted Irene's spirits. She'd seen young Azrael en masse before in the cave, but this was different. These were *her* Azrael.

All the girls rose to attention at the same instant.

"Can they see us?" The idea they could sent a thrill through her.

"No, the glass is one-way. I felt it important for experienced Azrael to observe and make suggestions for improvements."

Irene stared at her daughter. A flush of pride filled her. "The Lord has blessed us. He chose wisely when He chose you to lead."

Annabelle actually blushed. "I am but an earthbound servant of my Lord."

On the other side of the glass, the girls marched in place, perfectly synchronized. After marching, they touched their toes and did jumping jacks.

Irene wanted to gush praise but opted for a single pious nod. "Thank you for allowing me a glimpse of these new angels. I would love to stay longer, but I have an engagement this evening. I'll need time to pray and to dress, so I must return home." She walked out of the new building, back down the boardwalk toward the boat dock.

One of the Azrael—she couldn't be sure, but it looked like the same one that had brought her here—waited at the end of the dock where the moored flat-bottomed boat bobbed in the river's current.

Irene paused, turned a loving look on her adopted daughter. "By the way, darling, I have it on good authority that Counselor Matthews will be at his home after ten tomorrow night. Perhaps that would be a good time to take care of the Lord's—weeding?"

"His will shall be done."

Irene disguised the sudden twisting of her stomach with a smile, glad she was leaving. "Of course it will." She wanted to ask Annabelle to call her, to tell her when it was done, but her discomfort made those words stick in her throat. She swallowed, changed tactics. "I'll see you again soon." Her voice was too tight, but she'd done her best. She turned her back on Annabelle and walked toward the boat, acutely aware that something had changed in her daughter but uncertain what that change meant.

Chapter Thirty-Seven

Miranda had lost track of how long it had been since they'd brought Sandra to camp. At least it was still dark, but instead of being with and questioning Sandra, she stood outside Pokeweed's tent, relegated to listening. Her jaw was so tight her entire head ached. *I found Sandra. I know her. I'm the one who should question her.* Fortunately, tents weren't soundproof.

Pokeweed's questions were soft but clear. Sandra's answers were so soft Miranda didn't always get the whole thing. But his choice of little kid words would not force Sandra to answer with any detail. He didn't even ask about the Prophet and Irene's visit. He treated the child as if she were a china doll. An antique china doll who'd fall apart if he raised his voice or asked a tough question.

The voices inside fell silent. She could no longer hear whether anything was being said. Her skin and muscles itched to find out what was happening inside.

The tent flap opened. Pokeweed stepped out, turned toward the inside. "Are you sure you aren't hungry? Maybe an apple and some cheese or peanut butter?" He waited for an answer, his back to Miranda. "Okay, if you're sure." He faced Miranda and smiled. "Poor kid. She hasn't seen her parents in months."

"I know." Miranda stepped forward.

He stopped her with a hand on her arm. "Look, your niece is

exhausted. Let her get a few hours of sleep. You could probably use a few hours yourself."

Miranda smiled sweetly. "She wanted me to stay with her. I promised her I would."

"Won't your host family be worried?"

"I told them earlier that I'd be staying with a friend for a few days."

Pokeweed's expression clearly said he didn't believe her, but he shrugged and walked wearily away.

Miranda entered the tent.

Sandra lay inside a sleeping bag on one of the two cots, her eyes open, staring. Her grip on the top of the sleeping bag was white-knuckled. She smiled at Miranda. "I'm glad it's you."

"I told you I'd stay with you." Miranda crossed the four feet to the cot next to Sandra. "Okay if I sleep here?"

Sandra nodded.

Miranda sat. "So, did they let you go to school while you were at that house?"

She shook her head.

"Oh, did that make you sad?"

Sandra didn't respond or even move.

"Did you watch television or listen to the radio or go to the park or anything?"

Another negative head shake. A thick strand of blonde hair fell across her face.

"That's a long time to go with nothing fun to do." This time there was no reaction at all. "You're so smart, I'll bet you made your nanny work hard to teach you." Miranda reached out and brushed the hair out of Sandra's face.

Sandra flinched.

The movement was so eerily familiar, Miranda froze. She had to force herself to breathe. Force herself to repeat, my father can't touch me ever again.

Force herself to calmly bring her hand back to her side. "Did they hurt you?"

A slow head shake. "When will you take me to Mommy and Daddy?"

Miranda shifted her weight on the edge of the cot. "I'm sorry. It'll take a few days."

"A few days?" Sandra's voice cracked. Her chin quivered. "It's been for-ev-er already."

"I know. But your mommy and daddy don't want to talk to me, so I have to—um—send a friend. Because your father is the Prophet, it's not always simple to visit him."

"He'd see me right away."

Her pleading tone fed a current guilt through Miranda. But Nick and Beryl have been dead *forever* too. *I don't want to wait any longer either.* "I know you're tired of waiting. I don't blame you. I would be too. Maybe you can remember something that will help me—help my friend—get in to see your daddy faster."

"Like what?"

"Like, do you remember where you were when you last saw your mommy or daddy?"

Sandra gave her a puzzled look. "Of course."

"Where were you?"

"At home."

"Do you remember the address?"

"I'm not a kindergartner."

Miranda hid her irritation with a soft fake chuckle. "Of course not. So tell me the number and street name."

Sandra gave a great I'm-being-put-upon sigh. "Thirty-six, fifty-one Winfield Lane Northwest, Georgetown, Washington DC."

Maybe she was right earlier. She's been a captive in that house since before the caves? That would be ten, no, eleven months.

Sandra's expression turned puzzled. "I got it right. I know I did."

"Yes. Yes, you did," Miranda hastened to say.

Sandra stretched her mouth open in a never-ending yawn.

Oh no, you don't. Not yet. I need more information. "Stay awake a little longer, Sandra. I need to know the name of your father's secretary."

"I don't remember," Sandra mumbled. Her eyes drifted closed.

Miranda sprang up and yanked Sandra's sleeping bag open. "I can't reach your father if I don't know his secretary's name. Tell me her name."

Sandra gave Miranda a hurt glare and tugged at the sleeping bag to cover herself again.

"Come on, Sandra. Think. What's the name of your father's secretary?"

Sandra's hurt expression shifted. "I told you, I don't remember." Her lower lip stuck out.

Miranda dropped to a squat so her face was close to Sandra's. "Okay, you don't remember your daddy's secretary. How about your mommy's?"

"I don't know! Wait. That's a trick question. Mommy doesn't have a secretary." Sandra's tone changed from whining to belligerent. "If you want to talk to Daddy, call the Fellowship Center. Ask for Daddy's office, you'll get his secretary."

Miranda hid her surprise. "I can't." *She doesn't know about the explosion that destroyed the Fellowship Center.*

"Then call Mommy at home." Sandra rolled over, her back to Miranda, and wrapped her arms around her shivering form.

Miranda released her grip on Sandra's sleeping bag. Deep inside Miranda, memories burned. Memories of the caves collapsing, killing Beryl, burying Nick. She glared at her niece. *She's been at that house since before the holidays...maybe before the annulment? Eleven months with no television, not even the daily call to prayers? That's just not possible.*

She stiffened. *Sandra is lying. Irene and Felix would train her to. They wouldn't want their daughter to reveal the truth about the inner workings of the Fellowship.* She grabbed Sandra's shoulder, pulled her roughly to her back. "Sandra."

The girl's eyes were closed, her face slack.

"Sandra, wake up. I need answers." Miranda shook the girl's shoulders. "Sandra!"

Sandra opened her eyes, licked and then smacked her lips.

"Why are you lying to me?" Miranda demanded. "I saw them visit you. Just admit it, and you can sleep."

Sticking her lip out, Sandra glared. "I am not lying. I'm an elite, born a Fellowship member, *and* the daughter of the Prophet. I don't lie."

"You *are* lying." Miranda pulled the girl up by the shoulders, forced her to sit on the side of the cot. "I saw two visitors enter the house. Not one. Two."

"When Uncle Lucas came?" A frown creased Sandra's face. "He

always comes with his helpers and his agents." She sagged. "Now can I go to sleep?"

Should I tell Ethan this? Miranda scoffed softly. *Tell him what?* "Let's take them one at a time. When did you last see your mother?"

Sandra's lower lip quivered. "I told you, I haven't seen Mommy in two times forever. Not since Daddy sent Agent James to take me to that house."

Miranda cocked her head. "Since when? Do you know what day that was?"

"It was a school day a long, long time ago. Before summer, I think."

"This summer?"

Sandra huffed air through her nose. "No. Don't you listen? I said forever and ever ago."

Miranda had to know when. "What about your father?"

"I'm tired," Sandra whined. "I just want to sleep."

"Don't be a baby. You are old enough; I know you remember what day they took you to that house."

"Why are you being so awful to me?" Sandra's lower lip quivered. "You said you would take me to Mommy and Daddy. But you lied. You don't care." She crossed her arms over her chest. "You're a bully. I won't answer any more questions, bully." Sandra's voice grew louder. "You're just as evil as Mommy said you are. I hate you!"

"Stop that!" Miranda slapped Sandra across the mouth.

She wailed. Loudly.

The tent flap snapped open. "What on earth is going on in here?" Pokeweed stepped into the tent and glared at Miranda.

Sandra stopped crying and blinked at Pokeweed. "She's being mean to me."

Miranda lifted her chin. "She's throwing a tantrum to avoid answering my questions."

"She's your niece, not your prisoner." Pokeweed sounded shocked. He pressed his lips together and took Miranda's arm firmly, guiding her to stand up. "I came here to tell you Monkshood wants to speak with you."

She glared at him. "I have to finish—"

"Now." He didn't let go until they were at the fire ring in the center of camp.

Chapter Thirty-Eight

eslie carried a cardboard box full of paper cups and hand-lettered cardboard signs past the man-sized concrete urn and hesitated. The whirring of a swarm of anxious bees buzzed through her veins. She looked across the block-long War Memorial Plaza, a tribute to the soldiers lost in the Great War.

Dominating the center of the open landscape was a sunken grid of concrete and crushed black rock rectangles, a poignant representation of a military graveyard. Flanking the north and south sides of the grid were concrete benches alternating with black lampposts topped with acorn-shaped globes. It being mid-morning, only one bench had an occupant.

"Where do you want this, Miss Leslie?" Howard, the young man who cleaned the clinic every night, carried the large green thermal water dispenser she had borrowed.

"Follow me." She descended the steps to the crushed-stone path of the plaza, past the first of the light poles, and set her box on the bench. "Just put next to this."

He placed the water dispenser on the bench, wished her luck, and hurried back toward the bus stop.

"Thank you," she called after him, wondering who else would avoid the protest because of fear.

Leslie sat on the bench next to her box, wishing she hadn't gotten here so early. This was her first official act for SABR. For Monkshood. She didn't want to fail, but...getting the mayor to come out and talk to non-Fellowship protesters was a tall order. Even when the protest was outside his office. And all she could do for now was wait for the church bells to ring at the top of the hour and for the protesters she had hoped would fill the plaza.

She looked down the center of the plaza again, this time focused on the building that would make this protest a success or a failure, city hall.

Framed by the two flagpoles on the west end of the plaza, the city hall was an ornate and massive six-story brick building topped with an iron dome above a mansard roof. A split grand marble staircase led from street level up to a spacious landing and a ninety-degree turn for the steps to the large portico-covered porch and the extra-tall entrance doors. Six fluted columns and four multi-headed bronze lanterns on the concrete banister lined the porch.

The scents of car exhaust and hot concrete around her warned Leslie it would be a long, sultry morning and a hotter afternoon. She wished the benches were on the other side of the pathway, among the green boxwood bushes there. Not that the bushes or the retaining wall behind them provided any shade, but the trees flanking the street-level sidewalk on the other side of the wall offered a little relief from the heat.

The wait weighed on her. She swung her legs, rocked back and forth, and cast glances around for her fellow non-Fellowship citizens coming to join her protest. Protesters weren't showing up. The whirring buzz inside intensified.

A protest wasn't something one could announce in public. She had told a handful of people about it, and like the kids' game of telephone, each of those people spoke to a handful, and so on.

She exhaled heavily. *Maybe, like in the game, the message got scrambled.*

An agonizing ten minutes later, two of her coworkers from the clinic appeared.

They nodded at her.

She offered them a sign each. Signs that read, "Enough is enough!" and "Our lives. Our Choices. Our Voices."

They held the signs above their heads and strolled the wide perimeter walkway. Alone. They made one circuit, then another, and another.

Church bells rang out the half hour.

Leslie's shoulders drooped. According to Monkshood's instructions, she needed to gather enough non-Fellowship people to walk around the plaza holding signs and chanting. He wanted them to grab the attention of the mayor, the city council, and the news stations. She gave a last forlorn glance in each direction. She had failed. She understood people's hesitation. Taking a public stand against the Fellowship was dangerous.

She stood. Rummaged in her box for a sign to carry.

"May I have one of those?" a woman's voice asked.

Leslie faced the woman and smiled at the unfamiliar face framed with mousy brown hair. Behind that woman, another woman approached, and behind her, a gray-haired couple. And more men and women strode down the street behind them. People Leslie had never met.

A puff of air escaped Leslie. "Are you here to protest?"

Heads bobbed and voices chorused, "Yes."

Leslie grinned. "Welcome."

One by one, she handed out signs. Soon all twenty-four signs she'd made were gone.

She hitched her shoulders up and back, plastered a big smile on her face, and shouted, "The power of the people is greater than the people in power!" She joined those who walked around the central memorial and past the gathering crowd of Fellowship members who gaped at the protesters.

The sun reached overhead, stealing what little shade they'd had. Leslie's feet grew hot and tired, and her voice cracked and croaked. She stopped shouting.

Around her, the chanting faltered, their shouts discordant.

"No more silence. No more fear," a clear, resonant voice chanted. "The people rise—their voices clear." A few other voices echoed him.

"No more silence. No more fear," the lead voice called, louder. "The sphere's end is near."

More voices answered, repeating his words.

More and more people joined them on the pathway and raised their voices and clapped the beat. Some even carried their own signs. They clapped and shouted and filled the plaza with sound.

Leslie couldn't stop smiling. *So this is what a protest is like.* She clapped and shouted and wormed through the crowd, urging people to shout louder, to clap, to keep their energy up.

The sun traveled across the sky, and the trees along the north side of the plaza provided shade, but there was no shelter from the dense, muggy air.

She tugged to free her sweat-glued clothes from her skin. *Three hours. No one cares. How long does Monkshood expect us to go on?*

Whir-pop-snick. Whir-pop-snick.

Is that? She spun to see.

Whir-pop-snick. Flash.

A camera! She ducked her head, hoping his camera hadn't captured her. Peered up from under her brow and glimpsed a press pass dangling in front of a brown suit. Moved to put bodies between her and the reporter. *Monkshood didn't say what I should do when the reporters showed up.* She maneuvered closer to the reporter.

"Why did you come to the plaza? What are you trying to do?" The reporter held his pen ready over a stenographer's notebook.

"We want the mayor and the city council to hear us," a female voice answered.

Leslie frowned. She didn't recognize that voice, but the answer was good.

"The government is for all of us," another voice said.

"Not just for the Fellowship."

"Aren't you afraid…?"

Leslie's stomach went rock hard. That answer…would bring trouble.

The crowd shifted again. She had to move further away and couldn't hear the rest. Couldn't get closer. Couldn't risk being recognized.

A news reporter from the Baltimore Sun showed up. More reporters arrived.

We have the attention Monkshood wants. So why do I feel so shaky?

More and more non-Fellowship people joined them, invigorating the crowd. The shouting grew louder.

More and more Fellowship members watched from the far sides of the surrounding streets. And the BPD officers appeared. They stood on the outer sidewalk around the plaza, batons in hand, facing the protesters.

Some of the watching Fellowship shouted at the protesters. "The

Fellowship is the way!" "You are damned!" "Get thee behind me, Satan!"

The police didn't react to the crowd and continued to stare impassively at the protesters.

"Stay calm." Leslie urged her fellow protesters. "We must stay calm.

The BPD simply stood there. A silent threat. Waiting.

One by one, the protesters began to leave.

Leslie hurried after one woman and cried, "Please stay. We need you!"

The woman carried her little girl, who slept on her shoulder. She gave a pointed glance at the police, then looked Leslie in the eye. "My baby is tired. I've gotta take her home." She walked away.

Leslie turned back to the two or three dozen people remaining. Shouted as loud as her hoarse voice would go, "No more silence. No more fear..." Her voice gave out.

She ran to the planter bench that held the green thermal water dispenser on the east side of the plaza. Downed a cup of water. The cool water soothed her throat. She realized there were almost the same number of cups that she had brought this morning.

She filled two paper cups and offered the water to her fellow demonstrators with encouragement about how well they were doing. Over the next hour, she gave every protestor on the plaza a cup of water and a few words of encouragement. It seemed to work. The shouting grew louder.

She trudged back to the bench that held the empty water dispenser, wondering where she could get more water. Pulled up short. "Where did that come from?" She pointed at the stainless-steel water cooler sitting next to her smaller, green one.

A young woman wearing a bright-pink polka-dotted jumper turned and faced Leslie. The women carried a wooden tray filled with cups of water. Held it out.

Leslie gaped at the woman, at the tray, and back at the woman. "Where did this—you—come from?"

The woman tucked a stray strand of her long brunette hair back behind her ear and smiled. "I work across the street. But when I heard you guys and saw you running around two cups at a time, I knew I could help."

"But you're—" Leslie tried not to stare at the woman's clothing. "I mean…are you sure?"

"I wore these clothes so I could keep my job, but it's not worth it anymore. Not when I see what they are doing to people like you."

Overwhelmed, Leslie blinked back tears. "Thank you. This is amazing." *Maybe this protest stuff might actually work.* She took the tray and tried to get across the plaza, but people had pressed together more tightly. Hands reached for the water and quickly emptied her tray. She tucked the tray under one arm and started back toward the table.

Every time she made a few feet nearer the table, the movement of people around her forced her back. "What the heck?" she muttered. "Do people spring out of the concrete?"

A male voice from behind her said, "What a crowd."

"Why don't they spread out a little?" Leslie asked.

"Nobody wants to get too close to the police. But we're gonna spill into the street pretty soon."

"So many?" Leslie couldn't see anything but heads and shoulders around her.

He grinned and nodded. "Elbow-to-elbow non-Fellowship."

"Where'd they all come from?"

"Probably heard about it on KBAL's noon news. That's where I heard about it. Had to come see for myself."

A balloon of hope bubbled in her chest. She tried to keep it small against the inevitable pop. Instead, it grew and grew and grew until her tired-stiff cheeks lifted in a full-beam smile. Grew until she couldn't help but thrust a fist in the air. Couldn't help but shout a throat-ripping "No more silence. No more fear!"

Her raw throat made her fall silent again, but she continued to walk. Weary protesters sat elbow-to-elbow on the benches. Occasionally someone would rise and rejoin the walkers, and some other worn protester would take that seat.

Fourth time around, Leslie took one of those vacated seats. The burn in her hot and aching feet lessened a little. She frowned at city hall. *If only the mayor or the city council president would show.*

A gasp rippled through the crowd. Like a warm spring day in the mountains can change to a snow day in an instant, the air around her became charged with tension and fear you could taste.

The crowd in front of Leslie shifted. Gave her a clear view of

BPD officers placing sawhorse barriers around city hall and the sidewalk that ran along its perimeter.

Reporters with cameras and microphones moved behind the protection of the barriers and the police. Some of the reporters' cameras pointed at the protesters. Others raced up the steps of city hall.

"Ladies and gentlemen..." An amplified male voice rose above the singing. "Quiet, please. I have an announcement."

The protesters quieted and faced city hall.

On the building's upper landing, visible between each of the six Corinthian columns, stood Baltimore Police Officers, each holding a baton or stick so all could see. A young man stood behind a microphone in the center of the city hall's porch.

Leslie recognized him as the mayor's spokesman. *Not the mayor.* She worried her lower lip.

"The mayor has heard you, and he wants you to know that Baltimore will always be a place that supports its citizens, but we will not allow violence and lawlessness. Please be good citizens and return to your homes so your mayor and your city council may do their work in peace."

Arms linked with other officers, the police formed a living line, a wall, that moved forward and relentlessly pushed against the crowd.

"Move!" they commanded. "Move along!"

Grunts and yelps came from the people near the fountain.

The rhythmic chant around her stumbled and fractured into a chaotic jumble of noise.

The crowd surged eastward. Leslie's shoulders tightened and her pulse raced, but adrenaline chased all the bees inside away and she pushed westward. "It's okay. Be calm. Go home," she said to the people she passed.

"You heard him," an officer shouted. "Move! Move now!"

"Stay calm!" Leslie shouted, her voice stronger than it had been. "Do as they say."

Her fellow protesters threw over-the-shoulder looks at the police behind them but quieted and moved more calmly.

"It's okay, folks," Leslie said, her shout steadier than she felt. "We'll do as the mayor has asked. Stay calm. Go home." Under her breath she added, *for now.*

Chapter Thirty-Nine

Irene worried that her glove-covered palm was so damp the bottle of belladonna she concealed in her fist would slip out of her grasp before she'd had a chance to drop it in Mrs. Wynter's tea.

Mrs. Wynter had lapsed into a recollection of her late husband again. "He was a very intelligent man." Her characteristic gravelly wheeze seemed more prominent today. "So, I've always taken his words to heart. He predicted the Council would become so old and insular that it would threaten the stability of our country by holding onto archaic ideas and not inspiring our youth. And he was right." She drained her teacup with a noisy sip and put the cup down on the coffee table.

At last. "I see why you revered him." Irene set her own teacup down and topped off her cup. "Would you like me to pour more tea for you?"

"That would be delightful. You are such a dear friend, Irene. I look forward to the next few years as we work to restore our country's greatness." Mrs. Wynter's lips stretched over her teeth in an almost imperial smile.

Irene ignored the trickle of sweat down her back, tipped the silver teapot, and poured fresh tea into Mrs. Wynter's cup. Cupping her left hand around the teacup, she blocked Mrs. Wynter's view of the cup. Though she'd practiced opening the bottle and adding drops to the tea it was much more difficult now. "You like two sugars, is that correct?"

"Yes, dear, how observant."

She dropped two cubes of sugar into the drug-laced tea and stirred.

"The next time Lucas gives you an order," Mrs. Wynter said. "Add a statement from the Prophet about feeling the Lord direct him in a new direction."

"You're sounding a little hoarse. I don't want you to have one of your coughing fits because you're talking with me." Irene handed the drugged tea to Mrs. Wynter. "Here, this will soothe your throat."

"Thank you, dear." Mrs. Wynter took the cup and put it to her lips. "Oh, my. That's hot. It needs to cool a bit." She set it down.

Irene gritted her teeth and fixed a pleasant expression on her face.

"As I was saying, the Lord is directing him in a new direction, and soon he will have clearer guidance from the divine."

Irene eyed the teacup. Mrs. Wynter had to drink at least half of the cup for the drug to be effective.

"Then in a week or two—" Mrs. Wynter barked a hoarse cough. She dabbed her lips with her light blue lace handkerchief. "In a week or two, you will announce that Gabriel visited him."

"Oh? That will make the membership take notice." *The nerve of the old woman, telling me what to do.* "And what is Gabriel going to tell the Prophet?"

"It's better to—" cough cough. "To keep the next step—" cough cough cough. "Oh dear, my heart is racing..." She put a hand to her heart and another harsh coughing fit seized her.

Don't worry, Mrs. Wynter. At the right time, the Lord's spirit will fill me and I'll bring you back to life. Soon after, you and Lucas and the entire country will take orders from me, the new Prophet.

Mrs. Wynter's coughing slowed, and she struggled to catch her breath.

Irene drew her brows together in imitation of concern. "Please drink your tea and soothe your poor, irritated throat."

Shakily, Mrs. Wynter picked up the cup and drank.

"That's it," Irene said. "Drink it all up and rest a moment or two." She picked up her own teacup and faked a couple of sips.

Mrs. Wynter opened her mouth as if to continue but coughed

again and reached for her teacup. After a couple of swallows, she set the cup down again.

Irene patted Mrs. Wynter's hand. "Don't strain yourself. I am a patient woman and will wait for you to recover, however long that takes. Just close your eyes and rest a moment."

Mrs. Wynter smiled a wan smile. "Thank you. I'm afraid that coughing fit took my breath away." She leaned back against her sapphire sofa and closed her eyes.

Irene watched the rise and fall of the old woman's chest for long minutes. Listened to the old woman's open-mouthed breaths sigh in and out. Irene worried that the dosage hadn't been strong enough.

Mrs. Wynter took a sharp breath and dragged her hand up to her chest as if she barely had the strength to move. Her breath rattled. She sighed and went silent, unmoving.

Irene leaned forward, unable to hide her eagerness. Her driver had delivered the belladonna with a set of symptoms that would warn of the medication affecting the heart, and here it was happening in front of her. *Fascinating.*

She took off her right glove and fingered Mrs. Wynter's wrist—couldn't feel a pulse. Put her fingers on Mrs. Wynter's neck. The weak pulse there faded to nothing.

Irene enjoyed the swell of her pride in her chest, then stood and put on a distressed look. "Help! Jeeves, help!"

Jeeves appeared instantly. "How may I—"

"It's Mrs. Wynter. She had a coughing fit, then—I can't wake her... Is she—is she dead?"

Jeeves's expression changed from aloof to deeply concerned. He rushed to Mrs. Wynter's side. Placed his fingers on her neck, then hurried to the phone. "We need an ambulance immediately." Then he dialed a second number. After a moment he said, "It's Mrs. Wynter. She needs you." He listened. "Yes, I've already called for one, sir."

"Oh, Jeeves," Irene said in a sorrowful tone. "I'm afraid it's too late." *But the more witnesses to this miracle, the better. Now, they just have to respond as fast as they normally do.*

She didn't have to worry. The ambulance and a fire truck arrived in minutes.

Jeeves escorted the rescuers to Mrs. Wynter. The doctor followed. *Guess the rich really do get better service.*

The doctor delicately lifted one of Mrs. Wynter's eyelids. Then he took his stethoscope out of his bag and listened to her chest. "I'm sorry, she's gone."

"Oh." Irene kneeled beside Mrs. Wynter's body. Placed her clasped hands on the dead woman's lap and bowed her head. "Lord, I feel you. I am your willing instrument." Out of the corner of her eye, she took in the astonished looks on the men's faces. "Yes, Lord." She rose to her feet, the motion fluid enough to look as if the Spirit lifted her. Placed her sweaty right hand on Mrs. Wynter's cool forehead. "Let us pray. Dear Lord God in heaven, if it be our sister's time, take her to Your heavenly house, but if it's not her time, use me to restore her." She couldn't decide whether warmth was returning to the old woman's body or not. She took off her left glove and slipped her hand inside the "dead" woman's blouse. *Ah, yes.* There was a faint heartbeat. "Lord, I am Your instrument, Your vessel, ready to pour out Your love and healing energy into our sister." She moaned and swayed the way she'd seen Felix do during his miracles. That she had to fake it was a minor annoyance. "Yes, Lord. I feel it." She moaned once more and stopped swaying. She peered through her lashes at the men surrounding her, gaping at her. "Sister Wynter needs all our prayers. Open your hearts and souls and pray."

They exchanged wary glances and one by one bowed their heads.

"Lord, we bow before You." She moaned louder and shook harder and, under the cover of the blouse, jabbed Mrs. Wynter with her fingers.

Irene kept moaning and swaying until her muscles and throat ached, and she feared she'd given Mrs. Wynter too much belladonna.

Mrs. Wynter's eyes fluttered open.

"Thank you for this miracle, Lord!" Irene shouted. Then dropped back to her knees in a planned faint that nearly was an actual one.

"What's happened?" Mrs. Wynter croaked in a barely audible voice. Lifted her head and took them all in. "What are you doing here?"

The doctor dove forward, checked Mrs. Wynter's heart, and had the rescuers start an IV.

Jeeves appeared at Irene's side, took her arm, and helped her stand and move back to the armchair she'd sat in earlier. "That was a miracle," he whispered to her.

She smiled a demure smile. "I was simply the Lord's instrument doing His will."

"Load her up," the doctor instructed. "I'll meet you at the hospital."

The rescuers placed Mrs. Wynter on the stretcher. "We just witnessed history," a male voice behind her whispered. "A woman performing a miracle. Anointed."

The rescuers rolled the stretcher out of the room. "Do you think she'll become the next Prophet?"

"It's possible," whispered the first man. "If she performs two more, she'll have to be, won't she?"

That's the plan.

Chapter Forty

Miranda sat on the cot in the small tent. There'd been a time when she'd have thought a tent a luxury. Last night had not been one of those times. Even with its screen windows unzipped, the tent had been too stuffy and the SABR camp too quiet for sleep.

On the other side of the tent, Sandra tossed and turned. Her cot creaked with every movement.

Miranda stood, stretched, and rolled the stiffness out of her neck and back. She crossed over to kneel by Sandra's sleeping form. "Sandra. It's time to wake up."

Sandra rolled over and faced the tent wall.

Miranda tapped the little shoulder. "Come on, Sandra. Wake up. It's morning."

Sandra opened one eye. Looked around, confusion on her face. Made eye contact with Miranda. "Oh, yeah." She popped into a sitting position. "Are you taking me to Mommy and Daddy now?"

"Not until you tell me how to find your parents," Miranda said.

Sandra's pert little nose wrinkled. She laughed. "Silly. You know how to find them."

"No, I don't." Miranda struggled to sound patient. "They're hiding. Tell me, when were they going to visit you again?"

"What?" Sandra gave her a pained look. She wriggled her bottom on the cot. "You said you would take me home."

Miranda sucked her cheeks and counted three before she spoke. "I don't know where to take you, Sandra. You have to tell me."

Sandra grimaced. Put her hands low on her belly and rocked back and forth.

Miranda rubbed her mouth. "Do you need to use the ladies' room?"

Rapid, repetitive nods bounced blonde hair up and down.

"There's a bucket in the corner." Miranda pointed to the uncovered metal pail. A roll of toilet paper sat on the tent floor between the pail and a large white enamel bowl of water. A crumpled hand towel and a bar of soap sat beside the bowl. "Just be sure you hit the bucket and not the washbasin."

Sandra's eyes widened. "But what if I have to sit down?"

"Squat or don't." Miranda shrugged and resumed her morning stretching routine. The faint smell of wood smoke warned her that the entire camp would be awake soon.

After a few grunts, the sound of liquid hitting the pail reverberated in the tent.

Miranda gave Sandra privacy, finished her stretches, and then turned around.

Sandra haphazardly dried her hands on the hand towel, then returned to stand in front of and look up expectantly at Miranda.

"Bet you're hungry."

Her eyes widened. She gave three vigorous nods and asked, "Do you have any waffles?"

Miranda genuinely laughed. "You've never been camping before, have you? No electricity means no waffles." She made a show of sniffing the air. The aroma of fried biscuits and bacon and eggs made her stomach rumble. "Smell that? Cook is making bacon and eggs. And biscuits too."

"Ooh, I lo—ove biscuits."

"Okay. You can have some…after you answer my questions."

"More questions? Can't we eat first?"

Miranda gritted her teeth at Sandra's petulant tone. Took a breath and tried again. "When was the last time you saw your mommy and daddy?"

Sandra's mouth dropped open. "I told you last night. It's been forever. Only Uncle Lucas came to the house for months, and years maybe. And I had to hide, so he wouldn't see me."

A knot twisted and burned in Miranda's chest. She clenched her fists. "Don't lie. I saw them."

Sandra glared, stuck her lower lip out. "I am not lying. I'm an elite, born—"

Miranda took a step closer to Sandra. "I know. I know. You told me last night." Backing up, Miranda's calves hit the cot behind her. She sat heavily. *Lucas? The books and papers were his, not Felix's? No. Some of the writing looked like—but some of it didn't.*

From outside the tent, footsteps and mumblings meant she was running out of time.

"Can I eat now?"

"You hid where I found you while Lucas was there, didn't you?"

A guilty flush crept up Sandra's face. "Sometimes." She crossed her arms. "I hoped he'd bring Mommy or Daddy so I could surprise them." Her face fell. "But he never did."

"What did he say or do while you were there?"

Sandra sighed. "I don't know. Mostly, he wrote letters."

"Did you see any of the letters? Did he call anyone? Talk to anyone?"

"I was in the dark hole, silly. I couldn't see the letters."

"Did he make phone calls?"

"Sometimes."

"Who did he talk to? What did he say? What was he planning?"

"I don't know. He was boring. And it was boring in the dark. I'd fall asleep, and Nanny would be mad, and I'd have to write sentences and stay in my room." She heaved a long sigh. "I'm so hungry I'm dying."

"You said Agent James took you to the house. Your daddy visited you, didn't he? Did your mama visit too?"

Sandra frowned. "Daddy visited every other day and said Mommy couldn't come till later. But then he stopped coming. And nobody came. Not even for Christmas!" Tears slid down her cheeks.

So, the explosion that destroyed the Fellowship Center injured Felix. "Did anyone else visit?"

"No more questions." Sandra stomped her foot. "I'm starving!" she shouted, then wailed and sobbed.

The tent flap snapped open. "What on earth is going on in here?" Ethan stepped inside the tent and glared at Miranda. "This child announced her hunger to anyone in earshot, and now she's crying. Why?"

Miranda lifted her chin. "She's throwing a tantrum to avoid answering my questions."

Ethan gave her a look she didn't know how to interpret. "Pokeweed."

Pokeweed's head and shoulders appeared through the tent flap. "Yes, sir?"

"Take this child to the mess for breakfast."

"Uncle Ethan—"

"Don't." His look cut like edged steel.

Pokeweed stepped inside, held his hand out to Sandra.

Sandra raced to him. Took his hand. Turned and stuck her tongue out at Miranda, and they disappeared out the tent flap.

Miranda put her fists on her hips and glared at her uncle. "She would have told me everything if you hadn't interrupted."

Ethan didn't flinch. Returned her glare with one of his own. "What has happened to you that you would mistreat a child? Your own niece, no less."

Mistreat her? I told her over and over that she could eat when she answered my questions. Besides— "She can't starve over the course of a few hours. She has to earn her place around here, just like I did."

The breath he released through his nose sounded disapproving. "You *were* a child when you joined us. I think you still are." His tone added burn to his words.

The injustice that stormed deep inside Miranda intensified, red-lined the pressure behind her breastbone. "When I joined you, you were a courageous leader. Now you are spineless and unfit."

He pulled back as if she'd slapped him.

She waited for his apology.

He sighed heavily. "Miranda, I know Nick's death, and your Aunt Beryl's, affected you deeply. But you haven't allowed yourself to feel that pain. Instead, you inflict it on everyone around you. And for that reason, you are no longer active in SABR."

"You can't do that."

"I can, and I just did." He turned on his heel. "Go away, Miranda. Mourn. Come back when you can feel something other than anger." The tent flap fluttered closed.

Miranda huffed over and over. *Ethan never thought I had what it takes to be a rebel. But he doesn't have the guts to kill Irene or the Azrael. Fine.* She stomped out of the tent and searched for Wanda.

Pokeweed saw her first. Gently took her by the upper arm. "Monkshood said you need to leave. Please don't make me force you out."

"I'm not leaving until I find Wanda."

"Monkshood sent Wanda on an errand. She won't be back until after nightfall."

Miranda caught her breath. Wanted to scream obscenities. She whirled away. Strode into the forest. *I'll show him. I'll show them all.*

Chapter Forty-One

Irene paced behind the heavy black drapes that hid them from the audience seated in the Washington Coliseum. Instead of enjoying her elevated status as a known miracle worker, she clenched her jaw. Since Annabelle had told her Miranda had kidnapped Sandra, Irene could not calm her shaking limbs or her thoughts. *Miranda assumes that since she has Sandra, she has the upper hand. She has no idea what I will do to get my daughter back.*

She gave herself a mental shake. *I must get myself under control.* In minutes, she and Fake Felix would be on stage where the Prophet's Lady had to exude peace and love of all things Fellowship. She focused on the sound of Norma Zimmer's soprano.

"God will take care of me, Hushing my fear; When danger's 'round I see..."

Irene gave a self-satisfied smile. She'd requested Miss Zimmer sing this song in particular. *It was perfect. Everything would be perfect except for Miranda.*

Miranda expects I'll react like Momma. But I was there. I endured the press and the unendurable sympathy of the sycophants surrounding us. I won't make the same mistake.

The sound of Lucas's pompous voice echoed through the Washington Coliseum.

Not even Lucas expected the announcement she and Fake Felix

would make today. Under her breath she repeated her current favorite Bible verse: *"The LORD's enemies will be like the beauty of the fields; they will vanish—vanish like smoke."* Words that guided her. Gave her hope. Powered her choices.

Over the loudspeaker, Lucas said, "Ladies and gentlemen of the Fellowship, please stand for our Prophet and his Lady."

She smoothed the crisp fabric of her royal blue flare skirt and adjusted the bow of her matching calot hat so it wouldn't tickle her right ear so much. Took three deep calming breaths and forced the feral tiger of rage inside to crouch and wait in her belly.

Madonna smile in place, she took Fake Felix's arm, and they walked out into a wall of heat generated by dazzling stage and camera lights and a palpable wave of excitement.

Applause and cheers erupted.

She and Fake Felix made a quarter turn to bask in the adoration of their people, who sat in the stands on stage right. The audience was a sea of anonymous black that continued to applaud and cheer nonstop.

They made another quarter turn and another until each section of the people in the coliseum could gaze upon their holy faces.

They moved to center stage in front of the Council Members, whose seats filled the back half of the stage.

Fake Felix stood behind the microphone, lifted his arms above his head, and waved at the believers to sit.

The rumble of ten thousand souls taking their seats settled to a murmur punctuated by random coughing and throat clearing, until that too faded into attentive silence.

"Grace to you and peace from our Lord and Savior." Fake Felix had perfected his vocal imitation of real Felix's traditional greeting. "He sees how the unbelievers have tested us with denial and grievous transgressions and fiery trials. He knows how our disquiet had grown into fear and horror. And He has seen how our Fellowship has remained strong in our faith and good deeds despite the evil temptations, trials, and tribulations those who support SABR have cast at us."

The crowd roared their agreement.

Irene carefully kept her Madonna smile in place despite the swell of pride in her chest. *Those are my words they love.*

"What is this?" Lucas's stage whisper behind her held a touch of fear.

His fear and her anticipation sparked electric energy that zipped through her. Her smile broadened.

Fake Felix gave a loving description of the Fellowship Center and ended with a cry of grief at its destruction. He reminded the crowd of all the cities rocked by explosions and recent riots over the past ten months. In speaking her words, he fanned the crowd's fear until the grumbling from the audience nearly drowned him out.

"Fear not," he shouted. "The Lord has not abandoned us. Our Lady of the Fellowship will now share some of the Lord's words with us." He took two steps back.

Behind her, someone cleared their throat loudly. *Surprise, Lucas. I am not your puppet.* She stepped up to the microphone. "In Matthew 5:29 the Lord said, 'And if thy right eye offend thee, pluck it out, and cast it from thee; for it is profitable for thee that one of thy members should perish, and not that thy whole body should be cast into hell.'"

The audience applauded enthusiastically.

Irene thought their reactions lasted a smidge longer than the reactions for the fake.

Fake Felix joined her. "So sayeth the Lord." His voice boomed.

The crowd echoed his words.

He held one hand up.

Silence fell.

"Today is Judgment Day. Like removing the chaff from the wheat, our blessed Second Sphere agents are removing those who offend us and our Lord to Judgment Centers even as we speak."

Shocked whispers rippled through those seated behind her.

"Because the Lord is merciful..." Irene said. She held her Madonna smile and tone, but the tiger inside prepared for a powerful pounce. "Our most faithful Fellowship members will staff the Judgment Centers and will offer redemption to all non-Fellowship who turn themselves in." *Miranda has already failed redemption.*

"Should any unbelievers repent, we will send them to one of our nation's re-education centers," Fake Felix said. "If they show true repentance and earn redemption, we will welcome those pious members back into our Fellowship."

The coliseum erupted in sound. Thousands leaped to their feet, applauded and cheered and screamed, "Praise the Lord!"

The people want protection. The continuing applause filled her with warmth and a soaring euphoria and confidence. She beamed her smile over the seats filled with white-faced counselors. *The people have spoken. From this day forward, all sinners, apostates—or counselors—and Miranda will go to hell.*

Chapter Forty-Two

Leslie's smile made her face ache in the best possible way. At the end of the street, against a crisp blue sky, the dome of the Maryland State House towered above orange and gold treetops. Between her and the State House, men, women, and children chanted, waved signs, and clogged School Street in Annapolis.

"Freedom of religion means free for you and me," she shouted in chorus with the others. They'd been walking for forty-five minutes, and though her feet burned, the crowd around her and the sight in front of her gave her energy.

Two hours ago, she and nearly two hundred people in four trackless trolleys had arrived from Baltimore. They joined the crowd at Truxtun Park on Hilltop Lane. A crowd built by SABR cells across Maryland.

Folks willing to raise their voices against the Fellowship in front of the governor's mansion and the Maryland State House.

"No more silence. No more fear."

Leslie couldn't see who had started that familiar chant, but she happily repeated the phrase with the other voices.

"The people rise—their voices clear."

Maybe there was bravery in numbers; Leslie didn't care. She wished Ian could have been here to see and feel the determination and fierce hope these people had.

People jostled her, forced her to the edge of the street. A car parked at the curb blocked her. Forced the protesters to pack together more tightly. They hoisted their signs higher to avoid any injuries.

Some of their signs had slogans, but many had names and pictures. Pictures of family and friends who had already disappeared in the Fellowship's so-called Judgment Centers. So many pictures. Leslie's throat and chest ached. Monkshood's instructions ordered that she not carry a sign. Not one with pictures of Ma, Pop, and Junior. Not even one with only their names. Those close to Monkshood couldn't risk discovery.

She hurried onto the sidewalk around two parked vehicles and back on the street in time to follow the crowd around the corner to Circle Street.

Circle Street shop owners stood in the doorways of their Federal-style buildings, gawking at the protesters. Hotel guests hung out of the second- and third-story windows. Some raised their fists and shouted, but the voices of the protesters blotted out all but the loudest car horns. The noise vibrated Leslie's bones, re-energized her steps.

The crowd pressed in again. This time they pushed Leslie further toward the middle of the street before the crowd spread out. Moments later, they squeezed tight again, and Leslie had to walk so close to a turquoise Chevy Bel Air that she had to wiggle past the side-view mirror.

They marched past the entry points of Francis Street and Cornhill Street and East Street.

In the middle of Maryland Avenue, an older man in a beige Buick Century blasted his horn. Startled, ears ringing, Leslie hurried forward. Not that her scurrying allowed the man in the car to enter the street. The marching protesters had closed down all the roads leading into the circle.

A temporary gap between protesters opened. She glimpsed the gleaming white columns framing the Maryland State House's portico ahead. It held two rows of Capitol Police in white helmets and brandishing rifles. Barely visible were more helmets of more officers, probably on the steps up to the portico. Officers surrounded the State House as far as she could see.

"Stay calm, people," she whispered. *If we're calm, they'll stay calm.*

There'd been rumors things hadn't stayed calm in some state capitals. Protesters had been hurt, arrested, or never seen again.

Pop-pop.

She wasn't positive she had heard correctly at first.

But a silence, like a collective gasp of surprise, fell. Then angry voices shouted.

The crowd visibly surged forward as if they all wanted to see what had happened.

The too-close sound of fireworks knifed through the air, followed immediately by piercing screams of terror.

The crowd hurled toward her. People tumbled and disappeared in the crowd's panic. Bodies crashed into her. Spun her around. She stumbled, desperate to get to the sidewalk, to stay upright. Bricks scraped her shoulder. She turned sideways.

A pair of arms pinned her against the wall.

She ducked, but an arm wrapped around her waist. She wriggled to escape.

"Stay still. Safer here." The male voice in her ear was barely audible amid the screams and thumps and moans and pleas that filled the air.

The man's body jerked. He groaned and stiffened his arms around her. His body crushed her against the wall.

Back against the rough brick, Leslie struggled to breathe.

He strained. The pressure on her lessened.

Heartsick, Leslie watched.

The crowd moved in waves, stationary, then a jerk forward.

The press of people trying to escape trampled people who writhed and twisted under their feet, and trapped Leslie and her unknown protector.

She watched a wavy line of police officers with white helmets and linked arms press the crowd past her.

In their wake, two dozen or more bloodied men, women, and children lay on the pavement, strewn like fallen leaves.

A handful of police officers worked their way through the fallen. Striking anyone who stirred. The police officer closest to her raised his billy club over a middle school-aged child crumpled on the ground.

"No!" Leslie screamed.

Something hard came down on her shoulder.

A lightning bolt of pain shot from her shoulder to her fingertips.

Her vision exploded with light. Flash, total darkness. Flash, bright light, and pain.

Darkness and images of billy sticks and rifle butts striking people already on the ground flickered as if there was a projector malfunction.

A hand clamped around Leslie's upper arm and pulled.

She resisted.

A faraway voice said, "Let me help you."

She stopped resisting. Tried to wriggle toward the helping hands. The projector stopped.

———

THE ACHE OF A MILLION BRUISES MADE HER CATCH HER BREATH. SHE coughed, and knives pierced her shoulder.

"You're awake. Good," a barely audible voice said. "Don't move. Don't talk. Take slow breaths. It'll hurt less."

The voice was right. It didn't hurt as much. She blinked. Opened her eyes. Couldn't see a thing. "Where am I?"

"Shhh." Warm breath brushed her cheek. A hand gently covered her mouth.

Footsteps stomped across the floor overhead.

"You're certain there's no basement, no other rooms where the criminals that attacked the State House would hide?" a gruff voice asked.

"As the Lord is my witness, there is nowhere else," a second voice answered. "Besides, my wife and I wouldn't shelter those hoodlums. We're upstanding Fellowship members."

"Right. Well, thank you for your cooperation." The footsteps and voices moved away.

The hand over her mouth withdrew. "We can whisper now."

"Where am I? Are the lights off?"

"We're in the basement of an antiques shop on the circle. The owner's taken a terrible risk hiding us here."

"What happened?"

"What do you remember?"

"The police shot into the crowd. Then everyone panicked. I was trying to get out of the way, but someone—you?—stopped me."

"Yeah. People were getting knocked down, stepped on, crushed. We were safer against the wall until the troopers formed a wall with their shields and pushed. They didn't care that people were dying. If it weren't for the shop owner and his wife, we'd be trampled or in a jail cell—if we were lucky."

"But all those people. There were children—and older people. We've got to go help them." She raised up on an elbow. Gasped at the sharp pain that ripped through her shoulder.

"Stay down until I can look at you. They'll let us know when it's safe enough to turn on the light."

It took a few moments to get her breath back. She had to ask, "Who are you?"

"Drake. Drake Reed. What's your name?"

"Le—" She couldn't even see him. "You can call me Bluebonnet."

"Okay, Bluebonnet. Pretty name." His voice had a smile in it. "Are you breathing any easier?"

"Yeah—" Approaching footsteps stopped her cold.

"All clear," a gravelly voice called. A door latch clicked, followed by a heavy creaking sound, then an overhead bulb flashed on.

Leslie put her hand over her eyes, squinted through her fingers.

"Is the young woman still unconscious?" The woman's voice had a breathy quality with the tiniest bit of tremor. "Oh, she's awake. Thank goodness." She had an oval face with a square chin and wore a bun of abundant salt and pepper hair perched on the top of her head. She hurried from the steps to Leslie's side and kneeled on the floor, not minding her pink dress with lime-green squiggly lines. "How are you feeling, dear?" Her cool hand caressed Leslie's forehead.

"Sweetpea, leave the girl be." Behind his thick, round glasses, the man's toothy smile took the mild scold out of his words. Tall and lanky, he rubbed his bald head, bumping his elbow on the overhead floor joist. "Told you, son. Them Second Sphere men take one look at all the antiques crammed in the shop upstairs and they don't look for anything behind the furniture."

"We're more grateful than words can express." Drake's sincerity made Leslie bite back the 'we're not we' comment that nearly escaped her.

Leslie smiled and added, "I'm grateful, too. Are the injured still out there?"

"It's awful," Sweetpea said. "They're still picking up bodies—"

Leslie touched her fingers to her lips.

"Sweetpea!"

Sweetpea's face colored. "I'm sorry. My husband can tell you my mouth works before my brain's had time to think. I hope none of them were friends or family."

Leslie lifted a melancholy smile Sweetpea's way. She'd grown to know many of the protesters over the past few weeks of planning. No close friends, but none who deserved to die.

"Anyway." The shop owner took off his glasses, rubbed them with a corner of his shirt. "There's still a heavy police presence out there. Looks like you're down here until after dark."

"We can't stay." Leslie stood. Hot-cold dizziness overwhelmed her. She reached for support.

Drake put his arm under her good arm.

She studied him. He had short, chestnut brown hair, sharp features, and intense light green eyes; he didn't look at all like she'd imagined. She refocused on the shop owner and Sweetpea. "We are putting you in danger."

The shop owner put his glasses back on, focused a sober expression on her. "You go out, they'll know we hid you from them and they'll arrest us all."

"I'll bet you're hungry. And thirsty." Sweetpea pushed herself up to her feet. "I've got meatloaf leftovers. A couple of hearty sandwiches and some lemonade will make you both feel better." She rushed up the stairs.

The shop owner followed her, stopped at the base of the steps, and turned to them again. "Stay put. We knew what we signed up for when we pulled you inside. We'll get you out. *After* dark."

Drake nodded once. "Looking forward to those meatloaf sandwiches."

Leslie opened her mouth, ready to tear into the two strangers, two men who were assuming she'd just be the little woman and go along with their decisions. But arguing right now was pointless and dangerous. She closed her mouth. After dark, she'd probably never see either of them again.

<h1 style="text-align:center">Chapter Forty-Three</h1>

Miranda climbed the steps to the Baxters'. A deep ache knifed from her jaw to her neck to her back. She had hoped a walk would make the endless wait for a reaction from Irene more tolerable. It didn't.

At the back door, she paused. The house was never quiet, but the muffled noise coming from the other side of the door was more than she wanted to deal with right now. She peered through the door's window. *Good. No one in the kitchen. I can slip downstairs.* She stepped into the kitchen.

Shouts and wails filled the house.

Miranda froze. Tried to convince herself that she could still slip downstairs unnoticed. The desperate tone of the voices tugged at her. But she couldn't make sense of the sounds.

She gritted her teeth, crossed the room to the basement steps. Hesitated. Her right foot hovered over the first step down. *Maybe all the shouting is about Mimi delivering the letter.* She braced herself and moved down the hall, toward the sounds.

At the end of the hallway, ZeeZee yelled in a language Miranda didn't recognize, clung to the front door doorknob, and struggled to free himself from Bernie, who had his arms wrapped around ZeeZee's waist.

Red eyes welling with tears, Evelyn kneeled on the floor at the base of the stairs, an arm around each of her sobbing children.

Miranda watched the struggle but directed her question at Evelyn. "What's going on?"

"Mimi went to visit her friend, Sarah—" Her voice broke with a sob.

Gene cried, "Mimi, I want my Mimi."

Thea wailed.

Miranda's shoulders didn't feel strong enough for this. "And?"

Evelyn's glassy eyes were dark oceans. "Second Sphere agents took her."

Miranda's stomach tightened as if an icy fist had punched her. "Wh—" She couldn't speak.

ZeeZee's anguished shouts grew strained and breathy.

Miranda tried to remember. *Was Sarah the friend who works for the Prophet?* One shaky breath, two. *If Mimi didn't have time to deliver the letter, Irene doesn't know we have Sandra. If she didn't deliver the letter, did she have it on her?* "When—how did this happen?"

"No, ZeeZee, if you try to find her," Bernie said in English, "they'll take you too, and that won't help her. Please, ZeeZee— Papa, please. We'll figure something out. I promise."

The old man's shoulders dropped, and he deflated like a balloon.

Bernie and Evelyn exchanged meaningful looks. "Come, Papa, let's sit down." He guided ZeeZee into the living room and sank onto the sofa, exhaustion and fear on his face.

Evelyn gave her children a tight hug, then released them. "Go upstairs to your rooms. Your father and I must have an adults-only talk."

Gene crossed his arms and set his mouth in a pout.

Thea whispered in his ear, then took his hand, and they trudged up the steps.

"We don't even know if my Mimi is alive." ZeeZee's thin voice wavered on the verge of shattering.

Miranda ignored the ache in her chest. Turned to leave them alone, desperately hoping that Mimi had delivered the letter before she got caught.

"Please come into the living room." Evelyn's cool hand rested on Miranda's arm. "I'll tell you what happened. Then, we talk."

"I don't know what I can—"

"Please."

Evelyn's tone made Miranda's chest tighten even more. She

followed Evelyn and sat in the worn avocado-green armchair across from the sofa where Bernie sat next to his father. Evelyn sat next to ZeeZee and put a hand on his knee.

No one spoke for a painfully long time. Miranda couldn't stand it. "Did anyone see what happened?"

Evelyn shook her head. Took a shaky breath. "Mimi and Sarah meet at the deli at least once a week. Today, Mimi went to the deli —" Tears ran down her cheeks, dripped off onto her light-brown jumper, and added another splotch of wetness to the ones on each shoulder. "She didn't come home." Evelyn gave a wan smile. "She's always home in time to start dinner." Evelyn dabbed at her eyes with a sodden handkerchief. "I sent the children to the deli. They said the doors were open, but no one was there. Tables and chairs and food were—knocked over. They found the butcher crouched behind the counter with a cleaver in his hands. He was so frightened he swung at Thea. Blessed is God, the cleaver missed my babies." Tears strangled her words.

She dragged in a long breath. "He told them that as Mimi left the shop, two Second Sphere agents came in and heard Mimi wish him, *shalom aleichem*. They each grabbed one of Mimi's arms and asked her what this meant and who she said this to. Mimi refused to answer them. The butcher also would not answer. And though many customers had heard her talking with him, they were afraid for their lives and would not admit they understood Hebrew. The agents took Mimi to their car and drove away."

"What about her friend, Sarah?" Miranda asked. "Maybe her friend knows something."

Evelyn shook her head. "I tried calling Sarah and the deli. No one answers their telephone." She released a shaky sigh.

"No one knows where Mimi is," ZeeZee said in a high-pitched voice. "I need my Mimi home with me." A horrified look came over him. "What if they think she is a rebel?" He covered his face with his hands, and he whimpered and moaned and sobbed.

Miranda's stomach churned. *If they found the letter on her, they would torture the old woman. And if they torture her, she will die, or she will tell them everything.* "How long ago did this happen?"

"Three hours?" Bernie looked at his wife.

"Four," Evelyn said. "She left four and a half hours ago. Who knows how long she talked with Sarah."

"They probably just wanted to frighten her," Miranda said, wishing she believed that was true. *I should check the dead drop. If Irene left an answer there, then Mimi might be okay.* "You should go to the police, file a missing person's report."

Bernie gave a dismissive snort. "You know what our beliefs mean to the Fellowship. The police won't help us. And Mimi won't hide or pretend just to be safe. No, we need help from—from outside the Fellowship."

Miranda didn't react. *Do they suspect? I should...I can't. It would put all of us in danger.* "Where would you get that kind of help?"

Evelyn's eyes shimmered with tears and hope. "We think—hope —you might know someone who could bring her home before..."

Memories of Gert lying in a pool of her own blood overwhelmed Miranda, struck her speechless. She shook off those memories and refocused.

Across from her, Bernie and Evelyn fixated on her with a mixture of fear and hope on their faces.

I can't. "Mimi's tough." Miranda's voice squeaked through her tight throat. "I'm sure she'll be okay."

They looked lost, without hope.

"I wish there were something I could do, but I'm as powerless as you. There's nothing—"

"I knew it!" Thea stormed into the room. "You don't care about us."

Miranda leaped to her feet. "Don't say that!"

"If the agents took Mimi, they'll arrest all of us. They'll arrest me." She put her fists on her hips and glared defiantly. "You said you would protect me."

Miranda's heart thumped painfully. "I meant what I said to you, Thea. But I can't—"

"Teacher was right. Single women aren't nice. You're a liar." She crossed her arms and turned her back.

Thea's words robbed Miranda of breath. *That's the second time a child has called me a liar.* She sent a silent plea for help to the other adults in the room. But Bernie, Evelyn, and ZeeZee each reflected Thea's hurt and disappointment.

Miranda tried to swallow and choked on her own dry throat. She circled Thea and kneeled so they'd be eye-to-eye. "I meant what I said to you. But protecting you from bullies and finding Mimi—they aren't the same thing."

"Because you don't care about us—about Mimi or me." Tears streamed down her cheeks. She collapsed to her knees and buried her head in her mother's lap.

Nausea roiled in Miranda's stomach. "I care. I do. But I can't..."

Four pairs of eyes full of pain and fear bore into her.

They don't believe me. She bit her lower lip. *Thea's right. The letter to Irene was all I could think about. I sent an old woman into danger. More than that. I sent her to a murderer.* Miranda's cheeks burned. She ducked her head and rubbed her throbbing forehead.

Even if Mimi doesn't tell the agents about the letter, the Baxters are in danger. Agents will arrest the rest of them next. It's my fault. I have to fix this. But how do I do that without putting them and the rest of SABR in danger? She sank. Sat cross-legged on the large Persian rug. Ran a hand over the soft wool fibers that created once-vibrant red, blue, and green flowers on a cream background. Mimi had told her the rug was one of the only family heirlooms they still owned.

"We believe you—you have connections." Bernie's soft voice held an edge of desperation.

Miranda raised her eyes to his.

"Connections that could find Mimi. Rescue her."

"You shouldn't say things like that to a stranger." Her dry throat made her voice scratchy.

"But you're not a stranger," Evelyn said. "We've seen your kindness to Gene and Thea, and you—you've become part of the family."

"You don't know what you're asking." *Beryl wouldn't hesitate. She'd do what she thought was right even if her actions endangered the rest of SABR. Even if she lost friends and family.*

"We can pay," Bernie said. "We've got silver hidden away."

Miranda licked her lips. "The price won't just be silver. You will become fugitives from the Fellowship, the Second Sphere—there will be no safe place for you—for the rest of your lives."

The Baxters exchanged looks, then targeted Miranda with eyes full of hope and fear and resolve. "We understand," Bernie said. "Our people have survived being fugitives before."

"Mimi has been like a second mother to me," Evelyn's voice

cracked. "We will do whatever it takes to save her. Please don't let her die in their prisons."

Miranda lowered her eyes. The ache in her throat and chest made it hard to breathe. *How did Beryl make hard choices like this over and over again?*

She told herself to leave, but something anchored her to the floor.

I cannot let Mimi die because of me.

And I can't let Thea believe my word means nothing.

Miranda raised her chin. Locked eyes with Bernie. "I might know some people. I can't promise anything, but I'll ask around." She strode out of the room, out of the house. Determined to figure out how to infiltrate the Judgment Center, find Mimi, and bring her home.

Chapter Forty-Four

The counselor's updated Federal-style house, home to him and his wife, gleamed with bright white and soft neutrals. Large, clear windows without drapery surrounded the ground level. But it lacked security of any kind. They would be oblivious to Annabelle's intrusion when they returned. She explored the house in the dark.

The second floor held the master bedroom at one end and a massive study at the other end. A four-door closet lined a wall perpendicular to the heavy desk that sat before a large window.

She waited inside the dark closet, the door slightly ajar. Bore the weight of her jumpsuit and body armor for more than an hour. It felt right, balanced.

The soft tick-tock of the clock on the wall, the house's muted creaks and groans, and the occasional road noise of a passing vehicle kept her sharp.

Her Azrael eyesight penetrated the late hour's blanket of darkness. The masculine lines of the counselor's desk and lamp, centered on the large window behind them were visible.

The counselor and his wife might not be home for hours, but she would wait.

Her sixty-year-old target, Counselor Lucas Matthews, stood five feet nine inches tall. Carried almost three times her weight. He wore a white dress shirt and three-piece suit every day. Lighter materials and colors now than in the winter. He'd finish his suit with a navy-blue bowtie with white polka dots and a matching pocket square, his favorite black or brown wingtip shoes, and of course his walnut walking stick topped with an emerald-eyed silver owl's head. He brandished it with power and authority.

He'd once let her hold that walking stick. Before. When he only knew her as the adopted daughter of the man who'd performed miracles in Argentina. Back when she had called him Uncle Lucas. She closed her heart to her memories.

Tonight he and his wife had a late dinner with the counselor to the secretary of war and his wife at one of DC's premier restaurants.

After dinner, the chauffeur would deliver Counselor Matthews and his wife to the front door of their home. They'd enter the living room, not bothering to lock the front door behind them, and climb the staircase to the second floor where they would part.

Mrs. Matthews would take a long, hot shower and then retire for the night.

Counselor Matthews would enter his study. He wouldn't notice the closet door and would sit at his desk.

He had manipulated her mother and destroyed Annabelle's family. By her hand, his death would be righteous retribution for his wrongs.

The front door creaked. Counselor Matthews's heavy footsteps followed the clack of his wife's high heels. The high heels rang on every step, passed the study, and entered the bedroom. Huffing and puffing, the counselor's steps came closer. The overhead light clicked on.

He gasped for breath—whether from the exertion of climbing the stairs or from overfilling his rotund belly, Annabelle couldn't tell. He crossed in front of the closet. Took a seat at his desk.

Her angel within seized control, ready to spring.

He pulled an envelope out of the inside pocket of his suit coat. "Now, let's see what was so important the courier waited for me to come home."

Annabelle's blood thumped harder in her chest. She remembered a vehicle stopping nearby, but when the engine had shut off without further disturbance, she had dismissed it. *It was a courier who waited? How did I not know that?*

"They've got Sandra in that dead-body-dump, Leakin Park?" Lucas kept his voice low, but it held an edge of outrage.

Sandra! He found her. Annabelle grinned.

Doors opened in the bedroom behind Annabelle. A faucet squeaked, then the trickle of water turned into a rushing roar.

Lucas picked up the telephone receiver.

Oh, no you don't. She pushed the door open and took one step forward. "We are Azrael."

He glanced up at her, his mouth open.

She squeezed the trigger. The silenced three-round burst of polymer darts hit him in the center of his chest.

His body jerked. Bits of flesh and blood splattered his suit coat and the window behind him. A red stain blossomed on his shirt. His head lolled.

She reached him in two quick steps, catching his head before it banged onto his desk.

His open eyes stared vacantly at the wall beside her.

She straightened. Breathed in the odors of his death: acrid nitrates, hot sweet blood, and pungent excrement. An ethereal lift tingled across her skin, sped her pulse and her breath. Her inner angel crowed, and her soul floated to the ceiling. A tremendous swell of joy and gratitude made her tremble. She would leave this mortal soil at last.

Pain lanced through Annabelle's chest. *If I leave now, Mother will never find Sandra.* A trembling hit her, grew uncontrollable. Her body teetered. Instinctively, she put her hand out to the wall. She steadied. Feet solidly on the floor. Her inner angel wailed.

Annabelle raised her fist to her mouth, bit her gloved, curled finger, and stifled her sob.

You ruined it, her inner angel cried. *For an earthly child? All our work destroyed!*

Our Lord says even the smallest sparrow is important, she answered.

Her inner angel went silent.

Her chest ached with emptiness.

This was His will. To be here, Take this sinner at this time, and find my sister.

Purpose renewed, the ache vanished. She appraised the lifeless, powerless body before her. *May his family suffer the shame.* She curled her gloved hand into a fist, made the mark of the Azrael on his forehead. "Thy will be done."

In the room behind her, the water roared and rushed and spared the woman.

Annabelle burned the sign of the Fellowship into the wood of his desktop with her laser pen. Signaled her cleaners to take his body. Then slipped downstairs, out the door and into the night.

Chapter Forty-Five

The lights in the Memorial Stadium players' tunnel glared, and the rumble of sound from the other end of the tunnel grew louder with each step. Irene followed the Second Sphere agent out onto the field and gasped at the indistinct roar of voices that pummeled her eardrums. But it wasn't as bad as the sour stench that swarmed her.

A mass of people milled about on the field, with lines of six or seven people wide pouring in from both sides of the stadium.

She blinked, not quite believing her eyes. "You've only been open six hours. Where did they come from?"

"We started getting tips the night you announced the Judgment Centers."

She had never guessed there would be so many detainees rounded up in a little over three weeks.

"Filled the city's temporary detention centers by the end of the next week," the Captain continued. "Most of these are from those detention centers, but neighbors, coworkers have turned some in, and the like."

I did this. Me. And not even Lucas can call this flawed or failed. She did a slow turn to disguise her giddiness and take it all in.

Under the far goal post, extending past the end zone, stacked and tossed suitcases and crates and cardboard boxes of belongings made a pile taller than a man.

Irene waved her hand at a team of SS agents that examined the contents and sorted things into a small pile and a much larger one. "What are those agents doing down there?"

"They're sorting the donations into valuables and discards."

Irene's escort led her to a cleared section that ran the center length of the field. From her new perspective, the detainees clearly shuffled between barricade fence panels and concrete highway barriers that snaked down each side of the field.

A Second Sphere agent, who had shed his suit coat, stopped in front of her and saluted. "Lady Earnshaw. May I enquire when the Prophet will arrive for the inspection?" He spoke loudly enough to be heard over the constant murmur of voices.

"The Prophet has spiritual things that require his attention." She answered as loudly and in her haughtiest tone. "He asked me to oversee the more—secular—functions of the Fellowship. Things like this..." She gestured at the whole stadium with a sweep of her hand. *And this is only the first step. Wait until you see what else I will do.* "Walk me through the inspection as you would the Prophet, Captain."

"Of course, Your Ladyship." He inclined his head toward her. "This way to the check-in station."

She followed him across the sun-heated field to the head of one line, where a Second Sphere sergeant and a female civilian sat behind a card table with a half dozen trainees standing behind them. The line of detainees stretched from in front of the table all the way downfield and up into the stands.

A neatly dressed family of four—two adults, their teenage son, and school-aged daughter—held a suitcase each and waited in front of the table. A warm, spicy aroma of frankincense emanated from them.

No wonder agents detained them. They might as well have worn signs declaring they were non-Fellowship.

"Number 17,274," said the sergeant.

The female civilian repeated the number, waited for an acknowledgment, then wrote the number on a tag.

"This is the intake table," the captain said. "We give each family or single unbeliever an identification number. We tag them and their belongings. Then we send them to a specific area of the stands where they wait until we assign them a bus that will transport them to their assigned camp."

The father of the detainee family answered the sergeant's questions in a subdued voice with a strong accent. The sergeant instructed the family to put their belongings, including any wallets, purses, and IDs, in a pile to the right of the table. When the father hesitated, the sergeant promised he'd record everything they had brought and immediately scribbled information in a wide spreadsheet. Meanwhile, two trainees stepped forward and tied identification tags to a button on each unbeliever's shirt and each of their belongings.

"Your family number is 17,274. Go to upper section eight, rows twenty to twenty-five. Wait for instructions."

The family hummed an unfamiliar tune and melded into the anonymity of the crowded stands.

Irene hesitated, but she had to know. "Is their number random or—?"

"It's the actual count, Ma'am."

She ignored the beads of sweat that trickled down her back, hooked her fingers together at her waist, and sighed. Soon, Baltimore would be safe again.

The SS trainees carried the family's belongings downfield to the end zone. They tossed the wallets and purses onto an overflowing table. Tossed the suitcases onto a mountain of belongings that nearly touched the horizontal bar of the goalpost.

She and the captain followed but walked past the mountain of belongings to the sorters going through the luggage. Behind them, more Second Sphere trainees were packing diamond-crusted tiaras, silver menorahs, gold coins, and artwork in gilded frames into large packing crates.

"Where are these going?" She hadn't included this in her plans for the Judgment Centers.

The captain glanced at the pile of belongings. "Thirty percent of those are tithes these unbelievers owed to our Lord. The rest are compensation for the costs of establishing the Judgment Center here and for the use of Baltimore's detention camps."

Irene nodded. *I should've thought of that. Fake Felix must redirect some of this. And I'll have Annabelle and her angels collect tithes when they Take the wealthier sinners.*

"Attention. Attention." The voice on the loudspeaker had that buzzy echo all ballpark speakers had. "Lower Section two, rows one through five, report to gate four immediately. Anyone late for departure will be noncompliant and dealt with accordingly."

"How often do the trolleys leave?" Irene asked the captain.

"Every thirty minutes."

"That should empty this place fairly quickly."

"It should have, ma'am, but new detainees arrive faster than we can ship them off."

There were certainly more unbelievers here than Irene had expected to see. "I will speak to my husband, the Prophet, to see if he might consider opening another Judgment Center in town. Would you have the personnel to staff another Judgment Center, Captain?"

"We can arrange to." He turned toward her. "That concludes the tour unless you wish to go in the stands amongst the—"

"Not today." She gave him a saintly smile. "I've got—"

"Lady Earnshaw," a voice called.

A sudden chill prickled her skin. She wished she didn't have to turn in response, but she did.

The counselor to the secretary of war and the counselor to the attorney general caught up with them.

"Counselor Lucas Matthews has been Taken." The statement held an accusatory tone.

"Oh dear." Irene's gasp was only part acting. *At last.* "I hadn't believed those nasty rumors," she said in a quietly shocked voice. "I suppose they must have been true." *What had taken Annabelle so long?*

"Counselors are not Taken because of rumors." The counselor to the AG's nasal tones made Irene want to wince.

"This was not sanctioned." The counselor to the secretary of war peered at her over the top of his gold-rimmed glasses. "He was one of us. An elite and a member of the Council."

Irene did her best to look aghast. "Not sanctioned? If you didn't order this, who did?"

"We thought you would know."

"Me? How would I know anything?"

"Lady Earnshaw," that nasal voice whined, "we have not

forgotten who your parents were. Nor have we forgotten about your adopted daughter."

Irene's insides churned. Never privy to the Council's closed-door sessions, she had no clue what they knew or didn't know. But everyone had secrets. Even counselors kept secrets from one another. "I suppose Lucas's—um—resignation means you are looking for another counselor. I'm sure my husband, your Prophet, has a recommendation or two."

"Irene—you don't mind that we call you Irene, do you?" the counselor to the secretary of war asked in thinly veiled hostility. "Do not imagine that the remaining counselors won't be watching you closely."

"I am naught but the humble Lady of the Fellowship; I fear I shall bore anyone who watches me." *No doubt they think of themselves as wolves. They act like pigs. Hungry for whatever scraps of power they can find.*

"You should know Lucas did not decide alone," he continued. "The Council had a hand in your reinstatement." His tone grew darker. "You would be wise to play the role of the humble wife of the Prophet and be content with it."

"I am quite content with my role." *If they think I will allow them to steal that from me again, they don't know me at all.* "The people are grateful to the Prophet *and* me for freeing them from these dangers. Look around you. They turn in neighbors, friends, and even family." She gave them an arch look. "How well do you know *your* neighbors?"

The counselors stole glances at one another.

"Don't think you can get away with this."

"Gentlemen, I don't have a clue what you think I, the humble wife of the Fellowship Prophet, am trying to get away with." She entered the tunnel, grateful for its cool shade and for her escape from the overbearing men.

When I get home, I'll have Fake Felix direct the Second Sphere to investigate the extravagances of the Council. Extravagances often hid sins. And Lord knows the Azrael are very good at reducing the number of sinners in the world.

Chapter Forty-Six

The rough brick on the side of the row house pricked Miranda's back through her clothes. She peered around Wanda, across the street. There were more vehicles in the parking lot than she'd expected. The lot and the stadium itself were awash with bright light. Dozens of people milled around on the first tier of the closed end of Memorial Stadium. The brick and concrete acted like a megaphone, directing the people's frightened voices, their cries, and their moans toward the homes where Miranda and Wanda stood.

"I still think we should have gone to camp, at least gotten intel from them." Wanda's whisper was barely audible. "You don't even know if your friend's granny is in there." Her voice dripped with doubt.

Miranda darted a glance at Wanda. *I didn't think they'd arrest Mimi. She's harmless.* Balled her fists and refocused on the stadium. "She's there." *She has to be.*

"There's a hella lot of people in there. How will we find her?"

"I haven't figured that out yet. But if it were your grandma, you'd want me to try."

"Of course. I'm here to help you rescue her, even though we haven't got a gnat's chance of getting outta there."

Miranda chewed the inside of her cheek. With that many non-Fellowship, there had to be a lot of Second Sphere there too. She tugged at her shirt again and again, but she was too hot and sticky for comfort.

Wanda gave a resigned sigh. "We're going to get caught."

"They aren't expecting us."

"Do you suppose all them cars belong to people who drove themselves here? Turned themselves in?" Wanda's disbelief held an edge of how-could-anyone-be-that-foolish.

"Doubt it." She tried to read her friend's face, but Wanda's eyes were unreadable.

Brightly lit, concrete-paved parking lots surrounded the stadium. The parked vehicles provided some cover for their approach and maybe for their exit.

But getting inside the stadium might not be possible. There were three gates for spectators. The main one stood at the other end of the stadium, almost exactly opposite where they stood. Smaller gates opened on each side of the stadium for games. It was unlikely they were open today. And equally unlikely any of them were unguarded.

Miranda had hoped to enter through the outfield, but every one of the tall ballpark lights flooded the outfield with a white glow, making it bright as daylight. *They certainly chose a defensible location.*

"Well, well. Would you lookie there?" Wanda pointed. "The people didn't drive their cars here."

Across the street, a white car drove slowly into one of the few parking spaces available on the last row. A man exited the car. Even from this distance, his suit was unmistakable. The heat inside Miranda flared. "So they *are* confiscating the people's vehicles."

"And probably everything else they own."

Miranda's knuckles ached. She would get Mimi back even if she had to shoot every Fellowship member or Second Sphere agent in sight. Everything within her burned with a frightening intensity.

A metallic tang of her own blood filled her mouth. She ran her tongue over the now raw spot inside her cheek. She couldn't, wouldn't risk Wanda's life. "You're right," she said, working out a plan. "We need more intel. You head toward Ellerslie Avenue, check the perimeter for guard positions and the like. I'll sneak inside and see what we're facing."

Wanda audibly sucked in air. "Going in alone is suicide."

"It'll be dangerous. But we need more information than we can get standing here."

"You won't get past the Second Sphere. They'll recognize you and take you somewhere for interrogation—or worse." Wanda blew out a long breath through pursed lips. "I'll go with you. Watch your back."

"Don't worry. I'm not using a gate. I'll go through the tunnel. Besides, one of us has a better chance of getting inside unnoticed." *Not to mention that only I can pass as a Fellowship member.* "I'll just do recon inside. You do the recon on anything and everything you can learn about what we face outside. Then, when we know more, we'll make a better plan."

"Can't say as I like this." Wanda sighed. "You'll just do recon inside?"

"Uh-uh."

"How long before we meet up?"

"Thirty minutes. Whoever shows up here first waits ten more if it's safe. After that, go to Virgil's. If I don't show up in one hour, don't come looking for me."

Wanda put a warm, firm hand on Miranda's arm. "Show up."

Miranda gave a sharp nod. "I plan to."

She slipped from car to car across the parking lot easily. Ran to the nearest brick wall of the stadium. A low murmur came from inside the stadium. But it didn't sound like an agent or police officer was nearby.

She darted across the garage door of the vehicle tunnel to the windowless slab of the players' door beside it. She hoped it would be her way in. Opened it just enough to squeeze inside. Eased it shut behind her and paused. Let her eyes adjust to the sudden darkness.

No shouts raised an alarm. *So no guards here?* The dark lessened, but not enough she could see even a flicker of light. Arms outstretched, her fingertips grazed a cool, concrete wall in front of her and to her left. No wall on her right. She turned and shuffled one foot forward, hand on the wall, feeling her way.

She slid her left foot forward; the floor disappeared from under it. The beat in her temples sped faster. *Stairs?*

Cautiously, she lowered her foot and hit a step. Groped for and found a handrail. Followed the stairs until the handrail stopped. Stuck her foot out again. Discovered a landing.

Hugging the wall for guidance, she toe-tapped, searching for the next step down. Stubbed her toe hard enough to jar her shin bone. Explored it with her foot more gingerly. *Steps up?* She extended her right arm, cast about for another down staircase. But this landing only led to stairs going up. So she gripped the handrail and followed it to another landing. No, bigger than a landing.

The fingers of her left hand followed the long and slowly curving wall until light spilled down the hall toward her. She pulled back. Someone had turned those lights on. Could still be there. No noises of movement. In fact, even the crowd sounded no closer.

Her stomach fluttered. *Is that the players' locker room?* She put her hand on the butt of her pistol. But the sound of gunfire would alert the agents to her presence. *Where's a baseball bat when I need one?* Her throat was too tight to swallow. *Gotta try to make it into whatever room is up there and find a hiding place before anyone notices.*

She took a deep breath and dashed across a large doorway filled with light and into the shadows where she froze. Held her breath and listened. The sounds of the crowd were louder here but no more distinct.

She stood in an aisle lined with metal lockers. Under the pungent scent of pine cleaner, the vacant locker room also held the musty scents of sweat and dirt, wet towels and shaving cream. Opposite where she had come in stood an interior door; its gap glowed with light.

"Attention." The extra-loud announcer said.

Miranda cringed and covered her ears.

"Lower Section A, rows one to ten. Report to the Section A gate immediately." *How close am I to the Section A gate?*

Clumping footsteps and murmuring voices came from the direction of the doorway. She plastered her back against the wall. The edge of a locker handle dug into the middle of her back.

Why send people to the gate? The answer popped into her head. *They're already shipping them out to Redemption sites. Damn it. Gotta find Mimi fast.*

Once the footsteps faded, Miranda counted sixty heartbeats twice. Eased the door open. Squinted against the light.

Her vision flashed with red-edged echoes of the light. Her

muscles quivered. She gritted her teeth against a shout of frustration. *Uncle Ethan could have at least given me some equipment.* She backed away from the opening, deeper into the shadows. *Think. You cannot let the Baxters down.* But the thought that she would fail because of Uncle Ethan circled relentlessly in her brain. *Focus!*

She slowed her breathing. Her thoughts and her pulse steadied. *Assumptions kill. First, find Mimi. But how?* A smile tugged at the corner of her lips. One thing she knew for sure about the Fellowship, it loved lists.

She peered through a crack in the door. Allowed her eyes to adjust to the light. The door opened onto a corridor that ran under the bleachers in one direction; the other direction led to the brightly lit players' tunnel.

From the sound of it, the people who had passed the locker room were in the tunnel now.

She hurried down the corridor toward the bleachers. About every hundred yards, an aisle cut toward the front of the bleachers. She took the next turn under the bleachers and moved toward the field.

The lights and the sounds grew brighter, louder. The acrid stench of fear filled the cold night air. Six feet from the end of the shadows, she paused. Sobs and whispers surrounded her. People in the stands gave furtive glances around them but didn't notice Miranda.

Crouched under, she turned and inspected the bleachers behind and above her. Vacant.

The bleachers clattered.

She whirled. No one behind her. Looking through the aluminum stands of the next section over, she saw an agent leading a long line of people down the main aisle. The people filled the seats from the bottom row to the top.

After the noise settled, she crept forward and peered down at the field.

Portable metal fences and concrete barriers followed the out-of-bounds lines on each side of the field. Between the barriers, dozens of people followed one another to a table in one of the two corners of the end zone. Behind the goal posts, stacks and stacks of luggage and boxes and purses and teddy bears grew taller and wider.

Second Sphere agents and cadets manned the field. *If there's a list, it'll be on those tables. Do I dare?*

Miranda scanned for agents in her vicinity and on the opposite side of the field. None were in her line of sight. She had no doubt they patrolled the occupied sections. She'd have to be careful.

She ducked between the railings separating the two sections and approached the nearest person, a middle-aged man in greasy overalls. "Excuse me, sir."

"Huh?" The man gave her a wide-eyed look. "Who're you?"

"Nobody," she whispered. "I'm looking for someone. An older woman who goes by Mimi, last name Baxter. Have you seen her?"

Oceans of sadness filled his eyes. "They took me from work. I don't even know if my wife and kids are here. Hope they got out of the city."

"It's important that I find her," Miranda insisted. "Are they sorting people by last name or first name or location—or something?"

"You aren't gonna find her. Not unless you know her number."

"Number?"

He touched the brown paper tag tied to his top button. Handwritten in black marker was a six-digit number. His expression changed to suspicion. "Don't you have one?" He grabbed her wrist.

"Hey, you. What are you doing here?" The gruff voice came from the other side of the section.

Miranda sucked in a gasp. Blood rushed like the roar of the ocean. "I—uh"—she ducked her head away from the agent—"used the ladies' room."

"What's your ID number? Where's your escort?" The voice sounded closer.

She ducked back under the rails, back the way she had come.

"Alert!" A shrill whistle blew. "Runner. Home team tunnel section." The whistle sounded three more times.

She ducked under the bleachers. A police officer came down the aisle toward her, his hand on his pistol grip.

Miranda climbed back up and onto a bleacher. Ran up the empty seats as if they were stairs.

She reached the balcony wall. Turned and raced into the next section, heading to the entry arch there. People on each side of the aisle started and ducked. She took the hint, ducked as small as she could and ran faster.

Two agents appeared under the archway.

The one behind her was moving fast.

She whirled and ran across the top of an empty bleacher, toward the end of the stadium.

Agents thumped down the last aisle.

Arms pumping, she flew past the populated section.

Halfway up the next section, two Second Sphere agents appeared in the entry opening above her.

The agent behind her was closing in.

She slid through an opening and under the bleachers. Leaped cross beams. Ducked metal bracing. Reached the corridor.

The light of the locker room was a hundred yards away. A thundering herd of heavy footsteps followed too close. Shouted unintelligible orders.

Bang.

Shoulders tense, she kept running. She dashed past the lockers. Sped through the dark. Stumbled down steps, then up again. Slammed through the door. Ran into the parking lot.

The door banged open behind her. "Stop!" Gunfire echoed with the sound of an army.

She darted between cars and ran away from the row houses, and away from where Wanda waited.

Chapter Forty-Seven

Irene and Fake Felix stood at Lincoln's feet in the Lincoln Memorial on the National Mall, waiting for the Prophet to be introduced.

Fake Felix yawned, rolled his shoulders then rolled his head.

"Stop that. Someone will see you and know you aren't..."

He raised his eyebrow and gave a pointed glance out of the corner of his eye to where Annabelle and her Azrael stood.

"—well." She bore a dark look at him that carried more threat than he could understand.

Indistinct crowd noises came from outside.

"Bless them," Fake Felix said. "Looks like everyone in the District has come."

He was right. The VIPs—the counselors, their families, and various government and financial leaders—sat in the rows of wooden folding chairs at the foot of the steps. Even the wide concrete walkway surrounding the reflecting pool, all the way to the Washington Monument and back, held so many people that there was no open concrete visible.

In moments, they'd be standing in the sunlight in front of all those people. Irene's stomach pitched.

The fake had done well at his appearances so far, but this was different. The people out there were the laborers, the moms and dads, the grandparents, and Lord knew there could be rebels and all sorts of riff-raff. Maybe even people who once knew this man beside her in his former life as an actor.

A wave of dizziness swept over her. She took deep breaths. It didn't slow her out-of-control heart. She clasped her hands together, rubbed her right thumb across her left palm.

Applause rose from scattered to steady.

"Well, that's my cue." Fake Felix turned on a beatific expression, and with monk-like steps, walked out onto the apron to the waiting podium.

The applause grew thunderous.

So far, so good.

"Thank you for the warm welcome. First, I want to introduce a person who is my number one aide, the holiest person I know, my wife, my soulmate, the First Lady of the Fellowship."

Irene wished she could see the counselors' reactions. She joined Fake Felix at the podium. The roar from the crowd hit her like a tidal wave. *They're cheering for me?*

Fake Felix took two steps backward and, with arms open, invited the audience to welcome her.

She smiled a genuine, from-the-heart smile and waved. She had never seen so many people in her life. They sat pressed against each other on the concrete steps up the memorial and on the walkway and even under the trees that paralleled the walkway.

The roar of their voices and applause vibrated in every cell of her body.

They waved Fellowship flags and signs. "We love our Lady of the Fellowship." "Lord bless our Lady and the Prophet." And more that she couldn't see well enough to read. *They love me.* It was terrifying and exhilarating at the same time.

Fake Felix walked forward, joining her at the podium. He held his arms up and motioned for the crowd to quiet.

Slowly, the noise died down.

He launched into his statement about the recent violence perpetrated by apostates who claimed to be rebels.

Uneasy, Irene watched the crowd's upturned faces as he spoke. They seemed to hang on his words. None seemed to suspect he wasn't the real Prophet. Now, not fully the center of attention, she read more signs praising her return.

Pride swelled in her chest. She was certain there was no sin in it. After all, it was the Lord's reward for all she had suffered.

She turned her attention to the VIP section. The counselor to the sSecretary of war peered up at her through his gold-rimmed glasses.

The counselor to the attorney general sat in the row behind. His beady eyes fastened on her as if she were the devil incarnate.

She met his look with a self-assured smile made more confident by the crowd's adoration and the knowledge that the disappearance of Lucas had frightened him and all the remaining counselors.

She identified ten of the fifteen counselors in the VIP section. The Council had posted Second Sphere agents around the VIP section and throughout the crowd. Grim satisfaction washed over her, glad she'd had the foresight to have Annabelle and her sister Azrael stand behind her.

Fake Felix finally got to the announcement. "As I stand here, the President is signing an emergency declaration of martial law for the entire country. Every city, county, and state."

There were gasps and shouts of hallelujah and an indistinct murmur that rippled through the crowd.

Irene's eyes were on the counselors in the first and second rows.

"Alongside the agents of the Second Sphere, the Azrael"—he gestured at Annabelle and her sisters—"the Lord's angels here on earth, will monitor the streets of DC to keep our Fellowship members safe. So spake the Lord."

The crowd responded in unison, "So says the Lord. His will be done."

Fake Felix opened his arms as if embracing the crowd. "Go in peace and love and the knowledge that the Lord's angels will keep you."

The counselor to the secretary of war purpled and exchanged words with the counselor behind him.

The people on the steps rose to their feet, blocking Irene's view of her enemies.

Annabelle and her angels assembled themselves into an inverted V formation with Annabelle at the tip. They cut a path through the swarming crowd toward their limo.

Spectators made way for them but shouted, "Prophet, will you…" or "Lady, your blessing, please…"

Their progress was so slow that Irene's tension grew. She

expected the counselors would catch up and accost them. But the Azrael stayed in tight formation. She couldn't see anyone other than Annabelle's angels around her.

Hours later, Annabelle searched her home and declared it and its grounds safe.

Irene sank onto her sofa, kicked off her heels, and rubbed her aching toes. She relaxed into the corner of the sofa, comforted by knowing that Annabelle and her sister Azrael watched over her.

It wouldn't be long before the Azrael found Sandra or a rebel who broke the curfew. Soon she would have Sandra back, and the end of her misery would follow. She would end the cursed Council. And the rebels. And Miranda.

Chapter Forty-Eight

The night brought a full moon, a velvet and diamonds sky, and cooler air. In a past lifetime, Miranda would have enjoyed it. Instead, she stood against the wall of the Baxters' garage, the darkest corner of their tiny backyard. Her heartbeat competed with the speed of the crickets' nonstop chirruping, and the bright light in the Baxters' kitchen window blamed her for a family's anguish.

She couldn't make herself go to the door. Couldn't tear her eyes off the glowing kitchen window. *They're waiting up for me. Waiting for Mimi.* But she hadn't found Mimi.

She couldn't bear the thought that even if she and Wanda got Ethan's help, there was little hope of finding Mimi. The idea of Mimi in Redemption…

Miranda's muscles quivered. She ground her teeth. *Refused to remember that part of her life.*

Bernie knew the chances were slim. They all knew the Second Sphere could pick one of them up someday. It's not my fault the SS got Mimi. Not my fault I couldn't find her. I'm not a miracle worker.

A shadow moved in the kitchen. The kitchen door creaked. A rectangle of light grew. A woman's form stood dark against the light. "Miss Norwood? Is that you?"

I must focus on Irene. After Irene is gone, Mimi will be free. Miranda took a deep breath, raised one hand in a friendly wave, and moved forward.

Evelyn was all smiles until Miranda trudged up the steps... alone.

The rest of the family waited in the living room. Bernie and ZeeZee perched on the avocado sofa. Thea and Gene sat nearby on Mimi's rug. But ZeeZee's mournful face...

Stomach anchored far below, Miranda told them how she and Wanda, whom she didn't name, had tried to find Mimi. How she'd barely escaped being caught. And after hours of dodging Second Sphere agents, she and her friend made a plan to ask a rebel leader for help.

Miranda licked her lips. "I'm sorry."

Bernie turned away from her, focused on his father.

"There were thousands of people there. Men, women, children...."

"I knew it," Thea said in a cold, hard-edged voice. "I'll bet you didn't even try." She stomped out of the room. Thumped up the stairs.

"Thea—" Miranda took a step to follow. Stopped. *I will fix this after I take care of Irene.*

"I'll take care of her." Evelyn cut her off and trailed after Thea.

Miranda turned back to Bernie and ZeeZee. "You have to understand. The rebel leader might not agree. He has to protect his people. If he agrees to help, it will take time to find one woman out of the thousands being held."

ZeeZee stood and, without looking at her or saying a word, hobbled out of the room.

Bernie scrambled to stand also, finally made eye contact with her. "I understand." His voice cracked. Then he put a hand on his father's elbow and helped him up the stairs.

"ZeeZee's real sad." Gene spoke in a soft voice directed at his lap. "We love Mimi. We need her—even if she's old." He looked up. His eyes glistened; tears stained his cheeks. "Dad says if you don't find her soon, she'll be gone forever." He fell silent. Head down, Gene left the room.

Miranda swallowed the lump in her throat. This wasn't right. She had promised herself she would never go through this again— be this weak again. She strode out of the house. *One way or another, Ethan will help me stop Irene, then we will find Mimi.*

Chapter Forty-Nine

L eslie sat bolt upright on the cot. Her heart wanted to explode. She struggled to catch her breath, and her shoulder ached. She wiggled her shoulder gingerly. The doctor had said it didn't seem like any permanent damage. *Must have lain on it wrong.* She lay back down on the cot. Stared up, unable to see the tent's roof in the dark.

Sandra's ragged breathing filled the tent. Outside, the night was unnaturally quiet. Not a breath of air fluttered the tent walls. Even the cicadas had stopped their incessant chirping. *The guards would have alerted us to an attack. Sandra must have had a nightmare. Even scared the big, ugly bugs.*

Less than a yard and a half away, the shadowy-girl-shape sat up on her cot too.

After the way Miranda had treated the girl, Leslie had stayed the night to calm Sandra. "Did you have a bad dream?" she whispered.

The girl didn't answer.

Leslie reached for the battery-powered lantern she'd placed next to her cot.

A sound like a yelp in the distance choked off. Her body went rigid. Her stomach clenched in a rock-hard knot.

Lantern forgotten, she snapped up to sit on the edge of the cot again. *Not Sandra's nightmare.* Her throat pulsed with her heartbeat. She grabbed a shoe. Pulled it on.

Another strange sound choked off unnaturally.

"Alarm!"

Startled cries and strangled shouts and sickening thuds burst out all around them.

Leslie pulled on her other shoe. "Shoes on," she whispered to Sandra.

Bang!

Her ears rang.

Explosions of gunfire erupted.

Sandra squealed and curled into a ball on top of her cot.

Leslie hurried to her side. Leaned in close so Sandra could hear her. "We'll be all right." *We just have to follow the bug-out plan. If I can remember it.* Leslie forced a slow, deliberate breath. Then another one. Remembered.

"We're going to get out of here," she said as quietly and calmly as she could. "Did you get your shoes?" She jerked her head back to avoid a shoe being shoved in her face. "Okay. Give me your foot." She got it on her charge. Stood.

Outside the gunfire grew erratic, but the slaps and thuds meant their attackers were close. Too close.

"Stay with me. I'll protect you." Her voice shook too much to be very reassuring. She scanned the tent. No weapon inside. Not even something she could use as a weapon.

The sound of feet crashing through dry leaves came toward them.

She grabbed the small battery-operated lantern and stood at the entrance to the tent. Didn't think the lantern would do much damage, but she had to try. She raised it.

Behind her, Sandra screamed.

She whirled. The tent shook, and the side bowed toward her.

A knife tip and then blade penetrated the canvas and ripped downward.

A familiar hushed voice whispered, "Be quiet!"

"It's my brother, Ian." Leslie rushed forward, grabbed Sandra's hand.

"We have to go. Now!" Ian held the raw edges of the tent while they stepped through.

Three of Pokeweed's team stood in a semicircle around them, facing out.

"Follow me." Ian grabbed Leslie's hand.

Something in Leslie's shoulder popped, then blinding pain ripped through the shoulder to her fingertips. She tightened her hand around Sandra's, and the two of them ran surrounded by their protection squad.

They ran through the trees, dodging low-hanging limbs, protruding roots, and bushes that tugged at their clothes.

Awash with a confusion of pain, adrenaline, and fatigue, Leslie struggled to stay upright. Her lungs burned, and under Ian's urgent tow, her pulse became snare drums at full-throttle. Her hands grew slick with sweat.

Sandra stumbled. Her small hand slipped from Leslie's, and the girl fell to her knees.

"Sandra!"

Ian didn't allow Leslie to slow down.

Behind them, one of Pokeweed's men raced forward and, barely breaking stride, scooped Sandra up in his arms.

Their footsteps crunched dry leaves and thudded against drier ground. Leslie hoped they would leave their pursuers behind soon. She wasn't certain how much longer she could run.

A howl ended in a death rattle.

"Scatter!"

Ian released her.

She glanced back.

A dark shadow dogged the man carrying Sandra.

Leslie's steps faltered.

A twin of the shadow behind Sandra threw something at her.

"No!" A man leaped toward Leslie.

Thwack.

The man grunted and fell onto Leslie. Knocked to the ground, her head smacked something hard. Black dots spun in her vision. Something warm and wet trickled down her side.

In the distance, someone said, "Leslie?"

She couldn't. Keep. Her eyes. Open.

Chapter Fifty

Overhead, leaves whispered, but the breeze didn't touch Annabelle's sweaty face. She crouched in the relentless darkness behind a tree trunk and studied the enemy camp hidden deep in Baltimore's infamous Leakin Park.

Six camouflaged tents blended seamlessly with the surrounding foliage. They stood in an irregular hexagon around a firepit with four picnic tables.

This must be their central command. She would have kept a prisoner like Sandra here, had she been in charge. Yet, none of the tents had a guard or barrier that suggested it held a captive.

She dropped back into the trees. Her angels had scoured the park, discovered the encampment, and sent for her.

Annabelle and a dozen of her angels had broken every speed limit from DC to here. Had Taken every lookout. Now they waited for her orders.

She returned to where her lieutenants waited, crouched behind a fallen log.

They listened carefully to her plan, then ran to pass her orders to the other angels waiting near the dozen other tents they'd discovered secreted in the woods.

She moved in closer to the smallest tent in the command zone, the tent she figured held Sandra. And she waited. The humans snored, the cicadas resumed their buzzing, and her angel within trembled, impatient for the signal.

Who Whoo. Whoo.

Annabelle infiltrated the tent. Scanned it. A single rebel slept on top of a sleeping bag on the floor. No Sandra. She pressed her lips tight. Slashed his throat before he woke.

She stole across the clearing to the next tent. A discordant chorus of snores came from the larger tent. Annabelle slipped inside.

Two men lay parallel to the tent sides. Across from her lay a third man. Still no Sandra.

The rebel on her left rose to an elbow. Rubbed sleep from his eyes.

She slit his throat before he lowered his arms. Kneeled next to the man in the middle.

His eyes opened.

She slashed her blade, leaving a jagged crimson line across his neck.

His breath bubbled and gurgled, his face purpled.

"Breach!" the third man shouted and reached for his weapon.

She threw her knife. It sailed across the tent and lodged in the third man's abdomen.

He grabbed his stomach and writhed. Tried for his weapon.

She pulled her knife free and finished the job.

Lips pressed tightly, Annabelle wiped her blade on the man's pant leg. Drew herself to her full height. Then strode out of the tent, every inch of her determined to find her sister.

Outside, guns barked. Voices yelled, screamed, and moaned. The air smelled of cordite and sweat and fear.

A young girl's scream tore through the night air.

Annabelle whirled. Sprinted toward the sound.

Exiting his tent, a half-dressed man with a rifle stood between her and her goal. He swung his weapon toward her.

Knife ready, she bent low, barreled into him, slashed across his neck. Didn't wait to see him fall.

The little girl's voice went silent.

Annabelle ran faster.

Her angel within fought for release, to drink the deaths, but Annabelle resisted.

She approached a tent with a hole ripped in the side. Glimpsed a handful of adults running away. One male held the hand of a female who held a child's hand—Sandra. Two of the men fired blindly behind them. Then they disappeared into the woods.

She gave a high-pitched whistle and doubled her speed.

An Azrael appeared. Ran with her.

A second angel joined them.

In a *V* formation, they followed the thumps of their targets' footsteps through the trees, dodged drooping limbs, hopped over roots, and leaped over bushes. Stealthy and fast, they quickly caught up with and shadowed their targets.

Sandra stumbled. The woman released her, but a tall, bloodied man swooped forward, picked Sandra up, and kept going.

Annabelle signaled her angels.

They flanked the man carrying Sandra.

Fewer than fifty paces later, an angel leaped onto the back of the man, wrapped her arms around his neck, and snaked her legs around his.

Weaponless, he rose, still holding Sandra, and slammed backward into a tree trunk.

The angel made no sound and held fast.

He stumbled.

All three of them went down.

Sandra screamed, rolled downhill, and when she stopped, curled into a fetal ball.

Annabelle ran forward, grabbed Sandra's arm, and hoisted her to her feet.

Eyes squeezed tight, Sandra screamed and tried to pull away.

"Sandra, stop. It's me. Annabelle."

Sandra stopped. Opened her eyes and gaped. "Annabelle?"

"I've come to take you to Mother."

"Annabelle!" Sandra wrapped Annabelle in a fierce, desperate, never-let-go hug.

Behind them, the angel stood and freed her garrote from the man's neck.

Annabelle held out her hand. "Can you run?"

Sandra grabbed her hand, and they ran.

Chapter Fifty-One

Deep inside Leakin Park, Miranda signaled Wanda to stop and listen. No birds were singing. Instead, there was an odd assortment of muffled thuds and the occasional clang of metal. Closer to but still out of sight of the camp, the acrid odor of cordite made her heart speed like a bullet. She caught her breath, blew it out through pursed lips. Exchanged a look with Wanda and reached for her gun.

Wanda put a gentle hand on Miranda's. Cocked her head, questioning.

Miranda hesitated. With that much cordite, more than one gun fired—recently. But she and Wanda had heard no gunfire.

Whatever had happened, the gunfight was over. She bypassed her gun and grabbed her tactical folding knife. Readied the blade.

Wanda gripped her own knife and nodded—ready.

They crept to the edge of the camp.

Camp was a jumble of tents in various states of collapse. A handful of men scattered across the site took apart poles or folded tents or stuffed gear into rucksacks. The cordite-heavy air held traces of sweat and blood and fear.

Closest to them, a young man wearing a muddy t-shirt and jeans stuffed a wet tent into a carry bag.

"What happened?" Miranda asked.

He tossed a suspicious glance at her, hoisted the bag's strap over his shoulder, and darted into the trees.

Wanda gaped after him. "What does he think is chasing him? The devil?" She clipped her words, and the line between her eyes deepened.

A heavy lump landed in Miranda's gut. Crawled up into her throat. She did not like where her thoughts were going. *Azrael?* By the look on Wanda's face, she'd just had the same thought. *But we buried them under tons of rock.*

Miranda crossed over to a man struggling to put his rucksack on his back. "I can help." She lifted the pack while he got the straps over his shoulders.

"Thanks."

"Where's Monkshood?"

The man shrugged and hurried out of sight.

She exchanged glances with Wanda. Walked a few feet farther and saw a bloodied man on the ground. Dead. *Shit. Sandra.*

Miranda raced through the camp.

The half-collapsed tent in that clearing robbed her of breath.

"Sandra?"

She bent and entered. Lifting the collapsed portion, the rest of the tent came down on her. "Sandra." Holding the top of the tent with her back and neck, she searched for her niece. Sandra wasn't there, but someone had sliced open the side of the tent.

"*They* were here," Wanda said.

Miranda shook her head. There'd been no reports of any Azrael activity since the explosions and cave-in. Even Ethan had figured that the few who had escaped must have died of their injuries. *But what if…we missed a lab…or they built a new lab?* The nagging doubt that had crawled up to her throat sent the ghosts of thousands of ants across her skin. With a fierce tug, she freed herself from the tent.

Wanda's neck cords stood out. She swept her pistol back and forth, aiming at the tree line.

Miranda ignored the wormlike ripple of her skin. Put a hand on Wanda's gun hand and gently pushed the barrel down. "It couldn't have been the Azrael. Maybe the Second Sphere?"

Wanda cocked her head. "He was convinced. Said the Azrael attacked just before dawn. Took out the perimeter guards. Killed people in their sleep. Someone yelled breach. He figured the Azrael killed at least half of the team. The man I spoke to didn't know if

Monkshood was here. He said Pokeweed told him to bug out and that he, Pokeweed, would get the girl and the housekeeper woman. Said they'd meet up at Camp Tango."

A furnace blast roared inside. Miranda simply could not believe the Azrael had survived and attacked this place. Not after all this time. *He had to be mistaken.* Miranda forced herself to focus on finding Sandra. "Did Pokeweed get to her? Which way did they go?"

"The guy I spoke to said he ran for cover. Didn't see Pokeweed again."

I have to find her. "Look for tracks." But both hers and Wanda's footprints obliterated any others at the tent's entrance. *They must have left footprints somewhere.* She waved Wanda to take one side of the tent and slowly circled the other side.

"Here."

Miranda rushed to Wanda's side.

Wanda pointed at a faint confusion of footprint impressions on the mostly dry ground. "Pokeweed's maybe. And at least two others." She pointed again. "And they were followed."

Miranda focused on the ground. Followed the trail. Some prints were irregular, as if that person were running. Parallel to those were two or three sets of nearly identical prints, regular and relentless. The ground grew muddy. Some prints sank deeper as if for a stop or a turn. Others were smeared and elongated, their edges blurred in the slippery mud. And some were regular and relentless footprints parallel to the desperate runners. Miranda knew she was hours behind them, but she couldn't help searching, following the footprints a little faster.

The air fouled with an all-too-familiar scent. Miranda's footsteps slowed. The hair on the back of her neck stood. *Not Sandra. A dead animal, maybe.* She knew it wasn't.

Her heart drummed a bone-bruising beat against her ribs. Her thoughts spiraled like a leaf caught in an eddy. *I left her here…no, not my fault, Irene's…how many more…?*

Partly hidden by vines, a man lay crumpled in a heap. The mud surrounding him still churned up and splattered with droplets of mud and blood.

Miranda kneeled at his side. Peered at his mud-crusted face. One of Pokeweed's men.

Wanda searched in an expanding spiral pattern. She found more tracks. The others had kept running.

They followed the tracks deeper into the woods. The stench didn't clear. It grew stronger. A sour taste burned the back of Miranda's throat.

A hundred yards from the first body, Wanda stopped at the edge of a small clearing.

Choppy and bloody mud surrounded two deathly still bodies. Males. *Not Sandra.* Miranda huffed out a breath. But…

She tilted her head. Blinked. Blinked again. One man had three legs? She pinched her nose closed and moved closer. No, the extra leg was feminine. Miranda froze. She couldn't move. Couldn't breathe. Couldn't take her eyes off the leg.

Wanda crossed over to the tangle of bodies. Rolled the man over. Leslie lay beneath him, blood-smeared and unmoving. Paler than Miranda had ever seen her. The sight hit Miranda like a riptide sweeping her out to be lost at sea. Wrongheaded though Leslie was, she didn't deserve to die.

Leslie's foot twitched.

"She's alive!" Miranda dropped to Leslie's side. "Leslie?"

Leslie blinked once…twice. Her eyes fluttered, then stayed open. A puzzled look settled on her face.

Miranda took one side, Wanda the other, and they helped her into a sitting position.

Leslie put a hand to the back of her head. "Ow." She locked eyes with Miranda. "They took Sandra!"

Everything inside Miranda shrank. "She's—she's dead?"

"No. Not Taken. One of them grabbed her, and—and Sandra knew her. Called her Annabelle."

Blood sledgehammered in her ears. Her vision strobed bright then dark. "Annabelle." She ground the name out between gritted teeth. *That* she believed. One Azrael and helpers, likely Second Sphere agents. "How long ago? Which way did they go?"

"I don't know." Leslie's face creased in concentration. "I heard Sandra scream, turned toward her, and that's when he"—she nodded at the dead man—"slammed into me. The last thing I remember was hearing Sandra say Annabelle."

"We found your tracks," Miranda said. "We'll find hers."

"Can you walk?" Wanda asked.

"I think so." Leslie stood gingerly. Wriggled her head and shoulders in a checking-to-see-what-hurts way. Took a few steps and shot Miranda a determined look. "Let's do this."

Leslie refused to stay behind, so Miranda paired her with Wanda, then split the area into rough halves, and they agreed to alert the other one of a find with a warbling birdcall.

Crouched low, Miranda moved out from the edges of the churned mud. She climbed a small rise, and the ground grew firmer. Piles of leaves covered the earth, but here and there the leaves looked disturbed. Not footprints exactly, but odd little depressions and little mounds.

She straightened and scanned for Wanda and Leslie. Neither was in sight. *I'll give them a whistle if this turns into anything.* She followed the odd little depressions. They appeared in a pattern that had to be from a small adult or an older child—running.

Miranda nearly stepped on a small mound of blood-soaked leaves. The trail grew to an alarming amount of blood on the ground. A hint of copper scented the air. The trail circled back into the undergrowth toward the trees.

T*he strong* coppery scent left a tang on her tongue.

The crushed and bloody bushy undergrowth told a tale of someone losing strength. A few steps farther, something small and pale lay on the ground. A foot. Miranda gulped. *Too big for Sandra?*

Miranda steeled herself. Ignored the scent and taste in the air. In the bush, as if she'd fallen and crashed through it, lay the house-cleaner Miranda had interrogated a lifetime ago. Knees trembling, Miranda crouched beside the woman's body.

The woman lay face up, her long hair strewn across her face as if she'd fallen face forward and used the last of her strength to roll onto her back. Three stab wounds punctured her torso. Dark blood pooled beside her.

Stabbed? By Annabelle? Why? She was with the Fellowship.

A gurgling breath.

Startled, it took Miranda a moment to react. "Ma'am? Ma'am? Can you hear me?"

The woman's eyes fluttered open and focused on Miranda.

"Tried to tell her. I didn't say anything." The woman took several short catch-up breaths.

"Tell who? Annabelle? The Azrael?"

"Said I was tainted. Couldn't go with them."

Miranda leaned closer to the woman, spoke louder. "Was a little girl with you?"

The woman shuddered and closed her eyes.

"No, no. Not yet." Miranda shook the woman. "Wake up. Tell me. How many Azrael were there?"

Eyes fluttering, the woman took a deep, shuddering breath. "Six. More. Radio."

More? Miranda put a hand on the ground to steady herself. *They did it. They made more Azrael somehow.* Miranda gulped down several quick breaths. Noticed the woman's eyes were closed again and patted her face. "Stay with me. I need to know. Was my niece with you? Did the Azrael hurt her?"

The woman gave a slight nod. "To...Lady—rene..." She took a shuddering breath between each word. "Wear hush...four...one... one...one...Men...lo..." Her voice slurred into a mumble. Her eyes closed.

"No. Please," Miranda pleaded. "You can't go yet. What's Menlo? A road? In Baltimore?" She tapped the woman's cheek.

The woman's mouth opened a little, almost closed, opened again.

"I couldn't hear you." Miranda bent and positioned her ear close to the woman's mouth.

"Rr-Ricers..." She wheezed. Her breath rattled. "—ton... Don't..." She took another shuddering breath. Her eyes fluttered closed. Her breath whistled and stopped.

Miranda put an ear to the woman's chest. Unnaturally quiet. Not even the faintest breath. Not a single weak bump from her heart. Miranda rocked back on her knees and stared at the woman's body. *Annabelle's killing Fellowship members now? No one's safe.* The muscles in Miranda's jaw twitched. *Except maybe Sandra.*

What else were you going to tell me? Miranda shook her head. *Annabelle had to pay for this, and all the lives she had taken. Every one of them.*

Miranda burned to run and find Ricers Town. But without surveillance, without weapons... She lowered her head, stared without seeing the path. *I can't fail again. Especially after what they did to the camp. What they did to Ethan's…*

She rose and whistled for Wanda and Leslie. *After what Annabelle did to the camp, Ethan will give me everything I need. You've run out of time, Annabelle. I'm coming.*

Chapter Fifty-Two

Annabelle ran, not expecting Sandra could keep up. But she did.

Certain no one followed them, Annabelle led Sandra to the thicket where she'd hidden her motorbike.

Sandra eyed the black motorbike with a mix of fear and eagerness. "You want me to get on that?"

"This is how we get you to Mother." Annabelle straightened the bike, swung her leg over it. "Hop on behind me and put your arms around me."

On the second try, Sandra got her leg over the bike. She wrapped her arms around Annabelle's waist, and Annabelle walked the bike out of the trees.

The bike roared to life, jolted, and carried them over the bumpy ground.

Sandra's arms squeezed tighter. Her head pressed against Annabelle's back.

A puzzling but pleasant warmth spread through Annabelle's chest.

She pressed the gas pedal and bent down over the handlebars.

They zig-zagged across the city.

Dawn brightened the horizon. Streetlights winked off, and citizens stirred in their houses.

Annabelle parked her motorbike behind a dumpster in an alley. "Get off."

Sandra stared up at the walls of the factories on either side of the alley. "Mommy's here?"

"We walk from here." She led Sandra to the low warehouse building that housed Mother. Their footsteps crunched across the gravel parking lot.

A skeptical look from Sandra prompted Annabelle to say. "The outside is only a shell." She rang the bell. The door buzzed, and she opened it.

Sandra remained quiet and watchful through the hallway and the front office.

Annabelle opened the hidden door.

Sandra's eyes widened, but she followed without comment.

Annabelle led her through the fake warehouse space, opened the next door to the riot of color and shapes and sweet floral scents of Mother's garden.

Sandra ran down the path and spun in a circle. "Flowers! Beautiful flowers." She giggled and bent to sniff a bloom.

"Sandra. Is it really you?" Mother stood, agape, in the arch of the bushes surrounding her cottage.

"Mommy!" Sandra ran to embrace Mother.

Annabelle followed at her usual pace. Paused in front of Mother.

Mother freed herself from Sandra's arms and took a step back. "My goodness gracious," she said. "I think you've grown a half foot taller. But look how skinny you are."

"I *have* grown, Mommy. And Nanny says I am not skinny, I'm just right."

"For a growing child, you are just right, but as a woman…well, husbands like a—oh, never mind. I'm being silly. Let me show you your room." She led Sandra inside the cottage without a word or even a glance toward Annabelle.

Annabelle set her jaw and followed them.

Mother led Sandra straight through to a frilly pink bedroom filled with dolls and a bed piled high with stuffed animals.

"This is all mine?"

Mother nodded.

Sandra squealed, ran, and jumped into the pile of stuffed animals.

"I'm so happy you're home, Sandra, darling. But Mommy has some adult business to take care of, so stay here and play with your things. I'll come get you when I'm done."

"Can't you stay with me and play for a little while?" Sandra's voice quivered.

Mother put on her stern face. "Not now, Sandra. Maybe later. Do not leave this room until I come get you." Mother closed the door.

Annabelle's chest fluttered, and her throat tightened. But she had no time to puzzle over it; Mother had said something.

"—and how are the littlest angels doing? Their training going well?"

"Yes, Mother."

Mother crossed to the red sofa, sat in the center, and draped one arm across the back. "Your father has received instructions from our Lord. Those instructions will disturb some of the Council, so all the angels must be prepared to enforce His words."

Annabelle ignored the bizarre lightness in her chest and studied her mother's face. "Does this mean Papa is better? He's able to talk again?"

Mother's eyes shifted to the left. "Not exactly. He and I are very close, you know. So we've worked out a way to communicate."

"Tell me how. I must communicate with Papa."

Mother gave her a bright smile. "It's complicated. Besides, he's simply worn out today. Talking with our Lord and then passing that information on to me wears him out. Perhaps we can try teaching you the method another day."

Annabelle's muscles stiffened at Mother's tone.

She dares to keep us from the Prophet?

Annabelle's stomach and her thoughts swirled in an unsettled way.

No one may keep us from the Prophet, who guides us in our earthly duties.

Annabelle squared her shoulders. *The Lord chose Papa as Prophet. The Lord would not choose Papa if he had an unholy wife.* So Annabelle simply said, "Yes, Mother."

"Thank you for bringing Sandra home to me. You are a dutiful daughter to me, and to the Lord. Now, go and make your angels ready. Their greatest battle against the darkness is coming."

"Yes, Mother." Annabelle left quickly. Her uneasy stomach and thoughts tormented her all the way back to the compound.

306

Chapter Fifty-Three

L ips pressed in a tight line, Irene pried Sandra's arms from her waist and glared at her youngest daughter.

Tears streaked Sandra's upturned face, and her chin quivered. "Please, Mommy. Don't leave me alone."

"I am not leaving you alone. Our gardener and our maid will be here the entire time." *Fake Felix has been waiting in the limo for ten minutes, and I'm not even out of the living room.* "Sandra, sit down."

Arms crossed, lower lip jutting, Sandra plopped onto the vermilion couch.

Seething, Irene's cheek muscles twitched violently. She snapped her gaze upward and stared at the painting above the sofa. The pleasingly abstract shapes in vermillion, gold, green, black, and white calmed her. She looked down at her daughter with a softer smile. "Darling, you know I have important work to do. And you are old enough to know how to behave when I have to go to work." *She can't go with me; she doesn't understand, hasn't met Fake Felix yet.*

"*Please.*" Sandra's chin trembled. "I won't bother you. I'll be quiet. I promise."

"I'll come into your bedroom and give you a kiss when I get back."

"Mommy, please." Sandra popped up and wrapped her arms and the bubblegum scent of her favorite perfume around Irene's waist again.

Sandra's wheedling tone grated on every nerve in Irene's body. *I don't need this right now. I need to be calm.* "You have a lovely room and all the toys a little girl could ever want." Irene forced Sandra's hands loose. "Now, be the young lady I know you to be."

Sandra's brows drew together, and her frown deepened. "I'll call you a billion times if you leave me. And I'll—" She gave a desperate glance around them. "I'll break—everything! *Please.* Don't leave me."

Irene glanced at the starburst clock on her wall. If she didn't leave this minute, she and the fake Prophet would be late, and that just wouldn't do. She'd planned this down to the last detail. Details that didn't include Sandra's little conniption fit. *I cannot allow Sandra to derail my plan... Hmm. There* was *a way.* "All right," she said grudgingly. "I'll take you with me, but you will sit in the front seat" —*with Fake Felix hidden behind the privacy screen*—"and stay there the whole time I'm—we—are working." She took Sandra's chin in her hand and locked eyes with the child. "And I will not hear another peep from you all evening. Understood?"

Face brightening, Sandra nodded frantically.

"This isn't the end of this. We'll talk about punishment and behavior changes when we get back home. Now, get in the car before I change my mind."

Sandra snatched her rag doll and a book from the sofa and dashed out the door.

"You are a young lady; act like it," Irene called after her. Nodded when her daughter slowed to a walk.

Irene worried during the entire two-hour drive to the Carter Barron Amphitheater that Sandra would convince the driver to lower the privacy screen. She didn't. Or Paul knew Irene well enough to ignore Sandra's pleas.

They pulled into the performers' entrance to the amphitheater. The loudspeakers blasted Tennessee Ernie Ford's rich tones singing the last verse of "When the Roll is Called Up Yonder."

The roar of the crowd singing and clapping along made her ears ring and her heart soar. Her selection of music had whipped the in-person crowd into a religious fervor.

Irene got out, opened the front passenger door, and kept Sandra's attention with another warning to act like a young lady— to cover Fake Felix.

She glanced behind her.

Fake Felix slipped behind the backstage curtains.

Irene closed Sandra's door, waved goodbye, and waited until the limo disappeared into the adjacent parking area.

She mounted the steps backstage and crept forward to peer out at the audience. Adoring worshippers filled every seat. They filled the folding chairs on the apron, and there were people standing three or more deep behind the uppermost tier of seats. *Perfect*. If tonight went half as well as rehearsal, she would change the Fellowship and America forever.

The choir stood and began singing, "Holy, Holy, Holy." The intro music. She turned back to Fake Felix. He wore real Felix's robe and carried his Bible—in the wrong hand. She bit her tongue hard enough to taste copper. *I've told him and told him.*

She took his hand to get his attention, smiled, and moving only her eyes, looked pointedly at his left hand, the one holding the Bible, and slid her eyes to his right. Fake Felix gave her a Felix-smile, dropped her hand, and switched his Bible to the proper hand. She handed him a fresh white handkerchief folded in a neat square. "They're ready for the Lord's word." Felix never used a script. But Fake Felix didn't know the Bible. She had written all his superb sermons. But tonight's was extra special.

The music faded out.

"That's our cue."

She walked on stage, slightly behind and to Fake Felix's right. The people knew about the second "healing" she'd performed and expected her presence on the stage now.

"Good evening, everyone," Fake Felix said with just the right balance of reverence and familiarity.

The audience responded with a scattered "Good evening."

"I didn't hear you. Good evening, everyone."

"Good evening," the crowd shouted.

Fake Felix smiled benevolently. "That's more like it. Sounds like you're ready to hear the words of our Lord."

"Hallelujah." "Yes, Lord." "Ready."

"Tonight I'm here to—to speak the Truth." Fake Felix dabbed at his brow with the white handkerchief just like she'd shown him. "Twenty-five years ago, the Prophet Josiah and his Fellowship saved our country from the evil that ravaged our nation. He *saved* us!"

Fake Felix shook his head as if in great sorrow. "Some of your grandfathers and many of your fathers came forward during his crusades. They came forward and pledged to be part of the Fellowship and to follow the Lord. And they did—they did. But Adam's original sin doomed us—doomed us to be forever tempted by the devil. And I'm afraid—yes, I'm afraid there are some of us who have fallen—yes, they've fallen to temptation. Backsliders who surrendered to the lure of evil. Let's turn to Jeremiah 2:19, which says,

"Thine own wickedness shall correct thee, and thy backslidings shall reprove thee: know therefore and see that it is an evil thing and bitter, that thou hast forsaken the Lord thy God, and that my fear is not in thee, saith the Lord God of hosts."

Irene tuned out the words she knew by heart and scanned the upturned faces.

Shining eyes drank in the sight of their Prophet. They raised a hand or stood or bowed their heads amid shouts of "Not me," "Preach it," and "Lead us out of temptation."

Her chest swelled, and her fears vanished.

The only faces in the entire place that held expressions of polite disinterest were in the center eight chairs on the apron. The counselors. Her fingers curled. She couldn't make a fist on stage, so she brought her hands in front of her waist and hooked her fingers together.

"Brothers and sisters, if you are part of the Fellowship, if you believe in the Lord, let me hear a hallelujah."

The crowd roared, "Hallelujah!"

"Make a joyful noise!"

The crowd stomped and clapped and shouted. "Hallelujah, brother!"

With a pious expression, Irene pretended to make eye contact with the crowd but scrutinized the counselors' every movement.

"So, brothers and sisters, when you leave this worship service, when you go out into the world again, remember Proverbs 1:15, where it says, 'My son, walk not thou in the way with them; refrain thy foot from their path.'

"You know them. You live next door, or you shop at their store. Or you've seen them on the news. Now is the time to take your stand. Now is the time to be a soldier in the Lord's army and fight this blight on our land and our very souls. Join us. Stomp out the evil that calls themselves the Soldiers for the American Bill of Rights. Remove *all* the sinners from your lives. Fight for your country. Fight for your souls and for the souls of your children." Fake Felix's voice crescendoed in a fervent challenge. "Become a soldier of the Lord."

The piano chords introduced the anthem hymn, "Onward Christian Soldiers." Voices swelled with the music until the entire amphitheater reverberated with sound.

Every nerve tingling, Irene joined in and kept her eyes on the counselors, who were slipping out of their seats and vanishing into the night. *Run, you contemptible little men. You can run for now, but I'm not done with you yet.*

Chapter Fifty-Four

Stains darkened and dulled the yellow basalt walls of the two-and-a-half-story gatehouse to Baltimore's one-hundred-twenty-year-old historic Congressional Cemetery, Mount Olivet. Miranda strode through the grand arch over a cobblestone drive created for horse-drawn carriages. A stiff breeze that smelled of rain caught her skirt, lifted her hat as far as her hatpins allowed. She clamped one gloved hand onto her skirt and one onto her hat, irritated by the costume as much as by Ethan's insistence they meet in a place that required her to pass as a Fellowship member. She hadn't worn a dress since—*before I let the "Lady Angelfish" wreck.*

A stooped and bearded man stood inside, west of the entrance.

She quirked her mouth and walked a little taller. *He thinks he's fooled me with his old-man disguise.*

The old man followed her down the cobblestone path until it split into different asphalt paths.

She walked down the main path a few more rows, then paused and looked up at a tall obelisk grave marker. Watched from the corner of her eye, waited for Ethan.

The old man shuffled past her, down the path until he turned out of sight.

"This place used to be called 'The Resting Place of Methodist Bishops.'"

Miranda's insides tightened. *How did he sneak up on me?* She made a quarter turn.

"No, don't turn. Don't speak. Wait. Count to one hundred, then join me in the public vault."

She clamped her lips shut, firmly cutting off the demand that he stop scolding her as if she were a child.

He strolled past her and around a path that curved to the right.

She pretended a casual scan of the place. Grave markers stretched across the green expanse as far as she could see. Beyond them, a tree line they probably planted to protect residences from looking at gravestones. Her throat tightened. The stones that buried Nick and Beryl had no engravings and weren't in a graveyard. Miranda bit her lower lip. The sharp pain drove away the dull pain of memories. *Damn.* She hadn't counted the seconds. Figuring she'd waited long enough, she strode down the path.

The public vault was a rectangular building made of the same dull yellow basalt as the building at the entry. Scallops of water spray covered the bottom third of the building. She wrapped gloved fingers around the handle of the oversized iron door and tugged.

The door gave a soft groan that ended in a creak. She entered the cool silence lit by a rainbow of sunlight through the cathedral-style, stained-glass window that filled the far wall.

"What was so urgent you had to speak to me in person?" Ethan demanded.

Yeah, he's all business now. "Well, hello to you too. Glad to see you survived the attack on your camp."

He strode to the end of the room, where a vase of dead flowers sat upon a small table in front of the stained glass window. "I wasn't there." He whirled, tilted his head. "Where were you?"

"I was trying to rescue Mimi from the Judgment Center, but that's not—"

His right eyebrow raised. "Did you?"

She blinked. "Did I what?"

"Rescue her?"

A wave of heat swept the back of her neck. "Do you have any idea how many thousands of people they've taken to the Judgment Center? I—"

"Of course I know," Ethan said.

"Then why aren't you—why isn't SABR—doing something about it?"

"We aren't miracle workers. You're going to have to be patient; we're working on—"

"Patient?" Miranda couldn't keep the anger and disbelief from her voice. "There are families being split up, and heaven only knows where they go and what happens to them after they're shipped out of the center. We know where—"

The door groaned softly, and a ray of sunlight appeared, widened.

Miranda whirled toward the vault wall and touched one of the memorial plaques. The cold of the metal seeped through her gloves. Ethan moved close. Put an arm around her. It took an enormous effort, but she didn't pull away.

"Oh, sorry," a male voice said. The door groaned again and shut off the sunlight.

Ethan dropped his arm. "Grow up, Miranda." He spoke quietly, but his tone burned with fury. "Do you really think that the little skirmishes you've been on will actually stop the Fellowship? There's a bigger plan here. One that has started rolling, and we *must* keep rolling."

Breathing hard, she gaped at him. "Wait? A bigger plan? I've heard nothing about a bigger plan. Why are you keeping me in the dark?"

"Look at you." His look softened. He sighed. "You've been a reckless mess since the caves. You lash out without thinking. We're at the stage where that's not only dangerous on a personal level, but the wrong moves can scuttle our one chance at actually over-throwing the Fellowship and restoring our constitutional republic."

The chill that riddled her skin was from more than the tempera-ture inside the vault. *He's never trusted me. Will never stop treating me like a child.* She set her jaw. *When I bring Felix and Irene to him, he'll have to see me differently.* "I wish you'd trusted me earlier, but—" She kept her tone soft, controlled. "Tell me how I can help."

"You know it's not about trust. It's about keeping information tightly controlled so that no one person knows it all."

Except you know it all, and who else? Pokeweed? Leslie? More?

"You are important to me personally and to SABR, to the entire country."

Right. For once she was grateful she'd learned to wear a mask against her true feelings.

"Your time is coming. Soon. There are powerful people moving behind the scenes. Once they've gotten into position, we—you—will know. We'll need you then."

In the meantime, I do—what? Twiddle my thumbs while Felix and Irene do terrible things to people like Mimi... "Of course." She gave him a copy of her mother's sweeter-than-honey smile she used for the elite she had dirt on. "Send word when you need me." She moved to the door, turned back to Ethan. "For now, I guess I'll be—busy capturing Felix and Irene."

Ethan grabbed her arm. "What are you talking about?"

She wanted to smile a big gotcha smile. She didn't. She turned an innocent face to Ethan. "Remember the housekeeper I saved?"

His cheek twitched, and his chin lifted slightly. "I remember."

"The Azrael who attacked camp brought her out into the woods and decided she was unfaithful. Stabbed her. I found her dying." The memory sobered Miranda. "She knew where Felix and Irene were hiding. She told me before she died."

"When were you going to tell me that?"

"I tried to when I came in, but you had another agenda."

Ethan rubbed his mouth, took three paces away, turned, and came back. "You're sure this woman told you the truth?"

"She knew she was dying, Ethan. Why would she protect the secrets of those who killed her?"

"Tell me everything."

Chapter Fifty-Five

Every muscle aching with exhaustion, every nerve tingling with electric joy, Irene held her head high and glided along the flower-carpeted sacred processional route. Her white robe trimmed in gold was hers alone. The wind caught her royal purple chasuble and fluttered the gold stole embroidered with the Fellowship shield that hung around her neck.

She beamed at the hordes of Fellowship members lining her route. Their voices bathed her in waves of adoration. Flowers exploded from their fingers; petals—red roses, purple violets, and ivory jasmine—rained sweet perfume on her.

Euphoria threatened to crack her ribcage open. She was one breath closer to becoming the first female Prophet. But for now—First Apostle Irene—had a lovely sound.

Before her, the Council Steward turned onto Pennsylvania Avenue, then paused, halting the procession to announce her approach to the crowd. An exact duplicate of what he'd done at the construction site of the new Fellowship Center at the conclusion of her ordination and at every previous intersection, but she didn't tire of hearing it.

The fake Prophet and the counselors grudgingly trailed behind her, their footsteps clacking against the drive to the White House. Their decision, grudgingly unanimous. The Council had insisted she was the Prophet's helper, not replacement. And they vowed to keep Felix's failing health a secret.

She paused on the North Portico. Marble pillars flanked her like sentinels. Power radiated from the building behind her and seeped into her marrow. She burned this moment into her memory.

"First Apostle Earnshaw, look this way, please."

She turned that way.

Flash bulbs strobed. Camera shutters snapped and clicked. And more shouts asked her to turn this way and that.

She raised her right hand, then laid her hand on her left shoulder and gave a slight nod.

Twenty minutes later, the Steward led the way to the Green Room. Stopped at a vestibule table near the closed doors. He turned to Irene, tucked his elbows close to his sides, bent them at ninety degrees, and pressed his palms together.

Breathless anticipation fluttered in Irene's stomach. She hoped the councilors would remember this moment for the rest of their brief lives. She removed her stole and draped it over the Steward's hands.

He ceremoniously folded the stole and placed it on the vestibule table, then took the same palms-together pose.

She removed her chasuble, folded it once, and placed it in the Steward's hands, who finished folding it and placed it on the table beside the stole. He strode to the doors of the Green Room, opened the doors, and swept his hand toward the room.

Irene raised her chin and led the way into the room. She crossed to stand at the head of the U-shaped table she'd requested and waited for the counselors to file in. She savored the room's elegance with its vibrant green-velvet wallpaper, white trim and wainscoting, and the gold accents, from the gold-leafed frames of the portraits to the gold candelabras and the gold fireplace screen. *A fitting place to deliver the fatal blow to my enemies.*

Slowly, all fourteen old men filed in and stood behind the delicate antique chair at each man's assigned spot. And they waited.

She nodded regally to the Steward who pulled out her chair.

She sat.

Chairs scraped against the floor. The counselors sat, some with grace, others gracelessly.

The Steward thumped the floor with his staff three times. "Hear ye, hear ye. The Fellowship Council is in session. Introducing the First Apostle Earnshaw."

Her breath caught in her throat at the words. Words she never thought she'd hear.

"In light of the former Prophet's failure to heal," the former Chairman said. "I'd like to move our first item of business is a report on the state of the search for our next Prophet. Who seconds my motion?"

The Steward rapped his staff on the floor. "The Prophet hasn't recognized you, sir."

The Chairman squared his shoulders, glared at the Steward, then turned an insincere smile on Irene and Fake Felix.

Under the table, she nudged Fake Felix's foot.

"The Prophet must first welcome First Apostle Earnshaw and invite her to speak."

Irene returned the Chairman's smile with a Madonna one. "Gentlemen, in the intensity of recent events, we nearly overlooked our first order of business." She paused and scanned the room. She had their attention. "Our children need our help, our protection. On the table in front of you are copies of the Youth Spiritual Aptitude and Assignment Act. By adding your signature to that of the cabinet member you represent, you will help our children. Your signature will mean this act goes into effect on November second. It means that every twelve-year-old child in America will be tested on the tenets of the Fellowship. We will enroll worthy individuals in our schools to prepare them to serve the Fellowship. We will send the unworthy to Redemption centers to save the few we can." She swept her right hand in a gesture that included all the counselors.

The Steward thumped his staff on the floor.

Each counselor picked up a pen and scratched and scribbled his name onto the document, then placed the pen above the document.

The Steward gathered the signed documents and placed them on Irene's left.

She picked up one of the fourteen ceremonial pens in the tray before her and signed one document, placed it to her right, and picked up the next pen and document, until she had signed each document with a unique pen.

Irene laid her hands on the table in front of her and raised her chin. "The second order of business is not as pleasant as protecting our children but is just as sacred a duty. Before the terrifying raid that resulted in the kidnapping and death of our Prophet, he whispered a shocking revelation to me."

The counselors shot looks at each other, but no one made a sound.

"As your First Apostle, I fear I must report our Lord is not pleased." She swept a condemning stare around the room, sharing it equally with each of the counselors. "He has given us warning. First, it was via the Christmas flood in Louisiana, then the tornadoes in February, an earthquake in April, more tornadoes *on Palm Sunday,* and none of you noticed. So the Lord had airplanes fall out of the sky in June, delivered a devastating fire and explosion at that industrial plant in Arkansas in August, and then destroyed some of your summer homes in last month's Hurricane Betsy. Yet none of you paid attention. Some of you expressed concern when Counselor Lucas Matthews was Taken." She had to give them credit. The counselors kept their composure, though they pursed their lips or swallowed, or paled, or sweated. "Yet even then, not one of you repented. Not one of you made restitution." She let that sink in.

"Who here will confess to the sins of—addiction?" Silence. "Blasphemy?" No answer. "Violating the Sabbath?" She raised an eyebrow. Turned her skepticism on each counselor. "How about embezzlement? Gambling, gluttony, or drunkenness?" A brief glance up. "Pornography, forbidden relationships, adultery, envy and coveting, or idolatry?" She leveled her most judgmental leer at each of them. "No one?"

She tsked and shook her head as if she were sad. "That is unfortunate.

"The Lord directed the Prophet Josiah to create this Council to be the Lord's envoys to our government. It was to be a place of prayer and contemplation and decision for the people of the United States of America." She released a loud sigh, looked straight ahead, and announced, "In Galatians 5:21 the Lord said, 'Envyings, murders, drunkenness, revelling, and such like: of the which I tell you before, as I have also told you in time past, that they which do such things shall not inherit the kingdom of God.'

"Therefore, in the name of the Lord our God, I declare this Council null and void and dissolved immediately." She brought the gavel down. It gave a satisfying whack.

A cacophony of voices erupted. "I knew a woman First Apostle was a bad idea."

"We don't have to listen to this."

"This is preposterous."

"How dare she? Mr. Chairman, I object!"

The shouts continued. Words overlapped words until they were indistinguishable.

The Council Steward rapped his staff on the floor. "Order in the Council."

Irene folded her hands in front of her and waited serenely.

Thump. Thump. Thump. "The Council will come to order."

Slowly, the men quieted.

Chest charged and tingling with her new power, Irene sat with perfect posture and poise. "As I was saying, Mr. Chairman, this Council is disbanded. I pray you'll go home, repent, and do penance."

The counselors clambered to their feet, pointing at Irene, shaking fingers at her, and shouting even louder than before.

She ignored them all.

The Council Steward shouted, "Azrael, enter."

Irene's chest hollowed. Everything depended on the counselors' reactions in the next seconds.

Behind her, the doors banged open. Fourteen extra-large Azrael, wearing their black uniforms and goggles, marched in with weapons drawn, circled the table, and stood behind each counselor.

Eyes riveted on the angels, the counselors swiveled, following the angels' movements.

"The Azrael shall maintain order in the Council during its dissolution," the Steward said.

"Who dares defy the word of our Lord?" The lead angel's righteous tone held a deadly edge.

Irene's throat went dry. She hoped Paul's falsetto had that effect on the counselors.

The Chairman opened his mouth, and nothing came out. He cleared his throat. "All here are servants of the Lord, Blessed One."

"Then why must we appear to enforce our Lord's command?" The lead angel asked, puzzled. "Know you not that if you refuse to obey, you shall be Taken?"

The Chairman's mouth opened and closed again. He dropped

his gaze. "I am the Lord's willing servant." He sat heavily and reached for the documents spread on the table before him.

"Non-counselors have no right to any Council papers or property," Irene said in a mild tone. "Remove your robes of office and leave them. Leave all Council papers, pens, and the gavel. Take only your personal possessions."

In less than five minutes, every counselor had stood, shed his robe of office, and left the room empty-handed.

Irene gave Fake Felix a pointed look. "You can go now. Wait in the car."

Fake Felix nodded. His chair scraped the floor, and he walked out the door without hesitation.

Irene closed her eyes to savor the moment.

A gloved hand touched her arm.

She started.

Paul's disguise as an angel was intimidating. "Are you all right?" he whispered in his normal voice.

Irene scanned the chairs and table littered with sashes and robes and documents. Breathed in, then out. "Yes, I'm more than all right." *Too bad Annabelle wouldn't agree to this public appearance. She could have become more powerful.* Irene turned a thousand-watt smile on Paul. "Now we will obey the Lord. We will stop Miranda and the rest of the apostate rebels forevermore."

Chapter Fifty-Six

Annabelle arrived at the warehouse and dismissed the angels watching over Mother. They'd be back in the morning.

Even though she knew no humans lurked about, she was loath to enter through the same door every time. She entered through the last door on the dock, strode through the false dock area, and popped open the secret panel.

It was as dark inside the warehouse as it was out, but the air in here smelled surprisingly like the swamp did on damp days, though less pleasant. *Mother should have someone open all the doors to air this place out.* The silence of the warehouse made her human ears ring.

She walked around the fake Fellowship Center and hesitated. Papa's building stood on the alley side of the warehouse, its hospital interior hidden by the cottage-like facade. The sight of the lonely light above the door made something squeeze Annabelle's chest. She took two long strides toward the door, and the tightness in her chest got worse. *It's the middle of the night. Humans need sleep to heal. I should wait until morning.*

She hurried down the path past the wall of bushes. Mother's cottage glowed with light. *Good, Mother's still awake.*

She slid the patio door open. Silence greeted her. Then a strange choking-gasping sound came from the direction of the bedrooms.

She surged into the hallway. The choking sound repeated. It came from Sandra's bedroom. Annabelle nudged the door open.

Sitting on the floor in the corner, hugging her knees, Sandra raised a hopeful, tear-stained face. "Mommy? Oh—Annabelle." She made a strange gasping noise. "Are you here to take care of me?"

Annabelle cocked her head. "Do you *need* someone to take care of you?"

"Mommy left me." Sobs racked Sandra's body.

Sandra's tears twisted something inside Annabelle. She didn't understand why, but she had to make Sandra feel better.

She crossed the room and crouched beside Sandra. Awkwardly patted Sandra's hand.

Sandra started and gave Annabelle a tiny and tremulous smile.

Impulsively, Annabelle grabbed Sandra's cheeks between her hands.

Sandra's eyes widened.

Annabelle leaned forward and rubbed her nose against Sandra's.

"Ow! That's too hard," Sandra exclaimed.

Aghast that she, an Azrael, had done such a human thing, Annabelle recoiled, releasing Sandra.

"Eskimo kisses are soft." Sandra gently nuzzled Annabelle's nose with hers.

Annabelle submitted to Sandra's Eskimo kiss. The softer touch stirred her insides again. And somehow after the "kiss," Sandra's face had transformed.

Her lashes were wet, her cheeks damp, but her eyes shone with a light that lifted Annabelle. Not the same lift her inner angel got with the death of a sinner, but the rightness of this lift warmed Annabelle deep inside.

The human side of us is weak. Restore us. Feed us.

Annabelle ignored her inner angel.

———

After eating a peanut butter sandwich and a banana, Sandra had more color in her cheeks, but she was still quiet. Too quiet. The uncomfortable flutter in Annabelle's chest swirled.

Sandra asked Annabelle to play a board game with her. Annabelle agreed.

The game *Sorry!* required a beginner's-level strategy, which

Annabelle won easily. Winning the simple game warmed Annabelle's insides. One game became two, then three, then four.

An hour later, Annabelle sat opposite Sandra at the too-small child's table in Sandra's too-pink bedroom, waiting for Sandra to take her turn.

Sandra's blonde head bowed, and she hopped her blue pawn over the six squares the card she'd drawn said to move. She hesitated over a square that Annabelle's red pawn already occupied. Her shoulders slumped. "Again? I just can't win." She reluctantly put her blue pawn back on the square she'd just left.

A stab of pain drove the warmth Annabelle had been enjoying away. "It's just a board game. It's okay."

You wouldn't say this to our angel sisters, so why do you say it now?

Sandra is not an Azrael. We treat her as a human.

Sandra's plump pink lips pouted. "Do you think Mommy will be home soon?"

"Yes."

"Good." Sandra looked at her window with its fake night sky and sighed. "Do you think it's dark outside now?"

Annabelle glanced at the wall clock that was shaped like a black cat. It was seven minutes after midnight. "Yes, it's very dark. It's the middle of the night."

"Mommy won't be happy I'm still awake."

Annabelle didn't comment.

Sandra gave her a worried look. "You won't leave me alone if I go to sleep, will you?"

If we will not speak to the Prophet, we must return to the compound.

We will. First, Sandra needs my protection while she sleeps.

"Will you?" Sandra's voice held a plaintive note.

"I won't leave until Mother comes home."

"Promise?"

"I said I would stay. I will stay."

The other angels will know your human blood corrupted you.

Annabelle lifted her chin and waited for Sandra to change into her nightgown and climb under the fluffy pink bedspread.

Annabelle stopped at the doorway. Reached for the light switch.

"Aren't you going to kiss me good night?"

Her words stirred the memory of Mother's kiss at bedtime. "Sorry, I forgot." Went to the bedside, hesitated.

Sandra got on her knees, wrapped her arms around Annabelle's neck, and kissed her cheek. "Good night, sister," she whispered, her breath warm on Annabelle's ear. "Thank you for saving me."

A superheated flush swept up Annabelle's neck and face. She couldn't speak, couldn't move, couldn't understand what had happened.

Sandra tilted her head, exposing her cheek to Annabelle.

Annabelle forced herself to shift her weight.

"Please?" Sandra said sweetly.

Annabelle clumsily pecked at Sandra's forehead, then gently pried Sandra's arms away and twisted her lips into something that might resemble a smile. She patted Sandra's pillow.

Sandra climbed back into bed. "Good night." Her sleepy smile sent another wave of flutters through Annabelle.

"Good night." Annabelle closed the door behind her and returned to the living room. Everything inside her spun in an ephemeral way that warmed and confused her. It wasn't the beginning of ascension, yet it lifted her.

She paced between the red sofa and the cone-shaped dining room chairs and tried to focus. *How has Sandra unmoored us so?* The absence of a response from her inner angel shook her. She paced faster.

A loud click came from behind her.

Annabelle whirled.

The massive front door swung open. Mother stood with her hand on the doorknob but faced the fake. "Come on in. We'll talk about next steps and sip some soothing tea."

He dressed like the Prophet. Looked like the Prophet. Looked like Papa.

Each time Annabelle had seen the fake, the sight of him had caused a twisting pain in her chest. The pain was sharper and deeper now.

Mother turned. Faced Annabelle. Her mouth formed a silent O. "Annabelle?"

The fake Prophet entered quietly, closed the door.

The O-shape of Mother's mouth smoothed into a smile. "What brings you here at this hour?"

"I came to speak to Papa."

Mother's eyebrows drew together the tiniest bit. "Did you? Speak to him?"

"No, he slept. Sandra was alone and afraid." Matter of fact.

Mother's cheeks pinked. "She's too old to need a babysitter. Besides, I was only gone for a couple of hours." She strode past Annabelle. Dropped her purse on the end table. Faced Annabelle again. "It's too late to visit your father now. Do you want to stay overnight?" She waved her hand towards the sofa. "I can bring you a pillow and a blanket."

Chapter Fifty-Seven

Leslie blew out a quiet breath. Breathed in air that had a damp earth smell and a hint of something like machine oil. She couldn't believe her innocent comment about how Ricers Town sounded like Reisterstown Station, a neighborhood in northwest Baltimore, brought her here. Hiding in the dark. Waiting for the signal to infiltrate a warehouse. The thrum of her heart was louder in her ears than the hum of nighttime traffic crawling along the road one block over.

Forty-eight hours ago, she would have laughed at the idea that the Fellowship would ever give any woman a leadership role. That Miranda's obsession with pursuing her sister was the worst kind of sibling animosity.

But the Council had shattered their own traditions. Consecrated Irene as the First Apostle, her husband's helper.

Now, she feared Miranda's plan was the only sane response to a world gone mad.

Across a gravel parking lot, under the starless and cloud-choked sky, a single security light lit the front corner of the warehouse and part of the gravel driveway's padlocked gate. A flickering and dim streetlight in the alley on the northeast side of the building gave the alley side of the masonry building a kind of halo. The building was tall for a single story, but too short for a two-story.

Miranda's plan split them into seven small teams. One to breach

each of the three man-sized doors and the four garage-like doors on the docks.

Leslie's throat burned with acid. She had sworn she'd never fight again, but she couldn't miss finishing the Fellowship. She owed that much to her parents and older brother.

"Thornbush?" This close to Monkshood, her walkie-talkie echoed his spoken words.

"No sparkle."

"Winterberry?"

"No sparkle here either."

"Ruby." That meant wait.

"We can't wait all night. We need to move in," Miranda whispered from about a yard to the left. Her rigid, shadowy form stood between Leslie and Monkshood.

"I can't justify sending my men in there without some sign that the Prophet is in there."

"You think the housekeeper lied on her deathbed?" Miranda whispered. "Oh, I see. You think I'm the liar." If someone could shout a whisper, that's what Miranda did.

The rumble of a vehicle approaching made Leslie jump. The sound came from the southeast. She strained to see it.

"Miranda, you refuse to see the big picture."

A dark, slow-moving vehicle in the alley, moving toward Menlo Drive. Without its lights on. The hair on the back of Leslie's neck raised. "Quiet!"

In the sudden silence, the purr of the vehicle's engine grew louder.

Her pulse slammed against her throat.

A late-model limousine crept past and disappeared behind the building.

It reappeared on the south side of the building, pulled into the drive, and stopped in the pool of light at the gate.

The driver stepped out of the vehicle. Unlocked the gate. Pushed it open. The gate rattled and scraped gravel. He returned to his vehicle, and the limo crunched over the gravel. Parked nose into the dock.

The driver hopped out of the vehicle again and opened the passenger door. A robed figure exited the vehicle, walked to the dock stairs, and stood.

The driver circled behind the limo, opened the other passenger door, and reached into the vehicle. A woman in a long gown got out.

The Prophet and the First Apostle. Leslie's muscles tensed, ready to take up the lead position on the alley side of the building. She tilted her head toward the walkie-talkie secured to the shoulder strap of her overalls. Waited for the signal from Monkshood.

The gravel crunched softly with each step the Lady took until she joined the Prophet at the steps. Hand in hand, they climbed up to the dock. A door-shaped light glowed. They entered. The door closed, and all was dark again.

"Was that enough proof?" Miranda's triumphant whisper carried.

Leslie's walkie-talkie clicked.

"Diamond in the rough," Monkshood said. "Jade."

Leslie darted behind the building and into position next to the dock door. Ian, Kate, and Gordon appeared out of the dark.

The Fellowship will have to surrender after this. No more fighting, hiding, lying. Leslie's pulse settled into a fast but steady rate.

A click, then "shhh" came from her walkie-talkie. "Jade two."

This is it.

She and Ian climbed up onto the dock ledge.

Working together, they slid the heavy steel door open without a sound.

She drew her gun and entered the dark warehouse. Stopped. Exchanged a startled look with Ian.

Not ten feet ahead of them stood a building with another large sliding door.

Chapter Fifty-Eight

Miranda pressed her back against the cool concrete wall on the northwest side of the warehouse. Every muscle painfully tense but ready. *What is taking Ethan so long? We saw them enter.*

She glanced at Wanda, pressed against the wall behind her. Beyond Wanda, the two men who made up the rest of her team also pressed against the wall to avoid being on the camera over the dock door to Miranda's left.

The red light of the camera winked out. Expecting the go signal, Miranda took a half-step forward. No signal came. *Dammit, Ethan. Much longer, and I'll go without you.* Every second that passed hung like an anchor, rooting Miranda in place.

The buzz of her walkie-talkie startled her.

"Jade two."

Finally. She took a deep breath and led her team through the man door, into the dark warehouse that wasn't as completely dark as she'd expected.

Dozens of tiny white lights peppered the ceiling like starlight on a clear night. Random dim red lights divided the warehouse into sections.

The air smelled sweet and earthy.

Despite the raised hair on her arms, she led the way.

Two yards in, she stepped onto something soft, thick. She clicked her tongue, signaling halt. Didn't want the others to step on what-ever she had.

It definitely was not the concrete floor of a warehouse. *Grass?*

Gun trained ahead, she crouched and lowered her empty hand to the floor.

She swept her hand as far as she could reach. *Grass.*

Memories, twined with ice and pain, coiled in her gut.

She focused on the nearest red lights. They formed the corners of an imaginary rectangle. She crept forward. Tilted her head.

Realization slapped her. *It's a building inside the warehouse. Just like the cave...*

Mental images of the cave and falling rock rushed in, took her breath away.

I'm not in the cave. Not in Kansas City. I'm in Baltimore. In a ware-house—in Baltimore.

She shoved her memories back into a corner of her mind. Forced herself to breathe normally. *Okay. So they've turned this warehouse into a hideout.*

Calmed, she realized the red lights on the west side of the ware-house outlined a second building. *Why two buildings? To feed Irene's ego?* Miranda double-clicked her tongue and led the others toward the wall.

In the dim red gloom near the building, she signaled the two men to circle around the back and come up the southwest wall.

Inching down the wall, she took a quick peek around the corner. Gave a soft snort at the portico lined with marble columns before her.

Wanda followed her around the corner and muttered, "Waste of money."

Miranda kept moving, sliding along the wall of the wide porch. Froze at the sight of an unmistakable front door. *The Fellowship Center. Why?*

The two men on her team came around the southwest wall and stopped on that side of the door.

Beryl's voice whispered, *Be ready*, in Miranda's head. Miranda relaxed her grip on Beryl's gun and strode through the unlocked doors. Her team followed.

The cold coil in Miranda's stomach tightened. Every nerve in her skin tingled. From the replica of the statue, *Shield of Mercy, Hand of*

Justice, to the pink marble colonnade supporting fake balconies above, and the mural-painting on the illusion of a distant dome overhead, it was all there.

She forced herself to see through the ghosts of her past and realized this space was much smaller than it should be. She touched the marble walls, which were warmer than marble. Scratched the wall with her fingernail. Paint peeled. *It's fake.*

Miranda signaled one man to guard the entrance, then marched to the auditorium doors. Assumed they were also fake. Pushed. They opened.

Her stomach rolled. The seat-filled auditorium and red velvet-draped stage stood vacant. In her mind's eye, her father stood at the podium, called her name. And Mama forced her to accept Ryan's proposal. She swallowed her rising panic. *This is a fake. Like all things Fellowship.*

A closer look revealed there were fewer than a hundred seats. The rest were trompe l'oeil. *Fakes.*

She signaled Wanda and the second man to cover the side aisles; she walked the center one. They reach the stage.

Breathless and tingling all over, Miranda signaled Wanda to keep watch from the apron of the stage, then trotted up the steps onto the stage.

The vacant stage was near full-size, with wings on each side. She sent her fourth team member left. She went right. Ghostly prickles ran from her neck to her heels.

Stage right was the first area that looked significantly smaller, cheaper. Two doors stood open to what she guessed would be dressing rooms. She crept toward the first one, ready to find an enemy.

Inside, an upholstered armchair faced a small television set atop a narrow table. To her left stood a closet filled with men's slacks and sports jackets. To her right were an unmade twin bed and a chest of drawers. *An apartment? For Felix?*

Miranda searched the drawers, under the bed, the closet and found nothing. Moved to the second room.

A mirrored vanity against the back wall held a messy array of makeup, foundation, and powder. A roll-around rack held three Prophet's robes and an assortment of colorful stoles. With her free hand, she slid the robes first one way then the other. No one hid behind the robes.

Opposite the clothes rack, a shelving unit held wig stands that sported fake eyebrows and wigs styled the way Felix styled his mousy brown hair. Boxes of glue for the wigs and tons more makeup filled the lower shelves. Dumbfounded, Miranda gaped at it. *Felix wears all this? The explosion must have disfigured him.*

A faint sound came from outside the room. Miranda turned slowly toward the door.

Chapter Fifty-Nine

A nauseous stench of something rotten made Leslie gag. She covered her mouth and nose with her left hand. Tried to breathe only through her nose. Glanced at Ian.

Her brother wrinkled his nose. Nodded.

She signaled two of her team to advance on either side of the building, then moved to the sliding door. It moved easily, silently.

Inside, her skin crawled. Her stomach pitched and rolled, but she wouldn't give in. She walked up the hall.

Ian stood guard.

She entered the first room. Full of the ever-present, overpowering stench, it was a tidy, one-bedroom apartment with no personal items.

She continued forward. The air grew thick and oily and vile. She held her breath and passed through the next doorway. Came to an abrupt halt.

A swollen, almost unrecognizable woman's body lay face down as if she'd collapsed. Dried vomit pooled around her head.

Across the room, another bloated body lay on a soiled hospital bed. This one was only recognizable because it resembled the face that had been the image of the Fellowship plastered on newspapers, the walls of buildings, and the sides of trolleys for the past year. *No wonder we couldn't find him.*

Leslie ran out of the room and out the front door. Ian followed close after her and slammed the door shut behind them.

The two she'd sent around the building came running. They stopped at her hand signal and maintained operational silence but wore quizzical expressions.

Bent, hands braced on her knees, Leslie gasped for air. Though it wasn't as thick, the odor hung here too, clung to her, triggered a coughing fit.

The coughing quieted. She stood and wiped the tears from her eyes. She had to find Miranda. If Miranda confirmed the body on the bed was who she thought he was, Monkshood had to be informed. She glanced around, and her mouth dropped open.

The last third of the warehouse held lush gardens and two buildings. The building she'd just come from and a second one on the northwest side. Miranda's side.

Leslie squinted at Miranda's building. It had columns and looked kind of like a miniature Fellowship Center. *What the heck is going on here?*

Ian pulled up beside her. "What's wrong?" he whispered.

She sniffed. Pulled a face. "That smell. Ugh. It's sticking to me."

"Oh." He raised his elbow toward his nose. "Yeah. Me too, I guess." He shrugged.

She didn't move. *I don't want to be the one to tell Miranda. She acts like she hates her sister and her brother-in-law, but they are still family. What I have to ask—it'll be her last memory of him.*

Ian gave her a puzzled look. Glanced back at the other two, kept them back with a gesture. "Les, we've got to do this. If it's possible to positively identify that monster, Miranda's the only one of us who can do it."

Leslie sighed and led the way into the fake Fellowship Center.

Chapter Sixty

Rapid footsteps approached the dressing room. Miranda flattened herself against the wall beside the door. Her index finger pulled the slack out of the trigger of Beryl's gun.

"Miranda?" Leslie's strained whisper came before she appeared in the doorway.

Miranda pressed her lips together and re-holstered the gun.

"I'm so sorry, but you need to come with me." Leslie held her hand out as if she wanted Miranda to take hold.

"Look at this. It's probably the most important clue we've found." Miranda swept her hand toward the vanity and all the makeup. "Obviously, Felix was injured—"

"I think Felix is dead."

The words hit Miranda like a wall in a place it shouldn't be. "Did you shoot him?"

Leslie looked shocked. "No. I didn't shoot him. I wouldn't shoot —" She shook her head. "*No one* shot him. He's been dead. Long dead."

Miranda scoffed. "You aren't making any sense. We just saw him."

Leslie moved closer. "I don't know what we saw, but I don't think it was him."

What is Leslie up to now? Miranda sucked in her cheeks and got a whiff of something rotten. She eyed Leslie suspiciously.

Leslie gave an exasperated sigh. "Come with me. See for yourself." Her tone was urgent.

Miranda stepped closer. Leslie reeked of rottenness. "Okay, from the way you stink, someone is dead. It's not Felix."

"I'm not joking. You have to come and look." Leslie put her hands on her hips. "I'm not going to leave without you."

Fine, she can watch me.

The nauseating stench from Leslie filled the room.

Jaw clenched, Miranda looked around her. *If it's the only way she'll take her nasty self out of here, guess I'll have to go look, tell her it's not Felix, so I can figure this place out.* She gave a sharp nod and led Leslie out to the stage apron, where Wanda stood guard.

"Don't let anyone in there." Miranda jerked her head toward the dressing room she'd discovered. "I'll be back before you can sing 'Twinkle Twinkle.'" She left without waiting for Wanda's acknowledgment. Followed Leslie out of the building. Discovered Ian waiting on the portico.

The three of them strode across the warehouse.

Three yards from Leslie's building, the air turned so foul Miranda's eyes burned.

Ian held the door; Leslie led the way in. A few moments later, Leslie stepped aside.

Miranda stood in the doorway of a large room filled with hospital equipment. On the floor, a mound of flesh wore a stained nurse's uniform. *Definitely not Felix.*

"Sorry to subject you to this, but..." Leslie tipped her head toward the hospital bed behind her.

Another lump of flesh lay in the bed, sheets with huge oily stains pulled up to the armpits and neatly folded.

"You think that's Felix?" Miranda asked.

"You tell us."

Scarcely daring to breathe, Miranda moved closer to the bed. Grotesquely misshapen, the body in the bed's puffy face stared, unblinking, the mouth slack. The hair was shorter than she'd ever seen it, but the shape of the ears... She rubbed her watering eyes. Looked again. If Felix had been one hundred pounds heavier, the nose and the chin would... Tremors shook her.

Unable to look at him anymore, she spun away. A hurricane of grief and horror and a kind of glee, "Hooray, he's dead," and a wailing, "Who killed him before I could?" churned inside her. She swayed. Set her feet in a wider stance and steadied herself.

"Miranda." Leslie's hand landed softly on her shoulder. "Are you okay?"

Miranda whipped her head around and glared at the offending hand. "I'm fine. It's Felix. And he's exactly where he needs to be. Dead—rotting." She marched out of the room, out of the building. Far enough away that the stench wasn't so overwhelming.

Leslie trotted after her like a parasitic puppy, murmuring reassurances.

Miranda heaved huge breaths, refilling her lungs with better air, and struggled to understand. *How can Felix be dead and rotting? We saw him...* She stood straighter. *Death had disfigured the Felix in the bed, but he had a full head of hair. He didn't need a wig. The REAL Felix didn't need a wig.* "He's a fake," she whispered breathlessly.

"Who? But you just said..."

"I know what I said!" Miranda whirled. Faced Leslie. "I'm not talking about him." She pointed at the building they'd just left. "I mean the public one. The Prophet we saw enter this building. He's a fake. That's why all the makeup and wigs and auditorium. *He's a fake.*" Her mouth dropped open. "And Irene knows it." A blazing ball of fury filled her chest to bursting. *And she's First Apostle. She's planned this...*

Comprehension brightened Leslie's face. "Of course. They've been fooling everyone." She inhaled sharply.

Have to find Irene. She wasn't in the theater or the hospital building. Miranda scanned the wall of bushes. An archway peeked into another garden on the other side. *That's where Irene has to be. Crap. Ethan will find her first.* "We have to tell Eth—Monkshood—NOW."

Chapter Sixty-One

Annabelle stood in the space between the dining room and the living room. Some strange, invisible thing filled her chest and tightened her throat. Her attention bounced between scowling at the fake Prophet in Mother's dining room and puzzling over Mother's fretful fussing in the living room.

She glowered at the fake Prophet, who sat in one of the cone-shaped chairs in Mother's dining room, sipping a glass of wine he'd poured himself as if he did this often.

Across the room, Mother made the red sofa a place to sleep, tucking and re-tucking warm beige blankets under the cushions.

What more do you need to see to know this human is not holy?

I found Sandra and brought her home because Mother said she needed Sandra. Perhaps it's too soon for—

The fake sits here as if he belongs. The woman is hypocritical and deceitful. A sinner.

But she is Mother.

"Annabelle? You don't look well, darling. What's wrong?"

"I am Azrael. Azrael doesn't get unwell."

Almost imperceptibly, tension tightened the skin around Mother's eyes. "Of course, darling." She smiled, but her eyes were bright like those of a trapped bird. "So, you'll stay, yes?"

Annabelle tilted her head and stared at her mother and the sofa-turned-bed.

Every light in the room flashed three times. Mother's eyes went wide, and her mouth dropped open. "Someone's broken into the building."

Without thinking, Annabelle drew her pistol with her right hand, her knife in her left. She hesitated. *Lord? What is Thy will?* No answer came.

She faced the door again in a ready-to-fight stance, prepared to do her duty and protect the Prophet, his wife, and daughter.

"The angels guarding us will take care of them." The fake Prophet sounded as if he found pleasure in the idea.

Annabelle didn't tell him she'd dismissed the angels hours ago. He was not one of her charges. Glancing over her shoulder at Mother, she whispered, "What is your escape plan?"

"The pantry. Hidden passage." Mother's quiet voice held a tremor.

"Get Sandra and go there now."

"But—"

Annabelle half-turned to face Mother. "Now, Mother."

"You are overreacting," the fake said. "We are in no danger."

Sandra poked her head out from around the hallway. Her eyes were wide. "Mommy?"

Mother whirled. "Get some shoes on now." She pushed Sandra ahead of her, down the hallway.

"Hurry," Annabelle whispered. She repositioned herself so she could see the front door and the glass of the patio sliding doors, ready to respond in either direction. No one appeared in the dark gardens beyond the patio doors. No one came through the front door. Still, the warning light flashed. So she waited, alert, lethal.

A sliding sound came from behind her. She glanced toward it.

Mother dragged a tousle-haired, nightgown-wearing Sandra toward the kitchen.

Annabelle moved, keeping herself between her family and the doors where the intruders might appear. Tossed brief looks over her shoulder to check on their progress.

"You can't be serious," the fake whined. "Have you heard anyone breaking in? I haven't."

Mother threw open the pantry door and pushed Sandra inside before her.

Annabelle moved to stand in front of the pantry.

The fake gaped at her.

Mother fumbled under the middle shelf on the back wall. A portion of the shelving and wall swung open, revealing a hole in the floor and a ladder that stretched downward. "Get down there."

"It's too dark!" Sandra cried. "You go first."

Mother whispered, "Follow me," and disappeared down the ladder.

The front-door latch clicked.

The fake stood. His chair tipped and wobbled.

Annabelle spun toward the sound, holding fire until she could see her target.

A familiar face appeared in the doorway. A face from the wanted poster. The leader of SABR. She fired.

The SABR leader fired at the same time.

Annabelle's first bullet ripped through the center of his chest.

A bullet whined. Grazed her arm, burned. She fired again.

His knees buckled, and he fell forward.

A gun blazed from behind him.

Annabelle dropped the second intruder with one shot.

A third intruder followed. His shot went wide. She hit him, and he staggered inside. Her second shot made him fall like a puppet whose strings were severed.

A fourth man popped in and out of the doorway, firing wildly.

Annabelle steadied herself against the kitchen counter, took careful aim, and fired three times through the wall next to the door. A satisfying thud sounded, followed by a ringing silence. She advanced to the door.

The fourth man slumped on the porch near the door. He looked dead, but she took no chances. One shot to the heart for him and each of the others.

She spun toward the kitchen patio doors. The fake was on the floor surrounded by a puddle of blood. Through the glass, movement caught her eye. *More intruders. Coming here. Coming from Papa's place.* She hesitated. Checked her gun's magazine. Two bullets left. *Lord, protect your servant, my father. I'll take care of Mother and Sandra.*

She turned, walked calmly to the pantry, and pulled the door closed behind her. Took two steps down the ladder and spotted a leather strap at the bottom of the shelf-door. Pulled it shut. Felt her way down the ladder.

"Annabelle, is that you?"

"Yes, Mother." With her feet on solid ground, she pulled her tactical flashlight from her belt. Shone the light at Mother. They were in a large duct of brickwork with a wide river of water flowing through the bottom. She swung the light around, peering in the opposite direction. "How do I get to the Prophet?"

"It's impossible." Mother's sharp tone cut through Annabelle's fixed state of mind. "The wicked rebels have him by now. Get me out of here."

Annabelle hesitated. *Mother didn't see the SABR leader or the second wave of rebels coming, so why is she so certain the rebels have Papa?* Still, Annabelle had to admit the rebels outgunned her. She led Mother and Sandra away from the warehouse. Determined to reach her angels and send them all to find and save the real Prophet.

Chapter Sixty-Two

Miranda raced across the fake gardens. She couldn't wait to tell Ethan that Irene had a fake posing as her husband. Couldn't wait to expose her sister's lies to the world. Couldn't wait to celebrate the end of the Fellowship.

"Wait. Miranda, wait!"

Wanda's whisper reached her, but Miranda couldn't stop now; the archway was only steps away.

Bang. Bang.

Rapid gunfire answered the first shots.

The Azrael? Ethan! Hot energy surged through Miranda. Her hands and legs erupted into motion. Pistol in hand, she darted through the archway and zigzagged between fragrant rosebushes to the cottage-style walls of the third building inside the warehouse. *Irene must be inside.* Miranda gritted her teeth.

Wanda, Leslie, and the others, each with a gun in hand, caught up. They paused behind trellises, or bushes, or statues.

The cottage sat off-center from the path and had no windows on the nearest end. Close to the opposite end, a concrete patio and patio furniture stood before a pair of sliding doors. The lights were on inside.

Miranda signaled Leslie and her team to get positions on the other side of the cottage. Then, she waved her team to flank her.

She inched forward, reached the nearest wall of the fake house.

The gunfire went silent.

She flattened against the wall, slid to the frame of the sliding doors.

Bang. Silence. *Bang.* Silence. *Bang.* Silence.

A quick peek inside revealed no one in sight.

The silence deepened. The thump-bump of her heart filled Miranda's ears.

She took a longer look. Crumpled on the floor between a cone-shaped chair and the table lay a robed body. Miranda smirked.

Beyond him, neither Irene nor any Azrael stood in the visible part of the kitchen. The living room was vacant as well, but in a short hallway a door stood open, blocked by a body. Her throat tightened. *Ethan?*

She slid the door all the way open. Slipped inside. Scanned the area for hostiles. Her chest hurt; she was breathing too fast and couldn't slow down. She stood in a gleaming dining area open to the kitchen and living room. No Azrael was in sight. The robed body lay inert. But it wasn't one body slumped in the front doorway. It was three. Her chest hollowed.

A rustling sound came from beyond the bodies. She aimed at the sound, finger on the trigger.

Leslie stepped through the doorway. Her free hand flew to her mouth.

Miranda drew in a slow breath and released it just as slowly. She lowered her gun.

Leslie didn't move.

Trembling, Miranda walked toward the bodies. Halfway across the room, she knew.

She rushed forward, pausing only to check that no one lurked in the central hallway. Kneeled on the floor next to Ethan.

His breath gurgled.

She lifted his head to rest on her knees. "Ethan? Uncle Ethan?"

His eyes fluttered open. His mouth worked. Bloody bubbles rose, dribbled down his cheeks.

She glanced at Leslie. "Find something to carry him on. We have to get him help. Hurry!"

Ian rushed past Leslie, who started, then followed.

"No." Ethan's voice ended with a wet-sounding rattle.

She bent, her face close to his. Whispered, "Don't talk. Save your energy." Tears threatened. "My fault." Her breath hitched against the boulder in her throat.

"No...fault"—gasp—"war"—gasp—"some...die."

She forced a smile. "But not you. You aren't finished yet. SABR needs you."

"Pokeweed..."—gasp—"knows—"

"Knows what?"

His breathing stopped. His eyes closed. His mouth went slack.

"Uncle Ethan?" Hand shaking, she placed her fingers on his still-warm neck, tried three places on his neck. No pulse. She shook his shoulder again. His head lolled nervelessly.

Her breath rasped through the cave-in that constricted her throat, her chest, her heart. She rocked back and sat on her heels. Gulped air in short, shallow bursts. Unable to believe what she saw, what she felt with her own hand.

A faraway voice said, "All rooms are clear."

"What did you say?" Miranda jerked to her feet. "That can't be. *Someone* shot him. You missed something."

She stormed down the central hall, through a bedroom done up in royal blue velvet. Checked closets and under the bed and in the attached bathroom. Marched across the hall to a pink frilly little girl's room. No one there either.

She returned, stood between the kitchen and living room.

The surviving teams, hers and Leslie's, stood around the room, exchanged glances with one another and then, one by one, focused on her.

"Well, don't just stand there! Find them!"

"They're gone," Wanda said.

"Then we have to find them. I have to find them. They have to pay!"

Wanda and Leslie exchanged glances.

"We'll take Ethan back to camp," Leslie said in a strained voice.

Ian and another of Leslie's team picked up Ethan's body, carried it out. Leslie followed them without a word or a backward glance.

"You can't leave," Miranda said with more whine in her voice than she'd intended. "We have to find Irene. Stop Irene."

Wanda regarded her with pitying eyes. "You still don't understand, do you? That revenge costs too dearly. This fight is bigger than stopping your sister. We have to stop the Fellowship. To do that, we have to take back the government for good. Ethan saw it. Planned for it. He knew that when the Fellowship has no power, people like Irene won't have any power, and people like the Baxters, like me—heck, all of us—will survive. That's what we're fighting for." She paused as if waiting for Miranda to say something.

Miranda wanted to scream, "we'll only survive if Irene is dead." She wanted to say Irene *is* the Fellowship. But a small part of her knew it wasn't true.

She wanted to stand up and go with Wanda and the others. But saw it in Wanda's eyes. *They know I talked him into this. I caused this. He's dead. They. Are. All. Dead. Ethan, Beryl, Nick, and Gert. Dead because of me.*

The weight of so much blood, the weight of the mountain she ordered blown up, was too much. She couldn't move, couldn't say anything. Couldn't *do* anything except watch Wanda walk out the door.

Chapter Sixty-Three

Annabelle led Sandra and Mother single file down the winding underground tunnel on the wet and uneven stone and staggered brick of the hundred-year-old tunnel. Kept the water that rushed down the center to their left. Kicked unidentifiable clumps of gray debris off their path into the gray slime that clung to the edges of the water.

Sandra's heavy breathing worried her.

Annabelle slowed, tried to take Sandra's hand.

Sandra pulled away and hid her hands behind her back.

"Do you need to rest?"

Sandra didn't answer, kept walking.

"Don't be rude, Sandra." The tunnel's echo amplified Mother's sharp tone. "Your sister asked you a question."

"I'm fine." Though she didn't shout, Sandra's voice was distant, flat.

Annabelle wished she could see Sandra's face, but kept her light pointed at the walkway so they wouldn't slip and fall into the water.

Splashing sounds warned her before her light picked out the two-step terrace. "Steps," she said.

They descended the slick stone steps and followed a long, gentle curve still leading south-southeast without end.

"Where are you taking us?" Sandra and her echo asked.

"Somewhere safe." Annabelle suspected the tunnel would end at the bay. She planned to take them to the compound. But wouldn't share the location with anyone who might be listening in this echo chamber.

"I don't like this tunnel. It stinks, and it's dark."

"Be a big girl, Sandra." Mother's tone held edgy impatience. "We'll be out of here soon. Besides, it's dark outside too."

No answer, only the echo of their footsteps and the gushing water filled Annabelle's ears. She didn't like this tunnel either. It made her uneasy. She couldn't tell whether anyone was following them.

"I didn't tell that man anything, " Sandra said.

Annabelle stopped. Turned her flashlight onto Sandra's face. "What man?"

"The man you killed."

That funny hollow feeling emptied Annabelle's chest.

"Who Annabelle killed?" Mother asked. "You mean the men? The rebels?"

"The man with the silver in his hair."

Mother gasped. "Where did you see Eth—him? When?"

"The tent where Aunt Miranda took me. He was nice."

"Did he ask you any questions?" Mother asked in a tight whisper.

"No, he made Aunt Miranda leave me alone and asked another nice man to take me to breakfast. And he had a nice lady stay with me after that, so I wasn't alone." Her footsteps slapped the wet path. "Annabelle shouldn't have killed him. He was a nice man."

"You're confused," Mother said. "He was one of the bad men. A sinful man. It is a very good thing Annabelle was there."

"But he wasn't a bad man, Mommy. He brought me milk and cookies. And he said he was sorry that he couldn't let me come home until later."

Mother huffed. "If he really had been a good man, he would have brought you home right away, and he would have been one of us, one of the Fellowship."

"He was good to me—"

"He was evil. You'll understand better when you're a grown-up."

"Even if he was evil, the Bible says thou shall not kill. Doesn't that make it a sin to kill?"

"Enough, Sandra. Now is not the time for an intricate theological discussion you're too young to understand." Mother's voice rang with finality.

Sandra thinks I am a sinner. The fluttery feeling spilled from her chest to weaken her arms and legs. Annabelle frowned at the bright spot her flashlight made and kept walking.

The fluttering grew more intense and stuck in her throat. She couldn't stop swallowing. It hurt every time she swallowed.

They walked out of the tunnel at Leakin Park near Edmundson, where Annabelle commandeered a beat-up vehicle she found on the street, drove a circuitous route to the swamp, and walked them to the compound.

She reassigned the cabin near hers to her mother and sister. Still without sleep, Annabelle stood outside the bathhouse, her hands braced on the boardwalk railing. The strangeness of her throat and chest had dulled. Mother and Sandra were safe. That was all that mattered.

No, it's not, argued her inner angel. *We must find out what the rebels did with the Prophet.*

Annabelle agreed. *I must talk with the Prophet soon.* She resisted the urge to pace. *The rebels would not dare to kill him. The Lord would destroy them.*

He would. Would He also denounce Mother and the fake Prophet? What if He demands they be Taken?

Uneasy with her inner angel's question, Annabelle squirmed. She had many questions for the Prophet. *I must rescue him first.* That the rebels held Papa, the real Prophet, prisoner consumed her. *Once Mother is settled, I will find the Prophet.*

Freshly showered and all three of them in clean jumpsuits, Annabelle took them to the dining cabin. Mother refused to wait in the serving line. So Annabelle accompanied Sandra, who filled her tray with more than enough food for her and Mother.

Sandra stuffed the last bite of her third slice of banana bread into her mouth and, before she swallowed, mumbled, "May I go back and get another slice of banana bread?"

"No, you may not." Mother's firm voice ended the discussion. "We need a nap."

"But I'm not tired."

"You will feel different when your head hits the pillow."

After settling Mother and Sandra in their cabin, Annabelle hurried to the command center. Spread her angels across the city. When they found the Prophet, she would lead the raid to save him.

Hours later, their search had not been fruitful. She stood and stared at the Baltimore street map pinned to the wall behind her desk. Crossed off the latest block searched.

Knock. Knock. Knock.

"Come."

The door opened.

Sandra stumbled through the doorway, a hand on her shoulder.

Anna ZSP 2929 followed close behind, her hand gripping Sandra's shoulder. "This one steals food."

Sandra aimed a pouty glare at her captor. "I did not."

"There were crumbs on your face."

Annabelle stifled an amused smile. Crumbs still clung to the corners of Sandra's mouth.

Sandra's pout swung toward Annabelle. "I'm not a thief. It's free. Besides, it was on the counter. And I didn't eat the whole thing. I just had a taste."

ZSP 2929 tightened her grip on Sandra's shoulder.

Sandra winced.

"With your approval, Blessed One, I will put this sinner in holding."

The tightness in Annabelle's throat returned and swiftly spread to her chest. She couldn't breathe. *Sandra as fodder for the angels?* Words stuck in her throat.

Mother's lies taint the soul of this child. She must be Taken.

A gnawing, twisting pain made Annabelle want to grab her stomach.

An angel that is pure does not hesitate.

ZSP 2929 cleared her throat.

Annabelle held up an index finger. Took a sip of her hours old-iced tea and struggled to give the order she knew she should. But Sandra was too important to Mother to allow her to be Taken.

They both must be Taken. All that needs done is a nod.

No! Annabelle's breath came in hot gasps. *I hereby decree no angel may Take Sandra.*

You are the Chosen One. You deny your duty?

An inner angel who insists I Take my family is no angel. I denounce you and my duty if it means any of us Take my family. "ZSP 2929, she is my charge. I shall see to her punishment. That is all."

ZSP 2929's eyes flashed briefly. Then, she bowed her head slightly and left the room.

Annabelle gave Sandra a cool look that belied the jarring upheaval inside.

"I didn't do anything wrong." Ashen, hands jammed into her armpits, Sandra's tremors discredited her defiant expression.

The fluttery feeling in Annabelle's chest overtook her. She stood, crossed to Sandra, and wrapped her in an awkward hug. "Of course you didn't."

Annabelle swallowed, stunned by what she had just done. If ZSP 2929 had done such a thing, it would be insubordination, a sin punishable by crucifixion.

<h1 style="text-align:center">Chapter Sixty-Four</h1>

Miranda stepped into the Baxters' soft-blue kitchen. Mimi wasn't there, of course, but Evelyn wasn't preparing breakfast at the mint-green stove either. Neither Bernie nor ZeeZee sat on the avocado-green sofa in the living room reading the morning paper. No Thea or Gene stomped around upstairs, yelling at one another. Not a single light glowed. Not a whisper of sound other than a ticking clock and the hum of the refrigerator. A deathly hush filled the house as if it held its breath. Something was terribly wrong.

Miranda's breath came quicker. She drew her pistol, wary of a trap. No sign of the Fellowship burned into the door. No Second Sphere lurked in dark corners.

Inside each bedroom, dresser drawers and closet doors stood open and empty as if inviting new occupants to fill them.

The basement seemed unchanged. Her bedroom was untouched; even the multicolored quilt atop her bed remained. A white envelope sat on top of the quilt. She opened it.

Bernie's neat printing read, "Too dangerous for us to stay here. Suggest you find safer lodgings. Bernie." A childish P.S. scrawled at the bottom read, "I'm sorry. I'm not really mad. We know you tried to get Mimi. You are a good person. Thank you. Thea." Miranda's eyes burned. *They are gone.*

A piercing chill swept from her core to her fingers and toes. Her heart bashed against her chest. Her legs gave out. She sank onto the edge of the bed. Stared blankly at the floor. A cold, endless fog blanked all thought and memory. She didn't combat the fog. Wasn't sure she wanted to. If she came out of the fog, she'd have to face what she'd done. What she'd become.

A voice inside her head blasted through her like a foghorn. *I sent Mimi into danger. Now the whole family is in danger. They are gone because of me.*

She couldn't blame them. She'd failed them. Like she had failed Beryl and Nick and…and Ethan. Tears behind her eyelids leaked out. *Ethan was SABR. I took that away from everyone. Beryl would be so disappointed. Like Ethan was. I even disappointed my parents so much they would rather see me dead… They killed anyone who—*

Miranda sucked back a sob, horrified. *Wanda was right. I told myself I had the right to decide—that they owed me their lives…* Her breath hitched against knots in her throat and chest. *Even Sandra saw me for what I am. I am no better than they are.* She crumpled, lost in a bottomless ocean of black water.

Hours or maybe days later, a wrung-out calm settled over Miranda. Dried salt pulled at her cheeks. She ran a hand over her face without relief. Her mouth and throat were so gummed up she couldn't swallow. She sat up and swung her feet off the side of the bed. Lurched to the dresser. Her legs trembled with the effort.

The water pitcher on the dresser was full. The glass beside it was clean. "Thank you, Evelyn," Miranda said, her words more air than sound. She poured herself a glass of water. Downed it and half of the second one. But thirst was only part of the problem that made her knees rubbery.

She dragged herself up the stairs to the kitchen. There were no dry goods in the cupboards, but the refrigerator held a splash of milk at the bottom of the gallon jug and a pot of leftover stew.

The reheated savory stew practically melted in her mouth and warmed her stomach.

After she'd finished, she washed, dried, and put away the pot, then turned and leaned back against the counter. *If I don't pursue Irene, what do I do? I can't stay here. Bert was right; the Second Sphere will be back.* She glanced around at the soft-blue walls and cream-and-green tile floor. *I have no job. No money. I've alienated my friends.*

She rubbed her face. Rubbed off some dried tears. Sniffed and wrinkled her nose. Felix had gifted her a pungent addition to perspiration odor. *Definitely not fresh anymore.* She didn't remember when she'd last bathed or even changed clothes.

Miranda took a shower, put on a clean outfit, and returned to her room to gather her meager possessions. After scuttling the *Lady Angelfish*, all she had was a rucksack and three changes of clothes. She dug the rucksack out from under the bed; an unfamiliar weight tugged at it.

Reaching inside the rucksack, she closed her fingers around the smooth handle of Beryl's pistol case. Pulled it out. Sank on the edge of the bed, opened the case, and stared at the second pearl-handled pistol that rested inside. A small smile twitched on her lips. Miranda re-read the quote: "The fiery trial through which we pass will light us down in honor or dishonor, to the latest generation." Beryl had mentioned nothing about any honors she'd earned. Miranda sighed.

She packed her few belongings into her rucksack. Double-checked the dresser and closet and under the bed for anything she'd missed. The note from Bernie lay on the floor where she had dropped it. She picked it up. Thea's P.S. jumped out at her. "You are a good person."

I haven't been the person you see in me for a very long time.

At the back door, she gave the kitchen a last goodbye glance. She'd never see the Baxters again, but she vowed she'd change. For Thea. To be the person Thea saw in her. *Starting now. Starting with an apology to Wanda and Leslie and the others. Even if they can never forgive me.* Miranda closed the door behind her and headed out.

Chapter Sixty-Five

T he ceiling fans stirred the damp swamp air but did not cool Irene or the room. Mostly, it kept the disgusting rotten-egg stink swirling around them. Add to that Annabelle's insistence that she remain in this spartan, insect-infested place, and Irene struggled to keep her tone calm. "I must go to DC." *When I announce the rebels killed Felix and no one can find a counselor alive, the people will have no choice but to accept me as Prophet.*

In the glass cage she called her office, Annabelle continued reading reports without even a glance acknowledging Irene's presence.

"Did you hear what I said?" *I'll bet if I told her I am the First Apostle, I'd get her attention.*

"You know it's not safe right now." Annabelle turned a page.

Especially for the First Apostle. A muscle in Irene's jaw knotted. *Perhaps now isn't the time to tell her. Maybe a different approach...* "Thanks to you and your angels, the rebels are withdrawing from the city in record numbers. Killing Ethan broke them. Besides, you have an angel watching over me. She can come with me and protect me while I appear before the Council." *And make them quake in fear.* "If you think that's not enough, send two. Surely two angels can protect me." *Definitely two.*

"It will have to wait." Annabelle didn't look the least bit perturbed, though she had disrespected her mother.

Irene tightened her fists. *I do not take orders. I, the Prophet-to-be, give them.*

On the other side of the glass, an angel rose from her desk to mark the map on the wall. Beyond her, another Azrael listened intently to the radio.

They outnumber me three to one. She forced her lips to curl into a motherly smile.

"Blessed One."

Startled, Irene managed not to yelp and jump.

An angel came from behind and stepped closer to Annabelle without actually shoving Irene aside.

Annabelle raised and cocked her head. "You have finished questioning the prisoner?"

Irene pressed her tongue against the back of her lower teeth.

"What have you learned?" Annabelle asked.

The angel indicated Irene with a lift of her chin, not bothering to look at Irene. "Are we to speak of this in front of her?"

"Mother—our Lady—understands we are doing the Lord's work. Speak."

"The prisoner continues to insist that our Prophet was dead when he and the others arrived at the warehouse."

Irene's throat went desert dry. "Of course he would lie." Her voice rasped. She cleared her throat.

Annabelle cocked her head, finally made eye contact with a look that pierced Irene.

Her heart did little flip-flops in her chest, and the muscles in both jaws twitched. "It's a lie." Irene's voice was steady and firm.

The angel's eyes were hard. "He insists despite our most strenuous interrogation. He claims the camera he carried has pictures of the dead Prophet."

"I would know if the Prophet—my husband—was dead." Unfaltering. "Not even the rebels would kill the Prophet. Felix simply cannot be dead. The prisoner must be delirious."

"He is the one who attempted to retrieve the dead."

Irene spread her hands, palms up. "There you go. He's confused Fake Felix with the real one. Instead of questioning this confused person, find and free our Prophet."

"Mother!"

Irene sucked in a sharp breath at Annabelle's sharp tone. She glanced at her daughter's alarmed expression. *What did I do?* "I'm sorry, dear. I am overcome with worry about my dear husband, your father. Perhaps if I question the prisoner…"

The angel kept her focus on Annabelle. "It is not for the Lady to question prisoners. That is an Azrael's duty as ordained by our Lord through *our* Prophet."

Irene turned to Annabelle. "Then, *you* must question him again. Do not spare him pain. We must know where they took your father."

"Clearly this…human…does not understand the Blessed One's duties are to inform and guide her angel."

The Azrael's tone sent spidery shivers through Irene. She fought to keep still. *I must make them find Felix's body and blame the rebels for killing him. Then I can become the Prophet, and no one will dare question me.* She raised an eyebrow directed at the angel. "Surely, you understand the Blessed One's duty is first to our Lord and second to our Prophet's safety."

"The prisoner will not survive another round of…questioning," the angel said with even more of an edge in her voice.

Annabelle stood. "Thank you, Lieutenant. Replenish yourself. I will send for you shortly."

The angel stiffened, whirled, and strode out of the office, out of the control center.

Annabelle turned, threw an intense look at Irene. "Of course you may interview the prisoner, Mother. But we must allow the prisoner to consider what we might do next. And you need rest. You have been under a great strain. You must be strong to question him."

Irene knew a tone of dismissal when she heard it. She dipped her head. "Yes. Of course. I could use a brief rest." She left the control center. *I am the Prophet-to-be. I cannot cower before the Azrael. Not even Annabelle.*

Shaking inside, she controlled herself. Made it appear she strolled down the boardwalk, dignified despite the stench. *Ethan is dead. Miranda should be too. Surely the Azrael can find them and destroy all the rebels now. Them and Miranda. Why am I unable to convince Annabelle? Perhaps Annabelle was right. I'm tired. A little rest—* She opened the door to her cabin.

Sandra whirled toward her, shame-faced. The cobalt-blue bottle of belladonna in her hands. Behind her, the dresser drawer Irene had hidden it in stood open.

A bolt of electricity jolted the breath out of Irene. Her pulse spiked to I'm-going-to-pass-out speed. Froze her momentarily. She shook it off. Surged forward. Snatched the bottle away. Tucked it in her bra. "What are you doing going through my things?"

"I was looking for—"

"I don't care what you were looking for, young lady. You know better. You never get into my things without my express permission." Irene slammed the drawer shut.

"I'm not a baby anymore." Tears welled in Sandra's eyes. "I can read. I know it's poison. I wouldn't have tasted it."

Irene's throat knotted. *No one was supposed to see that bottle. Ever. If Ethan hadn't shown up when he did, Fake Felix would have drunk the rest of it in his tea. Instead, constantly shadowed* by Annabelle or her Azrael, I haven't had the chance to throw the bottle away.

Irene licked her lips with an extraordinarily dry tongue.

Sandra didn't move, but her expression had changed from caught-red-handed to curious.

Irene frantically considered and tossed aside explanation after explanation. Then it came to her. "I'm sorry I got upset." She put an arm around Sandra. Pulled her toward the bed.

She sat and patted the bed beside her.

Sandra sat too.

"When I opened the door and saw you with it, I was terrified you had tasted it. It *is* poisonous if you take too much. I know exactly how much to take, so it helps me sleep better."

"Why do you need medicine to sleep?"

This is going to work. Irene released her pent-up breath. Patted her daughter's hand. "Sometimes adults have too many things to think about. You'll understand these things when you get older." *I need to distract her.* "Mommy needs to rest for a bit. Why don't you see if our guardian angel will take you to the canteen for a snack?"

Sandra's eyes lit up. "But it's almost lunchtime."

"That's okay." Irene pretended she hadn't noticed Sandra's suspicious tone. "We've both had a really hard couple of days. Go on." She shoved Sandra off the bed. "You deserve an extra snack."

"Okay." Sandra hurried out the door.

Irene listened to Sandra's bouncy steps click across the boardwalk until they faded out of hearing. She peeked out the door and, seeing no one, slipped out to the railing at the water's edge. Did a slow, casual glance around, then took the bottle out of her bra and dropped it into the murky water. When it sank out of sight, she released a sigh of relief.

"Mother?"

Irene slapped her hand to her chest. Spun toward her daughter. *Did she see me? How does she—all of them—creep across this creaky boardwalk so silently?*

"Why aren't you resting? And where is your guardian?"

"Why—um, I—needed a breath of air. As for my guardian, Sandra was starving, so I sent them to find something to tide the girl over until lunch."

"It's just as well we are alone." Annabelle came to Irene's side. She held a photograph out for Irene to see. "Explain."

Slightly out of focus, the photograph showed Felix's bloated body on his hospital bed. Irene's knees weakened. She put icy fingers to her lips, her breath shortened, her pulse filled her ears. *Don't lose it. Have to play this right.* "Is that? No, no, no, that can't be!" She allowed her knees to buckle. Her bottom hit the boardwalk with a painful thwack.

"Mother!" Annabelle kneeled beside her. Whispered something into her mic. "Can you stand?"

Irene turned tear-filled eyes on her daughter. Grateful she'd learned tears were weapons early in life. "They killed him. Why would they kill him?"

"Let me help you to your room." Annabelle's voice sounded strange. She put an arm under Irene's and helped her to her feet.

Irene took a shaky step. *Heh. At least I don't have to fake the shakiness.*

Two other angels appeared; they took over for Annabelle. Got Irene onto her bed inside the cabin.

Irene pretended to be consumed with grief while watching and listening to them. Annabelle was more uncertain than Irene remembered her being since her first moments after Felix raised her from the dead.

It took longer than Irene thought necessary, but eventually Annabelle decided the Council needed to be informed immediately. Irene dabbed at her eyes. "I should do that. As the Prophet's Lady, as Felix's"—she made her voice crack—"widow, it's my duty. Oh!" She gulped. Put a hand to her heart. "The Prophet is dead. That makes me...oh. This can't be happening."

"Mother?" Annabelle peered at her. "It makes you what?"

Irene feigned a pained look. "Things happened so fast...I didn't have time to tell you...and it's been one thing after another..." She squared her shoulders and looked Annabelle in the eye. "The Council made me First Apostle last evening."

Annabelle's mouth dropped open. "First Apostle? Before Papa died?" Annabelle dipped her head and then jerked it back up. "That means you'll be—"

"The new Prophet," Irene said softly, adding a little sorrowful squeak to her voice. "It was just to help Felix until he was better." Irene smiled sadly. "I didn't ask for this. But," she scooted off the bed. "It is even more important that I fulfill my duties. Let me make myself presentable, and then we shall go."

Annabelle deferred to her and shooed the other two angels out of the cabin ahead of her.

Irene sucked in a big breath. Steadied herself. *From here on out, it will be easier.*

Chapter Sixty-Six

Lashing rain and a milky mist scattered the beam of Miranda's flashlight and blurred her view of the bent branches that marked her trail through Cedarville State Forest. The saturated earth clutched at one shoe. She tugged it free and then had to work her other shoe free of the mud. She paused and examined another bent branch. A cold, brown-green tide of mud seeped through her shoe leather. It was harder to yank her foot free, to take the next step.

Camp Tango wasn't really a camp, just a tarp shelter, buried in leaves against a tree near Zekiah Swamp Run. A place where SABR officers would regroup in the morning and plan their next steps. Pokeweed had marked the path with bent branches. Branches tossed by wind and rain. She studied a bent branch. The break was on the right side. She turned left.

Cold water trickled off her sodden headscarf and slithered down her back. Her teeth chattered so violently her jaw throbbed. But the deeper ache inside drove her ever forward. She had to reach Pokeweed before anyone else did. Ethan said to ask him. She had to ask, which meant she had to tell Pokeweed she had led Ethan to his death.

Miranda's foot slid. She teetered off-balance, nearly fell into the narrow stream. *Found you. So far, so good.* She followed the stream until it widened and turned in a more southerly direction. Measured off twenty-five paces into the trees and searched for Pokeweed's camp in earnest. Murky shadows and mounds of fallen hardwood leaves slowed her pace.

She swept her flashlight over another pile of leaves. The light blinked out. She shook it. A ghost of light came on, flickered, and died. Plunged her into a gloom made sickly yellow by predawn light.

She shook the flashlight again. Nothing happened. "Damn it. The batteries aren't that old." She tucked the flashlight in her coat pocket and forged ahead. Branches clawed at her oilcloth coat.

A brief orange flicker caught her eye and vanished before she could focus on it. She eased forward, caught another orange burst that extinguished as quickly as it had appeared. It could be fatigue or the rain playing tricks on her, or it was Pokeweed's camp. Only one way to know for sure. She tried to call out. Rain filled her throat. Her shout was barely louder than the pounding of the rain.

She slogged another four steps. The orange light pulsed. She put two fingers to her lips—the way Beryl had taught her—and whistled the pattern of long and short notes Pokeweed would recognize as from a friendly.

A whistle came out of the fog, repeating the pattern.

Relief sluiced over her.

As if the rain had opened like a curtain, orange light formed a rough triangle. It wasn't as far away as it had seemed.

She ducked her head. Entered the shelter. A blanket of warmer air wrapped around her. She took off her headscarf, swiped at the rainwater dripping from her hair into her eyes.

"Miranda?" Pokeweed's expression matched his puzzled tone. "What are you doing out here at this hour? We don't meet for another couple of hours." He crawled a couple of feet deeper into the hut and sat cross-legged by a small fire of twigs burning inside a coffee can that sat in the center of a beat-up pail surrounded by packed dirt.

"I had to—there's something you need to know before then." Unable to look at him, she raised her chin, studied the shelter. The tarp overhead was taut; the space underneath not quite tall enough for her to stand upright.

"Okay. I'm listening."

Miranda darted a glance at Pokeweed. Took a deep breath. Swallowed the lump in her throat, which was so much drier than her clothes and skin. Blurted, "Monkshood died early this morning."

Pokeweed didn't react. His gaze focused somewhere past the walls of the shelter.

She waited respectfully. And waited.

The flicker of light from the fire dimmed, leaving only glowing coals.

"Do you want to know how he died?" She asked softly, almost in a whisper.

"What?" Pokeweed focused on her. "Oh. No, I don't need to know how he died. I've seen how people die in this war." He cocked his head. "Were you with him?"

She had no more tears to shed, but the knot of pain deep inside twisted tighter. Broken, she couldn't speak. She jerked her head in a series of tiny nods.

"Good," he said. "He was with someone he loved deeply."

Breathing hurt. She tried to focus on why she had come to Pokeweed. "Before he died, Monkshood told me to come to you. He didn't"—a shaky breath in—"couldn't say more." She didn't think the lump in her throat would ever go away. "Do you know why he said that?"

Pokeweed's lips curved slightly. "He had me hold a letter for you, in case…"

Ice flooded her veins with a bone-deep chill. She sucked in air through a throat so tight a collapsed drinking straw would seem like a firehose. *Uncle Ethan left me his in-case letter?*

Pokeweed pulled a rucksack out from the back of the hut, dug around in it. "Here it is." He held out a thick white envelope, her name written on it in Ethan's scrawl.

She reached out, took it with a shaky hand.

Pokeweed crawled toward the door.

"Where are you going?"

"Outside—to give you some privacy."

She wanted to say, "You don't need to get soaked," but could only squeeze out, "Don't."

Pokeweed quirked an eyebrow, then said, "Okay," and tended the fire.

Barely able to breathe, she slid her finger under the flap and opened the envelope. Pulled out the handwritten pages. Ethan's handwriting. Her hands shook. Her vision blurred. She blinked and sucked air until she could read what he'd written.

If you're reading this letter, I didn't make it back from a mission. I'm sorry I had to leave you. There's so much I want you to know. I had hoped I'd have the time.

I was so angry that Beryl had gotten herself killed. That I had gotten her killed. That this damn resistance took everything and everyone from me. Angry that I didn't figure out what was important before it was too late.

Miranda sat frozen to the ground. Not hearing. Not feeling. Re-read the phrase 'I was so angry' over and over and over again. *How could I not know he felt to blame? He had to know it was my fault…that's probably what he's about to say.* Hands shaking, she continued reading.

Our cause was and is important, but shouldn't always be the most important thing. War is hell and leaves scars on everyone, no matter what side they're on. Some of those scars may never completely heal. I have some scars. I inflicted more.

I hope I was able to counter some of the wrongs I've done by doing the right thing. Guess I won't know.

I trust you will understand. That you can put aside your anger and grief and work with Pokeweed. I've listed the pieces that are in place for you, Miranda. But Pokeweed needs your help. You are better known and more admired among our soldiers than you know. They will look to you for leadership.

My friends in the north woods, and my friends where the wattle blooms, especially my friend sitting in the lavender fields, will all recognize the captain of the Lady Angelfish. Pokeweed will explain. He knows the plan. Trust him. But you will have to steer the ship, lead and inspire our people to victory over the Fellowship.

Miranda's breath snagged in her throat. *He can't mean that.* She read the section about her leading SABR again. Put a hand to her mouth. Tried to catch her breath. But short and shallow was all she could do. On the third reading of the paragraph about how she needed to steer the ship, she finished the letter.

I pray that you won't spend your whole life like I did, angry and fighting. Believe in yourself. Love yourself. You owe it to yourself. Signed, your loving uncle, Ethan.

Owe myself? She covered her face with her hands, drew them down to cover her mouth. *No, Uncle Ethan. I owe you. And Beryl. And Nick.*

"Are you all right? Miranda?" Louder. "Miranda?"

Does he know what Uncle Ethan wrote? That it was about how badly I failed him? She forced herself to look Pokeweed in the eye. "I'm fine." Her voice cracked. She coughed and cleared her throat. "I'm fine." *That sounded better.* "Did you read this?"

"God, no. I would never. It was his private message to you."

"Thank you."

"Of course." Pokeweed studied her as if weighing something on his mind. "Ethan left me instructions too. In them he said he'd asked you to lead SABR, but he wasn't certain you would." He paused.

Miranda stifled her impulse to shout I am no leader.

"You know…" Pokeweed chose sticks from a pile near the door. Snapped them into smaller pieces and fed the coffee-can fire. "You can decide to do this and change your mind if it's not for you." He shrugged. "No one will think less of you. Least of all your uncle, or me."

She ran a hand through her still-wet hair plastered to her scalp. "I think my uncle had an inflated opinion of how important I am to SABR."

A grin spread across Pokeweed's face. "I think you have no idea how much everyone admires your courage. You left a high society life, defied your parents, shared the worst moments of your life with the world for a greater good. Miranda, you are an incredibly strong woman. They will follow you willingly if you let them."

Tongues of orange and red flames flickered out of the coffee can.

Miranda drew her knees up, rested her arms on them, then her chin on her arms. Her thoughts flickered as unevenly as the flames. *Thea, Uncle Ethan, and Pokeweed. How can they still believe in me?*

How can I refuse Uncle Ethan's last request? I owe him…

And I owe it to myself. I swore I'd quit fighting him. Quit arguing with everyone. Still…

"Why don't you believe me?" Pokeweed asked softly. "Monks-hood told me you captained a boat, developed an entire network of boats, and rescued hundreds of people."

And I scuttled my boat at the first sign of trouble. She gave a laugh she hoped was dismissive. "I had lots of help."

"You'll have lots of help leading SABR too. But don't let me pressure you," he said. "It's a big responsibility." He crawled to the door again.

"Wait. Where are you going?"

Pokeweed looked over his shoulder at her. "Sun's up, and it stopped raining a while ago. I want to make sure the storm didn't change the trail markings. I'll be back in fifteen, twenty minutes." He lifted the flap that was his makeshift door, turned back to her again. "It'll give you time to think. Make your decision. Whatever you decide, lead or not, it'll be the right choice." And he was gone.

She stared after him. Wondered how he could think that whatever she decided would be the right choice when she'd made so many wrong ones.

The fire sputtered.

She fed it more sticks. Uncle Ethan and Pokeweed were wrong about her. She hadn't meant to build a freedom waterway. It just sort of happened. The flames steadied, and she picked up Uncle Ethan's chronicle of SABR.

The more she read, the more she realized that from the beginning Uncle Ethan had known that killing the Prophet or even members of the Council wouldn't stop the Fellowship but would strengthen it by making their dead leaders martyrs. *If I had killed Irene, they might have turned her into a martyr.*

Stunned, Miranda re-read her uncle's letter and what he'd accomplished with a new perspective. Understood he'd acted much like a boat's captain, thinking ahead, planning for changes. She'd planned for water levels and currents. He'd planned for politics and popular opinion and so much more.

By the time Pokeweed returned, she was ready to talk.

He shocked her with news about Irene becoming the First Apostle and the upcoming Youth Spiritual Aptitude and Assignment Act.

She shocked him with the news that the Prophet Felix was dead.

He told her his real name was Oliver.

They planned how to tell the team about Ethan and all the rest.

FOUR HOURS LATER, MIRANDA STOOD BESIDE OLIVER IN THE CENTER OF a clearing that barely fit the definition. Six feet wide and a little less than six feet long, it was clear of trees but filled with knee-high grasses and waist-high saplings reaching for the weak autumn sunlight. The air, still damp from the night's rain, held the chill of autumn and did nothing to warm her fingers or stiffen the shakiness of her legs. She felt like an over-saturated sponge. Still trying to absorb everything she'd read. Everything Oliver had told her.

People trickled in, gathered around them.

She recognized some faces turned toward her. Leslie and Wanda, and a lieutenant she'd seen before but whose name she didn't remember. More lieutenants crowded behind them.

All eyes were on her. Part of her wanted to look away, wanted to run away, waited for someone to ask what the hell she thought she was doing. But part of her remembered how much she owed Uncle Ethan. So she stayed.

"You're alive? Miranda! You're alive!"

"David?"

David burst through the crowd. He slammed into her, wrapped his arms around her, and lifted her from the ground. "Leslie and Wanda last saw you in the warehouse and didn't know for sure. I'm so glad to see you."

Breath crushed out of her and her feet dangling off the ground, she couldn't speak, and not just because he hugged her so tight. So many questions she wanted to ask. Then, a hand squeezed hers.

Leslie laughed, released her hand. "David, put her down. Let her breathe."

"Sorry." David lowered her until her feet hit the ground, then released her. "I'm just so damned relieved."

"Glad to see you too." She gave him a tremulous smile.

Wanda stood nearby. She raised two fingers to her forehead, made a small salute, mouthed the word, "Captain."

Leslie gave Wanda a nod and saluted Miranda as well. So did David.

Miranda stood quietly. Shock reverberated inside. *Oliver was right. I was the captain. No one had questioned it. Not them. Not Beryl. Not even me. I captained my boat, my crew, and the whole waterway rescue system.*

Oliver greeted the gathering. Acknowledged the rumor they'd all heard. Monkshood was dead. Then he introduced Leslie.

She turned slightly to address everyone. "The team buried

Monkshood in Leakin Park. The one place the Fellowship will never look for him, never find him, and never desecrate his memory or his body."

"In remembrance," Oliver said solemnly, "let's observe a moment of silence."

Some bowed their heads; others gazed upward as if they could see Uncle Ethan somewhere in the clouds.

A few moments later, Miranda broke the silence. "Thank you. Monkshood was a strong and courageous leader. He will be missed." Her voice gave out.

Oliver spoke up as if they'd planned it this way. "He's gone on to a place of eternal peace."

She looked out over the leaders standing in front of her. Leaders, whose silence and rapt attention focused on her. She looked pointedly at Oliver.

"Monkshood knew the dangers of this fight firsthand," he continued. "So he left Miranda and me instructions for a future without him."

"In his letters," she said. "Monkshood shared plans he's been working on since before SABR existed. He recruited friends and friends of friends back then. Over time, he found supporters in both houses of Congress, in the justice system, and in the military—"

"We need a whole fucking army, not some *friends*," a voice called out.

Miranda shot a glance at Oliver. He didn't look at her, so she continued, "These friends have given SABR money—"

"It takes a shitload of money to feed an army and to buy a ton of bullets," an unfamiliar voice shouted.

"We need names!" a fretful voice demanded.

Miranda found the owner of the voice. It belonged to a young man with a dusting of peach fuzz on his chin. "A few of us know their names, but for obvious reasons we can't share them."

"Without names, how do we know they aren't Fellowship infiltrators?" a man asked, his paranoia showing. "Maybe they're setting a trap for us."

"So what if they have?" Wanda asked with a smirk. "We'll just send some of them to hell ahead of us."

Overlapping shouts erupted. "Maybe we are—"

Oliver raised his hand, motioned stop.

"A trap could kill us all," a voice from the back said.

Oliver raised both hands. Motioned for them to stop more emphatically.

But it was too late; the lieutenants, including Leslie and David and Wanda, had broken into small arguing groups.

Miranda waited for Oliver to raise his voice or something.

The arguments got louder.

Miranda put two fingers to her lips and gave a sharp whistle.

Everyone fell silent.

"Look"—Miranda couldn't keep her irritation out of her voice—"in sixteen days, the Fellowship's Youth Spiritual Aptitude and Assignment Act will go into effect. If you don't want them deciding which twelve-year-old goes to Fellowship school and which goes to a workhouse, listen up."

She looked straight ahead. Waited for Oliver to continue. Scanned the twenty-some faces of the lieutenants whose expectant looks rested on her. She shot a glance at Oliver.

He raised an eyebrow in a you-can-do-this expression. "You've got their attention, Captain."

She pressed her tongue against the back of her teeth. *Okay. You want to play it that way.* "No one person could take Monkshood's place. I know why he trusted Oliver. I don't know why he trusted me. I've made a lot of mistakes. Especially in recent months." She let her gaze linger on Leslie for a few seconds, then Wanda, and Ian, and David. "I made those mistakes because I acted alone. But leadership isn't about being perfect—it's about learning from failure. Uncle—sorry, Monkshood—believed I could learn from my mistakes, my failures. He believed I could help lead you into this battle." She rubbed her throat, but the lump there didn't move. "I'll understand if you don't believe I've changed. And if you want to choose someone else in my place, now is the time to voice your objections." She swept her gaze across the faces of those gathered around her.

There was an expectant silence, and the lieutenants and her friends glanced at one another.

"Sounds like you're afraid you'll make more mistakes," Leslie said in a kind voice. "Like leading us wasn't your first choice. Good. The best leaders are usually the ones who don't want the job."

The tall lieutenant standing next to Leslie nodded.

Another one said, "Here, here."

More voices added, "Right."

"You said it."

Others nodded their heads. No one objected.

Miranda's mouth fell open. *Damn. Well, if they all believe in me, I'd better prove I'm worth their faith.* She squared her shoulders and made eye contact with as many of them as she could. "Each of us has kin who's twelve or knows a twelve-year-old, you're on edge, and to lose Monkshood on top of that—it's beyond hard. I don't mind telling you I'm scared, but Monkshood was a brilliant strategist. Unfortunately, he didn't share very well.

"As the new leaders of SABR, Oliver and I decided to share what we could with you." She nodded to Oliver.

"For those of you concerned about money," he began, "let's just say the people who have invested in us have very deep pockets."

"And in case you think our friends can't be as invested in our cause as you are," Miranda added, "I want to remind you that a certain governor and his family barely escaped a fire-bombing last month."

Murmurs ripped through the lieutenants.

"Yes, you can guess who that was. He secretly sent his family to Canada to escape future attempts by the Fellowship and its supporters."

"We face four moving parts," Oliver said and counted on his fingers. "Political, military, legal, and spiritual. We hit all four simultaneously, or the Fellowship adapts and erases us forever."

"We have supporters in the Court—" Miranda's voice cracked. She touched her lips, cleared her throat. "Forgive me. There are justices who've waited more than twenty years for this moment, ready to right our laws and restore the Constitution."

Cheers startled her silent. Then she realized they were cheering the taking back of the government. She held up a hand. Amazingly, they settled down.

Oliver gave her a crooked smile, then said, "Believe us. We have influential public figures, people at every level, from every state, that will help us pull this off." He eyed two of the men in the group. "Plus, we have help from two friendly countries."

Miranda had suspected Ethan's frequent trips to New York and Texas meant he had recruited some powerful allies there, so Rockefeller and Senator Lyndon B. Johnson hadn't surprised her. Now she remembered Ethan's letter had referenced the wattle, the north woods, and lavender fields. That had to mean Australia, Canada, and England would supply weapons or armed forces or both.

"All these people," Miranda said, her voice cutting through the growing murmurs of the surrounding lieutenants, "governors, justices, congressmen, and foreign allies—they are betting everything—including their lives—on SABR." She looked around the circle of faces. "On all of us here, now."

The weight of her own words settled on her in a familiar way. It was the same feeling she'd had when boat captains from three different states started following her lead without her asking them to. People believing in her before she believed in herself.

"If they have that much faith in us," she continued, "maybe we should start acting like we deserve it." *I'm trying to, Uncle Ethan.*

"I will—we will—miss Monkshood," Oliver said. "But he left us everything we need." Oliver gave Miranda an encouraging nod.

"Oliver and I appreciate your confidence," she said in a somber voice. "I want to remind you, Monkshood did not want SABR to become an involuntary enlistment. If you are tired of fighting or are needed at home or simply no longer agree with our goals, you're free to leave. Go home. Be with your loved ones. But leave now. Before we talk about our next steps."

"No one here is going anywhere," the tallest lieutenant said. "Tell us what you want us to do."

Miranda smiled, wondering how many of them would survive the next few weeks. Tried not to think about how many wouldn't. "Oliver's going to hand you an envelope with your name on it. These are your assignments. It is imperative that you not discuss your assignment with anyone other than your own team. Your safety and the safety of all our teams depend on your silence. Memorize them and return them in the envelope to Oliver or me. We will destroy them."

Oliver moved through the group of men and women, handed each of them an envelope with their name on it.

A few minutes later, David was the first to hand her his envelope.

She tried to read his expression.

He flashed her a smile, but the haunted look in his eyes weighed on her like an anchor dragging her soul to the bottom of the ocean. She wanted to hug him, to make him promise he'd survive. She knew that was a promise none of them could make, but she had to make one, anyway. "In case we're too busy to meet before, let's promise to meet up at Virgil's Grocery on President George Washington's Birthday, February twenty-first. Deal?"

His smile brightened a little. He nodded and disappeared into the crush of the others waiting to return their envelopes.

Whether they handed their envelope off right away or took a while to memorize the contents, gave the envelope to her or to Oliver, each of them had that weariness and fear in their eyes.

Miranda made Wanda, Leslie, Ian, and Oliver promise to meet in March as well. Each of them reflected a silent hope of being there despite knowing the odds against them.

After everyone else had left, she and Oliver burned the letters to ashes, smothered the fire, took down the tarp, and swept away evidence it had ever been there.

Oliver shrugged his rucksack on, shook her hand, and said, "See you soon."

She hoped she would.

Chapter Sixty-Seven

Annabelle threaded her way past the vacant jungle gym, swings, and slides into the trees. Between Mother, Sandra, and the angels, Annabelle hadn't had a minute to herself since they ordained Mother the First Apostle. No thinking time for two and a half weeks made Annabelle willing to take a risk outside of the Azrael campus.

Even though it was early afternoon, Annabelle hid in the shade of a cluster of tall pine trees nearer the playground than the city street. The temperature was shirtsleeve comfortable, and the air filled with the fresh scent of pine. She settled down cross-legged in a nest of fallen needles.

Mother performed three miracles. The Council decided she is Chosen. Anointed her First Apostle. Then Mother said the counselors were evil. Now everyone is dead. The Prophet, the fake, and all the counselors. And Mother will become the Prophetess.

Annabelle rubbed her upper lip. The dampness there surprised her. She stared at her hand. Both hands. Dampness on both. She swiped her palms across her pants. It had always been her inner angel who guided her. But she no longer heard her inner angel's voice or felt her presence. Not even to answer the questions that haunted Annabelle. *Is the fluttery feeling I get a sign I've fallen from Grace? How could an evil Council rightly determine Mother is worthy?*

Annabelle put her hands together and prayed for guidance.

Finally whispered, "Amen." Looked up at the clear blue sky. No shafts of radiance. No voice from within or above.

She prayed a prayer of supplication, then listened to the pines sighing in the wind in case the Lord would speak through them.

Waiting, listening, and smelling the pines eased her troubled spirit. She felt more at peace than she had for weeks.

The faint sound of a soft, bubbly giggle disturbed Annabelle's peace.

The giggly little girl's voice grew nearer and nearer.

Annabelle peered between pine boughs.

The giggle came from a girl with sandy brown pigtails. She held the hand of a woman younger than Mother. The woman carried a small woven basket on her other arm.

A few yards from the cluster of trees that hid Annabelle, the woman took a red checkered blanket, arranged it on the ground.

"We eat first, then I can play. Right, Mommy?"

"Yes, darling." Mommy lifted the lid of the basket, pulled out two plates, a thermos, and a pair of drinking glasses. She unwrapped waxed paper and placed fried chicken and carrot sticks, thick slices of homemade bread, and an apple on each of their plates.

The aroma of the fried chicken made Annabelle's stomach twitch and growl. She considered moving away, but she was confident she had hidden well.

With full plates and drink glasses before them, Mommy and the child shared a brief prayer. The child ate with gusto, barely pausing long enough for her mother to wipe her hands before she raced to the swings.

Keeping an eye on the two humans, Annabelle refocused on her prayers. Every once in a while, a child's laugh or shout of "higher" would distract her. But no matter how fervent her prayers, she received no clear answer.

Movement a few yards away alerted her.

Mommy bent, picked the blanket up off the ground. Shook it out, folded it, and placed it in the basket. Then she turned, cupped her hands around her mouth, and shouted, "Patty, it's time to go."

The girl in pigtails stopped her swing and swiveled toward the woman.

"Come on, Patty."

Patty hopped off the swing and ran toward Mommy, arms spread wide.

Annabelle didn't understand. *Did not Mommy teach Patty that exposing herself like that is dangerous?*

Mommy kneeled, arms open until the child arrived and they wrapped their arms around one another. "Mommy, can't we stay for a while?"

Mommy put her hands gently on each side of Patty's face and, smiling broadly, rubbed the tip of her nose against the tip of Patty's nose. "We've already been here a while, Pumpkin."

"But you haven't swinged on the swings with me yet."

Mommy stood and picked up her basket.

"Please?" Little Patty wheedled.

Annabelle shook her head. If she had dared to plead for what she wanted, she would have received a backhanded slap.

Mommy put her basket down and gave her daughter a stern look. "Do you want me to get in trouble?"

Patty's face fell. She looked down at the ground. "No."

"I'm gonna—" Mommy said in a mischievous tone, "—beat you to the swings!"

Patty's face lit up. "You cheater!" Laughing, she chased Mommy to the swing set. But Mommy got there first and hopped on a swing. Patty tried to push her but could only move the swing a short distance. Mommy said something to her, and Patty jumped up and down, then crawled into her mother's lap, and Mommy walked the swing way back, then lifted her feet off the ground. She pumped and pumped, urging the swing higher and higher until they both squealed.

Annabelle's mouth fell open, and the flutter in her chest returned forcefully. *Mother had never ever done anything like that with me or Sandra.*

Mommy slowed the swing, and Patty hopped off her mother's lap. Then Mommy gathered Patty in her arms and showered the little girl's face with kisses, sending the girl into fits of giggles. "Darling, we've got to go now. I'm going to be late."

Patty pouted. "I don't want you to go."

Mommy hugged Patty and said, "Sometimes Mommies have to do Mommy things." She bopped the tip of Patty's nose with her finger. "Besides, you love being with Grandma."

"I love being with Grandma this much." Patty held her hands shoulder-width apart. "But I love being with you this much." She spread her hands far apart.

"It's only for two hours, darling. You'll have lots of fun, and I'll be back before you know it."

Patty gave an enormous sigh and hugged Mommy. "You'll hurry back?"

"Of course, darling."

Mommy retrieved her basket, and hand in hand, the two of them skipped out of the park.

Annabelle watched from the trees. Deep inside her, the flutter morphed into a tingle. Kind of like the tingle that came right before the energy of the Taken one lifted her. *How could that be?*

Mother had never taken her and Sandra to a park. Never once played with them. A kiss on the forehead had to be earned by good behavior. Yet Mommy gave Patty kisses and hugs freely. Joyfully. That had renewed Annabelle's fluttery feeling. Made Annabelle realize she'd gotten flutters with Sandra but not Mother. Never Mother.

Mommy even hugged and kissed Patty when the girl did punishable things.

Punishable things like being late. Annabelle checked her wristwatch. She gasped. The tingle was gone. Its absence left an overwhelming emptiness. But it was almost time for the meeting with Mother.

Annabelle sighed. Forced herself to move. *I'll have to hurry to get to the compound on time.*

Chapter Sixty-Eight

Miranda shuffled down 27th Street Northwest, part of a river of the District's poorest people. Sad, worn-out people—disposable in the eyes of the Fellowship. After a sleepless night, it wasn't difficult for her to look wornout too. A gust of icy wind cut through her wool coat. She grabbed the brim of her straw hat. Her other hand held down the skirt of her loose-fitting green-and-white polka-dot housedress.

She stopped at a narrow alleyway crowded with hand-built, run-down houses that sat between the broken-down apartment buildings and the alley. Garbage overflowed trashcans. White laundry hung on clotheslines the way rich people strung their patios with fancy lights. A quiet voice inside warned her: today will not end well. Her throat tightened, and a new chill ran down her back. She ignored the voice and walked down the alley.

Midway down the block, she climbed wobbly wooden steps to the second floor of a beat-up apartment building. Entered a tiny apartment.

A black woman sat at a card table, her drinking glass half-full of the brown water that passed for coffee among the occupants of this so-called "tough" neighborhood. Her brief, disinterested look was a reminder of what Miranda was fighting for.

She hurried through the room crowded with its tiny kitchenette, table, and double bed. Stopped at the doorless entry closet filled with raggedy clothes and two winter coats. Reached through the coats to the closet's back wall and knocked a double knock four times.

A portion of the wall popped open. The young man on the other side of the wall waited for her to enter, then pulled the door closed with a rope rigged so it also slid the coats back into place.

She walked through his apartment to the inside corner of a bedroom painted with colorful graffiti. Rapped her knuckles against the wall. *Knock knock knock.* Pause. *Knock. Pause. Knock knock.*

The reply came. *Knock.* Pause. *Knock knock.* Pause *Knock.* All clear.

She pushed open the door and entered SABR's ham shack and command center. An assortment of dining tables stood against the walls in an L-shape. A jumble of homemade and purchased ham radio equipment, speaker cones, and wires lined the back half of each table. The two transmitters sat at opposite ends of the table. Six people stood at attention in a civilian way along the one wall without tables shoved up against it.

Pinned high on the fourth wall, a map with colored push-pins showed the location of each of the teams. A petite older woman, the plotter, stood in front of the map where she would track SABR team movements. She saluted Miranda.

Oliver rose from his chair and saluted too. "Welcome, Captain." He gestured to the chair he'd vacated, the one in front of the transmitter with a mike. "Did you have any difficulties getting here?" His tone was casual, his smile tense.

"No." She couldn't manage even a tense smile. "You've received the last of the notifications?"

"Yes, ma'am. The teams are ready and waiting for your orders."

"Thank you." His phrase "waiting for your orders" took her breath away. Soon, she would send people she knew and people she'd never met to injury, death, or the deaths of loved ones. And it wasn't just SABR soldiers. The likelihood of civilians being injured or killed… She brought her clasped hands to her mouth. Blew on her hands to control her nervous breathing. Couldn't control how her heart bruised her ribs with each thump. *How did Uncle Ethan do this? Knowingly send people into danger.* She figured he did what she had to do now—ignore her own feelings. She relaxed her hands and turned to the lieutenant in charge of safe houses. "All locations secure and stocked?"

"They are, ma'am, but I still think we need more." He'd argued for more for the past six weeks.

She gave him a tired smile. "Do we have the supplies or extra personnel for more yet?"

His gaze and chin dipped down. "No, ma'am."

She took his calloused hands in hers. "I can't delay any longer." Six weeks before the law went into effect was cutting it too short. She'd barely had time in the ten previous weeks for courier messages to reach all of SABR's state supervisors and learn all the moving parts of their four-phase attack. "Keep me informed."

He gave her a tight smile and nodded. "Will do, ma'am."

She wished Uncle Ethan were here. He'd know how to stop the Youth Spiritual Aptitude and Assignment Act. "We'll find a way to help everyone."

The round black clock on the wall read 8:00 a.m.

Oliver gave her an encouraging smile.

She heaved a sigh. It didn't soften the jackhammer blows of her heart. She locked eyes with the young lieutenant. "Deliver the milk."

He nodded and ducked into a hidden passage that led out to the street. There, he'd get in his milk truck and deliver milk bottles with green seals to the local leaders of the four-phase assault.

The plotter, the communications technician, and three volunteer runners side-eyed each other with everything from anxiety to excitement.

She sat in front of the transmitter. Picked up the ham radio's microphone, held down the push-to-talk button, and said, "Bible Study friends, today we'll study the book of Ephesians." She released the button.

Static punctuated responses came. "I'll bring extra candles," "I'll bring some extra Bibles," "I'll bring the flowers," and "My study notes are ready." Each of them would now notify seven other state supervisors. And at 0900, every SABR member reached by the message chain would perform their role in the revolution. At least, that was the plan. The success of this assault depended on all of them doing their part.

Now all Miranda could do was wait out the next ninety minutes.

She tucked her hands under her arms and shivered despite the heat of a dozen or more vacuum tubes in the radio equipment baking the unheated apartment. She didn't think she'd ever get warm enough.

A courier disguised as a maintenance worker knocked on the front door at 0930. "I'll be working on the water heater for the next two hours." A message that meant the political team was evacuating the Capitol Building.

The ham radio lit up with the dits and dahs of Morse code, a warning of an incoming message. Miranda moved out of the way so Oliver could interpret. He was much better, faster than she. The message from the leader of the judicial team read, "The package weighed four pounds."

Miranda nodded at Oliver. Surprised that they hadn't found five of the Supreme Court justices, she blurted out, "Send: Thank you. I knew it was heavy." She bit the inside of her cheek as it flamed red outside. *Oliver knows the correct response better than I do.*

Oliver simply nodded and did it.

She didn't have time to apologize or worry about that because another courier waited anxiously for her attention.

The courier's gaze darted back and forth between Miranda and Oliver. He ran a finger around his T-shirt collar and bounced on his toes.

"What is it?" Miranda asked.

"You need to turn on the radio or television for an announcement. It's probably already started."

Miranda exchanged a glance with Oliver, who reached up to the radio perched on top of his transmitter and turned it on.

Flutes and drums and piano notes struck the familiar chords of *Symphony of Psalms* by Igor Stravinsky. Miranda gave the courier a puzzled look.

He glanced at his wristwatch. "It's supposed to repeat every half hour."

Less than a minute later, the music swelled dramatically and stopped mid-note.

"Ladies and gentlemen, we interrupt our program featuring the Boston Symphony Orchestra to repeat the special announcement we received just an hour ago. And now a message from the Prophetess Earnshaw."

Miranda's chest buzzed as if a world of angry bees swarmed inside.

"The Lord of Grace and Wisdom and Glory be praised." Irene's confidence and arrogance were obvious even on the crappy radio. "The Most High keeps His covenant and lavishes His love on all who love Him and obey His commands. And He does not hesitate to punish and destroy those who reject Him. He sent His angel Gabriel to me. The Lord's wondrous patience has grown thin. Those apostates who hate Him and all that His people of the Fellowship have shown their true selves. He requires the public execution of any who harbors or helps the apostates, until Miranda Clarke and all her rebels and her supporters have been destroyed. But any who turns in Miranda or the other apostates will be spared.

"The first executions will be of the traitorous Baxter family, who hid Miranda from the authorities. At five pm today, we will execute a member of the Baxter family in front of the Capitol Building each hour the apostate doesn't show, starting with Mimi Baxter, who carried messages for the apostate."

Miranda's lungs pushed air out between her lips in rapid, explosive bursts. A chill shook her. She couldn't believe her little sister had just ordered the deaths of hundreds of people, starting with the Baxters.

I can't let Mimi, of all people, die because of me. But I promised Uncle Ethan... She looked around the command center. Realized everyone —Oliver, the plotter, the communications technician, even the courier—stared at her. Her stomach hollowed out. *They remember I gave the order to blow up Irene's cave in Kansas City. That people died— because of me.* She focused on the map, one group of colored pins at a time.

"Miranda?"

She whirled to face Oliver and her guilt. "Yes?"

His mouth quirked into a smile that wasn't really a smile.

It was three-thirty p.m., one and a half hours before the first execution. The urge to pace, to do something, screamed in her head, but she didn't move. She would take responsibility for what she'd done. She would wait for Oliver to unload his anger and blame on her.

"Your sister is really something." His eyes didn't leave her face.

The angry bees inside swirled like a buzzing tornado. *What does he want from me?*

He took a deep breath. "We can't send a team to help them. You understand, don't you? There's too much at stake." His eyes pleaded with her.

The scream in her head to do something competed with the buzzing in her chest. If she opened her mouth, the scream would come out.

"I know how hard this must be for you." He swallowed. "You know as well as I do, if you try to help them, Irene will have you killed. Don't you?"

His words penetrated the screaming and buzzing. "Yes, I— wait." She searched his face. "Are you saying you'd be okay with my going there? Helping them?"

His face clouded. He shifted his weight and scratched the back of his neck. Then, squared his shoulders and looked her in the eye again. "I'm saying I know I couldn't live with myself if I allowed a family I cared about to die. And maybe—your showing up in front of Irene could distract her from SABR's—from our operation. Am I okay with sending you to your death? Heck no. Am I okay with you choosing to help your friends even if it means your death? No, but...I won't stop you."

Time froze.

Memories flooded her. Memories of the Baxters—of Mimi, Evelyn, ZeeZee, Bernie, Gene, and Thea—her family for the past six months. Memories of broken promises. She had promised to protect Thea. And broke that promise once already. She couldn't break it again. Couldn't let Thea, and the rest, die. *Even if I must die to save them.* The scream inside transformed into *I don't want to die.* But hell, she couldn't let the Baxters die because she was afraid. She pushed her shoulders back, lifted her chin. The screaming and buzzing inside quieted.

"Thank you." Her voice was steadier than she'd thought it would be.

"For what?" Oliver sounded confused.

"Free will. That's what you're giving me. Something the Fellowship and my sister don't believe in. But we do. In a way, that's what we're fighting for, isn't it?"

Oliver's face remained clouded.

"I'm choosing to go. I will find a way to free the Baxters, and I'll try my damnedest to survive." She gave him a tight-lipped smile. "Now, how distracted do you want Irene?"

———

BRACED FOR A GUNFIGHT, LESLIE APPROACHED THE VACANT GUARD shack at the gate across the private drive leading to the home of the counselor to the secretary of state in the prestigious Kalorama neighborhood of Northwest DC. The lack of guards was unexpected and worrisome. Though grateful she had avoided a gunfight, every nerve in her body prickled with the sense that something was wrong. Intelligence had said there would be a guard or two at the shack outside and the counselor, his wife, and their two Second Sphere bodyguards inside. Capturing them wasn't supposed to be easy.

Leslie gawked at the enormous house, bigger than anything Leslie had ever seen. It had an arched double-door entry, tons of windows, a colonnade, and chimneys. Searching it for Fellowship documents would take longer than expected. Her walkie-talkie beeped. She stopped admiring the mansion. It was ten a.m. sharp, and Miranda had given the go for Phase Two.

Inside the gate, Leslie's team split up. The plan was to control the property's main house, including its six exits, the guest house, and the pool house.

Leslie and the burliest member of her team approached the front.

The front doors opened soundlessly onto a stunning, wide foyer lined with white bookcases and window seats on one side and a staircase and soft yellow walls studded with gold-framed paintings on the other. The central hallway looked as if it stretched on for at least a mile.

The house had such a clean, almost sterile smell, Leslie wondered how many maids it took to keep the house this clean.

She wiped such silly thoughts from her mind and sent her second up the stairs, then crept forward across the gleaming tile floors down the hall. Cleared two sitting rooms larger than her parents' whole house.

Next was a narrow room that held a restaurant's worth of glassware and wine bottles. The once sterile air held a hint of a bitter, ashy scent she couldn't identify.

About ten feet farther down the hall, she entered a sun-filled garden room. Going deeper into the room, the bitter smell grew stronger. Dried remains of a partially eaten breakfast sat on fine china on the glass tabletop. Of the eight wicker chairs neatly pushed in, one chair on each side of the table was out of position, as if the occupants had left the table in a hurry.

On the opposite side of the room, a serving cart held a glass carafe on a warming plate. Blackened coffee filled the bottom quarter of the glass carafe. Leslie guessed the carafe had sat there for at least a full day, maybe more. The prickle increased. *Anything can cause someone to leave their breakfast half-eaten, but who would leave the coffee pot on and not notice the smell? Have we been watching an empty house?* She unplugged the warmer and returned to the hallway.

Past the garden room, the bitter, ashy smell grew less. She entered an enormous kitchen with restaurant-sized appliances that was immaculate except for a sink full of dirty dishes in sudsless, gray water. The prickles raced up and down her skin. *What the heck happened here?* She hurried into the next room, hoping to find answers…people…something.

The room's soft yellow walls and white trim were the same as in the rest of the house. But the sofas and drapes were pink and yellow floral prints. And on the far side of the room, a pair of French doors. *Another room. Does this house never end?*

She approached the doors. Soft voices sang "Just a Closer Walk with Thee." She adjusted her grip on her pistol and took another step. Got a whiff of a nauseatingly familiar odor. Froze. Clapped her hand across her nose and mouth. She knew what that smell meant. She'd barely gotten it scrubbed off her skin and out of her nose. She definitely did not want to open those French doors. But she had to, to fulfill her mission—for her parents, her older brother, and all who had lost loved ones to the Fellowship's insane rules.

The doorknob turned easily. The shock of oily, putrid air and the singing from a nearby radio froze her again. A suit-clad, bloated body sat on an overstuffed sofa to the left of the doorway. His head lolled to one side, his neck sliced open, and his dried blood sprayed about the room. The sign of the Azrael was on his forehead, in his own dried blood.

Next to him, his wife had suffered the same fate.

Leslie stared at the remains of the two people, unable to shed a tear.

"Don't waste your time feeling sorry for them," a deep voice said from behind her.

Startled, Leslie gave a strangled scream, leaped left, and whirled to face her number two man. She released a long, relieved breath. Propped her fists on her hips and scowled at him. "Don't sneak up on me like that!"

"I'm just saying, he must have pissed someone off good. Good riddance." He shrugged.

His callousness shook her. *Two people died. Have we been fighting so long we've lost our compassion?*

"No one upstairs and no papers. So, where do we go next?" He gave her an expectant look. "To the Capital or the White House?"

She led him out into the hallway, where the odor of decay was less and the air was more breathable. She turned to him again. "We fulfill our secondary mission. I'll search this room. You take the next one."

He didn't say a word, just strode down the hall.

She took a couple of deep breaths, then re-entered the stench. Other than an oily film on everything, the game table and liquor cabinet were undisturbed. Reluctantly, she stepped over dried blood and searched the trophy case behind the sofa. It held a dozen awards for baseball played two decades ago. No documents.

She turned. It was a little easier to look at the dead from behind. A massive white-brick fireplace filled the opposite wall. The screen sat to the side of the fireplace, but it held charred wood and a pile of charred paper on the grate.

Kneeling in front of the fireplace, the smell of burnt wood diminished the other odor that dominated the room. She grabbed the poker. Poked the pile of paper. The top layers crumbled into blackened flakes, but beneath them lay a thick stack of documents with blackened edges, otherwise intact. She gingerly picked up the papers. Fragile edges broke into flyaway pieces.

She gently placed the papers on the rosewood coffee table between her and the corpses.

From what she could read, the charred papers were proposals presented to the Fellowship Council. She scanned proposals about changes to public school libraries, a tax increase on gasoline, and a proposal to create a law forbidding pets in city parks.

The next page had a single word on it. In large red type, it said, "Classified."

Her pulse sped. *Could this be what will bring SABR victory?*

She turned the page too fast. The fragile edges broke into flyaway pieces. She blew off the ashes that had landed on the next page.

"Notice to all Counselors: Beginning October 22, 1964, the War Department will start an offensive against bad actors known as SABR. We advise you to close all windows, lock your doors, and seek shelter in a safe space inside your home. This offensive will continue until the notorious SABR member, Miranda Clarke, is captured or dead."

Leslie covered her mouth and gasped for breath. *That's today. Every member of SABR—across every major city—today. We're all in danger.* Gasp. *Miranda needs to know…*

Leslie pulled her walkie-talkie off her belt. She turned the talk button on and off. Signaled "SOS Trap for Silverthorn." Dit-dah-dit-dah-dit (end of message).

The response from headquarters said Miranda's ETA was ten minutes.

ETA? To where? Here?

On the radio, the choir stopped singing mid-chorus. "Ladies and gentlemen. We interrupt our scheduled…" Leslie listened to Irene's threat to kill the Baxters one at a time until Miranda turned herself in. Her thoughts scrambled to keep up with her pulse.

At the Capitol Building? That must be where Miranda's headed. She doesn't know it's a trap. I have to warn her. She turned her walkie-talkie to her team's channel and signaled them to regroup. Then sprinted out of the house to their designated meet spot by the gate.

Chapter Sixty-Nine

The weather had turned. Storm clouds shrouded the skies above the Capitol Building and sent a fine mist through the chilly gusts of a westerly wind. Annabelle and four of her best Azrael, in their black uniforms and goggles, formed a line across the back of the stage under the canopy that sheltered the people on the stage. The stage sat elevated on the western edge of the plaza. Everything from the soaked and shackled prisoners huddled in the street-level, steel cage on the east side of the stage, to the Capitol steps behind them, and the hundreds of Fellowship faithful spread across the lawn set up to Mother's best advantage.

A dreadful weight in Annabelle's stomach plunged into an endless, inescapable pit of dread. She stood as still as the buried secrets of the dead. Each minute that passed heightened her sense that her angels waited to Take Mother. She could not allow that. She was the only mother Annabelle knew. The other Azrael didn't understand. They had never had a mother.

Mother sat in her celebrant's chair under a spotlight, her gold-trimmed Prophetess robe gleaming. The placement of her chair gave her command of the stage, of the mayor of the district, the three city commissioners, DC's Fellowship Bishop, and Sandra, who sat in the first of two rows of metal folding chairs. Plus, the six other prominent figures sitting behind them and the family of agnostics she'd soon order executed.

The resonant bells of the Robert A. Taft Memorial and Carillon played ten seconds of an almost recognizable hymn, then tolled its bells four times. Four p.m. One hour until Mother would order the executions to begin. The hair on the back of Annabelle's neck lifted.

She stared past the motionless executioner. Anonymous in his black hood, powerful arms crossed over his chest, he easily held his heavy, two-handed sword in one hand.

Across the plaza and the east lawn, hundreds of the faithful in their raincoats of red or yellow or black, or under umbrellas of red or black, sang "Onward Christian Soldiers" energetically. The damp fog blurred the famous sights behind them.

In the middle of the third stanza of the song, the crowd stirred. Their singing faltered and died.

A wave of gasps and murmurs parted the crowd to reveal a single person at the other end of the plaza. She walked toward the stage. Miranda. Arms held up in surrender. Unarmed. Unescorted. Annabelle shifted from her attention stance to a readiness position.

Mother stood and crossed to the microphone five feet in front of her chair. She raised her arms, opened them in a benevolent Lord-like pose. "Coming to save someone else is the last thing I'd expect from you."

Twenty feet from the stage, Miranda stopped, shouted, "I'm here." She pointed at the soaked and shackled family huddled in the steel cage. "Release the prisoners."

"They sinned against the Lord and the Fellowship. As have you. The wages of sin is death." The microphone projected Mother's righteous tone.

"Did you hear that?" Miranda swept a glance across the crowd to her right, then to the people to her left. "This woman, who represents herself as a true Prophet, made a false promise. How can she be worthy of those robes?"

"I speak for the Lord, not myself." Mother's voice cracked. "He chose me. I am His vessel." She gripped the microphone stand. Her knuckles whitened. "I never chose this, but I will not fail Him."

Mother's glance darted from the crowd to Miranda. Her forehead glistened under the harsh light. "He wills for the Azrael to bring you to me now." Mother whipped her head around to glare at Annabelle.

Annabelle lifted her chin toward the two angels on her right. The two angels hesitated—just for a second. Annabelle doubted the crowd noticed, but she did. And it sent a chill through her.

Miranda walked past the Azrael, led them up the stairs, across the stage, and finally stopped an arm's length away from Mother. "I am here. Release them. Or do you plan to kill them as you did your own husband, the real Prophet?" The microphone in front of Mother amplified her words.

The outcry from the crowd drowned out anything Mother said.

A roar echoed inside Annabelle.

"Do not believe the lies of an apostate, a sinner by her own admission!" Mother shouted against the wall of voices.

Annabelle heard the strained note in Mother's voice, stepped forward, and grabbed Miranda's upper arm. "I was there. The rebels kidnapped the Prophet. If any poisoned him, your apostates did." Though she'd spoken softly, the microphone carried her words to the faithful.

Miranda faced Annabelle with an incredulous look. "How could you be there? See his rotting body? Smell the stench of his death? And say that?"

Annabelle remembered that night. The stale swamp smell when she walked past Papa's hospital-cottage. Her decision not to disturb Papa for fear of slowing his healing. Mother's nervousness when she realized I was waiting for her. Annabelle's trained response warred with a growing unease. *Mother performed miracles, lived a spiritual life, and spoke with assured righteousness. Why do her words ring so hollow now?* An intense, burning buildup of pressure threatened to burst Annabelle's ribs.

Mother threw her head back and raised both arms in the air. Staring skyward, she shouted, "I hear you, Lord." She brought her gaze down, glared at Miranda. "The Lord demands this sinner's death for her awful lies." Her anger focused on Annabelle. "Azrael, do your duty!"

Mother's hate-filled glare hit Annabelle like a physical blow that stopped her heart. In Mother's look, Annabelle saw nothing like the looks the mother in the park gave Patty. Nothing like the look of a loving mother. Nothing like the look of a benevolent religious leader like Papa.

The weight of her pistol, her angels' expectations, and the expectations of the crowd grew. But Annabelle's training hadn't prepared her for this. She refocused on the real woman who claimed to be her adoptive mother. Finally saw Mother as the unloving mother, the barely tolerant wife, and the fake Prophet.

Annabelle raised her chin, swiveled on her heel, and returned to her position in line. Her disobedience hung in the air like a ghost, invisible to the crowd, but unmistakable to Mother, the angels, and herself. Her gaze fixed on a distant point above the heads of the audience. She had just publicly chosen Miranda over Mother. Truth over loyalty. Love over obedience. Even if it meant her death.

Chapter Seventy

The misty rain dampened the earth and the usual traffic sounds around the Capitol. But it was the hundreds, maybe thousands, of people on the lawn of the Capitol building, who stared up at the stage silently, as if they held their breath, that was most unnerving. Miranda's hands grew clammy. Her knees trembled. *There are too many enemies here.* She wouldn't survive a fight.

She waited.

Seconds? Minutes?

Irene glared at Annabelle.

Maybe I can still give Oliver the time he needs. Miranda squared her shoulders, took one step forward. "Look, her own daughter walks away full of doubt, so how can any of you not have doubts too?"

Irene fixed a blistering gaze on her. "The Lord has condemned you."

Of course, He has. Unbidden, Miranda's lips twitched into a wry smirk. She forced them smooth. Wouldn't do to set Irene off too soon.

She had to stay alive until the Carillion bells rang at five fifteen. Keep Irene distracted. *How long has it been? Two minutes? Three?* Miranda's heart thrashed in her chest. *How am I going to last another dozen minutes?* She raised her voice, hoping the microphone in front of Irene would pick up her words. "I never would have dreamed my snot-nosed little sister would be so presumptuous as to think she could fool the entire country into believing God chose her to be Prophet."

Irene fiddled with the microphone as if she were looking for a switch. Finally, she put one gloved hand over the mike, lowered her chin, and spoke over her shoulder. "Shut her up."

"As a kid, she had a tendency to exaggerate so much that it became an outright lie. She even used to tell lies to her dolls, for goodness' sake. Maybe that's why she was Daddy's favorite. You all remember him, don't you? The former First Apostle, exiled because he was such a deceitful man. I guess dishonesty is in our blood. Irene has told some whoppers. And you all believed her."

Miranda's muscles tightened, bracing for the Azrael's attack.

It didn't happen.

She glanced at the line of Azrael. Unmoving and in those black uniforms and black goggles, they looked like bug-eyed statues. Even Annabelle ignored Irene's harsh, angry whispers and continued to stare straight ahead.

Unexpected. But I'll take it. Miranda faced the audience. "I've known her longer than any of you, and I believed the lie she told me today—told everyone. She *said* she would release the prisoners if I turned myself in." Arms at her sides, she spread them out as if ready for an embrace. "Here I am. Yet they're still shackled prisoners."

The crowd moved and murmured like an uneasy animal.

Miranda worked her dry tongue loose, faced Irene again, and raised her scratchy voice. "Gee whiz, Irene. Even the Azrael seem to want to hear what I have to say."

Irene snatched the microphone out of its stand. It squealed. She threw it offstage. Whirled to face the row of Azrael. "Obey the Lord's command now!" Her lips kept moving, but the crowd's roar drowned her words.

"Your own daughter and the Azrael won't listen to you," Miranda shouted. The shakiness in her knees spread to her lungs. She expected Irene to order the Second Sphere to kill her any minute. *Don't look at them. Don't look at your watch. Don't give them a hint.* "If they won't listen to you, why should any of us?"

Gasps and murmurs rippled across the people nearest the stage. Some raised their fists in the air.

Are doubts finally creeping in?

Irene whirled to face the audience, threw her arms in the air, and lifted her face to the heavens. "Oh, ye of little faith." The booming bass voice that came from her sent shock waves across the audience.

Miranda's skin crawled. *It's a trick. It must be a trick.* But even this close, that voice sounded as if it came from Irene's mouth.

Silenced, many in the crowd fell to their knees or raised their hands in supplication.

Irene turned a benevolent gaze to stage left, where a startled Sandra sat in a metal folding chair. "Come to me, child."

Miranda's stomach dropped. She hadn't seen Sandra there. *She shouldn't be here. She's a child.*

Wide-eyed, Sandra slowly rose from her seat and crossed to her mother's side.

Swallow after swallow, Miranda couldn't get rid of the cold lump caught in her throat.

"Why do you fear my messenger when a child is fearless?" Irene took Sandra's hand and faced the crowd. "Be not afraid. For ye who are in my Fellowship shall receive the gift of eternal life."

Sandra looked up at her mother. "Why are you talking like that?"

Irene cleared her throat and looked down at her daughter. "The Lord is speaking through me," she whispered in her normal voice.

She's altering her voice. Damn. I'll bet she has one of those new throat mics. But if I can't see it, how do I convince everyone else it's a trick?

Irene straightened and stiffened in her possessed-by-the-Lord stance. "Why do you doubt? Be not like the apostates. The wages of their sin is death."

"Amen!" The word rippled across the audience.

"Mommy?" Sandra tugged on her mother's hand. "Mommy? You mean Aunt Miranda?"

Irene's possessed expression wavered. "Bring the apostate to the executioner."

Miranda pivoted.

A Second Sphere agent gripped an arm on each side of tiny, white-haired Mimi. She marched up the steps, pale, head high, expression defiant.

Miranda's chest pulsed in a hollow somewhere deep inside. *When will the damn clock ring its bells?* Desperate, she turned to the audience. Shouted, "If I am evil, then what does your Lord say about a woman who poses with a False Prophet to protect the image of her sick husband?"

An audible gasp came from behind Miranda. *The Azrael didn't know?*

"Lies. Nothing but lies. The Lord demands we rid the world of apostates and sinners. Executioner, do your duty."

Cold rain plastered her clothes to her skin, but Miranda sweated anyway. "I wonder how long you followed the False Prophet?" Her voice shook. She hoped Irene thought it shook out of fear for herself. "How far did she take her pretense? Did she bed the fake like a husband?" Miranda wiped sweat from her upper lip with frozen fingers. "Whose idea was it to poison her sick husband, the proclaimed Prophet, then leave his body to rot for days—the fake's or hers?"

Gasps rippled through the audience.

"Guards, stop her baseless lies. Seize her!"

A hand grabbed Miranda's shoulder, spun her around. She faced a clean-shaven young man whose face should have held innocence, but held not a flicker of warmth or humanity.

A prick from the tip of a knife drove Miranda's chin up.

She whipped her hands above her head, clasped them together, and brought them down on the arm holding the knife at the same time she rammed her knee into his soft parts.

"Oof!" He dropped the knife, covered himself with both hands, and dropped to the stage floor, writhing.

She whirled, tucked her chin, and barreled toward the Executioner.

He raised his axe high above Mimi's head.

Miranda smashed into him.

They, and his axe, crashed onto the stage floor with a resounding thud.

Dazed, Miranda sucked in air and caught a blurry glimpse of the axe before it slid off the back of the stage. She turned on the downed agent and tunneled in on the knife that lay an arm's length away. Lurched to her feet. Staggered forward, then sideways. Bent. Snatched the knife. Straightened, swayed, and struggled to stay upright.

Something slammed into her back. Drove the wind out of her and threw her face-first onto the stage floor. Blinding pain slammed into her back, her chin, her nose, her mouth. Tears filled her eyes. Her head snapped back, and her face hit the floor again. A salty, metallic liquid filled her mouth. She fought for breath. Fought against the weight on top of her. Fought to get to her knees.

"Mommy!" Sandra screamed.

Irene's hands snatched at Miranda's hair, but the short strands slid through her fingers.

Miranda threw her head back, connected with Irene's face. Rolled over, faced Irene. Bright pinpoints of twinkling light surrounded her sister.

Irene's hands covered her nose and chin. Blood dripped from beneath her hands. Menace flashed in her eyes. She grabbed Miranda's wrists and pinned them to the stage.

A memory flashed through Miranda. Beryl teaching her...*I don't remember.* Then she did. Miranda planted her feet flat, bucked her hips up, and swept her arms in a snow-angel movement. Knocked Irene off her.

Irene sprawled on the stage but recovered and got to her feet as quickly as Miranda did.

Miranda circled her sister, backing toward center stage. "Stop. I don't want to hurt you, Irene." *She can't possibly think she can beat...*

Irene snarled. Whipped off her stole and robe in one violent motion. A heap of black and red fabric puddled on the floor. Then she was moving, closing the distance between them with a predatory focus. Her eyes lit. She dove forward.

The knife.

Irene's hand closed around it. She flicked off her heels. They flew across the stage, and she charged toward Miranda again.

Miranda backed away. Eyes on the knife. But glimpsed something that sent chills down to her fingers and toes.

Her sister's distorted face belonged to someone or something else. Something long hidden. Something empty of everything but molten hatred.

Miranda's throat closed. Her heart threw itself against her ribs—a desperate, wild thrashing of something that knew it was prey. This wasn't Irene anymore. This was someone who came to end Miranda. And if the Azrael decided to help...

The Azrael. *Where were*— She couldn't see them. The knife. Irene.

Miranda's hip banged into the podium. She grabbed it, swung it between them. Bought herself a little time. *Mimi? Where...*

There. Hand in hand with Annabelle, Sandra ran down the steps and into the scattering crowd.

Good. At least Sandra won't have to watch...

Irene drove forward.

Miranda's heel clacked against metal. Chairs exploded around her—clattered and skittered and crashed off the edge of the stage. *Too close. Can't keep backing up. Can't let Irene catch me. Not until they're safe. Not until the bells ring.*

The Beryl-in-Miranda's-head whispered, "*Be strong. Go all out.*" Miranda grabbed a fallen chair, held it in front of her, and charged Irene.

The legs of the chair trapped Irene's knife behind the seat.

Irene gave a raw, primal scream. Lunged.

They battled for the chair. Twisting, wrenching it back and forth.

Irene pressed hard against the chair.

Miranda took a step back. Her heel hung over the edge of the stage. She wobbled.

Irene yanked the chair from Miranda's grasp. Threw it off stage.

Miranda darted across the stage. Leaped over the mound of Irene's robe and stole. Swiveled and snatched at the stole. *Got it!* She ran and wound the red silk around her left hand and wrist twice, then Irene cornered her again.

With her knife hand extended, Irene dove forward.

Miranda sidestepped and, despite a burning in her left arm, whipped the end of the stole over and around Irene's neck. Failed to catch the free end.

Irene caught the loose end. Stripped it from her neck. Spun. Murderous intent oozed from her.

Miranda took three quick steps back. *When did she get so fast?*

The knife came at Miranda's gut.

Miranda threw her left arm across her body. Blocked Irene's arm. The impact sent a jolt clear up to Miranda's neck and drove her arm down. She tried to spin away, but something caught—jerked her to a stop. *Damn. The stole.* Trapped under Irene's foot.

One sharp tug.

Irene's leg slid out. She dropped hard. Tailbone cracked against the stage. Then, her skull hit.

The low thunk vibrated through Miranda's jaw. Made her teeth ache, but she was already in motion. Dropped. Knees on either side of Irene's ribs. Caught and pinned both of Irene's wrists to the stage floor.

Arms trembling, Irene pitted her strength against Miranda's.

The glint of the knife inched toward Miranda's face.

"Let it go, Irene." Miranda's injured arm trembled.

Irene rocked and bucked like a wild animal. The stage shuddered.

"Irene, please stop. I don't want to hurt you."

Another buck nearly unseated Miranda, but she held on, forced the knife a few inches closer to the floor. "Release the prisoners," she said through gritted teeth. "Release them, and I'll surrender."

Irene stopped bucking but didn't relinquish control of the knife

That look. God, that look. Something broke inside Miranda. She had seen her sister hurt, disappointed, and even furious. But never like this. Never so full of hatred. Never so personal, so physical a thing. It hurt more than the burning of her screaming muscles.

"You're willing to die for them?"

Where's the damn bell? Please let Wanda be winning. Let SABR win. Don't let them fail because I can't drive the knife into my sister's flesh. Miranda released a long, weary sigh. She could do this last thing. "Let them go first. Then you can do whatever you're going to do. I won't hurt you. I won't fight anymore." *At least the Baxters would have a chance.*

"Deal." Irene's smile was worse than any nightmare Miranda had ever had.

Miranda softened her arms. Just a fraction.

Irene went slack.

Miranda shifted her weight to stand.

The knife bit through the fabric, her skin. Fire erupted across her chest. She gasped. Instinct took over. Her hands shot out. Grabbed the knife just above the hilt. The tough silk wrapped around her left hand protected her fingers. Right hand over left, Miranda threw her weight backward, wrenched the knife away from her body.

Two-handed now, Irene fought for the blade.

I won't kill you. Miranda's muscles screamed. Her hands and arms shook so badly she could barely hold on. *I. Won't. Kill —*

Irene twisted, and they rolled.

Miranda let Irene's twenty extra pounds roll them full circle once. Twice. Miranda was on top again. "Stop. I don't want to hurt you." She pushed the knife down toward the floor. Made it as far as Irene's shoulder. Couldn't move it another inch.

Irene shoved back.

The blade rose. Quivered between their chests.

Irene twisted and turned Miranda's wrists, angling the knife's edge toward Miranda's neck.

With every last scrap of strength, Miranda forced the knife's tip back toward Irene.

Then, Irene stopped pushing.

Miranda fell forward. The knife slid off Irene's sternum, between her ribs, and plunged into Irene before Miranda could stop it. Before she could do anything but feel the knife pop through Irene's skin and bury itself in Irene's chest.

Irene drew in a gasp. The breath left her body in a long, weighted sigh. Her arms and then her face went slack. The hilt of the knife protruded from her blood-stained chest. Astonishing plumes of crimson feathered the floor, as if in death, Irene had grown wings.

No. No. This wasn't supposed to... Tears streamed down Miranda's face. *I didn't want to kill you. I wasn't supposed to...not my little sister.*

Strength gone, Miranda sagged onto her sister. The heavy thumps of her heartbeat rocked her entire body. Gulping and sobbing, she whispered, "I'm sorry. I'm so sorry."

Gunfire erupted.

I didn't even give Wanda and the others enough time. Miranda's breath rasped through her. *I killed her. I killed them all. Irene and Wanda, Ethan...Beryl...and Nick. What kind of person am I? I killed my family?*

The gunfire grew closer, louder.

A distant part of Miranda figured she'd just wait. They'd shoot her eventually.

The peal of the carillon bells competed with the sharp retorts of guns. The quarter hour.

Chapter Seventy-One

Leslie didn't even try to find a parking place near the Capitol building. She double-parked and sprinted to the edge of the Capitol's lawn, followed by two of her team. She signaled her teammates to go. They'd find the Baxters. She'd find Miranda.

Her fingers tightened around the grip of her pistol, but she didn't pull it from its holster. She slipped quietly into the crowd. Wormed her way toward the stage. She'd expected speeches over loudspeakers. But only low murmuring and shuffling surrounded her.

"Oh, ye of little faith." The deep voice boomed over the crowd.

Gasps rippled through the crowd ahead of Leslie. The hair on the back of her neck raised. Every instinct screamed danger. She stood on tiptoe but couldn't see over the people in front of her. She picked up her pace.

Metal crashed on metal. Screams erupted, and hundreds of people stampeded toward her.

Each time she surged forward, the panicked crowd forced her back.

She pushed through on a diagonal. Gained ground slowly, steadily. Finally, broke through to a vacant area in front of a raised stage at the bottom of the Capitol's steps.

Two bloody bodies lay in a crumpled pile on the stage. Her pulse played a drumbeat against her ribs. She scanned the stage for steps. *There.* She dashed to them.

Beyond the steps, an old woman was trying to open the containment cell that held the Baxters. Leslie hesitated.

Just then, her teammates reached the old woman.

Leslie bolted up the stairs.

On stage, the odor of iron thickened the air, and the sight of dark red blood pooling around the bodies knotted Leslie's throat. She took tiny, out-of-control gasps for air. Her pulse went into overdrive. "Miranda?" Neither body stirred. "Can you speak?" Her voice shook.

She stepped closer.

Miranda lay face down and unmoving over Irene.

So much blood. Too much. Miranda must be— Leslie closed her eyes for a second, steeling herself. She took a deep breath and blew it out. Her rapid heartbeat slowed to a heavy thump-thud.

She didn't want to, but just in case—she had to.

She reached out a shaky hand. Touched Miranda's neck.

Miranda twitched and gave a raw, strangled cry.

Leslie yelped and leaped backward. Her heart sprinted again.

Miranda rolled to an unsteady fighting stance. Knife in her right hand. Her left arm, dripping blood, hung limp at her side.

Leslie huffed out a breath. Her muscles released her tension, leaving her weak and shaky. Adrenaline kept her standing. "Thank God, you're alive!"

Miranda's blouse was bloody and torn at the neckline and along her right side.

"Your arm is bleeding." Leslie took a step toward Miranda. "Are you hurt anywhere else?"

"I don't want to kill you!" Miranda swayed and waved a gory knife at Leslie.

Miranda's haunted look flooded Leslie with chills. She gave a short, nervous laugh. "It's me, Leslie." She reached out hesitantly. "Give me the knife."

Staggering and off-balance, Miranda lunged clumsily at Leslie.

Leslie sidestepped and grabbed Miranda's knife-wielding arm. Easily forced it down, but Miranda's grip on the knife was strong.

"I don't want to kill you." Tears streaked Miranda's bloody face.

"Miranda, it's Leslie. The fight is over. You're safe."

Confusion clouded Miranda's face. She blinked and blinked. Tilted her head and stared. "Leslie?" Miranda's shoulders sagged. She dropped the knife and collapsed to her knees.

Leslie kneeled with her. "It's all right. You're safe." Miranda's arm trembled. *Or maybe that's me.* Leslie took a shaky breath. "Let me see your wounds." She gently opened the edge of the tear in Miranda's sleeve.

A three-inch-long wound gaped a few inches below Miranda's shoulder. Dark blood streamed down her arm.

Leslie pulled at the torn fabric, ripping Miranda's ruined sleeve into strips. Wrapped one strip above the wound. Tied it tight. "Can you tell me what happened?"

Miranda stared off into the distance.

It was a look Leslie remembered all too well. She blinked away the tears that threatened and examined Miranda's neckline. A superficial cut dotted with beads of blood made a macabre necklace that dripped down Miranda's chest. The only other wound Leslie could find was an angry red line that ran from the bottom of Miranda's ribcage to her hip.

"We've got to get you to a medic. That arm needs stitches. Can you stand?" Leslie rose partially, waited for Miranda to get up.

Miranda cast a darting glance around. "The Baxters?"

Relieved Miranda had stirred from her stupor, Leslie gave her a faint smile. "The Baxters are on their way to safety."

"Mimi?"

"The old woman too."

Miranda gave a nod and sighed wearily. She attempted to stand. Wobbled and sank to her knees again.

Leslie put Miranda's right arm over her shoulders and wrapped her own arm around Miranda. "On three. One. Two. Three. Up."

They stood as one and staggered off the stage.

Chapter Seventy-Two

E very movement spawned a new explosion of pain, but Miranda dug in, took another step down 27th Street Northwest. She wouldn't fail Uncle Ethan again, even if the medic disapproved. Even if she had to wall off the tidal wave of emotions that threatened to drown her. Even if she had to ignore the needs of her own body. She. Would. Not. Fail.

She pulled herself up the stairs and paused outside the vacant second-floor apartment to wipe sweat from her face and to prepare herself for seeing Oliver and the rest.

Moments later, she stepped into the stifling heat of SABR's ham radio command center and the unforgiving heat of five pairs of eyes focused on her.

Miranda's skin tightened, pulled at her stitches. *Do they know what I did?* A dozen vacuum tubes hummed in the background.

She couldn't make eye contact with the plotter, the technician, and the two runners in the room. *She couldn't imagine Uncle Ethan in this kind of situation.* But she remembered how distant he'd become. She pulled herself together and strode across the room to Oliver.

Still seated at the voice and Morse code transceiver, Oliver studied her. Worry lines creased his forehead. He moved one of his headphone earcups behind his ear. "Didn't the medic tell you to rest until morning?"

"I'm fine," she muttered. *They know.* An extra wave of heat swept over her. Her forehead grew damp. She silently damned the H Street Corridor medic for telling Oliver. "Bring me up to date so you can get some rest."

"It's only nine o'clock," he said in a too-casual tone. "I'm good. Why don't you grab a couple of hours in the room next door?"

She gave Oliver a dirty look. "You've been handling it for almost five hours. You need a break. I am still the captain, right?"

Oliver's cheek muscle jumped, and he gave a reluctant nod.

"Give me your report, then take a break," Miranda said. "That's an order."

He scraped a hand down his mouth and chin, wiping away the tension that had been there. "As expected, twenty-five governors called out the Army National Guard and have achieved control over their states, though there are still plenty of hot spots. Four of the governors in our 'Maybe' states joined it."

"Twenty-nine states?" Miranda's mouth dropped open. "So we're winning."

Oliver gave her an odd look, as if she should know better. "Got a long way to go before we can say that." He took a breath. "Senator Johnson's coalition has taken control of the Senate floor. But Representative Quick is still working on members of the House."

"General Carlyle has most of the army on the eastern seaboard behind us, and he's—" Lights flashed on the receiver. "Excuse me." Oliver pressed the earcup on his ear, listened, and studied the map on the opposite wall where the silver-haired plotter waited. "WA3I72 has control of National's air traffic tower."

The plotter moved a wooden stepladder, placed one and then the other of her practical low pumps squarely on it, and pressed a flag pin in the map at the airport's location.

"Where was I?" Oliver refocused on Miranda.

"General Carlyle…"

"Right. He's secured the cooperation of the marine commanders in the DC area. The Marines have a protective blockade running from Boston to Charleston. But that's not half of the US armed forces. The Air Force is on alert but hasn't launched. The Navy has been maneuvering but staying out of range." He gestured at an arch of red pushpins in the Atlantic from south of Charleston Harbor to Boston. "Plus, there's still a lot of DC and the rest of the forty-eight states to be concerned about."

Miranda sank into the chair beside him. The movement pulled at the glue holding the edges of her necklace-shaped wound together. She tightened her lips against a wince and glanced down at her blouse. *Damn medic.* She'd tried to convince him he didn't need to "keep the scarring minimal." He hadn't listened. She quirked her mouth, but even that hurt. She drew in a breath, trying to relax before she spoke. "This is gonna take longer than we'd hoped."

"'Fraid so."

"Then it's even more important that you rest when you can," Miranda told him. "Go. Take two hours. I'll take my turn after yours."

Oliver reluctantly took off his headphones, stood, and stretched his neck right and left.

Dit-dit-dit. Dah-dah-dah. Dit-dit-dit. The SOS signal repeated.

Oliver had his headphones on again and translated the dits and dahs into words far faster than Miranda could. "SS to torch one thousand prisoners. Judgment Center East Capitol Street. ETA fifteen minutes. Send help. Stop."

"Fifteen minutes?" Miranda's heart kicked into high gear. She stared at the map on the wall. "General Carlyle's close. Maybe he has some spare soldiers." She reached for the microphone.

The weight of Oliver's hand on her arm restrained her and triggered her inner alarms.

"If he can get someone there…"

His voice faded away, and the map blurred. The hair on her neck raised. Enemies surrounded her. Her muscles crackled with energy. She grabbed her knife. The world spun like a manic merry-go-round, and a chill swept over her. *Have to defend myself.* She whirled into a fighting crouch. Knife ready.

"Miranda?" Oliver's voice sounded far away. "Miranda, stop!"

"I don't want to kill you," she muttered.

"Miranda! It's me. Oliver." He gripped her shoulders. "Breathe. In and out. That's better. In and out." He spoke over his shoulder. "Find a medic for her."

Queasy acid bubbled up and into her throat. Her vision snapped clear. "No!" She tore out of his grasp. "I'm okay." Glanced down at her knife hand. But it wasn't a knife she held. It was an ink pen. She dropped the pen. It clacked on the floor. She twitched, fingers flexing, reaching for a non-existent weapon.

"Miranda, stay with me. Breathe. In…"

She focused on slowing her frantic, shaky breaths. Her heart still raced as if she were in mortal danger. "I am okay. I—I thought I heard something."

Oliver murmured, "Sit down. You're not okay. You should lie down—"

"I told you, I'm fine." *Too loud.* She pressed her tongue against the back of her bottom teeth rather than let another heated protest burst from her. Suppressed a shiver and took a more normal breath. "I'm fine. Go! I'll get you additional help from Wanda's team and anyone else that's near enough."

"Are you…"

"I'm sure. I'll hold down the fort."

She glared up at him, hoping she at least *looked* steady.

He hesitated.

"You can't let those people burn. Go. Now!"

He hesitated. Mouthed the words "watch her" to the plotter and hurried out the front door.

Eyes cast down, Miranda sat in front of the voice transceiver. Picked up the mike and called out Wanda's code.

Less than five minutes later, a signal came to WA3722R. "Rescue underway. Pokeweed out."

She frowned at the radio. *Rescue underway?* Wished she could ask Oliver if the SS were there, but if they were, signaling him would bring them down on him. Not being able to see what was going on…her stomach churned. *No wonder Uncle Ethan grew so distant.*

The call sign came over the radio again. "Request additional medical staff and space."

The caller reported that the H Corridor safe house was over-flowing with wounded and safety requests. She promised she'd divert the incoming to another location. Then she received a request for more ammo from David's team in Northwest DC. So did the team near the White House and a team near the old Fellowship Center site. She sent her runners to the general's hidden stash. They'd get that ammo where it needed to be. After that, the reports and needs came in so fast she barely moved from her chair.

Oliver stumbled in after dawn. He'd helped rescue most of the detainees at the Judgment Center and had filled all the safe houses in the Anacostia neighborhoods. They worked on getting the rest of the refugees to safe places and keeping their fighters supplied until Miranda lost her voice. She drank some hot tea and took a two-hour nap.

Weeks of two-hour shifts on and off duty, of managing the militia, the refugees, and the wounded blurred together. Requests poured in on the ham radio. Miranda heard someone ask if she was unwell. She heard herself respond, "I'm just tired. After another cup of coffee, I'll be fine." But something in her mind whispered she couldn't remember what "fine" felt like anymore. She knew she'd been someone else before. She was almost certain she'd been someone else, someone who didn't hear voices, someone whose hands were clean.

Chapter Seventy-Three

Leslie pressed through the sea of people that filled Baltimore's streets. Arms waved in the air. Some waved handheld flags, the Stars and Stripes, above their heads. The impending swearing-in of the president-elect—a leader they'd chosen at the ballot box—had them laughing and crying and singing and dancing. Leslie was glad for that too but couldn't feel the joy until she knew Ian—and Miranda and Wanda—survived.

Their jubilant voices washed over her, deafened her, made her long for the quiet of the mountains. Someone clapped her on the back or shoulder. She flinched. Her memories of fighting for her life were too fresh for her to feel safe. It had been forty days of endless terror. But they'd succeeded. SABR and the military had partnered to maintain order and to restore all constitutional rights, including the right to vote for the country's leadership.

Closing Virgil's front door behind her muted the singing and shouting. Leslie's thoughts instantly filled the void. *Ian has always struggled to keep in touch.* The knot in her stomach grew larger, heavier. *I'm sure he's fine. He's waiting in the back room.*

Virgil wasn't at the register.

Not a single shopper roamed the grocery store's aisles.

The curtain over the door to the back room stood open. Murmurs came from the other room. The cadence and excitement of the voice sounded like they belonged to a news anchor. She held her breath and stepped into the back room. Wanda and Virgil turned from the portable black-and-white television on the table to face her.

Wanda's wide smile brightened her face. "Good to see you."

"And you." Leslie scanned the room, but there was no Ian. Her throat tightened. Still, she smiled at Wanda. "It's been—"

"You've come just in time. President Johnson is about to hold a press conference."

She couldn't help it. "Have you heard from Ian?"

Wanda's smile faded. "Not yet. But don't worry; the crowds are crazy out there. I'm sure he's on his way."

"You're probably right." But Leslie's chest ached.

The news anchor's voice rose again. "Earlier today, Lyndon B. Johnson was sworn in as the thirty-sixth president of the United States. And in just a few minutes, he will speak here outside on the West Terrace of the White House."

The first bars of "Hail to the Chief" swelled.

President Lyndon B. Johnson appeared in the doorway. Dressed in a custom-tailored navy-blue suit, he paused and faced the camera. He crossed to the podium peppered with microphones.

"Good morning, friends and reporters. I am so glad you all are here this morning. Let me get the business done first, then we'll have time for your questions.

"On the evening of October twenty-second, the good people of these United States of America had had enough of oppression, of bias, and of prejudice and bigotry. They were no longer willing to endure one more day of the tyrants of the Fellowship inflicting yet more pain on the poor and disenfranchised, who had already suffered so much. They suffered under Fellowship rules and regulations; they suffered acts of hostility against their persons, at their jobs, in their homes and in their neighborhoods. Nowhere was safe.

"This morning, I am proud to salute my fellow citizens. I am proud that they confronted the tyrants on that fateful day. But to our great sorrow, that confrontation turned bloody. No matter which side you took or fought on, to *all* who have been injured, to *all* who have lost a loved one or friend or neighbor, we send our love and support. Know that from this day forward, America will not accept tyranny, despotism, oppression or bias, prejudice and bigotry. We want change. We believe all men and women are created equal. That they have unalienable rights, that among these are life, liberty, and the pursuit of happiness. So thank you to my fellow Americans, thank you for giving us the chance to be Americans again."

Cheers and applause erupted. The camera swept over a group of men and women standing to the right of the president. In the front row stood a young, dark-headed man with a long face dominated by a not-quite-straight nose, his right arm in a white sling.

Leslie sank to her knees. Tears filled her eyes. "Ian," she whispered. Arms crossed, hands pressed to her shoulders, she took in and blew out the huge breaths of someone long afraid to breathe.

Virgil stood, uncertainty on his face.

Wanda kneeled next to her. Put a supportive arm around her. "It's okay, Leslie. He's alive. He's okay."

Leslie swiped at her nonstop tears and stood, breathing easy for the first time in weeks."Yes. Yes, he is." She smiled a head-to-toe smile.

Virgil's face smoothed, and he settled back into his chair.

"Now we just have to hear from Miranda." Leslie's voice was still a little shaky.

"I don't know if she'll come," Wanda said.

"Oh?"

"She's…different. You heard what happened, didn't you?"

"I was there. I saw what her sister did to her. I got her to the medic."

Wanda's lips quirked. "Not then. After. I don't know the whole story, but—killing Irene affected Miranda's mind. Sometimes she—I don't know—I guess she thinks she's surrounded by enemies trying to kill her and tries to kill them. She wounded several people in the command center before they got her settled down."

Leslie put a hand over her mouth. Memories of meeting Miranda on the Lady Angelfish flooded Leslie. Memories of the boat trip upriver, of when they'd discovered they'd each known Gert. Memories of living with Gert on her mountainside farm. "Is there something we can do for Miranda?"

The bell over the front door jingled.

"Just one moment," Virgil called. He nodded for Wanda to go on.

"I figure it'll take time, a peaceful place, and family to help her. 'Cept David's in DC and I don't know if he knows…"

"She needs a place like Mama Gert's." After her parents and older brother were Taken, Gert's cabin had been a refuge for her and her brothers. A second family. A wave of longing washed over Leslie.

Memories of her three brothers clowning around with Gert's old mule blossomed into a smile. *Lots of political repair and restructuring needs to happen, but that's not my part of this. I can go back home, to Ambrose. We can be a family again.*

Chapter Seventy-Four

Jostled this way and that, Miranda gritted her teeth and plowed through the crowd that sang an enthusiastic if off-key version of "America the Beautiful." She'd spent March under treatment for exhaustion. After she hid her ongoing panic attacks and nightmares from the doctor and nurses and acted as if she had slept well every night, they released her. But here she could only manage ragged gasps and a tenuous hold on reality. *Just let me get to Virgil's. I'll be fine there.*

The shakes struck. *No, I can't, not now.* She darted across the street and took shelter in the doorway to Virgil's. Focused on feeling the ground beneath her shoes. Took slow, deep breaths. Held her hand out. It trembled, but the attack was letting go. Her heart rate settled from panic to mildly alarmed. Steadier, she opened the door and stepped inside.

The bell sounded overhead.

No one stood behind the register.

"Just one moment," Virgil called from the back room.

Sweat popped out on her upper lip. *I'm not ready for this.*

Someone had pushed the curtain to the back room to one side. Some shelves were visible, but nothing and no one else.

Voices came from back there.

"...it'll take time, a peaceful place, and family to help her. 'Cept David's in DC and I don't know if he knows..."

Miranda white-knuckle gripped the counter. *Wanda is talking about me.*

"She needs a place like Mama Gert's..."

And Leslie. Miranda's chest contracted painfully. She turned and reached for the front door.

"May I help you—?" Virgil's voice asked.

Miranda looked over her shoulder.

Virgil stood in the doorway to the storeroom. His eyes lit up, and his smile broadened. "It's good to—"

She put a finger to her lips.

He cocked his head.

She turned to him and forced her stiff lips to curve in some semblance of a smile. Motioned she needed to write something down.

He hurried to the cashier's stand, reached below the register, and pulled out an ink pen and a scrap of paper.

She took them, unable to hide how badly her hand shook. Scribbled: *Dear Wanda and Leslie, Glad you survived. I'm a little under the weather, so I won't stay. Going to the mountains for a while. I'll let you know when I'm back.* She folded the paper in half and in half again. Handed it wordlessly to Virgil, turned, and walked out the door.

Chapter Seventy-Five

nnabelle took off her boots on the porch of the old farmhouse, entered through the kitchen, and hung the rifle over the door. After a full day in the relentless Kansas heat, hunting and then cleaning the three rabbits and two squirrels she'd shot, she needed a shower. She went straight upstairs.

She stood at the mint-green kitchen countertop chopping the remaining end-of-the-year vegetables when the beep-beep from the school bus let her know Sandra had gotten off at the intersection a half mile away.

The rhythmic crunch of gravel reached Annabelle's ears long before Sandra arrived.

"I'm home," Sandra called. The screen door banged shut behind her.

Annabelle swept the carrots and celery off the cutting board and into the steaming pot of leftover stew.

"I'm beat," Sandra said. "School is *hard*. Especially science." She sat at the rickety old kitchen table, propped her elbows on the surface, her chin in her hands. "It makes me hungry." She sniffed the air. "Are we having stew again?"

She's always hungry. Annabelle gave a strangled laugh. *I am too.* Ever since her inner angel had rejected her, she hungered for food, not souls. "The neighbor lady brought some green beans over. In the bowl by the sink. You can snack on them while you snap them."

Sandra brought the bowl of beans to the table. "Why don't you ever call Mrs. Miller by her name?"

Sandra had the strange idea that Annabelle should be friends with their next-door neighbors, who lived a mile down the road. *True, we wouldn't have survived the past sixteen months without our neighbor's kindness and generosity.*

The neighbor lady had even insisted Sandra needed to go to school. Helped Annabelle figure out the paperwork, even when she suspected much of what Annabelle wrote was untrue. *But friends?* Annabelle couldn't explain what she didn't understand, so she switched topics. "I heard every step you took once you got off the bus."

"No, you didn't."

Annabelle gritted her teeth. "You're right. I did not hear every step. But you weren't practicing silent walking, were you?"

"Why do you always want me to walk that way?"

Annabelle slammed the wooden spoon down. The cast-iron stovetop rang.

Behind her, Sandra squeaked.

Annabelle closed her eyes and took a breath. *That's what the neighbor lady said to do when she grew angry.* It helped a little. She opened her eyes and turned to Sandra. The alarm on Sandra's face stopped her from giving the usual lecture.

"You think some of the Second Sphere survived?" Sandra asked in a quiet voice. "That they might come and take me away, don't you?"

"We're safe here." *For now.* Annabelle's stomach hardened. She didn't say that selling animal pelts didn't earn enough to buy the propane they needed. Didn't say that even though two years had passed since the Fellowship's defeat, surviving Azrael might still hunt her. Didn't say the reformed government might hunt them both.

Only the sound of beans snapping and the stove hissing filled the room.

Annabelle stirred the stew again, then mopped her sweaty forehead with the corner of the old apron she wore. She hated Kansas. Summers were too hot, and winters were too cold.

The scrape of Sandra's chair legs against the floor grated. Annabelle tightened her grip on the wooden spoon, determined not to lash out again. "Sandra, you couldn't possibly have snapped enough beans for dinner yet."

"You were hunting all day, weren't you?" Sandra asked softly.

A pair of arms snaked around Annabelle's waist. The gentle squeeze from those arms filled Annabelle with a fluttery warmth that melted her irritation.

"Let me do the cooking," Sandra said. "You can sit and snap beans."

Annabelle handed Sandra the wooden spoon and sat at the table. She snapped beans and watched Sandra. She'd grown into a strong young woman who cooked better than Annabelle did. And even though being a mother-not-mother was the most difficult thing she'd ever done, Annabelle finally understood why the mother in the park let her daughter play a little longer.

Chapter Seventy-Six

With her shopping bag slung over her shoulder and her unopened mail in her hand, Miranda paused at the entrance to Gert's labyrinth. Her throat ached. "Guess I should quit calling you Gert's." Gert had willed her property to Beryl, and Beryl to Miranda. She'd finished the paperwork in town. Gert's place was now hers. Except...

"This cabin, this glen, will always be Gert's." The ache in her throat eased. "Gert's Glen. It's a good name." She strode through the disarmed labyrinth.

She'd known coming here would be full of memories. What she hadn't expected was how much she missed hearing Frank, Gert's old mule, greet her every morning.

Gert's mule, Frank, and all of Gert's other animals were gone before Miranda had returned. She hoped they had found a good home.

"Hello, girls." Her first little brood of chickens clucked and scratched the dirt where Gert's collection of rusting appliances and junk once stood. That collection of other people's junk now made a decent, if unconventional, fence around the property. The cabin was still a little lopsided, but fresh sealant over wood patched the tarp-covered holes.

Miranda climbed the steps of the now-strong and steady porch and patted the rusted commercial dryer sitting on the porch. "I'm home, Gert. Thank you for keeping your eye on the place while I was gone."

The kitchen looked the same, from the unplumbed porcelain sink to the white tile countertop and the battered white metal cabinets.

Miranda tossed the unopened, unexamined letter onto the chrome dinette table and put away her flour, sugar, and rice. Placed the second-hand romance novel she wanted to read on the table and then crossed to the cast-iron stove. Picked up the cold coffee pot that held one more cup of coffee, took it to the table. Tipped the spout over her empty mug.

Her heart twitched; its regular rhythm became a weird series of flip-flop jumps.

Her knees went weak.

The tin coffeepot clattered onto the tabletop.

She gripped the edge of the table with both hands. Repeated her mantra: *Eyes open. Feel the ground. Be present.* It didn't help.

The ghostly newsreel of Gert, Ethan, Beryl, and Nick replayed in her head. Echoes of flashing lights, the bang of guns, and clattering rocks made her duck and flinch. Reawakened the ache inside that reached from her throat to oceanic depths. It hurt to breathe.

The sounds and sights of twisted memories faded slowly. Her heart restored its normal rhythm, and she could catch her breath, feel the ground, and hear the normal world again.

Drip, drip, drip.

A puddle of coffee trickled downhill across the table, missing her romance novel and the envelope by less than a half inch. She put the envelope on top of the book and picked them up with one hand. Then with one finger, she touched the coffee. "It's still wet." She wasn't certain that was a sign she was better.

She got her dishcloth and cleaned up the mess.

When she'd finished, she reached for the latched wooden box that sat atop the icebox.

The wreath of dogwood flowers carved into the wooden top suggested it had been someone's jewelry box once. She didn't have any jewelry anymore, but it was just the right size to hold unopened envelopes.

She carried the box, the romance book, and the envelope into the living room. Placed them on the green, second-hand sofa she'd bought and placed between Gert's armchairs. Lit one of the kerosene lamps that still sat on the familiar spindle-legged tables.

She sat on the couch, placed the box on the seat beside her, and faced the stone fireplace that rose majestically to the exposed rafters overhead. The warm breeze from the window on each side meant she didn't need a fire tonight.

Box on her lap and open, Miranda looked at the envelope. Sure enough, Leslie had written Miranda's name and address. *Leslie is sure persistent.* Miranda pressed her lips together. *I wish you'd kept your big mouth closed, David. Leslie doesn't understand.*

Miranda knew that she and her fits would have been a constant reminder to them. This way, none of them would feel forced to forgive her, and she had a place to figure out how to live with what she'd done. With the ghosts.

She tapped the corner of the envelope on her lap, a habit that preceded slipping the latest letter into the box with the others.

A slight weight shifted inside the envelope. Miranda held the envelope up in the hurricane lamp's light. *A polaroid?* Her breath caught, and she dropped the envelope. *I'm not ready.* With shaky hands, she slid the envelope into the box, returned it to its resting place atop the icebox, and went outside to work on the next of the endless list of chores this place needed.

After tending the garden, Miranda cleaned out soiled straw and put a fresh layer of straw into the chicken coop nesting boxes. It was the kind of chore that she'd learned to do without thinking about it. The kind where her mind worried over that envelope like a tongue touching a bad tooth.

She dumped the last wheelbarrow of straw clotted with chicken droppings into her waste yard behind the old mule's shed and carried six buckets of water to the cabin.

She checked her bathwater heating on the stove and somehow ended up staring at the box atop the icebox over and over again.

After her bath, she sat on the couch with the romance novel she'd bought in Lynchburg earlier. The kerosene lamps hissed. Curtains over the windows on each side of the fireplace stirred, and the cabin creaked in the evening breeze.

Hours later, Miranda closed the book. At the end, the heroine, who adored her true love's children, realized that the children loved her. That they didn't need her to replace their mom. That being part of a family wasn't about being perfect, and being a mom wasn't about whose blood ran in their veins. Blood didn't make a family; love did.

Miranda put the book on the side table. Stared out the window at the night-cloaked mountain. An owl hooted. Nothing had ever sounded so lonely.

Without thinking about it, Miranda retrieved the box of letters. Found the latest one. Opened it.

Chapter Seventy-Seven

Miranda walked from the bus depot to Leslie's street address. She stopped and gaped at the little powder-blue house perched on the slope. Its two dark-blue dormer windows and peaked porch roof with white trim stirred memories of a dream Cape Cod cottage. White rails and a banister led up concrete steps to an inviting dark-blue door with its three windows trimmed in white. Her muscles ached with tension. She waited for the shakes that usually came with those memories. Tried to breathe slowly, deeply.

Muted sounds of laughter chased the memories and shakes away. *I should have called first.* Miranda turned and walked away. Stopped. *I can't go back. Spent all my cash on my bus ticket.*

Besides, Leslie said they wanted to see me. She squared her shoulders. Hurried up the steps, knocked on the door before her courage failed completely.

The doorknob turned, and Miranda's tension cranked up a notch; her chest vibrated with the wings of frantic hummingbirds.

The door opened. A fruity aroma wafted out. Leslie stood with one hand on the inside doorknob, looking over her shoulder, saying, "I've got it." She faced Miranda, and her smile grew. "You came."

Miranda released the breath she held. "I did."

At least a dozen people stood inside, surrounded by birthday streamers and pastel pink balloons with Happy 1st Birthday embla-zoned on them.

Miranda shook her head. "I'm sorry. This was a bad idea...."

Leslie's smile broadened even more. "Nonsense. Come on in. Everyone has been waiting for you." She turned her head slightly and called, "Hey everybody, she's here!"

Oliver and a half dozen others turned.

A scream. "Miss Norwood!"

People shifted, and a body came hurtling out of the group.

A long-haired teen slammed into Miranda, wrapped her in a tight embrace. Thea looked up at Miranda with a tear-stained face. "You saved us, Miss Nor—I mean, Miranda. Thank you."

"My turn." David wrapped her in a bear hug, then drew her inside with him on one arm and Wanda on the other. Hands clapped her back, and overlapping familiar voices said, "Good to see you" and "Glad you could make it."

Everyone spoke at once, introducing her to partners, to Leslie's daughter, and asking her questions.

Miranda looked around at the familiar and joyful faces of David, Wanda, the Baxters, and people she once fought alongside. Gave a blissful sigh. "Looks like everyone is here."

Wanda laughed and said, "Yes, the whole family is finally together again."

Dear Reader,

Thank you for reading *And When I Wake*.

I moved at least seventeen times before I graduated from high school. That made for a lonely and unpredictable childhood. Fortunately, I discovered early on that books held stories that could lift me out of my troubles. Reading became a lifelong obsession.

I love stories that explore the complexities of being a female struggling to survive in a world that doesn't quite fit. You can see this in the histories of forgotten or ignored women on my blog and in the stories and books I write.

Creating stories is my happy place. But nothing gives me more pleasure than knowing a story I wrote touched a reader's heart.

Did *And When I Wake* touch you? I'd love to hear from you!

Give the book a review. You can review the book on its page of the online store where you purchased it, or on a reader-centric site like Goodreads or LibraryThing, or even on my website.

Write a comment or two about what you liked or didn't like. Comments in the review section help books get noticed. Positive or negative, I am grateful for *all* reviews.

You can join my readers' group, Reading Rebels, at lynettembur rows.com.

As a Reading Rebel, you'll get a free e-book of Fellowship plus weekly emails linking to Monday blog posts. Once a month, Lynette shares details of her writing life—the breakthrough moments, the research rabbit holes, the late-night revelations that shape her characters' fates. Be the first to know about upcoming appearances, book signings, and special events.

This isn't just a mailing list—it's a rebellion of readers who demand more from their fiction.

No matter what you choose to do or not do, thank you. May you ever be a reading rebel who keeps on reading!

Thank you,

Lynette M. Burrows

Books by Lynette M. Burrows

My Soul to Keep, the Fellowship Dystopia Book One https://books2read.com/MySoultoKeep

If I Should Die, the Fellowship Dystopia Book Two https://books2read.com/IfIShoulddie/

Fellowship, a companion novel to the Fellowship Dystopia series. https://books2read.com/fellowship/

9 798986 143316